D0786691

BENDING THE LANDSCAPE

SCIENCE FICTION

BENDING THE LANDSCAPE

SCIENCE FICTION

EDITED BY NICOLA GRIFFITH
AND STEPHEN PAGEL

THE OVERLOOK PRESS
WOODSTOCK & NEW YORK

First published in the United States in 1998 by
The Overlook Press, Peter Mayer Publishers, Inc.
Lewis Hollow Road
Woodstock, New York 12498

Copyright © 1998 Nicola Griffith and Stephen Pagel

All Rights Reserved. No part of this publication may be
reproduced or transmitted in any form or by any means, electronic
or mechanical, including photocopy, recording, or any information
storage and retrieval system now known or to be invented without
permission in writing from the publisher, except by a reviewer who
wishes to quote brief passages in connection with a review written
for inclusion in a magazine, newspaper, or broadcast.

Library of Congress Cataloging-in-Publication Data

Science Fiction / edited by Nicola Griffith and Stephen Pagel.
p. cm. — (Bending the landscape : original gay and lesbian writing : v. 1
1. Science Fiction, American. 2. Gays' writings, American.
I. Griffith, Nicola. II. Pagel, Stephen. III. Series.
PS648.S3S265 1998 813'.0876208920664—dc21 98-9855

Manufactured in the United States of America

Book design and type formatting by Bernard Schleifer

ISBN 0-87951-856-1
FIRST EDITION

1 3 5 7 9 8 6 4 2

3 3056 00573 7211

CONTENTS

6   *Contents*

inTRODUCTiOn

This volume of all-original Science Fiction stories is the second in the
Bending the Landscape series. As with the first (which was Fantasy), we
asked a wide range of writers—gay and straight, mainstream and old
genre hands, multiple-award winners and brand new authors—to con-
tribute. We gave each contributor one objective and one rule.

The objective was to combine, in any way they liked, the main formal device of science fiction with one of its major preoccupations.
Darko Suvin has defined science fiction's main formal device as "an
imaginative framework alternative to the author's empirical environment." In other words, we wanted the writer to imagine a different
landscape. The difference could one of time, or place, or attitude—past
or future, on Earth or off, altered or unchanged social mores. It just had
to be some milieu that had not happened. That milieu then had to be
combined with one of science fiction's major preoccupations, its most
enduring theme, which is that of the Alien, the Not-Self, the Other.

Our rule was that the Other had to be a lesbian or gay man. (In a
largely heterosexual society we are, after all, often treated as aliens.)
This rule was, of course, interpreted liberally.

With all of time and space to play with, roughly a quarter of these
stories take place outside our solar system. In these pieces, physical

landscape is less important than the social in the shaping of the characters' lives—the creation of their Othering. In Jim Grimsley's "Free in Asveroth," for example, the shaping force is not atmospheric pressure or a light spectrum tending towards the ultra-violet, it is greed: humans have come to a planet to strip it of one particular agricultural product, and the sentient life forms are either destroyed, or captured and put to work. Grimsley focuses not on the greed-driven humans, but on the three jumpers who escape. He shows us how rationalization by the greedy leads to an intelligent species being marginalized, alienated, and treated with inhuman brutality. Auschwitz in space. Mark W. Tiedemann's gaze, in "Surfaces," is more subtle. His focus is responsibility: at some point in our lives, we have to choose to become ourselves—not the person our parents, or friends or government, would like us to be. The primary shaping force in Charles Sheffield's deliciously sly poke at Clinton's *Don't Ask, Don't Tell* military policy, "Brooks Too Broad For Leaping," is hypocrisy; in Kathleen O'Malley's "Silent Passion" it is fear masquerading as fundamentalist faith. In "Lonely Land," Denise Lopes Heald's wrenching portrait of bonded servitude, the driving factor is the suffocation of personal desire by ironclad dictates of custom; for Wendy Rathbone's "Beautiful People" it is fashion.

Closer to home, we have two stories of men in traditionally manly occupations—Steve Baxter's moon-walking astronaut and Allen Steele's satellite beamjack—who find out what it is to be different. Each reaches the same conclusion: fear gets you nowhere.

Other people's fear and its lesser cousin, intolerance, are dealt with by lesbians and gay men on an almost daily basis. Three of our writers have given it their particular attention, taking us just a few years into the future and asking What If. In "Sex, Guns, and Baptists," Keith Hartman wonders what would change if the political christian fundamentalists continue to gain ground. According to his private investigator narrator, the answer is that gay men would still be gay men, they would just have to lie more often—and be lied to. Don Bassingthwaite, also writing from the viewpoint of a gay PI, asks roughly the same question but from the angle of corporate culture rather than religion. His conclusion is that everyone lies, and it's up to us to stay one step ahead.

There are some who believe that Science never lies, that—like Justice—it is blind. But science is just a tool; the results depend upon those who wield it. Richard Bamberg gives us a poignant vision of the possibilities of gene therapy. The first science fiction novel, *Frankenstein*, gave us our first scientifically created alien. In less than five hundred words, Mark McLaughlin takes a light but chilling look at some of Shelley's assumptions: just because you create something, does that give you the right to destroy it?

There is, of course, no law that says all aliens are monsters. In Ralph Sperry's delightful "On Vacation," we see that the aliens are not that different: shy workaholics; exasperated lovers; good with machines. Some alien life forms want to be human, like the artificial intelligence in Shariann Lewitt's "A Real Girl." But what is reality? Rebecca Ore's "Half in Love With Easeful Rock and Roll" asks that question, and then another: can we change our personal reality? Are we born with our sexual orientation or can we change it by an act of will?

It is often our perception of the world that makes us different from those around us. In "The City in Morning," Carrie Richerson takes a look at life in a city where reality is in constant flux. How do you know if something you perceive is real? L. Timmel Duchamp turns that around. In "Dance at the Edge" she gives us a double dose of frustration, sexual and social. Her narrator *knows* that what she sees is real; she *knows* that others see it too; she refuses to pretend as they do. But different perceptions are not always pretense. What happens when two women who love each other see their futures differently? In Nancy Kress's "State of Nature," one woman believes it is important to live in the world; the other thinks sequestering herself in a safe place is the only option. Both believe they are right; both *are* right, to some extent. Different people in different situations make different choices. Nancy Johnston, in her pseudo-academic paper, "The Rendez-Vous," gives us a wickedly funny glimpse of the way people twist the truth when they don't want to see it. Who did what to whom? Blame an alien life form.

What exactly is an alien life form? In the future it might not be easy to tell the difference between a work of art, a machine, and a living being. In "Stay Thy Flight," Elisabeth Vonarburg uses the variable perception of time to give us an elegant portrait of difference and two female creatures bonding. Time, more specifically, time travel, is also used to great effect in the longest story in the book, "Time Gypsy." Ellen Klages takes a '90s dyke back forty years to 1950s San Francisco where she discovers her modern sensibilities are utterly alien to the lesbians of the time. What makes sense in her own time is lunacy here; something as simple and human as a touch is dangerous.

Lesbians and gay men have, in our twentieth century western culture, been the Other; as the century is about to change, we believe we are becoming less so. The writers in this volume have different views about how things might turn out. We'll have to wait and see. One thing is certain: some of them are wrong.

BENDING THE LANDSCAPE

SCIENCE FICTION

SEX, GUNS, AND BAPTISTS

KEITH HARTMAN

*I*n "Sex, Guns, and Baptists" Keith Hartman tells of the struggle
between two people whose desire to know the truth has forced them to
rely upon one another, even though each dislikes what the other is.

Daniel smiled at us from across the lobby. Blond and cute and playful
as a puppy. I frowned and looked past him. He kept staring at me. Still
not making eye contact, I mouthed the words "Knock it off." He
winked. I glared back, trying to shake him off without calling any more
attention to myself or the nice lady who was paying us. Daniel feigned
a hurt look and turned his attention to the glass elevators.

I glanced over at my client. Ms. Churchill was staring at Daniel,
a mixture of contempt and curiosity on her face. "You shouldn't look
directly at him," I said. She was wearing dark sunglasses and a big
floppy hat, but I didn't want to take any chances on the mark recog-
nizing her.

"Why in the world is he wearing that shirt?" she asked, ignoring my
advice about staring. Daniel was wearing his usual work clothes, ripped
jeans and white tank top printed with a disturbingly realistic crucifix.
Christ's final agonies, captured in vivid color and full anatomic detail,
over the slogan *And you think you've had a rough day?* "Isn't it a bit...?"

"Trust me, Daniel's a pro, and he knows exactly what signals he's sending. The crucifix is part of his advertising."

"Advertising?"

"Yeah. If he were older, he'd probably wear a rainbow flag or a pink triangle on his T-shirt. But since most of the gay men under 23 are Roman Catholic, the kids have all adopted Catholic regalia as a sort of uniform."

She looked at me as if I were making the whole thing up just to test her gullibility. "Roman Catholic? Why in the world would they be converting to that?" I guess Baptist women don't follow demographic trends in the gay subculture that closely.

"They don't convert, they're just born that way," I explained. "It's one of the side-effects of the test." She continued to look at me as if I were out of my mind. At least she wasn't looking at Daniel anymore. "Think of it this way. What would you do if the test came back saying that your fetus was gay?"

She didn't say anything, but we both knew what would happen. The Southern Baptist Convention doesn't like abortions. But it really doesn't like homosexuals.

"That's why there haven't been a lot of gay Baptists born in the last 23 years," I went on. "Or Methodists. Or Mormons. Or Presbyterians. You all make a lot of noise about being pro-life, but in the clinch... you make 'exceptions'. Not the Catholics though. You gotta love the Pope. She may be a reactionary old cow who's trying to drag the world back into the middle ages, but at least she's consistent."

Ms. Churchill turned her cold stare back to Daniel. I don't know why I kept baiting her like that. I hated the case, but that wasn't her fault.

"How do you know if he's even Joseph's type, anyway?" she asked.

"Because I did my job," I said flatly. For the past several weeks I had been shadowing Joseph Thompson, and I knew him inside and out. I knew which people got that second glance when he passed them in the hall. I knew the sort of person that he was likely to strike up a conversation with in an elevator. I even knew which waiters he over-tipped at his favorite restaurants. I had also been into his financial records, and knew that Thompson was in the habit of withdrawing several hundred dollars in cash every few weeks, usually right before one of his business trips. No one uses cash anymore. Not unless you're trying to hide something. Like hiring a private detective. Or a hustler. I had a feeling that Thompson knew what boys like Daniel were for.

I felt Ms. Churchill stiffen next to me. Thompson had just come in through the hotel's big revolving doors. He was still dressed for his job—tailored jacket, bright tie, expensive shoes. He worked for a Southern Baptist advertising firm, doing PR work for one of their congressmen. He was 34, the same age as me, a little too attractive, and not married. I'll bet the gossip was already becoming a problem.

Maybe I was wrong about Thompson. Maybe he was just a 34 year old man who had decided it was time to settle down and start a family. Maybe he was in love and getting married for all the right reasons.

He did trip my gaydar, but that didn't necessarily mean anything. Evangelical Christians have been known to scramble my sixth sense about men. They do all the same things as a guy who's trying to pick you up. They smile too much. They stand a little too close. They look directly into your eyes. And then they say something stupid.

Daniel intercepted Thompson while the man was waiting for an elevator. I wasn't close enough to make out their conversation, but Thompson looked at his watch, so I guess Daniel must have asked for the time. I watched Thompson's eyes drift from his watch to Daniel's shoes, up Daniel's rather pleasant physique, and finally come to rest on the saint medallion around Daniel's neck. I could tell from Thompson's smile that he knew what it meant.

In adopting the Catholic roster of Saints, the gay community has added a few of its own. There's Saint Marilyn, patron of blonds and the blond at heart. Saint Judy, the patron of drag queens and twelve step programs. Saint Liz, patron of marriage and other hopeless causes. Saint Dolly, patron of big dreams and silicone. Daniel was wearing a medallion depicting the Madonna—not the holy virgin, but the like-a-virgin. She who is the patron saint and protector of all sex workers.

Beside me, Ms. Churchill was staring straight at them. Luckily, no one seemed to have noticed. She had insisted on witnessing this for herself, but I did not like having her here. There was always the chance that Thompson would spot her. Or that she might snap and blow the operation. I tried to read her expression. How much of this did she understand? Could she read the body language of the transaction that was taking place? The way that Thompson stepped into Daniel's space, so close that they were almost touching. The way that Daniel laughed a little too hard at some joke of Thompson's. The way he steadied himself on Thompson's shoulder. Soon, Daniel would ask some inane question about the man's family. Ask to see a picture of his sister, or something else that would give Thompson an excuse to pull out his wallet. An excuse to show that he was carrying cash.

Ms. Churchill's voice startled me. "Doesn't it bother you to exploit Daniel like this?" She had not taken her eyes off them.

"Daniel is a twenty-two year old with a public high school education," I told her. "He's bright, so he's taught himself to read, a little. What do you expect him to do? Become a programmer? A journalist? A quantum physicist? Who's really exploiting Daniel—the guy who'll pay him $250 an hour for sex, or the one who'll pay him $5.85 an hour for flipping burgers?" I should have stopped there. I didn't. "And if I were in your shoes, I wouldn't complain about other people using Daniel."

She turned. The look she gave me would have made a cobra curl up and whimper.

Ms. Churchill had never pretended to like me, but she did need me. For now, at least. My firm has three listings in the yellow pages. There's the number for "Fortress Security", which we use to solicit corporate clients. Then there's "McClintock Investigations—licensed psychic detective", which my partner Jen uses to pull in the new age crowd. Ms. Churchill had known what skills her particular job required. She had called on our third line, the one for "Drew Parker, PI—proudly serving the gay and lesbian community."

Ms. Churchill stared at Daniel and Thompson again, looking as though she could control the situation through sheer force of will.

"You don't have to be here," I said. "I can meet you later with the pictures."

"No," she said emphatically. "I told you. I have to see it with my own eyes. I have to be sure."

I can't say that I blamed her. Images are too easy to play with. I know more than a few private detectives who have found it cheaper to invest in a good graphics program than in good legwork. An overlay here, a deletion there, and voilà, incriminating photos made to order.

Right on schedule, Thompson pulled out his wallet and showed a picture to Daniel. I could feel the tension building in Ms. Churchill. Screw the bonus.

"Forget this," I told her. "Go home. Ask him to get a blood test before the wedding. Other people have done it."

She looked at me again, her eyes flashing. For a second I thought she was going to scream at me, but when she spoke it was very slowly, as if she was picking each word carefully. "Mr. Parker, you may not understand this, but I am very much in love with Joseph. I have never felt this way about anyone else, and I can't imagine that I ever will again. What would some DNA test tell me? We all have a disposition to some form of evil. Our own demon. But not all of us act on it. I don't care what's in Joseph's genes. I care what's in his heart. I have to know if he loves me, or is just using me."

I knew I shouldn't say it. But I did. "With men, it's always a little of both."

We looked back in time to see Daniel and Thompson get on an elevator together. The doors closed. I watched Ms. Churchill's face slowly fall. Her mouth go slack. Her lips tremble. Her eyelashes grow damp with half-formed tears. When she started toward the elevators, I grabbed her arm. She shook it free, angry.

"Look," I said, "if you've seen enough, go home. I'll make a full report. You'll have your answer. But if we do this, we do it right. No unresolved questions. No doubts. No ambiguous situations that he can talk his way out of. And that means we give them a head start. Fifteen minutes. To let things... develop."

For a moment I thought she might actually take my advice and leave. Go to the airport. Fly home. Wait for my call. Instead, she gave me an icy "Fine", and flopped down on a bench. While she sat there thinking about... No. I didn't want to guess at what she was thinking about. I sat down a few feet away and flipped on the throat mike under my tie. I had some final preparations to make.

"Alex," I said under my breath.

There was a slight buzz as the speaker in my left ear came to life, and then Alex's sullen voice. "Yeah boss, what is it this time?" The company that I purchased Alex from claims that the program is supposed to adapt its word choice and inflection to suit its user. I am not sure what it means, but in my hands Alex seems to be evolving into an insolent manic-depressive.

I took the palm display out of my jacket pocket. "Alex, pull up the photos I shot this morning."

"Yeah, whatever."

Alex displayed the first shot: a hotel maid about to clean a room. The angle wasn't right.

"Next."

Alex obliged and produced an image I had shot a couple seconds later. Still not the one I was looking for.

"Next."

Bingo. I touched a spot on the display and said, "Enlarge on this."

Alex zeroed in on the maid's pass key. I pulled a piece of cardboard and a hole punch out of my pocket and began work on a duplicate. I glanced at Ms. Churchill. I had no idea what was going on behind those eyes.

I checked my watch. Five minutes. Upstairs, it would be starting. Daniel and Thompson. A first kiss. Daniel would taste like that wintergreen gum he always chews. Thompson would run his fingers through Daniel's curls. Clothed bodies moving against each other.

Thompson had never crossed me. Never hurt me. Never given me any reason to hate him. But I was about to destroy his life. Oh, he'd probably get over losing Ms. Churchill. But his secret would be out. He'd be finished at his job. They'd never let him in a Southern Baptist church again. He'd lose his friends, his family. Maybe he'd be able to start over again. Get a job in a gay firm, move into the gay subculture, build a new life. It might even turn out good for him. But I wasn't giving him a choice.

Eight minutes. Daniel would be loosening the man's tie. Thompson would be lifting Daniel's tank top, sliding a hand over the muscles of Daniel's stomach. Daniel's arms around his waist. Daniel's jeans pressed up against Thompson's khakis.

I had not wanted to take the case. When Ms. Churchill called, I turned her down. Then I turned her down again. And again. But she had been relentless. She just kept saying it over and over again, "I have a right to know." Ten minutes. Their clothing would be in piles on the floor, thrown over the backs of chairs, lying on the bed. They would be learning each other's secrets. Does Thompson like to kiss, or to be kissed? Does Daniel like to have his ears nibbled on? His neck? His fingers?

I hoped that Thompson was a jerk. I hoped that this woman beside me meant nothing to him, that she was just a convenient bit of camouflage he had acquired so that he could go on working at his wonderful job and fucking his beautiful men. I didn't want it to be anything more complicated.

But then, I would never know what he really felt for her. On bad days, did he think of her and smile? Were there special things he had never told anyone else but her? Moments they had shared? Did he daydream about the children they would have? About kicking a soccer ball with their daughter? Telling a bedtime story to their son?

Twelve minutes. By now they would know each other's private sounds. The little gasps, or moans, or growls a man makes when he forgets himself in sex. His intimate sounds, as unique as fingerprints. I wonder if the FBI keeps a file of them. They seem to know everything else about us.

"I have a right to know." She had said, and she was right, damn it.

Fifteen minutes. I stood up. Ms. Churchill followed me into an elevator. I pressed the button for the 47th floor. She leaned her face against the glass, watching the lobby drop away beneath us.

"Have you ever been in love, Mr. Parker?"

The question surprised me. She had not looked up. The trees in the lobby grew smaller as we rose.

"Yes."

"With Daniel?"

I laughed. "Lord no. Whatever gave you that idea?"

"I've seen the way he acts around you."

Maybe she understood more than I had given her credit for.

"I just pulled him out of a bar fight once, and he's been following me around ever since."

"Are you two sleeping together?"

Ah. I could see where this was going now. She was hurt, and looking for some way to get under my skin.

"No. Daniel's too... cheerful. I mean, all the time. It would be like having sex with a cocker spaniel."

She thought about that answer for a while. "Don't you worry about him?"

"Daniel's a smart boy. He carries a taser when he works."

"That's not what I meant."

Another elevator passed us going down. A man and a woman, dressed for a party. Our own glass cage raced silently upward.

"You two aren't...?"

"No." I said. For the first time since we got on the elevator, she looked up at me.

"Why not?"

I almost took the easy way out and said that Daniel was too young for me. But that wasn't quite it. The truth was complicated, and I didn't know how to make her understand it. Hell, I couldn't even make Daniel himself understand it. Daniel is just too... innocent? No, that's not right. Daniel has slept with more men than Mata Hari. And yet, somehow Daniel has never managed to fall in love.

And I don't want to be the first. I don't want to be the one who ruins the fantasy for him. I don't want to be the one who can't live up to all his impossible twenty-two year-old expectations of love.

In his overly dramatic way, Daniel had once told me that while his body might have racked up the mileage, his heart was still virgin territory. But I don't want a virgin. I want someone who's been through the whole show before. Someone who's been hurt, and stepped on, and had every last illusion shattered. Someone who comes to me cautiously, knowing that falling in love is easy and staying in love is hard, that passion dies and most relationships are doomed before they start. Someone I can love as an equal, not a student.

I could never explain all that to her, so I lied. "I think his work would get in the way."

The elevator stopped at the 47th floor. We stepped off and walked down the hall to 4717, the room in which Mr. Thompson was staying. I got the fiber-optic snake out of my pocket and unlooped it. I slid a strand under the door.

"What's that?" asked Ms. Churchill.

"It's a camera on a fiber-optic cable," I explained, as I plugged the free end into my palm display. Then, under my breath, I said, "Record."

She grabbed my wrist. "I told you. With my eyes. I have to see it with my eyes."

I shrugged, and then glanced at the image on my palm display anyway—I don't go into a room blind. She was certainly going to get an eyeful. I put the palm display down on the floor, and slid the duplicate pass key into the lock. The indicator light flashed from red to green.

The door opened quietly. Well, quietly enough. Daniel and Thompson were making more than enough noise to cover our movements. From the doorway, I could see a pair of feet hanging over the edge of the bed. I stepped forward into the room and saw the whole picture. Daniel, on his back, a look of ecstasy on his face. Thompson, his back to us, his face buried in Daniel's neck, his hips grinding into Daniel. I stood there, looking at them, reminding myself that I am not a jealous person. Looking at Daniel's beautiful muscles, tensing and relaxing in time to Thompson's hips. Looking at the expression on

Daniel's face, how it changed with every twinge of pleasure. How he bit his lip, how he opened his mouth, and arched his neck. I wondered if it was an act, or if he really enjoyed his work this much. I must have stared at Daniel a little too long, because when I glanced back at Ms. Churchill she already had the gun out.

It was a .32. A small gun, the sort of thing you could fit in a lady's handbag, but still quite capable of punching a nice sized hole in someone. At the moment, this particular .32 was about to blow a nice sized hole in the back of Mr. Thompson. And from the angle she was shooting at, it stood a good chance of blowing a nice size hole in Daniel as well. I lunged.

The gun went off and then I knocked her arm back. Or maybe I knocked her arm back and then the gun went off. My brain wasn't working quite fast enough to tell which had happened first. She hadn't been ready for the gun's recoil, and my shove had put her further off balance. Ms. Churchill caught herself on the wall and looked up at me, her eyes cold with hate. She brought the gun back around towards me.

I caught her full in the jaw with an uppercut. It didn't knock her out, but it did take her mind off shooting me for a few seconds. While she was disoriented, I risked a quick glance at the bed. Just in time to see Thompson barreling up at me.

I grabbed his arm and tried to roll him into one of those fancy aikido throws that would have sent him flying across the room and smashing into a wall. You know, it's a real shame that I never had a chance to finish those aikido lessons. I keep meaning to, but something always comes up. My feet got tangled and I wound up flat on my back with a hundred and eighty pounds of fully aroused naked Baptist on top of me with his hands around my neck. It could have been fun under better circumstances.

"What the Hell are you doing here?!" he screamed at me, and slammed my head into the floor for emphasis.

Even if I'd had a good answer to that question, I couldn't say much while he was throttling me. So when he lifted me up for another blow I settled on a good head butt to his face. There was a satisfying crunch as my forehead connected with his nose. Unfortunately, all it made him do was grunt and start strangling me even harder. I have got to start charging more for cases like this.

There was no room to throw a punch, and it felt like Thompson was going to rip my head off by brute strength. I tried to get my hands at his face, but the blood from his nose was dripping into my eyes and I couldn't see what I was doing. He smashed my head into the floor again, and the world exploded into reds and yellows.

I heard the shot and felt his weight shift. This time my brain was working fast enough to pick up the small delay between the two events. Somehow, it even knew what that delay meant: Thompson hadn't been hit, he was only turning to look in the direction of the shot. It wasn't much, but it did give me an opening.

While Thompson was off balance, I braced an arm under his ribcage and managed to roll him off me. I still couldn't see anything and my head felt like a piñata after a birthday party, so I scrambled in the opposite direction until I found a wall. Steadying myself against it with one hand, I tried to wipe the blood out of my eyes with the other. Standing up I saw... The Last Supper. I knew it was the last supper because it was just like the painting. You know, Leonardo Da Vinci and all. Except Jesus was playing a guitar, and Judas and Matthew seemed to be having a fight over the bill. Everything had a red tint to it, and my brain decided that the painting itself must be on fire. And then St. Peter stood up and walked over to me, and smiled. And then he decked me.

Great. There's a loaded gun and at least two crazy people in the room, and my mind has decided to fly south for the winter. Well I may be crazy, but I'm not stupid. When I saw St. Peter lining up another haymaker, I ducked. There was a sound of breaking plaster, and when I looked back up I saw Thompson, cursing, his fist stuck in the wall. He looked at me and screamed something incomprehensible.

I smiled back at him. I hit him once in the solar plexus, which kind of took the fight out of him. A second blow to the nerve center in the small of his back pretty much stopped his misbehaving. I should have hit him again, just to make sure, but my heart wasn't in it anymore.

Turning to take in the rest of the room, I noticed that Ms. Churchill seemed to be suffering the aftereffects of a taser dart. Daniel had relieved her of the .32, which must have gone off when he zapped her. He looked indecently pleased with himself.

"Gee," he said with a grin, "and you complain about my line of work being dangerous."

I ignored him and picked up my client. Daniel grabbed his clothes in one hand and my optical cable in the other and caught up with us as I was loading Ms. Churchill into one of the glass elevators. We started down. As we approached the lobby, I pressed the emergency stop button to give her a few more minutes to come around. I could have just carried her through the lobby and out to a cab, but I did not feel like trying to explain the whole situation to the concierge.

A group of women in an ascending elevator pointed at Daniel and started giggling. He smiled back, flexing his arms in a muscle-man pose.

I frowned at him. "Put on your clothes and stop flirting." Daniel pouted as he got dressed. Daniel has raised pouting to an art form.

"You fucking bastard!"

My client had regained consciousness.

"How nice to have you with us again, Ms. Churchill," I said. "I believe our business has been successfully completed." I handed her the bill. "Payment of the agreed-upon bonus may be wired to this account number or delivered in cash to my place of business no later than..."

She tore up the bill and screamed at me some more. Something about damnation and burning in hell.

"People often have that reaction to my fees. Alex, another copy of the bill please."

While my wallet printed out another copy of the document, I held the palm display in front of her.

"Before you tear up this copy, you might want to take a look at the video feed from the snake. Alex, play the last recording."

She stared at the tiny screen, watching the whole affair played out again. The camera's position wasn't very good, and even with a wide angle lens it had missed some of the action. Still, there was easily enough there to warrant a couple of charges of attempted murder. And the whole situation would take a long, long time to explain to her friends and family. She glared at me when I handed her the second bill. But she didn't tear it up.

I started the elevator again, and Daniel and I left her in the lobby. A couple of hours later, he and I caught the evening train back to Atlanta. Daniel sat next to me, and fell asleep within five minutes of leaving the station. I watched him, as the train raced silently through the night, gliding over its single rail, with only the sound of the wind to let you know that you're moving at a hundred and fifty miles an hour. Daniel sleeps so easily.

Life is strange. You do all the right things. You expose the villain. You save the damsel in distress. You beat up the bad guy, and you take some knocks doing it. And somehow, when the day is over, you still can't sleep.

HALF IN LOVE WITH EASEFUL ROCK AND ROLL

REBECCA ORE

*T*here are some who think sexual orientation is matter of choice, others who believe it to be innate, or a matter of circumstance, or variable throughout one's lifetime. In this story of a mother whose child lives with his adopted parents, Rebecca Ore shows us how we might use the technologies of the future—in this case, virtual reality—to aid in our personal musings on the subject.

> Please can't I be happy being one of the girls, one night
> under monster cracking moonlight.
>
> *from* Creature

Black knocks behind the eyeballs down on Shattuck Avenue. When my son came for the weekend, I'd been rocking and rolling with Janis Joplin back in the 1960's Fillmore Auditorium, *ah, baby, don't you want some acid, some El Ess Dee*, then backstage, going down, saying *bye, Janis.* Knock against my door? I pulled the VR goggles up and stared at the glitter ceiling of the *faux moderne* apartment. The door knocks kept on as I pulled off the VR gloves, still dressed in the power suit. "Mom, I'm here. What the fuck are you doing?"

Me being the biological mom, and him now a teenager, I was beginning to get lots of advice, like last year's "Why didn't you raise me yourself, Mom. We could have had such fun on welfare."

"Wait, wait," I said to the door where he was knocking. "I'm taking
a shower."

"Yeah," he said. "Why don't you get hooked up with a real guy or do
the honest thing with Em?"

"Children always think things would be better if they were different." I pulled off the VR muff patch, wiped between my legs, blushed
furiously, and wished I had been taking a shower. "Aren't you're a day
early?"

"You forgot, Mom. Friday's a holiday. Da and Ma told you."

Many times, I felt like his parents, Dr. and Mrs. Rogers, were mine,
too. "Okay, okay, just let me get dried off."

"I'll be back in fifteen minutes," my son told me.

Rather a relief. I slipped Janis back into her polycarbonate jewel
box, turned the VR suit inside out and hid it. For a moment I wondered
if I wanted to replace the goggles with retina painters. They'd be a bit
lighter. Fifteen minutes, he said. I slid the Janis CD-ROM, her label
to the rear, between a VOGUE and a MIRABELLA. Still time for a
shower.

When my son came back, the Issey Miyake blouse and pants
covered me. Instant cookies in the microwave. Could he smell anything? I remembered my mother telling me, "They smell like chlorine.
We don't smell like anything." I had found the Vogue pattern for my
clothes down in a thrift store that specialized in 90's memorabilia. I let
my son in and said, "Sorry I forgot, but it's been so hectic." The
microwave delivered the cookies after a final blast of pure heat to
brown them.

"Yeah," my son said. "Em and I were talking about you."

What were Em and my son planning for me? "I wish you wouldn't
bother my friends."

"She called me."

The bitch. "Still, you don't have to talk to her." The silk maybe wasn't quite thick enough, but then I had put on panties and a bra, not really being up to incest even if my son was willing. I guess if I'd raised him myself, he'd seem less like a stranger. "So what did you two say about me that I've got to know about?"

"She says you ought to look for something better in life."

"That's so easy for other people to say."

For an instant, I felt like a female impersonator, impersonating a straight woman or a lesbian, I wasn't quite sure which. Janis must have known that feeling well.

We went silent, into our memories, as we ate the cookies and drank the milk like a real mother and child.

I'd gotten pregnant when I went looking for a guy to fuck so I could be just like my non-virgin friends. I'd fallen in love with an art printer's married assistant who gave me an esoteric venereal disease, fortunately easy to cure. Twice, I wanted to try sex with two very particular women, one of whom became a dyke but not with me.

A predator uncertain of her prey, I began to go to dyke bars. Em picked me up in one. I'd stolen her diary entry with a scanning wand. . . .

I met her in a bar. It was fairly dark and she seemed older than later it turned out she really was. A little dominating, she likes to talk with nice inclusive and sweeping gestures of her arms. It was only later when the evening paled on us both that I would see the freckles on her nose.

The whole of the several hours we spent together was some sort of regression starting from her coming in the door. Confidence, nicely dressed but not loud. But soon Joanna and I knew that she was Maude Tudor the author. Joanna had one of her books—yes, she'd run across more. Interest made a current between them and I doggedly tried to hang into a conversation in which I wasn't at all included. Boredom and I played with the dog while listening to a little informational name dropping. Nobody I'd heard of except one.

I was driving her home yet we turned up at La Salamandra. The vibes were heavy loud rock. Nerve bombing sound. Left then and went to the freak scene at the White Horse. She ended up in the ladies too often and

*finally she pried me away from some domineering black fellow who want-
ed to dance, just dance.*

    *Home then. She was talking a star spangled blue streak and didn't even
know where we were when we got there. Inside with Mandrake the happy
dog, she settled heavily into a chair, closed up at home. Almost safe, she
trusted me enough to give me a copy of her novel. And then leaving. First
I stole a kiss, then gave a warm hug and I was out the door.*

Often, I played the scene in VR, with me as Janis, with more nerve,
with sex. Or turned Em into a man and played myself as Janis, but that
never quite fit.

The dog had died a few weeks later, lethally injected at the vet's
because I couldn't pay to have his leg rebuilt. He'd been running loose
when a truck hit him.

Em and my son both screamed at me for being too proud to ask for
a loan. That's when they met. Sad about the dog, because a couple
months later, I started getting credit card applications again. Seven
years of credit limbo. With the new credit cards and my credit report
finally purged of the earlier defaults, I bought Janis VR and the rig.
While I can't stiff my friends on a loan, I felt no need to be faithful to
bank cards. But I'd pay them if I could.

So, what's better in life?

I never really wanted to know what plans my son had for me. As
soon as the milk and cookies vanished, I said, "I'm working now as a
security person. I can legally carry a .357 magnum."

"You're acting like a redneck. You've got an Ivy League education.
You've been published."

"Cool. I am a redneck." I sat down in a chair and put one foot over
the arm. What was I going to do with him for the whole weekend?
"And it wasn't Ivy League, just Columbia University General Studies.
It doesn't count. A porn novel. That doesn't count either."

"You didn't abort me. You didn't abandon me. Em says she'd help
you go back to graduate school."

Handguns take a year to become one with the household and the owner's psyche. At first, they semiotically whisper about death, the temporary and permanent stretch cavities their bullets blast into human flesh (from all the shit the NRA handgun instructors diagram with their shooting range ballpoints). Then, if it's a blued gun, it gets its first corrosion patches and turns into another metallic thing, like a car or the computer's casing, that can kill you if you're not careful. Which is something only weird people think about a lot. But I was still getting used to the gun, and taking on another adjustment project, especially one as scary as grad school, seemed a stretch.

So my son wasn't impressed that I was finally working. "It's a nice job. I just watch screens and terminals and respond if need be."

"Okay, let's not spoil the weekend," my son said as though he hadn't brought all this up. "Em wishes you weren't scared of sex. She said you haven't gotten over my dad."

"What's there to get over? Your egg was ready. Lost in hormones, I fucked him. Meat sex has consequences sometimes."

"Em said she'd been really interested one time, but you weren't even there. Like emotionally a void."

"When?" I couldn't remember. I'd seen Em plenty of times since I met her, but I couldn't remember when she felt like she was ready for me. Probably nobody was. Ah, Janis.

"Dinner in September," my son said. He went to my CD's and began to check what I had. From the back, he was a bit like his father, blond, medium build now. They'd both be stocky in middle age. Whatever my ancestral stock had been, blue-eyed blonds arrived to dominate us. Blond guys—I don't think they outnumbered dark haired people in the cities I'd lived in, but that's what I ended up fucking except for a Romanian who became famous. Men. Why shouldn't I think about trying women? I had wanted to sleep with two of them, once, but hadn't known how to make the right approach or something.

So I became a female female impersonator, but I still had problems. "Dinner in September?" I remembered going to Em's, then nothing. "I don't remember much about that." I thought it odd that I couldn't remember anything. A voided memory for dealing with Em's sexual interest in me. The Kink's song, *Lola*, affected me the same way. Friends played it for me, but I couldn't remember it at all. Memory void. *Do not enter this data into long term memory; self image can't deal with it.*

"She's seeing someone else. You better not get jealous."

"But she was never seeing me. Is this person good for her?"

He looked at me as though he didn't want to discuss my lack of a sex life anymore. "I wanna go out and play basketball."

Maybe I am the noncustodial parent, but I'd go with him. He needed, I thought, to be watched. I slipped into a jacket made out of cloth I'd woven in my Shattuck Avenue weaving class from threads I spun myself. I felt guilty about not watching Mandrake, but now I had credit cards. . .no, my son had real parents who carried him on their health insurance policy.

> You die, cockroach. Energy want to stay high
> like life. I put fresh washed glasses on my nose
> and look through the spectacles.
> All this sweat, to crawl through a gaudy fairy tale
> Where you go with your baby cutter through mutters.
>
> *from* Rumplestilskin

When we met, Em had just broken up with a woman she'd loved for fourteen years. A relationship as old as my son, and I, who didn't know whether I was coming or going, was supposed to replace that? Even a casual man-fucker like I'd been knows some people are wired for maximum commitment. This woman was. No way was I going to stick myself into that sawed-off devotion that ached to be re-attached.

Em came by during the week. She was a tall thin woman who scared me with her intensity. My fear that she'd break her neck in my shallows kept me too chilled to react to her. Now that my son told me she'd been attracted once, tried to seduce me to find my body stiff and my mind blanking each overture, I was embarrassed, awkward. "Come in. I'm working now. Security job." She came in the door and stared at me. Did she know my son relayed the information about the failed September seduction?

Having Em look at you was like having history look at you. One of those Indians who'd hated her grandfather must have gotten to one of her female ancestors. Tall, angular, she had straight black hair, not Oriental heavy but touched with that, and eyes that could have come from very old British stock or from a trek across a land bridge 14,000 years back.

"You need more than a part-time security job. I could help you get into graduate school. Maybe help you with the rent some if you need it."

"I'm just getting used to working again. Em, I heard you have a new friend," I said.

"I don't know how serious it's going to get. She's pretty intense."

But so are you, Em. "Tommy said I wasn't to get jealous."

"Don't have any right to, do you?" Em said. She looked around my living room, then sat down on the sofa. "You ought to get another dog."

"Or give the fellows another chance?"

"Start writing again."

"Olympia Press went out of business and I wasn't fast enough for the Mafia porn shops. You know they want 40 pages a day?"

"Get a journalism job. Go back to graduate school."

"What is this, bash Maude week?"

"Sorry." She wiped her hand across her eyes.

"How's the new friend? Where did you meet her?"

"She says she remembers meeting you. She's a photographer."

"Great," I said. "You really like her?"

Em didn't answer for a few minutes which made me nervous, like I'd flunked Lesbian Social Graces One. I remembered watching various gay women encounter each other in a bar. With signals too subliminal for me, they'd decide to go to Afghanistan together, to never bother each other again, to meet secretly behind a third lover's back, or something equally arcane. I always ended up feeling not just more heterosexual than ever, but dumb. Here was one of those gay things. If I was really acute, I'd be able to read this silence as either the woman had a tongue that could clean her own nostrils or she branded her lovers. Then a wave of sensitivity hit that both made me feel like a self-centered shit and made me realize that Em's new friend was really difficult. I said, "Oh," meaning, *I'm sorry.*

Em smiled slightly and said, "Hey, I've got the car. Let's go out."

"Want to share Janis with me?" I said.

Em looked at the computer as though visualizing what sorts of stretch cavities my .357 would put in it. Have to be permanent—metal, plastic and silicon lack flesh's elasticity. "No. You need to get out. We've got some daylight left. We could go up to Tamalpais."

"You said you'd take me to the Sierras once."

Am I just a car to you? Her expression wasn't subliminal now. How did I miss the signals back in September, or was my utter lack of memory for the time after dinner telling me precisely what my brain thought about her attempt at seducing me. *Forget this ever happened.* She said, "All I'm offering right now is somewhere close before dark."

"Tilden Park is even closer. I'll help with the gasoline."

"Put you on full time, did they?"

"Almost," I said. I'd found that even though I was two months behind on one of my cards, the bank machines still let me take money out. So I fished my Asolos from out of the closet, over-booted for Tilden, but I was breaking them in for the Sierras. "I'm glad you found a new friend. Really."

Takes pressure off you, doesn't it, her look said. I used the same card I'd gotten cash on to pay for the gasoline, then we drove up and walked through Tilden Park until sunset. The usual Berkeley thing was to watch from Lawrence Laboratory overlook, but here we were, looking out at a different angle. I wanted to cuddle with her without it meaning anything, but it would. She sighed and moved away from me. I wanted to tell her I was sorry about September, but that wouldn't work, either. I was a bold coward.

A leaf crashed to the sidewalk,
I crush it with my left boot foot,
Not thinking of it but thinking of A —
all women are A or B, guilty to feel confident,
guilty to be so kind people bring huge glasses of cognac,
Guilty not to have noticed the leaf until too late.
Of slightly subnormal intelligence
in a world of fingerpainting idiots.

from All Women are A or B

I began to write poetry then, the kind women write after indulging too much in Janis Joplin CD's. My son seemed happier to see me typing on the computer than jacked in, eyes in the goggles, body flinching and twisting to the power suit's caresses. He said, "So you're working again." He'd brought his fishing rods and two vests with him. I remembered I'd promised to take him fishing but I had forgotten to arrange a ride with Em. Was the Berkeley Pier so bad? Yes. Bay fish were inedible.

"Poetry," I said, "isn't real work."

"Can we go fishing this weekend?"

I'd promised him fishing, but I couldn't get Em to come with us. The indulgent credit card was about max'ed out, but I had some additional hours scheduled for next week. "Yes, we'll go fishing. Would you want to hitch or rent a car?"

Hitching—his eyes glowed, quite the teenager. Then he said, "Ma and Pa would kill me."

"It's safer these days than it was when I was a kid. We'll stop by Rides and pick up GPD's." Global Positioning Device. Any hitcher who did-n't have one wanted to be a serial killer victim or rape victim, so the killers and rapists ran their scanners while looking for riders. I always wondered what happened if someone who wanted to be a serial killer victim got picked up by a rapist. I supposed one could goad a rapist into killing.

"We should have gotten another dog," my son said.

"It's only *we* on weekends, Tommy," I said. But he was eager to try something his parents warned him against, using his own biological mom as a bad example. I wasn't supposed to know, but I found out that the Rogers disapproved when I was still hitching around regularly, before Global Positioning Devices, even before the dog. One of their friends told me the Rogers and all their friends resented my open adoption if I was going to get myself killed and upset Tommy.

Almost hurt my feelings that what would bother them would be my death's effect on my son. I must have seemed like the placenta that wouldn't let go.

"You know," my son told me, "I really do have the best of both worlds."

"That's what I wanted for you," I said.

"I get all this stuff from my parents and I can get you to help me play with it."

When would they be getting him a car? We stopped by Rides to pick up GPD's, turned them on so the bad guys knew we'd been registered, then walked down to where the cars headed out of town would pass us.

"Lake Berryessa," my son said.

"It's the most whacked-up looking lake I've ever seen," I said. "Like a lake with a plastic lining dropped in the middle of a desert."

"Chaparral, " my son corrected me.

"Very Californian," I said, meaning both my son and the lake. He did seem enchanted with me today, his unwed mother who played like a big kid. Well, if he believed hard enough, I could become his happy but hooky natural mother instead of this twisted thing I really was. And, if I threw him too weird, why then his safe parents could catch him.

Of course, we didn't catch a fish, but we had fun scrambling around the rip rap. We walked up a canyon I remembered to a place pocked with deer tracks. I said, "Mandrake took me here when I went fishing with him. Dogs don't understand temporary visits, so he tried to find me someplace I could live."

"Here?" my son asked.

"The little rush-like thing has a bulb. I took some home and did the whole routine on them: tongue touch, chew a bit and spit, eat a little bit. Well, I didn't get beyond eat a little bit, but if they'd been death camus, I'd have known by then."

"Did you learn that growing up in the South?" my son asked.

"No, from a Gary Snyder book," I said. That, to him, was just as romantic. His mom, the hippie outlaw, bearing him alive against everyone's wishes, insisting on the open adoption. If only I could step outside my skin, I could become my own heroine.

Here was my life, a mess with a few good things. Now how do I pull out the good things and step away from the mess?

We hitched out and turned our GPD's back into Rides, then he went home. I suited and goggled up and went back to Janis.

Janis was sitting in a red velvet chair, playing her guitar and singing "Me and Bobby McGee." I sat down on the virtual floor and leaned my head against her. Actually, the suit stiffened against my head and shoulder. The feel was either a little off, which meant a repair bill, or I was being hypersensitive, not giving that imaginary inch that made the VR rig really mess with the proprioceptors.

Janis put the guitar down and said, "Huh, baby. If you are such a dyke, how'a come I got a cock?"

Because I get off better that way.

Janis, being a computer's reaction to my needs, grunted. She said, "Am I still gonna O.D.?"

The suit could be loaded with syringes. We just sat there together after I got her playing "Me and Bobby McGee" again. The subliminal pick-ups in the suit seemed to be developing a life of their own. I thought about calling one of the guys I'd slept with in New York. Janis scratched me with her guitar pick. I turned around and looked at her, but the program wasn't paying any more attention to me than I'd paid to Em when she was willing.

"Bye, Janis," I said, logging out. I changed out of the suit and called Charlie from when.

And got his new girl friend. And heard about another ex-sex partner who was married now to a college professor. Charlie's new friend, the bitch, knew who I'd been, either from Charlie's talking about me, or just my voice tones. *Fence, fence, keep the old girlfriends off.*

That's what I liked about gay women. Not their needs, but their kindness toward women of any persuasion, the big *maybe* of their lives. I'd been using that kindness as a refuge, not that I hadn't been willing twice, with unwilling women.

Maybe all the guys had been perfectly fine guys. *Not the guys, me.* I'd been the one to storm and drang everything. Could have been. Could have been. Well, here I was, having dropped two perfectly okay guys who went on to marry women that I'd wanted to be when I grew up. Careers and guys, those women won. And here I was, a broke former porn novelist, depending on the kindness of a gay woman.

"Yes, I am of the race that sings under torture"
Revenuers boiled me in oil and I sang top forty.
They pricked my thumbs and operas fell off
my vocal cords—torn out with stainless steel tongs
they sang on by themselves—ivory songs so fabulous
the ocean crept up on the shore and wept.
My kin laughed, my uncle sang, crawling
through the moonshine under barbed wire
while revenuers ran into the barbs full tilt.

from After Rimbaud

So, if not capable of appreciating or giving commitment, I needed to be a virtuous ear and kind tongue. If not the heroine of the story, then I should try to be a reliable supporting citizen.

Then Em called and asked if she could come over. I heard background noises that sounded like large facility—hospital, cafeteria, the interior large room where functionaries keyboard. "Yes," I said.

When she came over, I could tell immediately that she needed someone now who wasn't sexual threat or coy eluder. I could be that virtuous ear and kind tongue. "Something happened," I said.

"Yes, indeed," Em said. "Do I attract crazy women?"

Wanting to be a comfort gave being a comfort a metal taste. "Was your last lover crazy?"

"No, but this one is. She's one half prescription of sedatives close to death."

For a second, I envied the woman. Gun owners can't play games with razors or pills without being quite obvious. Want emergency crews, chiding psychiatric aides, nervous professionals arriving at 10 p.m. to make sure this never happens again? Got to sell the gun.

Next instant, I kicked myself halfway to virtual Sonoma County for thinking that. "Em, are you going to be all right?"

"I didn't tell you she drank," Em said. "You weren't there. She seemed to love me. Does love me, if alcoholics can. I don't know if this stunt was about me or about finally getting someone like me who'd care enough to react."

"Em, please, I'm sorry."

Her eyes locked on mine as though she could port by eyeball into my thoughts. I needed desperately to do the right thing.

"I've been at the hospital all day," she said.

"So, let's walk," I said. "Through campus." Em didn't seem to notice she was shivering, goosefleshed. I got on my shoes and got out two sweaters against the night fog.

Finally, I realized Em was real, not a romantic outlaw image for me to play at being in love with, maybe seducing or being seduced by some day in the never-becoming future.

Oh, please don't let me do this wrong, I prayed to whatever graces I had left. We just walked through Berkeley, not speaking in the crowds, weaving together and apart like dust in Brownian motion, hit visibly by invisible things. Then we found a place to sit alone by a creek. Em said, "Why can't I get it right? You. Sandra."

"Am I as bad?"

"Promise you'll never do that to me."

"Em, I promise." And the promise locked me into a future I'd now have to make possible.

"Fourteen years, then I can't..."

"You scare me. One thing to experiment, but not with someone who was that intense, in a relationship for fourteen years. I'm sorry."

"Sandra was jealous of you."

"Why?"

"Some people you can't tell. The more you try to reassure them, the more they know you must be lying. And she was also jealous of your son. She wants a surrogate child."

"Em, do you?"

"You're only too eager to think of me as your gay friend. I've had male lovers, too. If I wanted a baby, I'd do it with someone I knew."

"Was she jealous of that?"

"Yes, of course. She told me that saying you're bisexual is like promising to be unfaithful."

I sighed. "Is she a successful photographer?" My own jealous twinge.

"Decent living, not great. Can we just sit here?" *Shut up, but don't go away,* her body language said.

"Yeah."

Above us in the hills, the sunset tribe celebrated another rotation that put the sun behind the Pacific shore. The fog bank rolled off the Pacific at us. Nothing I could say would make Em's pain go away any faster.

"You've now promised you'd never do what she did."

I didn't say, *I have a gun. I'd look foolish farking around with pills and I hate making myself more foolish than I already am.* I said, "Em, I would never do such a thing to my friends."

Em said, "It matters to me that you wouldn't."

I said, "And it could infect my son with suicide, if I did it." And realized I'd just promised away escape by gun. I had been flirting with it, but not committing to suicide seemed healthy.

"Is your virtual Janis going to die by overdosing?"

"How can a CD-ROM die?" I asked.

"Ah," then no more. "Can we sit for a while longer?"

"Why don't we go for coffee or something?" This time, I did feel the need coming off her, also the wish that we not end up in bed despite the need. Body to body, not mind to mind. As I'd proved by my relationship with my son, I could only partially be trusted.

Just a joke to die into a column of fine black print —
Air gone. Touch gone, light gone. Time to be
almost instantaneous.
Jet tracks unknown four million years from this electric
    glitter.
Jet stream leaving its wake in clouds—shifting snow
    somewhere else.
A photo—that stands after the man—under glass—
tracks of light captured from those times —
fired a gun and almost burnt out the film.

from Seals and Photographs

So I, not the lover but the confident, promised Em and the virtual son in my own brain that I'd walk away from the edge I realized I'd been courting only after I so promised. The reasons for the open adoption shouldn't be to make my son feel guilty that I'd birthed him, not killed him.

I said to Janis, "I owe him a more successful mother."

She, painting her toenails, looked up at me cynically. "So, how can you keep me from OD'ing?"

"How much narrative traction can you have on your own if I gave you a cock?" The new computers re-write CD's from VR suit postures, fine-tuning from pupil dilations to give me precisely what I craved. I went over, helped her finish painting her toenails.

"What I really want," Janis said, "is to become someone completely different."

Walking smoke in the goggles resolved into a thin version of me when I wrote poetry seriously. Here were all the chips of self: the me who got pregnant at 18, me with eyes in a wolf bitch flirt in a photograph at 24, me hitching to see friends in Bolinas, me listening to Em, me drawn by the gun, me watching the printer's assistant having pseudo guilt heart attacks after adultery with me, me at fifteen, sixteen, seventeen, and eighteen not getting asked to the proms. She said, "You have to integrate us all."

So the hotel in California formed around Janis where we saw her fixing ready to die. We rushed into Janis's room, cop sirens screaming through the night. Pulled the needle out of her arm and I was sitting beside her shaking her, *don't even think about it*.

And I shuddered and we shuddered and merged. I became different but would I be different with the goggles off? How to become whole, not to break off identity parts and hate them? Now the computer and goggles remembered when I was a young Bella Abzug in a velvet hat on acid in the loft of a divorced-off wife of a famous artist, looking absolutely gone and registering every minute of the folks tip-toeing around my glazed eyeballs. I was one of two people I knew who dropped all pretense of paranoia on acid. *I'm sure you're not Bella Abzug in your head*, the man had said. The suit and goggles fed me my memories, reacting at 180,000 miles per second. But I couldn't revoke the clichés in the brains whirling in that New York City loft, so then I could not be a young Columbia U redneck on acid, but had to be a Jewish girl, from Brooklyn.

And I'd tried to make my gay friends into romantic outlaws, but here was Em, a responsible woman with her job and her long term commitments, and real hurt.

As was done to me, I was doing to. . . .

Janis said, "They wrote you like you did me." She was sitting in the rattan chair that hung from the wall. "So, how do you revoke their clichés now?"

"Only thing counts is the attention paid, not the attention not paid. Follow the sound of hands clapping."

And we walked out, clapping ahead of us, got a taxi with enough other people from the party to be safe, and drove home to Shattuck Avenue.

Janis, who looked more and more like me, said, "I don't know if following the hands clapping works either. So, girlfriend, we got a way to revoke these clichés?"

Once upon a time on acid. Once in virtual reality. "Janis," I began to say the jack-out words.

"Oh, no," Janis said. "Not until you're all one person."

"I think I am," I said, looking around me. The smoky poet looked back at me from my left. "Okay, I've still got work to do."

"You've got to change yourself when the goggles are off. But there's one thing you can do from here. Make me go on to be a little old lady singer, fat-bellied on skinny legs, cackling at the young kids' woes."

The smoky poet looked like the Marilyn Monroe of scuzz poetry. I flinched, then embraced her without knowing if she was any good or not. No applause.

An old lady Janis Joplin cackled.

Fog twangs through the bridge strings—it smells safer here
I lost my purple hat and Jaeger skirt—
                                  the dog calms down
and ravels my stockings, brambles in the yard finish them.
"People in the East must be charming acquaintances,
but they seem like life's a flirt." Peter who says is is serious,
checks pre-amps and stereo devices, plans law suits.
I think, but don't say, *it is a flirt.Is isn't permanent.*
                        from "They Seem like Life's a Flirt."

Em came by when I was looking through a couple of graduate school catalogues. I said, "I could begin with a Masters from San Francisco State. I've got friends there, I think."

She said, "You can always work security part-time."

"How's Sandra? You know that if she'd really wanted to die, she'd have finished the bottle or waited for her next prescription."

"She found someone else to go the AI route with. I'm back where I started, I guess. I don't have what I want. You weren't even aware of when I wanted you."

"I knew once, but you. . . If you helped me, what would that mean?"

"It would mean I'm helping you. Nothing more."

"I feel a bit weird about you helping me. I'm not anything to you. I don't know."

Em said, "Yeah, you don't know. Look, if you ever end up in bed with a woman, you'd need to be raped. The money had no implications, no strings attached. Nothing to it."

I said, "I think I've been using you. For shelter. Do some women do that to gay women?"

"But you were there for me once."

"When Sandra played her pill game. I listened."

"Frankly, I was really surprised that you could. Most of the time, you make me worry about you."

"Sorry. Do you want to see what I've done with Janis in VR?"

Em couldn't fit into my VR suit, so she just put on the goggles and glasses. I turned on the computer and loaded the Joplin program, suddenly apprehensive. Would the Janis I left be the Janis Em saw? For a moment, what I could see of Em's face was stern.

Then Em laughed. "She's a little old lady running her own club," Em said, "and she still has an eye for young boys. She's teaching your virtual son to play the guitar."

My cynical self said, *ah, but that's just virtual reality.* I said, "But it's not as easy to fix real life."

Em said, "Or easier. The programming is looser."

"But in the life program, nothing can be completely erased," I said.

Em pulled the goggles away from her eyes and said, "Nor should it be. Who is the smoky woman?"

I said, "The poet I used to be. I thought I was gay."

"Who I love defines me, not how I make love," Em said. She pulled off the gloves and downloaded the changes she might have made in Janis while in VR with her.

So here I am, changing, adopting my former selves, evading images other people want to impose on me. I haven't checked to see what changes Em made in Janis.

All poem fragments from 3-WAY SPLIT, copyright 1978 by Rebecca Brown/Rebecca Ore.

POWERTOOL

MARK McLAUGHLIN

Whardhen asked for his thoughts on why he wrote this story, Mark McLaughlin says, "I think plastic surgery is, as Martha Stewart would say, A Good Thing. People should do whatever it takes to feel happy, attractive and self-assured." But the surgery has to be performed by someone, and that someone is bound to have opinions. What happens when those who create come to believe they also have the right to destroy?

He had been selected and so

Having found the street (in parked convertibles, aging funboys stared up at green stars constellated into dollar signs), he located the right building, opened the door and

Welcome, they said with practiced sneers, to the Bancroft Academy for the Study of Personality Enhancement, where today's young man—that's you—will discover the latest advances in the science of ego augmentation. Make us proud.

Quick as any given moment of ecstasy, they strapped him down and lubed him up and began the regimen. Withdrawing fat from his only slightly ample buttocks, they injected the creamy dollops beneath the skin in selected areas: their technique was so adroit, so practiced, that even the most skilled plastic surgeon would have been hard-pressed to determine where nature ended and bio-art began.

Having sculpted this raw clay into something worth dying for, they began to feed sparking wires into every orifice, to synchronize his various beatings and pumpings and churnings and yearnings and

They dyed his hair and his eyes and lowered his voice and raised his IQ and deleted a few of the more unpleasant memories (so long, Daddy: kind of you to buy that baseball mitt, but the kidney punches were a bit much) and they even smoothed out the broken half-moon in the bed of his left thumbnail, until

He was ready to star in his first full-length (tee hee) adult feature, complete with twin platinum-blonde cowboys, a horse-hair trunk filled with sextoys, and a mass murderer released from jail on a technicality. And with that stunning credential under his belt (among other things) and after a post-production whirlwind affair with said murderer, he was ready to write his guaranteed bestseller and hit the talkshow circuit—and his tutors, the sneering professionals at the Bancroft Academy, were so pleased that they decided to advance their star pupil to the next level.

And the campaign funds poured like steaming stallion-climax into the throbbing power-coffers, and his various dalliances with a variety of recording artists and pockmarked dictators only served to reinforce the myth and the magick that was our hero and

Eventually he was elected, and married to an airline pilot with fascinating tattoos, and when at last, AT LAST he was happy (for you see, he had once been the lowly burger boy at the Fry-Pappy Grill on 17th Street), the tutors at the Bancroft Academy handed a loaded rifle with laser tracking to their next star pupil and said, with practiced sneers, *A pretty toy for a pretty boy. Make us proud.*

TIME GYPSY

ELLEN KLAGES

Forty or fifty years ago, the concepts of gender and sexuality were radically different and the world was a much more dangerous and repressive place for lesbians and gay men. Ellen Klages, one of the early members of the San Francisco Gay and Lesbian Historical Society, tells us that the raid at Hazel's was quite real, and that there really is an article by Chandrasekhar in the '45 Astrophysical Journal. This lesbian-time travel-romance-revenge story is for all those who believe the lot of oppressed groups never improves.

Friday, February 10, 1995. 5:00 p.m.

As soon as I walk in the door, my officemate Ted starts in on me. Again. "What do you know about radiation equilibrium?" he asks.

"Nothing. Why?"

"That figures." He holds up a faded green volume. "I just found this insanely great article by Chandrasekhar in the '45 *Astrophysical Journal*. And get this—when I go to check it out, the librarian tells me I'm the first person to take it off the shelf since 1955. Can you believe that? Nobody reads anymore." He opens the book again. "Oh, by the way, Chambers was here looking for you."

I drop my armload of books on my desk with a thud. Dr. Raymond Chambers is the chairman of the Physics department, and a Nobel Prize winner, which even at Berkeley is a very, very big deal. Rumor has it he's working on some top secret government project that's a shoe-in for a second trip to Sweden.

"Yeah, he wants to see you in his office, pronto. He said something about Sara Baxter Clarke. She's that crackpot from the 50s, right? The one who died mysteriously?"

I wince. "That's her. I did my dissertation on her and her work." I wish I'd brought another sweater. This one has holes in both elbows. I'd planned a day in the library, not a visit with the head of the department.

Ted looks at me with his mouth open. "Not many chick scientists to choose from, huh? And you got a post-doc here doing that? Crazy world." He puts his book down and stretches. "Gotta run. I'm a week behind in my lab work. Real science, you know?"

I don't even react. It's only a month into the term, and he's been on my case about one thing or another—being woman, being a dyke, being close to 30—from day one. He's a jerk, but I've got other things to worry about. Like Dr. Chambers, and whether I'm about to lose my job because he found out I'm an expert on a crackpot.

Sara Baxter Clarke has been my hero since I was a kid. My pop was an army technician. He worked on radar systems, and we traveled a lot—six months in Reykjavik, then the next six in Fort Lee, New Jersey. Mom always told us we were gypsies, and tried to make it seem like an adventure. But when I was eight, mom and my brother Jeff were killed in a bus accident on Guam. After that it didn't seem like an adventure any more.

Pop was a lot better with radar than he was with little girls. He couldn't quite figure me out. I think I had too many variables for him. When I was ten, he bought me dresses and dolls, and couldn't understand why I wanted a stack of old physics magazines the base library was throwing out. I liked science. It was about the only thing that stayed the same wherever we moved. I told Pop I wanted to be a scientist when I grew up, but he said scientists were men, and I'd just get married.

I believed him, until I discovered Sara Baxter Clarke in one of those old magazines. She was British, went to MIT, had her doctorate in theoretical physics at 22. At Berkeley, she published three brilliant articles in very, very obscure journals. In 1956, she was scheduled to deliver a controversial fourth paper at an international physics conference at Stanford. She was the only woman on the program, and she was just 28.

No one knows what was in her last paper. The night before she was supposed to speak, her car went out of control and plunged over a cliff at Devil's Slide—a remote stretch of coast south of San Francisco. Her body was washed out to sea. The accident rated two inches on the inside of the paper the next day—right under a headline about some vice raid—but made a small uproar in the physics world. None of her papers or notes were ever found; her lab had been ransacked. The mystery was never solved.

I was fascinated by the mystery of her the way other kids were intrigued by Amelia Earhart. Except nobody'd ever heard of my hero. In my imagination, Sara Baxter Clarke and I were very much alike. I spent a lot of days pretending I was a scientist just like her, and even more lonely nights talking to her until I fell asleep.

So after a master's in Physics, I got a Ph.D. in the History of Science—studying her. Maybe if my obsession had been a little more practical, I wouldn't be sitting on a couch outside Dr. Chambers's office, picking imaginary lint off my sweater, trying to pretend I'm not panicking. I taught science in a junior high for a year. If I lose this fellowship, I suppose I could do that again. It's a depressing thought.

The great man's secretary finally buzzes me into his office. Dr. Chambers is a balding, pouchy man in an immaculate, perfect suit. His office smells like lemon furniture polish and pipe tobacco. It's wood paneled, plushly carpeted, with about an acre of mahogany desk. A copy of my dissertation sits on one corner.

"Dr. McCullough." He waves me to a chair. "You seem to be quite an expert on Sara Baxter Clarke."

"She was a brilliant woman," I say nervously, and hope that's the right direction for the conversation.

"Indeed. What do you make of her last paper, the one she never presented?" He picks up my work and turns to a page marked with a pale green Post-It. "'An Argument for a Practical Tempokinetics?'" He lights his pipe and looks at me through the smoke.

"I'd certainly love to read it," I say, taking a gamble. I'd give anything for a copy of that paper. I wait for the inevitable lecture about wasting my academic career studying a long-dead crackpot.

"You would? Do you actually believe Clarke had discovered a method for time travel?" he asks. "Time travel, Dr. McCullough?"

I take a bigger gamble. "Yes, I do."

Then Dr. Chambers surprises me. "So do I. I'm certain of it. I was working with her assistant, Jim Kennedy. He retired a few months after the accident. It's taken me forty years to rediscover what was tragically lost back then."

I stare at him in disbelief. "You've perfected time travel?"

He shakes his head. "Not perfected. But I assure you, tempokinetics is a reality."

Suddenly my knees won't quite hold me. I sit down in the padded leather chair next to his desk and stare at him. "You've actually done it?"

He nods. "There's been a great deal of research on tempokinetics in the last 40 years. Very hush-hush, of course. A lot of government money. But recently, several key discoveries in high-intensity gravitational field theory have made it possible to for us to finally construct a working tempokinetic chamber."

I'm having a hard time taking this all in. "Why did you want to see *me*?" I ask.

He leans against the corner of his desk. "We need someone to talk to Dr. Clarke."

"She's alive?" My heart skips several beats.

He shakes his head. "No."

"Then—?"

"Dr. McCullough, I approved your application to this university because you know more about Sara Clarke and her work than anyone else we've found. I'm offering you a once in a lifetime opportunity." He clears his throat. "I'm offering to send you back in time to attend the 1956 International Conference for Experimental Physics. I need a copy of Clarke's last paper."

I just stare at him. This feels likes some sort of test, but I have no idea what the right response is. "Why?" I ask finally.

"Because our apparatus works, but it's not practical," Dr. Chambers says, tamping his pipe. "The energy requirements for the gravitational field are enormous. The only material that's even remotely feasible is an isotope they've developed up at the Lawrence lab, and there's only enough of it for one round trip. I believe Clarke's missing paper contains the solution to our energy problem."

After all these years, it's confusing to hear someone taking Dr. Clarke's work seriously. I'm so used to being on the defensive about her, I don't know how to react. I slip automatically into scientist mode— detached and rational. "Assuming your tempokinetic chamber is operational, how do you propose that I locate Dr. Clarke?"

He picks up a piece of stiff ivory paper and hands it to me. "This is my invitation to the opening reception of the conference Friday night, at the St. Francis Hotel. Unfortunately I couldn't attend. I was back east that week. Family matters."

I look at the engraved paper in my hand. Somewhere in my files is a Xerox copy of one of these invitations. It's odd to hold a real one. "This will get me into the party. Then you'd like me to introduce myself to Sara Baxter Clarke, and ask her for a copy of her unpublished paper?"

"In a nutshell. I can give you some cash to help, er, convince her if necessary. Frankly, I don't care how you do it. I *want* that paper, Dr. McCullough."

He looks a little agitated now, and there's a shrill undertone to his voice. I suspect Dr. Chambers is planning to take credit for what's in the paper, maybe even hoping for that second Nobel. I think for a minute. Dr. Clarke's will left everything to Jim Kennedy, her assistant and fiancé. Even if Chambers gets the credit, maybe there's a way to reward the people who actually did the work. I make up a large, random number.

"I think $30,000 should do it." I clutch the arm of the chair and rub my thumb nervously over the smooth polished wood.

Dr. Chambers starts to protest, then just waves his hand. "Fine. Fine. Whatever it takes. Funding for this project is not an issue. As I said, we only have enough of the isotope to power one trip into the past and back— yours. If you recover the paper successfully, we'll be able to develop the technology for many, many more excursions. If not—" he lets his sentence trail off.

"Other people *have* tried this?" I ask, warily. It occurs to me I may be the guinea pig, usually an expendable item.

He pauses for a long moment. "No. You'll be the first. Your records indicate you have no family, is that correct?"

I nod. My father died two years ago, and the longest relationship I've ever had only lasted six months. But Chambers doesn't strike me as a liberal. Even if I was still living with Nancy, I doubt if he would count her as family. "It's a big risk. What if I decline?"

"Your post-doc application will be reviewed," he shrugs. "I'm sure you'll be happy at some other university."

So it's all or nothing. I try to weigh all the variables, make a reasoned decision. But I can't. I don't feel like a scientist right now. I feel like a ten year old kid, being offered the only thing I've ever wanted— the chance to meet Sara Baxter Clarke.

"I'll do it," I say.

"Excellent." Chambers switches gears, assuming a brisk, businesslike manner. "You'll leave a week from today at precisely 6:32 a.m. You can cannot take anything—underwear, clothes, shoes, watch—that was manufactured after 1956. My secretary has a list of antique clothing stores in the area, and some fashion magazines of the times." He looks at my jeans with distaste. "Please choose something appropriate for the reception. Can you do anything with your hair?"

My hair is short. Nothing radical, not in Berkeley in the 90s. It's more like early Beatles—what they called a pixie cut when I was a little girl—except I was always too tall and gawky to be a pixie. I run my fingers self consciously through it and shake my head.

Chambers sighs and continues. "Very well. Now, since we have to allow for the return of Clarke's manuscript, you must take something of equivalent mass—and also of that era. I'll give you the draft copy of my own dissertation. You will be also be supplied with a driver's license and university faculty card from the period, along with packets of vintage currency. You'll return with the manuscript at exactly 11:37 Monday morning. There will be no second chance. Do you understand?"

I nod, a little annoyed at his patronizing tone of voice. "If I miss the deadline, I'll be stuck in the past forever. Dr. Clarke is the only other person who could possibly send me home, and she won't be around on Monday morning. Unless—?" I let the question hang in the air.

"Absolutely not. There is one immutable law of tempokinetics, Dr. McCullough. You cannot change the past. I trust you'll remember that?" he says, standing.

Our meeting is over. I leave his office with the biggest news of my life. I wish I had someone to call and share it with. I'd settle for someone to help me shop for clothes.

Friday, February 17, 1995. 6:20 a.m.

The supply closet on the ground floor of LeConte Hall is narrow and dimly lit, filled with boxes of rubber gloves, lab coats, shop towels. Unlike many places on campus, the Physics building hasn't been remodeled in the last forty years. This has always been a closet, and it isn't likely to be occupied at 6:30 on any Friday morning.

I sit on the linoleum floor, my back against a wall, dressed in an appropriate period costume. I think I should feel nervous, but I feel oddly detached. I sip from a cup of lukewarm 7-11 coffee and observe. I don't have any role in this part of the experiment—I'm just the guinea pig. Dr. Chambers's assistants step carefully over my outstretched legs and make the final adjustments to the battery of apparatus that surrounds me.

At exactly 6:28 by my antique Timex, Dr. Chambers himself appears in the doorway. He shows me a thick packet of worn bills and the bulky, rubber-banded typescript of his dissertation, then slips both of them into a battered leather briefcase. He places the case on my lap and extends his hand. But when I reach up to shake it, he frowns and takes the 7-11 cup.

"Good luck, Dr. McCullough," he says formally. Nothing more. What more would he say to a guinea pig? He looks at his watch, then hands the cup to a young man in a black t-shirt, who types in one last line of code, turns off the light, and closes the door.

I sit in the dark and begin to get the willies. No one has ever done this. I don't know if the cool linoleum under my legs is the last thing I will ever feel. Sweat drips down between my breasts as the apparatus begins to hum. There is a moment of intense—sensation. It's not sound, or vibration, or anything I can quantify. It's as if all the fingernails in the world are suddenly raked down all the blackboards, and in the same moment oxygen is transmuted to lead. I am pressed to the floor by a monstrous force, but every hair on my body is erect. Just when I feel I can't stand it any more, the humming stops.

My pulse is racing, and I feel dizzy, a little nauseous. I sit for a minute, half-expecting Dr. Chambers to come in and tell me the experiment has failed, but no one comes. I try to stand—my right leg has fallen asleep—and grope for the light switch near the door.

In the light from the single bulb, I see that the apparatus is gone, but the gray metal shelves are stacked with the same boxes of gloves and shop towels. My leg all pins and needles, I lean against a brown cardboard box stenciled Bayside Laundry Service, San Francisco, 3, California.

It takes me a minute before I realize that's odd. Either those are very old towels, or I'm somewhere pre-ZIP code.

I let myself out of the closet, and walk awkwardly down the empty hallway, my spectator pumps echoing on the linoleum. I search for further confirmation. The first room I peer into is a lab—high stools in front of black slab tables with Bunsen burners, gray boxes full of dials and switches. A slide rule at every station.

I've made it.

Friday, February 17, 1956. 7:00 a.m.

The campus is deserted on this drizzly February dawn, as is Telegraph Avenue. The streetlights are still on—white lights, not yellow sodium—and through the mist I can see faint lines of red and green neon on stores down the avenue. I feel like Marco Polo as I navigate through a world that is both alien and familiar. The buildings are the same, but the storefronts and signs look like stage sets or photos from old *Life* magazines.

It takes me more than an hour to walk downtown. I am disoriented by each shop window, each passing car. I feel as if I'm a little drunk, walking too attentively through the landscape, and not connected to it. Maybe it's the colors. Everything looks too real. I grew up with grainy black-and-white TV reruns and 50s technicolor films that have faded over time, and it's disconcerting that this world is not overlaid with that pink orange tinge.

The warm aromas of coffee and bacon lure me into a hole-in-the-wall cafe. I order the special—eggs, bacon, hash browns and toast. The toast comes dripping with butter and the jelly is in a glass jar, not a little plastic tub. When the bill comes it is 55¢. I leave a generous dime tip then catch the yellow F bus and ride down Shattuck Avenue, staring at the round-fendered black Chevys and occasional pink Studebakers that fill the streets.

The bus is full of morning commuters—men in dark jackets and hats, women in dresses and hats. In my tailored suit I fit right in. I'm surprised that no one looks 50s—retro 50s—the 50s that filtered down to the 90s. No poodle skirts, no DA haircuts. All the men remind me of my pop. A man in a gray felt hat has the *Chronicle,* and I read over his shoulder. Eisenhower is considering a second term. The San Francisco police chief promises a crackdown on vice. *Peanuts* tops the comics page and there's a Rock Hudson movie playing at the Castro Theatre. Nothing new there.

As we cross the Bay Bridge I'm amazed at how small San Francisco looks—the skyline is carved stone, not glass and steel towers. A green Muni streetcar takes me down the middle of Market Street to Powell. I check into the St. Francis, the city's finest hotel. My room costs less than I've paid for a night in a Motel 6.

All my worldly goods fit on the desktop—Chambers's manuscript; a brown leather wallet with a driver's license, a Berkeley faculty card, and twenty-three dollars in small bills; the invitation to the reception tonight; and 30,000 dollars in banded stacks of 50-dollar bills. I pull three bills off the top of one stack and put the rest in the drawer, under the cream-colored hotel stationery. I have to get out of this suit and these shoes.

Woolworth's has a toothbrush and other plastic toiletries, and a tin "Tom Corbett, Space Cadet" alarm clock. I find a pair of pleated pants, an Oxford cloth shirt, and wool sweater at the City of Paris. Macy's Men's Shop yields a pair of "dungarees" and two t-shirts I can sleep in— 69 cents each. A snippy clerk gives me the eye in the Boys department, so I invent a nephew, little Billy, and buy him black basketball sneakers that are just my size.

After a shower and a change of clothes, I try to collect my thoughts, but I'm too keyed up to sit still. In a few hours I'll actually be in the same room as Sara Baxter Clarke. I can't distinguish between fear and excitement, and spend the afternoon wandering aimlessly around the city, gawking like a tourist.

Friday, February 17, 1956. 7:00 p.m.

Back in my spectator pumps and my tailored navy suit, I present myself at the doorway of the reception ballroom and surrender my invitation. The tuxedoed young man looks over my shoulder, as if he's expecting someone behind me. After a moment he clears his throat.

"And you're Mrs.—?" he asks, looking down at his typewritten list.

"Dr. McCullough," I say coolly, and give him an even stare. "Mr. Chambers is out of town. He asked me to take his place."

After a moment's hesitation he nods, and writes my name on a white card, pinning it to my lapel like a corsage.

Ballroom A is a sea of gray suits, crew cuts, bow-ties and heavy black-rimmed glasses. Almost everyone is male, as I expected, and almost everyone is smoking, which surprises me. Over in one corner is a knot of women in bright cocktail dresses, each with a lacquered football helmet of hair. Barbie's cultural foremothers.

I accept a canapé from a passing waiter and ease my way to the corner. Which one is Dr. Clarke? I stand a few feet back, scanning nametags. Mrs. Niels Bohr. Mrs. Richard Feynman. Mrs. Ernest Lawrence. I am impressed by the company I'm in, and dismayed that none of the women has a name of her own. I smile an empty cocktail party smile as I move away from the wives and scan the room. Gray suits with a sprinkling of blue, but all male. Did I arrive too early?

I am looking for a safe corner, one with a large, sheltering potted palm, when I hear a blustery male voice say, "So, Dr. Clarke. Trying the H.G. Wells route, are you? Waste of the taxpayer's money, all that science fiction stuff, don't you think?"

A woman's voice answers. "Not at all. Perhaps I can change your mind at Monday's session." I can't see her yet, but her voice is smooth and rich, with a bit of a lilt or a brogue—one of those vocal clues that says "I'm not an American." I stand rooted to the carpet, so awestruck I'm unable to move.

"Jimmy, will you see if there's more champagne about?" I hear her ask. I see a motion in the sea of gray and astonish myself by flagging a waiter and taking two slender flutes from his tray. I step forward in the direction of her voice. "Here you go," I say, trying to keep my hand from shaking. "I've got an extra."

"How very resourceful of you," she laughs. I am surprised that she is a few inches shorter than me. I'd forgotten she'd be about my age. She takes the glass and offers me her other hand. "Sara Clarke," she says.

"Carol McCullough." I touch her palm. The room seems suddenly bright and the voices around me fade into a murmur. I think for a moment that I'm dematerializing back to 1995, but nothing so dramatic happens. I'm just so stunned that I forget to breathe while I look at her.

Since I was ten years old, no matter where we lived, I have had a picture of Sara Baxter Clarke over my desk. I cut it out of that old physics magazine. It is grainy, black and white, the only photo of her I've ever found. In it, she's who I always wanted to be—competent, serious, every inch a scientist. She wears a white lab coat and a pair of rimless glasses, her hair pulled back from her face. A bald man in an identical lab coat is showing her a piece of equipment. Neither of them is smiling.

I know every inch of that picture by heart. But I didn't know that her hair was a coppery red, or that her eyes were such a deep, clear green. And until this moment, it had never occurred to me that she could laugh.

The slender blond man standing next to her interrupts my reverie. "I'm Jim Kennedy, Sara's assistant."

Jim Kennedy. Her fiancé. I feel like the characters in my favorite novel are all coming to life, one by one.

"You're not a wife, are you?" he asks.

I shake my head. "Post doc. I've only been at Cal a month."

"We're neighbors, then. What's your field?"

I take a deep breath. "Tempokinetics. I'm a great admirer of Dr. Clarke's work."

"Really?" Dr. Clarke turns, raising one eyebrow in surprise. "Well then we should have a chat. Are you—?" She stops in mid-sentence and swears almost inaudibly. "Damn. It's Dr. Wilkins and I must be pleasant. He's quite a muckety-muck at the NSF, and I need the funding." She takes a long swallow of champagne, draining the crystal flute. "Jimmy, why don't you get Dr. McCullough another drink and see if you can persuade her to join us for supper."

I start to make a polite protest, but Jimmy takes my elbow and steers me through the crowd to an unoccupied sofa. Half an hour later we are deep in a discussion of quantum field theory when Dr. Clarke appears and says, "Let's make a discreet exit, shall we? I'm famished."

Like conspirators, we slip out a side door and down a flight of service stairs. The Powell Street cable car takes us over Nob Hill into North Beach, the Italian section of town. We walk up Columbus to one of my favorite restaurants—the New Pisa—where I discover that nothing much has changed in forty years except the prices.

The waiter brings a carafe of red wine and a trio of squat drinking glasses and we eat family style—bowls of pasta with red sauce and steaming loaves of crusty garlic bread. I am speechless as Sara Baxter Clarke talks about her work, blithely answering questions I have wanted to ask my whole life. She is brilliant, fascinating. And beautiful. My food disappears without me noticing a single mouthful.

Over coffee and spumoni she insists, for the third time, that I call her Sara, and asks me about my own studies. I have to catch myself a few times, biting back citations from Stephen Hawking and other works that won't be published for decades. It is such an engrossing, exhilarating conversation, I can't bring myself to shift it to Chambers's agenda. We leave when we notice the restaurant has no other customers.

"How about a nightcap?" she suggests when we reach the sidewalk.

"Not for me," Jimmy begs off. "I've got an 8:30 symposium tomorrow morning. But why don't you two go on ahead. The Paper Doll is just around the corner."

Sara gives him an odd, cold look and shakes her head. "Not funny, James," she says and glances over at me. I shrug noncommittally. It's seems they have a private joke I'm not in on.

"Just a thought," he says, then kisses her on the cheek and leaves. Sara and I walk down to Vesuvio's, one of the bars where Kerouac, Ferlinghetti, and Ginsberg spawned the Beat Generation. Make that *will* spawn. I think we're a few months too early.

Sara orders another carafe of raw red wine. I feel shy around her, intimidated, I guess. I've dreamed of meeting her for so long, and I want her to like me. As we begin to talk, we discover how similar, and lonely, our childhoods were. We were raised as only children. We both begged for chemistry sets we never got. We were expected to know how to iron, not know about ions. Midway through her second glass of wine, Sara sighs.

"Oh, bugger it all. Nothing's really changed, you know. It's still just snickers and snubs. I'm tired of fighting for a seat in the old boys' club. Monday's paper represents five years of hard work, and there aren't a handful of people at this entire conference who've had the decency to treat me as anything but a joke." She squeezes her napkin into a tighter and tighter wad, and a tear trickles down her cheek. "How do you stand it, Carol?"

How can I tell her? I've stood it because of you. You're my hero. I've always asked myself what Sara Baxter Clarke would do, and steeled myself to push through. But now she's not a hero. She's real, this woman across the table from me. This Sara's not the invincible, ever-practical scientist I always thought she was. She's as young and as vulnerable as I am.

I want to ease her pain the way that she, as my imaginary mentor, has always eased mine. I reach over and put my hand over hers; she stiffens, but she doesn't pull away. Her hand is soft under mine, and I think of touching her hair, gently brushing the red tendrils off the back of her neck, kissing the salty tears on her cheek.

Maybe I've always had a crush on Sara Baxter Clarke. But I can't be falling in love with her. She's straight. She's 40 years older than I am. And in the back of my mind, the chilling voice of reality reminds me that she'll also be dead in two days. I can't reconcile that with the vibrant woman sitting in this smoky North Beach bar. I don't want to. I drink two more glasses of wine and hope that will silence the voice long enough for me to enjoy these few moments.

We are still talking, our fingertips brushing on the scarred wooden tabletop, when the bartender announces last call. "Oh, bloody hell," Sara says. "I've been having such a lovely time I've gone and missed the ferry. I hope I have enough for the cab fare. My Chevy's over in the car park at Berkeley."

"That's ridiculous," I hear myself say. "I've got a room at the hotel. Come back with me and catch the ferry in the morning." It's the wine talking. I don't know what I'll do if she says yes. I want her to say yes so much .

"No, I couldn't impose. I'll simply—" she protests, and then stops.

"Oh, yes, then. Thank you. It's very generous."

So here we are. At 2:00 a.m. the hotel lobby is plush and utterly empty. We ride up in the elevator in a sleepy silence that becomes awkward as soon as we are alone in the room. I nervously gather my new clothes off the only bed and gesture to her to sit down. I pull a t-shirt out of its crinkly cellophane wrapper. "Here," I hand it to her. "It's not elegant, but it'll have to do as a nightgown."

She looks at the t-shirt in her lap, and at the dungarees and black sneakers in my arms, an odd expression on her face. Then she sighs, a deep, achey sounding sigh. It's the oddest reaction to a t-shirt I've ever heard .

"The Paper Doll would have been all right, wouldn't it?" she asks softly.

Puzzled, I stop crinkling the other cellophane wrapper and lean against the dresser. "I guess so. I've never been there." She looks worried, so I keep talking. "But there are a lot of places I haven't been. I'm new in town. Just got here. Don't know anybody yet, haven't really gotten around. What kind of place is it?"

She freezes for a moment, then says, almost in a whisper, "It's a bar for women."

"Oh," I nod. "Well, that's okay." Why would Jimmy suggest a gay bar? It's an odd thing to tell your fiancée. Did he guess about me somehow? Or maybe he just thought we'd be safer there late at night, since—

My musings—and any other rational thoughts—come to a dead stop when Sara Baxter Clarke stands up, cups my face in both her hands and kisses me gently on the lips. She pulls away, just a few inches, and looks at me.

I can't believe this is happening. "Aren't you—isn't Jimmy—?"

"He's my dearest chum, and my partner in the lab. But romantically? No. Protective camouflage. For both of us," she answers, stroking my face.

I don't know what to do. Every dream I've ever had is coming true tonight. But how can I kiss her? How can I begin something I know is doomed? She must see the indecision in my face, because she looks scared, and starts to take a step backwards. And I can't let her go. Not yet. I put my hand on the back of her neck and pull her into a second, longer kiss.

We move to the bed after a few minutes. I feel shy, not wanting to make a wrong move. But she kisses my face, my neck, and pulls me down onto her. We begin slowly, cautiously undressing each other. I fumble at the unfamiliar garter belts and stockings, and she smiles, undoing the rubber clasps for me. Her slender body is pale and freckled, her breasts small with dusty pink nipples.

Her fingers gently stroke my arms, my thighs. When I hesitantly put my mouth on her breast, she moans, deep in her throat, and laces her fingers through my hair. After a minute her hands ease my head down her body. The hair between her legs is ginger, the ends dark and wet. I taste the salty musk of her when I part her lips with my tongue. She moans again, almost a growl. When she comes it is a single, fierce explosion.

We finally fall into an exhausted sleep, spooned around each other, both t-shirts still crumpled on the floor.

Saturday, February 18, 1956. 7:00 a.m.

Light comes through a crack in the curtains. I'm alone in a strange bed. I'm sure last night was a dream, but then I hear the shower come on in the bathroom. Sara emerges a few minutes later, toweling her hair. She smiles and leans over me—warm and wet and smelling of soap.

"I have to go," she whispers, and kisses me.

I want to ask if I'll see her again, want to pull her down next to me and hold her for hours. But I just stroke her hair and say nothing.

She sits on the edge of the bed. "I've got an eleven o'clock lab, and there's another dreadful cocktail thing at Stanford this evening. I'd give it a miss, but Shockley's going to be there, and he's front runner for the next Nobel, so I have to make an appearance. Meet me after?"

"Yes," I say, breathing again. "Where?"

"Why don't you take the train down. I'll pick you up at the Palo Alto station at half-past seven and we can drive to the coast for dinner. Wear those nice black trousers. If it's not too dreary, we'll walk on the beach."

She picks up her wrinkled suit from the floor where it landed last night, and gets dressed. "Half past seven, then?" she says, and kisses my cheek. The door clicks shut and she's gone.

I lie tangled in the sheets, and curl up into the pillow like a contented cat. I am almost asleep again when an image intrudes— a crumpled Chevy on the rocks below Devil's Slide. It's like a fragment of a nightmare, not quite real in the morning light. But which dream is real now?

Until last night, part of what had made Sara Baxter Clarke so compelling was her enigmatic death. Like Amelia Earhart or James Dean, she had been a brilliant star that ended so abruptly she became legendary. Larger than life. But I can still feel where her lips brushed my cheek. Now she's very much life-size, and despite Chambers's warnings, I will do anything to keep her that way.

Saturday, February 18, 1956. 7:20 p.m.
The platform at the Palo Alto train station is cold and windy. I'm glad I've got a sweater, but it makes my suit jacket uncomfortably tight across my shoulders. I've finished the newspaper and am reading the train schedule when Sara comes up behind me.

"Hullo there." She's wearing a nubby beige dress under a dark wool coat and looks quite elegant.

"Hi." I reach to give her a hug, but she steps back.

"Have you gone mad?" she says, scowling. She crosses her arms over her chest. "What on earth were you thinking?"

"Sorry." I'm not sure what I've done. "It's nice to see you," I say hesitantly.

"Yes, well, me too. But you can't just—oh, you know," she says, waving her hand.

I don't, so I shrug. She gives me an annoyed look, then turns and opens the car door. I stand on the pavement for a minute, bewildered, then get in.

Her Chevy feels huge compared to the Toyota I drive at home, and there are no seatbelts. We drive in uncomfortable silence all through Palo Alto and onto the winding, two-lane road that leads to the coast. Our second date isn't going well.

After about ten minutes, I can't stand it any more. "I'm sorry about the hug. I guess it's still a big deal here, huh?"

She turns her head slightly, still keeping her eyes on the road. "Here?" she asks. "What utopia are you from, then?"

I spent the day wandering the city in a kind of haze, alternately giddy in love and worrying about this moment. How can I tell her where—when—I'm from? And how much should I tell her about why? I count to three, and then count again before I answer. "From the future."

"Very funny," she says. I can hear in her voice that she's hurt. She stares straight ahead again.

"Sara, I'm serious. Your work on time travel isn't just theory. I'm a post-doc at Cal. In 1995. The head of the physics department, Dr. Chambers, sent me back here to talk to you. He says he worked with you and Jimmy, back before he won the Nobel Prize."

She doesn't say anything for a minute, then pulls over onto a wide place at the side of the road. She switches off the engine and turns towards me.

"Ray Chambers? The Nobel Prize? Jimmy says he can barely do his own lab work." She shakes her head, then lights a cigarette, flicking the match out the window into the darkness. "Ray set you up for this, didn't he? To get back at Jimmy for last term's grade? Well it's a terrible joke," she says turning away, "and you are one of the cruelest people I have ever met."

"Sara, it's not a joke. Please believe me." I reach across the seat to take her hand, but she jerks it away.

I take a deep breath, trying desperately to think of something that will convince her. "Look, I know it sounds crazy, but hear me out. In September, *Modern Physics* is going to publish an article about you and your work. When I was ten years old—in 1975—I read it sitting on the back porch of my father's quarters at Fort Ord. That article inspired me to go into science. I read about you, and I knew when I grew up I wanted to travel through time."

She stubs out her cigarette. "Go on."

So I tell her all about my academic career, and my "assignment" from Chambers. She listens without interrupting me. I can't see her expression in the darkened car.

After I finish, she says nothing, then sighs. "This is rather a lot to digest, you know. But I can't very well believe in my work without giving your story some credence, can I?" She lights another cigarette, then asks the question I've been dreading. "So if you've come all this way to offer me an enormous sum for my paper, does that mean something happened to it—or to me?" I still can't see her face, but her voice is shaking.

I can't do it. I can't tell her. I grope for a convincing lie. "There was a fire. A lot of papers were lost. Yours is the one they want."

"I'm not a faculty member at *your* Cal, am I?"

"No."

She takes a long drag on her cigarette, then asks, so softly I can barely hear her, "Am I—?" She lets her question trail off and is silent for a minute, then sighs again. "No, I won't ask. I think I prefer to bumble about like other mortals. You're a dangerous woman, Carol McCullough. I'm afraid you can tell me too many things I have no right to know." She reaches for the ignition key, then stops. "There is one thing I must know, though. Was last night as carefully planned as everything else?"

"Jesus, no." I reach over and touch her hand. She lets me hold it this time. "No, I had no idea. Other than finding you at the reception, last night had nothing to do with science."

To my great relief, she chuckles. "Well, perhaps chemistry, don't you think?" She glances in the rearview mirror then pulls me across the wide front seat and into her arms. We hold each other in the darkness for a long time, and kiss for even longer. Her lips taste faintly of gin.

We have a leisurely dinner at a restaurant overlooking the beach in Half Moon Bay. Fresh fish and a dry white wine. I have the urge to tell her about the picture, about how important she's been to me. But as I start to speak, I realize she's more important to me now, so I just tell her that. We finish the meal gazing at each other as if we were ordinary lovers.

Outside the restaurant, the sky is cloudy and cold, the breeze tangy with salt and kelp. Sara pulls off her high heels and we walk down a sandy path, holding hands in the darkness. Within minutes we are both freezing. I pull her to me and lean down to kiss her on the deserted beach. "You know what I'd like," I say, over the roar of the surf.

"What?" she murmurs into my neck.

"I'd like to take you dancing."

She shakes her head. "We can't. Not here. Not now. It's against the law, you know. Or perhaps you don't. But it is, I'm afraid. And the police have been on a rampage in the city lately. One bar lost its license just because two men were holding hands. They arrested both as sexual vagrants and for being—oh, what was the phrase—lewd and dissolute persons."

"Sexual vagrants? That's outrageous!"

"Exactly what the newspapers said. An outrage to public decency. Jimmy knew one of the poor chaps. He was in Engineering at Stanford, but after his name and address were published in the paper, he lost his job. Does that still go on where you're from?"

"I don't think so. Maybe in some places. I don't really know. I'm afraid I don't pay any attention to politics. I've never needed to."

Sara sighs. "What a wonderful luxury that must be, not having to be so careful all the time."

"I guess so." I feel a little guilty that it's not something I worry about. But I was four years old when Stonewall happened. By the time I came out, in college, being gay was more of a lifestyle than a perversion. At least in San Francisco.

"It's sure a lot more public," I say after a minute. "Last year there were a quarter of a million people at the Gay Pride parade. Dancing down Market Street and carrying signs about how great it is to be queer."

"You're pulling my leg now. Aren't you?" When I shake my head she smiles. "Well, I'm glad. I'm glad that this witch hunt ends. And in a few months, when I get my equipment up and running, perhaps I shall travel to dance at your parade. But for tonight, why don't we just go to my house? At least I've got a new hi-fi."

So we head back up the coast. One advantage to these old cars, the front seat is as big as a couch; we drive up Highway 1 sitting next to each other, my arm resting on her thigh. The ocean is a flat, black void on our left, until the road begins to climb and the water disappears behind jagged cliffs. On the driver's side the road drops off steeply as we approach Devil's Slide.

I feel like I'm coming to the scary part of a movie I've seen before. I'm afraid I know what happens next. My right hand grips the upholstery and I brace myself for the oncoming car or the loose patch of gravel or whatever it is that will send us skidding off the road and onto the rocks.

But nothing happens. Sara hums as she drives, and I realize that although this is the spot I dread, it means nothing to her. At least not tonight.

As the road levels out again, it is desolate, with few traces of civilization. Just beyond a sign that says "Sharp Park" is a trailer camp with a string of bare lightbulbs outlining its perimeter. Across the road is a seedy looking roadhouse with a neon sign that blinks "Hazel's." The parking lot is jammed with cars. Saturday night in the middle of nowhere.

We drive another hundred yards when Sara suddenly snaps her fingers and does a U-turn.

Please don't go back to the cliffs, I beg silently. "What's up?" I ask out loud.

"Hazel's. Jimmy was telling me about it last week. It's become a rather gay club, and since it's over the county line, out here in the boondocks, he says anything goes. Including dancing. Besides, I thought I spotted his car."

"Are you sure?"

"No, but there aren't that many '39 Packards still on the road. If it isn't, we'll just continue on." She pulls into the parking lot and finds a space at the back, between the trash cans and the ocean.

Hazel's is a noisy, smoky place—a small, single room with a bar along one side—jammed wall-to-wall with people. Hundreds of them, mostly men, but more than a few women. When I look closer, I realize that some of the "men" are actually women with slicked-back hair, ties, and sportcoats.

We manage to get two beers, and find Jimmy on the edge of the dance floor—a minuscule square of linoleum, not more than 10 x 10, where dozens of people are dancing to Bill Haley & the Comets blasting from the jukebox. Jimmy's in a tweed jacket and chinos, his arm around the waist of a young Latino man in a tight white t-shirt and even tighter blue jeans. We elbow our way through to them and Sara gives Jimmy a kiss on the cheek. "Hullo, love," she says.

He's obviously surprised—shocked—to see Sara, but when he sees me behind her, he grins. "I told you so."

"James, you don't know the half of it," Sara says, smiling, and puts her arm around me.

We dance for a few songs in the hot, crowded bar. I take off my jacket, then my sweater, draping them over the railing next to the bottles of beer. After the next song I roll up the sleeves of my button-down shirt. When Jimmy offers to buy another round of beers, I look at my watch and shake my head. It's midnight, and as much as I wanted to dance with Sara, I want to sleep with her even more.

"One last dance, then let's go, okay?" I ask, shouting to be heard over the noise of the crowd and the jukebox. "I'm bushed."

She nods. Johnny Mathis starts to sing, and we slow dance, our arms around each other. My eyes are closed and Sara's head is resting on my shoulder when the first of the cops bursts through the front door.

Sunday, February 19, 1956. 12:05 a.m.

A small army of uniformed men storms into the bar. Everywhere around us people are screaming in panic, and I'm buffeted by the bodies running in all directions. People near the back race for the rear door. A red faced, heavy-set man in khaki, a gold star on his chest, climbs onto the bar. "This is a raid," he shouts. He has brought reporters with him, and flashbulbs suddenly illuminate the stunned, terrified faces of people who had been sipping their drinks moments before.

Khaki-shirted deputies, nightsticks in hand, block the front door. There are so many uniforms. At least forty men—highway patrol, sheriff's department, and even some army MPs—begin to form a gauntlet leading to the back door, now the only exit.

Jimmy grabs my shoulders. "Dance with Antonio," he says urgently. "I've just met him, but it's our best chance of getting out of here. I'll take Sara."

I nod and the Latino man's muscular arms are around my waist. He smiles shyly just as someone pulls the plug on the jukebox and Johnny Mathis stops in mid-croon. The room is quiet for a moment, then the cops begin barking orders. We stand against the railing, Jimmy's arm curled protectively around Sara's shoulders, Antonio's around mine. Other people have done the same thing, but there are not enough women, and men who had been dancing now stand apart from each other, looking scared.

The uniforms are lining people up, herding them like sheep toward the back. We join the line and inch forward. The glare of headlights through the half-open back door cuts through the smoky room like the beam from a movie projector. There is an icy draft and I reach back for my sweater, but the railing is too far away, and the crush of people too solid to move any direction but forward. Jimmy sees me shivering and drapes his sportcoat over my shoulders.

We are in line for more than an hour, as the cops at the back door check everyone's ID. Sara leans against Jimmy's chest, squeezing my hand tightly once or twice, when no one's looking. I am scared, shaking, but the uniforms seem to be letting most people go. Every few seconds, a car starts up in the parking lot, and I can hear the crunch of tires on gravel as someone leaves Hazel's for the freedom of the highway.

As we get closer to the door, I can see a line of black vans parked just outside, ringing the exit. They are paneled with wooden benches, filled with the men who are not going home, most of them sitting with their shoulders sagging. One van holds a few women with crewcuts or slicked back-hair, who glare defiantly into the night.

We are ten people back from the door when Jimmy slips a key into my hand and whispers into my ear. "We'll have to take separate cars. Drive Sara's back to the city and we'll meet at the lobby bar in your hotel."

"The bar will be closed," I whisper back. "Take my key and meet me in the room. I'll get another at the desk." He nods as I hand it to him.

The cop at the door looks at Sara's elegant dress and coat, barely glances at her outstretched ID, and waves her and Jimmy outside without a word. She pauses at the door and looks back at me, but an MP shakes his head and points to the parking lot. "Now or never, lady," he says, and Sara and Jimmy disappear into the night.

I'm alone. Antonio is a total stranger, but his strong arm is my only support until a man in a suit pulls him away. "Nice try, sweetie," the man says to him. "But I've seen you in here before, dancing with your pansy friends." He turns to the khaki-shirted deputy and says, "He's one of the perverts. Book him." The cop pulls Antonio's arm up between his shoulder blades, then cuffs his hands behind his back. "Time for a little ride, pretty boy," he grins, and drags Antonio out into one of the black vans.

Without thinking, I take a step towards his retreating back. "Not so fast," says another cop, with acne scars across both cheeks. He looks at Jimmy's jacket, and down at my pants and my black basketball shoes with a sneer. Then he puts his hands on my breasts, groping me. "Loose ones. Not all tied down like those other he-shes. I like that." He leers and pinches one of my nipples.

I yell for help, and try to pull away, but he laughs and shoves me up against the stack of beer cases that line the back hallway. He pokes his nightstick between my legs. "So you want to be a man, huh, butchie? Well just what do you think you've got in there?" He jerks his night-stick up into my crotch so hard tears come to my eyes.

I stare at him, in pain, in disbelief. I am too stunned to move or to say anything. He cuffs my hands and pushes me out the back door and into the van with the other glaring women.

Sunday, February 19, 1956. 10:00 a.m.

I plead guilty to being a sex offender, and pay the $50 fine. Being arrested can't ruin my life. I don't even exist here.

Sara and Jimmy are waiting on a wooden bench outside the holding cell of the San Mateo County jail. "Are you all right, love?" she asks.

I shrug. "I'm exhausted. I didn't sleep. There were ten of us in one cell. The woman next to me—a stone butch?—really tough, Frankie— she had a pompadour—two cops took her down the hall—when she came back the whole side of her face was swollen, and after that she didn't say anything to anyone, but I'm okay, I just—" I start to shake. Sara takes one arm and Jimmy takes the other, and they walk me gen-tly out to the parking lot.

The three of us sit in the front seat of Jimmy's car, and as soon as we are out of sight of the jail, Sara puts her arms around me and holds me, brushing the hair off my forehead. When Jimmy takes the turnoff to the San Mateo bridge, she says, "We checked you out of the hotel this morning. Precious little to check, actually, except for the briefcase. Anyway, I thought you'd be more comfortable at my house. We need to get you some breakfast and a bed." She kisses me on the cheek. "I've told Jimmy everything, by the way."

I nod sleepily, and the next thing I know we're standing on the front steps of a brown shingled cottage and Jimmy's pulling away. I don't think I'm hungry, but Sara makes scrambled eggs and bacon and toast, and I eat every scrap of it. She runs a hot bath, grimacing at the purpling, thumb shaped bruises on my upper arms, and gently washes my hair and my back. When she tucks me into bed, pulling a blue quilt around me, and curls up beside me, I start to cry. I feel so battered and so fragile, and I can't remember the last time someone took care of me this way.

Sunday, February 19, 1956. 5:00 p.m.

I wake up to the sound of rain and the enticing smell of pot roast baking in the oven. Sara has laid out my jeans and a brown sweater at the end of the bed. I put them on, then pad barefoot into the kitchen. There are cardboard boxes piled in one corner, and Jimmy and Sara are sitting at the yellow formica table with cups of tea, talking intently.

"Oh good, you're awake." She stands and gives me a hug. "There's tea in the pot. If you think you're up to it, Jimmy and I need to tell you a few things."

"I'm a little sore, but I'll be okay. I'm not crazy about the 50s, though." I pour from the heavy ceramic pot. The tea is some sort of Chinese blend, fragrant and smoky. "What's up?"

"First a question. If my paper isn't entirely—complete—could there possibly be any repercussions for you?"

I think for a minute. "I don't think so. If anyone knew exactly what was in it, they wouldn't have sent me."

"Splendid. In that case, I've come to a decision." She pats the battered brown briefcase. "In exchange for the extraordinary wad of cash in here, we shall send back a perfectly reasonable sounding paper. What only the three of us will know is that I have left a few things out. This, for example." She picks up a pen, scribbles a complex series of numbers and symbols on a piece of paper, and hands it to me.

I study it for a minute. It's very high-level stuff, but I know enough physics to get the gist of it. "If this really works, it's the answer to the energy problem. It's exactly the piece Chambers needs."

"Very, very good," she says smiling. "It's also the part I will never give him."

I raise one eyebrow.

"I read the first few chapters of his dissertation this afternoon while you were sleeping," she says, tapping the manuscript with her pen. "It's a bit uneven, although parts of it are quite good. Unfortunately, the good parts were written by a graduate student named Gilbert Young."

I raise the other eyebrow. "But that paper's what Chambers wins the Nobel for."

"Son of a bitch." Jimmy slaps his hand down onto the table. "Gil was working for me while he finished the last of his dissertation. He was a bright guy, original research, solid future—but he started having these headaches. The tumor was inoperable, and he died six months ago. Ray said he'd clean out Gil's office for me. I just figured he was trying to get back on my good side."

"We can't change what Ray does with Gil's work. But I won't give him my work to steal in the future." Sara shoves Chambers's manuscript to the other side of the table. "Or now. I've decided not to present my paper in the morning."

I feel very lightheaded. I *know* she doesn't give her paper, but— "Why not?" I ask.

"While I was reading the manuscript this afternoon, I heard that fat sheriff interviewed on the radio. They arrested 90 people at Hazel's last night, Carol, people like us. People who only wanted to dance with each other. But he kept bragging about how they cleaned out a nest of perverts. And I realized—in a blinding moment of clarity—that the university is a branch of the state, and the sheriff is enforcing the state's laws. I'm working for people who believe it's morally right to abuse you—or me—or Jimmy. And I can't do that any more."

"Here, here!" Jimmy says, smiling. "The only problem is, as I explained to her this morning, the administration is likely to take a very dim view of being embarrassed in front of every major physicist in the country. Not to mention they feel Sara's research is university property." He looks at me and takes a sip of tea. "So we decided it might be best if Sara disappeared for a while."

I stare at both of them, my mouth open. I have that same odd feeling of déjà vu that I did in the car last night.

"I've cleaned everything that's hers out our office and the lab,"

Jimmy says. "It's all in the trunk of my car."

"And those," Sara says, gesturing to the boxes in the corner, "are what I value from my desk and my library here. Other than my Nana's teapot and some clothes, it's all I'll really need for a while. Jimmy's family has a vacation home out in West Marin, so I won't have to worry about rent—or privacy."

I'm still staring. "What about your career?"

Sara puts down her teacup with a bang and begins pacing the floor. "Oh, bugger my career. I'm not giving up my *work*, just the university— and its hypocrisy. If one of my colleagues had a little fling, nothing much would come of it. But as a woman, I'm supposed to be some sort of paragon of unsullied Victorian virtue. Just by being *in* that bar last night, I put my 'career' in jeopardy. They'd crucify me if they knew who—or what—I am. I don't want to live that way any more."

She brings the teapot to the table and sits down, pouring us each another cup. "End of tirade. But that's why I had to ask about your money. It's enough to live on for a good long while, and to buy all the equipment I need. In a few months, with a decent lab, I should be this close," she says, holding her thumb and forefinger together, "to time travel in practice as well as in theory. And that discovery will be mine—ours. Not the university's. Not the government's."

Jimmy nods. "I'll stay down here and finish this term. That way I can keep tabs on things and order equipment without arousing suspicion."

"Won't they come looking for you?" I ask Sara. I feel very surreal. Part of me has always wanted to know *why* this all happened, and part of me feels like I'm just prompting the part I know comes next.

"Not if they think there's no reason to look," Jimmy says. "We'll take my car back to Hazel's and pick up hers. Devil's Slide is only a few miles up the road. It's—"

"It's a rainy night," I finish. "Treacherous stretch of highway. Accidents happen there all the time. They'll find Sara's car in the morning, but no body. Washed out to sea. Everyone will think it's tragic that she died so young," I say softly. My throat is tight and I'm fighting back tears. "At least I always have."

They both stare at me. Sara gets up and stands behind me, wrapping her arms around my shoulders. "So that *is* how it happens?" she asks, hugging me tight. "All along you've assumed I'd be dead in the morning?"

I nod. I don't trust my voice enough to say anything.

To my great surprise, she laughs. "Well, I'm not going to be. One of the first lessons you should have learned as a scientist is never assume," she says, kissing the top of my head. "But what a terrible secret for you to have been carting about. Thank you for not telling me. It would have ruined a perfectly lovely weekend. Now let's all have some supper. We've a lot to do tonight."

Monday, February 20, 1956. 12:05 a.m.

"What on earth are you doing?" Sara asks, coming into the kitchen and talking around the toothbrush in her mouth. "It's our last night—at least for a while. I was rather hoping you'd be waiting in bed when I came out of the bathroom."

"I will. Two more minutes." I'm sitting at the kitchen table, rolling a blank sheet of paper into her typewriter. I haven't let myself think about going back in the morning, about leaving Sara, and I'm delaying our inevitable conversation about it for as long as I can. "While we were driving back from wrecking your car, I had an idea about how to nail Chambers."

She takes the toothbrush out of her mouth. "It's a lovely thought, but you know you can't change anything that happens."

"I can't change the past," I agree. "But I *can* set a bomb with a very long fuse. Like 40 years."

"What? You look like the cat that's eaten the canary." She sits down next to me.

"I've retyped the title page to Chambers's dissertation—with your name on it. First thing in the morning, I'm going to rent a large safe deposit box at the Wells Fargo Bank downtown, and pay the rent in advance. Sometime in 1995, there'll be a miraculous discovery of a complete Sara Baxter Clarke manuscript. The bomb is that, after her tragic death, the esteemed Dr. Chambers appears to have published it under his own name—and won the Nobel Prize for it."

"No, you can't. It's not my work either, it's Gil's and—" stops in mid-sentence, staring at me. "And he really *is* dead. I don't suppose I dare give a fig about academic credit anymore, do I?"

"I hope not. Besides, Chambers can't prove it's *not* yours. What's he going to say—Carol McCullough went back to the past and set me up? He'll look like a total idiot. Without your formula, all he's got is a time machine that won't work. Remember, you never present your paper. Where I come from it may be okay to be queer, but time travel is still just science fiction."

She laughs. "Well, given a choice, I suppose that's preferable, isn't it?"

I nod and pull the sheet of paper out of the typewriter.

"You're quite a resourceful girl, aren't you?" Sara says, smiling. "I could use an assistant like you." Then her smile fades and she puts her hand over mine. "I don't suppose you'd consider staying on for a few months and helping me set up the lab? I know we've only known each other for two days. But this—I—us— Oh, dammit, what I'm trying to say is I'm going to miss you."

I squeeze her hand in return, and we sit silent for a few minutes. I don't know what to say. Or to do. I don't want to go back to my own time. There's nothing for me in that life. A dissertation that I now know isn't true. An office with a black and white photo of the only person I've ever really loved—who's sitting next to me, holding my hand. I could sit like this forever. But could I stand to live the rest of my life in the closet, hiding who I am and who I love? I'm used to the 90s— I've never done research without a computer, or cooked much without a microwave. I'm afraid if I don't go back tomorrow, I'll be trapped in this reactionary past forever.

"Sara," I ask finally. "Are you sure your experiments will work?"

She looks at me, her eyes warm and gentle. "If you're asking if I can promise you an escape back to your own time someday, the answer is no. I can't promise you anything, love. But if you're asking if I believe in my work, then yes. I do. Are you thinking of staying, then?"

I nod. "I want to. I just don't know if I can."

"Because of last night?" she asks softly.

"That's part of it. And I was raised in a world that's so different. I don't feel right here. I don't belong."

She kisses my cheek. "I know. But gypsies never belong to the places they travel. They only belong to other gypsies."

My eyes are misty and she takes my hand and leads me to the bedroom.

Monday, February 20, 1956. 11:30 a.m.

I put the battered leather briefcase on the floor of the supply closet in LeConte Hall and close the door behind me. At 11:37 exactly, I hear the humming start, and when it stops, my shoulders sag with relief. What's done is done, and all the dies are cast. In Palo Alto an audience of restless physicists is waiting to hear a paper that will never be read. And in Berkeley, far in the future, an equally restless physicist is waiting for a messenger to finally deliver that paper.

But the messenger isn't coming back. And that may be the least of Chambers's worries.

This morning I taped the key to the safe deposit box—and a little note about the dissertation inside—into the 1945 bound volume of *The Astrophysical Journal*. My officemate Ted was outraged that no one had checked it out of the Physics library since 1955. I'm hoping he'll be even more outraged when he discovers the secret that's hidden inside it.

I walk out of LeConte and across campus to the coffee shop where Sara is waiting for me. I don't like the political climate here, but at least I know that it will change, slowly but surely. Besides, we don't have to stay in the 50s all the time—in a few months, Sara and I plan to do a lot of traveling. Maybe one day some graduate student will want to study the mysterious disappearance of Dr. Carol McCullough. Stranger things have happened.

My only regret is not being able to see Chambers's face when he opens that briefcase and there's no manuscript. Sara and I decided that even sending back an incomplete version of her paper was dangerous. It would give Chambers enough proof that his tempokinetic experiment worked for him to get more funding and try again. So the only thing in the case is an anonymous, undated postcard of the St. Francis Hotel that says:

"Having a wonderful time. Thanks for the ride."

LONELY LAND

DENISE LOPES HEALD

A ll of us face recurring struggles with our definition of our
selves, both as individuals and as part of society. When that
society is rigidly class-divided—almost feudal—it can be hard to do
anything but fill an expected role. Of this unflinching portrait of bonded
servitude, Denise Lopes Heald says, "Even when the story is written,
waiting and searching is required before the proper conclusion arrives.
For "Lonely Land" it took three years."

Markus's new slave stared out at the encompassing hills, his long
hair whipping in the wind. So early in the year the highlands wore
more mud than grass, but the sunnier banks were green and dotted with
purple ice flowers. Alien to this world, shirtless, his overalls worn thin,
body worn too so that every skitter of the floater wobbled him, the
slave cupped his hands over his nose to ward off the chill.

Markus glanced forward to see if his neighbors and hosts, the Jiggs,
were watching. The older couple rode stiff-backed, sheltered and warm
inside the cab. He could ride inside too, but wouldn't abandon the
slave. No, he would not. Gods forgive him, the alien was pretty—pret-
tier for all his size than Dara even before she birthed their child.

Markus scooted against the floater's window, blocking the view
through it, then spread his arms about the slave, holding his great coat

open. Dark eyes stared at him—old eyes in a pale young face, thick lashes fluttering and shedding wind tears.

The man ducked his head. Big-boned shoulders hunched against Markus's chest, and Markus wrapped his coat about the slave's back. It was like clasping an iceberg. Markus ignored the other's bitter soiled odor, pressed his cheek to the alien's and breathed warm breath against the slave's shoulder. The Jiggs must think him mad for going to market to sell a floater for seed money, but heading home with only three-quarters the seed he needed and this strange battered silent creature.

The wind whooshed against Markus's ears. He tucked down tighter. The slave shivered, but hadn't the strength to keep it up, nodded, and slept.

Cradling the alien's limp body, Markus stared from beneath his hood at dark mud, last year's limp grey grass, patches of green shoots, rock outcroppings that sported lichen mosaics of startling orange and yellow. The alien stirred, and his slave collar rubbed chill against Markus's chin. This spring, Markus thought, would be different.

Riding down the long slope of the hollow that cupped his fields, Markus stared at the solitary dot of Mother's homestead surrounded by an ocean of grass and bleached stubble. Mother was waiting, an even smaller dot on the front porch.

"Why?" She stared at the slave after the Jiggs had left.

"Because we need help."

"He'll die first. He's the look." She turned her broad back to him, and her ankle cast scraped a soft hiss across the porch boards. The screen door closed behind her, *thunk-thunk*.

She could have said nothing crueler. But Markus expected nothing kinder, swallowed his rage as always. Mother hadn't killed Dara and his child. If you lived, you died.

There was no proper place for the slave anywhere on the homestead. Old Boon, the only other slave they had ever owned, had lived in a shed near the house. When he died, they burned it around him. Mother planted herbs on the spot now. So, headed for the barn, Markus was conscious of the absurdity of buying the limping alien creature at his side. But he wasn't sorry. He had been alone with Mother for five years now, needed another face to look at, another ear to talk into.

At market, he had stopped to watch a string of slaves run up on the block. The bidding went three times past what he had just received for his floater, so he wandered through the stalls of private slave merchants. A glance down into dark eyes and a scarred face stopped him.

He put his alien in the barn's warmest stall and keyed the keeper on his wrist so the slave collar would confine the man to the stall's interior. Next he fetched bread and cheese from the house, a bucket of warm water, a clean blanket, and an old towel.

The alien was burrowed into the straw when he returned. Settling the water in the manger, Markus hung the towel from a harness hook and motioned the slave toward him. The man only stared, lips drawn tight, eyes frightened.

"Come on." Markus coaxed. "You're safe. Com'ona here."

The dark eyes rounded. Markus took off his coat, slung it over the stall door, and knelt in the straw, staring the man back. That close to the floor, old animal scents engulfed him, mixed with the man's bitter odor. A sow squealed in another stall. The man's eyes flinched, but didn't look away.

The slave knew. Gods forgive, the man knew. It shamed Markus, but he couldn't be beaten so early or the slave would be unmanageable. He caught the alien's leg and tugged.

"What's your name?"

The slave stared.

"Not telling?" If he took off the man's collar would the slave kill him? Was it hate in those beautiful eyes? "I'll call you Runner," Markus said. "That's what's on your papers. They say you're a runner, sold you cheap."

The man stared harder. Markus tugged on the leg again.

"Bath." Markus waved at the bucket. "We'll clean you up. Find clothes for you and something to drink. Some food."

The man's bottom lip trembled. "F-f-food?" An alien accent made the word sound like *fod*.

Markus nodded. "Food. Wash and *then* food."

The man's expression went tortured, and Markus cursed himself. He hadn't thought to feed his new responsibility on the way out, had begun their relationship with unintentional cruelty. He tugged again. Runner curled onto his knees, shoulders hunched, skin pimpled with chill.

"Here." Markus reached for the man's overall strap.

Runner stiffened, but held still. Markus unsnapped the strap. The slave's rags fell straight off, leaving the poor creature naked—beautifully naked.

Markus shuddered. He had never touched man or boy before in his life, but had wanted to since sighting this slave. His breath sighed out. His hand stroked the younger man's shoulder.

Runner's eyes closed, and his throat worked. Sweat filmed his cheeks. The man's terror drove the desire right out of Markus, but not the pain, not the need.

For now, he only slipped his hands beneath Runner's elbows and stood, lifting the slave erect, dipped a rag in the water bucket, and began to bathe the man, head-to-foot. He was gentle and careful, did nothing more than scrub the alien's bruised skin; but by the time he finished, he had learned his slave's every scar and the man was crying. He hated himself for that, but life was cruel.

He gave Runner's hair a final scrub and rinse, making sure the insecticidal soap did its job. Then he toweled the pale body dry, taking his time, stroking muscled thighs that had been thinned by poor diet, but were oh so hard. Runner's chest was broad and hairless. Markus finished by wiping beneath the imprisoning slave collar.

"Lie down." He wrapped the slave in a blanket.

The alien folded into the straw, trembling, eyes unfocused. Markus watched with a knot in his chest. Who knew what had been done to the slave in the past. Markus lifted his great coat, spread it over the man's legs and the alien sobbed aloud.

Later, Markus brought out a mug of hot broth and a biscuit saved from his own meal. Mother hadn't mentioned the slave all through dinner, only voiced her estimates of how best to plant their limited seed supply to produce the maximum crop. Runner roused at Markus's entrance, face pinching when he sighted the food. The bread and cheese left earlier were gone. Markus upturned an empty bucket and placed the steaming broth on it.

"Come." Markus waved the slave up.

Runner's eyes danced and his jaw quivered.

"Come on now. It's getting cold."

Runner curled out of the straw and crawled to the bucket, hands shaking as they encircled the broth mug. Markus shook out a pair of pants and a shirt he had outgrown through the middle, plus socks and underwear he would soon miss.

"Well?" He cocked his head. "Will they do?"

Runner's broth-wet lip trembled.

"Best get them on. The wind's rising. Tonight'll be chill. I'll find another blanket."

He left the clothes on the straw. By the time he returned with a stock tarp—Mother wouldn't spare more from the house— Runner was dressed. The shirt was fine in the shoulders, but flapped around his waist. The pants were baggy, but the outfit was an improvement.

"You look almost civilized."

Runner blinked, eyes glazed with exhaustion.

Markus dropped the tarp. "Finish eating."

Runner sat, but his head drooped toward the straw.

"Here now."

Markus caught the man's slumped shoulders and tipped him backwards, protecting the slave's head with his hand until it was down. Then he covered Runner with the blanket and tarp and mounded straw over him for added warmth. For water, he left a stoppered bottle. For sanitation, he righted the empty bucket, hoped the man had sense enough to use it and not the straw.

* * *

Markus woke to the sounds of birds on the roof. Was the alien warm enough? Was he frightened alone in the barn? Was he, Markus, going to touch him today as he had all night in his dreams? Would it be like his dreams? Odd that in the end, it had been Dara he envisioned in his arms, the first pleasant dream he'd had of her—since her death or before.

He was up before Mother, which was unusual, and coaxed heat from the meager residue in the thermal storage bank beneath the house. With cold biscuits, a tube of honey, and a withered apple stuffed in his pockets, he headed for the barn.

Everything in the slave's stall was as he had left it: the man asleep, water bottle untouched, bucket empty. Markus slipped inside and squatted where he could watch the man's face, see the faint stir of Runner's breathing in the straw.

He could not live with this man without touching him. How could he live with himself or Mother if he did? It was crazy. So why did he feel like this? The man was pretty, but he *was* a man. And there were scars right across the slave's cheek, over his eye, down his chin, a flawed beauty, a—

The eyes flipped open. The slave shuddered, and his breathing quickened.

"Easy," Markus said. "You're safe. I brought food."

The runner blinked. Markus lay down eye-to-eye with his possession, the two of them so close, he could feel the man's exhalations. A cow stamped and snorted. Markus should be at chores. But he stared into the man's eyes, helpless and lost. When he was younger, sometimes he had felt ...

"I'm sorry I frighten you," he said softly. Runner blinked. "It's just that my wife died and my boy—" Markus's voice failed for a breath. "And I'm so lonely. I couldn't—" He couldn't afford a woman if he wanted one.

Runner closed his eyes, lips compressed, his breathing purposeful. Markus reached out and stroked the long scar on the man's cheek. Runner flinched.

"I'm sorry anyone ever hurt you," Markus said.

The eyes flipped open, glittering and lost, and Runner's hand slipped over Markus's wrist. It took all Markus's strength to lie still.

"Sssor..." The man's voice choked off.

Markus didn't know who or what Runner was sorry for. "May I hold you?" Markus breathed. "Just hold you a little?"

Runner's jaw worked.

"Then I have chores." Markus thought to reassure the man that there were other things on his mind.

Runner nodded agreement. Without that collar, he would run.

Markus gathered the strange, hard bundle of bone and muscle into his arms again. The man's bitter stench was replaced this morning by soap perfume, the scent of grass straw, and something exotic. Markus nuzzled Runner's hair, twined a soft curl around one finger. "May I cut this?" he asked, tugging on it gently.

The man's head moved against his shoulder, agreeing again. How much would he gain from the slave one slow step at a time? It frightened him, what he was doing. Markus eased away, helped Runner to sit, dug a biscuit from his pocket, split it, and dabbed syrup on it from the honey tube. Runner took it in both hands and swallowed it whole.

"Good." Markus smiled at the man's sticky face. "You eat. I'll go work."

He didn't return to the stall until the animals were fed and his own breakfast eaten. Mother was trapped in her usual morning silence. Her broken ankle pained her. Pray that it healed soon. They had no credit for the operation the med suggested might be necessary—which made his extravagance with the slave all the more insane. Even still ... no regrets.

He found a pair of through-at-the-toe boots, and fashioned a poncho for Runner from feed sacks. The sun was warm by the time he led the man out of the barn, but Runner shivered in his wraps. Mother was right, there was no strength in the alien.

Markus pointed out the stock pens, the stream course, the trees marking the reservoir that generated power for the farm. He explained his plans for planting and showed Runner the hedge hen's nest alongside the field path. The alien listened, shoulders slumped. It paled the sunshine for Markus to see this still young man, a fighter and a runner, so reduced.

He steadied Runner as they crossed the board over the stream. The plank was wide enough, but the movement of the water held the alien's eyes and undid his balance. On the other side, out of sight of the house, Markus slipped his arm about the man's waist. Runner stiffened, eyes on the ground, but didn't pull away. Markus walked him to the upper field, thrilling to the simple pleasure of another living body against his own.

"See these tufts?" Markus kicked a clump of new-grown grass. "They pull out easy now." He released Runner's waist and stooped. "Later they won't budge even with a shovel." He held a wad of roots up for the slave to examine, pulled a square of plastic from his pocket and unfurled it. "Kneel on this. I've manuring to do. Pull the grass, and I'll be back by lunch."

So he left Runner in the sunshine, keyed the keeper to give the man room to roam, and went off to work.

Shoveling and hauling were easier this morning, riding the solar/methane powered spreader was less boring. He daydreamed of Runner's body against his own, dark eyes and pale skin. Except for scars, that skin was flawless. And alone in the morning sunlight, Markus didn't let guilt bother him, only whistled, worked, and forced himself to stay away from the upper field.

At lunch time, he left the spreader, walked over the hill to the higher field surrounded by the piping of savannah birds and filled with quiet anticipation of the slave's company. But as he topped the hill, Markus's gut lurched. A scavenger hawk croaked away above the empty field. Where—

A movement drew his eyes, and he spotted Runner at the far limit of the slave's keeper-proscribed circle pulling grass in great hanks. The field all about Markus was weeded, the grass tufts piled in mounds. Oh no.

Markus ran. The slave heard him and turned, face haggard and reddened. Markus slowed, hands in the air.

Runner's eyes widened. He gasped in rapid pants, and a broken cry sounded as he lunged to his feet. Markus froze.

But the keeper alarm sounded on its own, and Runner dropped flat on the ground, curled into a ball, arms over his head.

"Runner?" Markus knelt near the man's head. "Runner?" His fists flexed. "Oh, man, I didn't mean for you to do it all." He brushed at Runner's tangled sweat-wet hair. "Gods. I'm stupid."

Runner thought he was to clear to the limits of the keeper barrier— which would challenge Markus's energy let alone this starved creature's. Fighting Runner's tensed muscles, Markus unwound the man, wrapped his arms about the alien and held on while the slave shook and shuddered.

"Easy. It's all right." Markus murmured into the man's ear. "My mistake. Shouldn't have worked you today. Thought the sun would be good for you." Markus coaxed Runner to drink water, used what was left in the canteen to wash the man's torn hands. "No more today," Markus said.

Runner's eyes closed. Markus carried him to the barn.

Mother was feeding the chickens. "Dead already?"

Runner roused while Markus tended his blistered hands.

"You rest now," Markus said. "You rest tomorrow."

The man stared, still frightened. There would be no simple way to gain this one's trust.

"Has he the fever?" Mother asked at breakfast.

"No." Markus refused to be angry. "He's only tired."

Her expression went strange, but she said nothing.

On the third day, Markus took Runner to the upper field again. This time they tackled the weeds together and Markus stopped Runner when the man tired. Mother arrived on their one seated floater with lunch, found the master weeding and the slave napping. She said nothing, which surprised Markus. It surprised him more that she had brought a slice of pie for Runner. The next day Runner helped Mother in the herb garden.

Spring flowered around them; and in spite of Mother's dire prediction, Runner blossomed too, put on weight, relaxed into the homestead's quiet routine. Markus felt a warm surge every time he looked at the man, and they furnished Runner's stall with a cot and a shelf, Father's small mirror, a dented pitcher, and a wash bowl fashioned from a plastene jug bottom. Runner seemed overwhelmed by the luxury.

Days and days passed. During the quiet of evening, Markus indulged himself, sat on the brow of the hill and watched the sunset sift color through the growing grain while he held Runner. He thought of taking things farther; but as evenings passed and he didn't, Runner relaxed. Did Runner enjoy the closeness?

The fields were weeded in record time. Mother's herbs grew tall. She worked Runner freely, but no harder than herself. In spite of which, her ankle healed. When the med examined it again, the woman replaced the hard cast with a brace so Mother could wear a shoe. After that, Runner worked longer in the fields; and he and Markus finished the planting. Then it was back to weeding. The days progressed—slow, silent and identical. Still, this spring was different.

Runner didn't talk, but would smile if Markus was very clever. And Runner was always there, quick to help, and considerate. Of course, wearing a slave collar left the man little choice. Still, Runner's silence was companionable. They shared meals, patched each other's scrapes and blisters, mended machinery and fences, and walked the fields. Markus taught Runner to handle the stock. Runner wordlessly showed Markus how to service the floater in half the time it had always taken.

The slave was wary, but they made a good team. Mother became so accustomed to seeing them together that her face turned worried if Markus walked into the yard alone. For a hard woman, she was kind to Runner. Markus realized she was lonely too.

One early summer evening, Markus stood with the slave at the trough behind the barn, scrubbing dried clay from their hands and arms. Runner sniffed beneath one armpit, stripped his shirt, and began a general bath. Markus's breath caught. Heat surged through his groin and he caught Runner's wrist.

The younger man froze, eyes rounding.

Markus felt paralyzed, ached in so many different ways, saw the water bucket come up in Runner's free hand. *Now he'll kill me*, Markus thought. But—

Water hit him, ice chill and straight in the face. He choked and backed, dropped Runner's wrist, *whoofed* with shock, pawed his eyes clear in time to see the slave at the corner of the barn. He reached for his wristband.

"Runner! Wait! Please. Wait!"

Runner stumbled ... and stopped.

Markus shivered as the evening breeze filtered through his wet clothes. "I'm sorry," he called. "I won't. I promise. Not ever against your will."

Runner stood with his back to Markus. The wind whispered beneath the barn's eaves. Insects chirruped. Runner turned, walked back to the trough. Scars stood out pale against the new golden tan of his skin.

"I ... " Runner tried to meet Markus's eyes. "I ... " He folded down on his knees in the mud beside the trough and bowed his head to the toes of Markus's boots.

It tore Markus's gut and shredded his heart. Two months of progress, and he had wasted it all.

"Up." He lifted Runner by the elbows. "Up." They stood chest to dripping chest. "Look at me," he said, lifting Runner's chin with a finger. "We have to decide about this. I can't be panicking you. You can't be panicking me." He stroked the damp hair off Runner's forehead. "I love you," he said and meant it with his every fiber. "I just love you."

And feather-lashed alien lids closed. A weary head dropped on Markus's shoulder. He stroked the man's hair and hugged him, knew he had total advantage now. But now he couldn't push it.

"It's all right," he said. "Don't worry about it. Mother has dinner waiting."

When they sat to eat, Mother eyed them, said nothing.

It was a long hot summer with lots of rain, and the scantily seeded fields grew thick with grain as if some magician had blessed them. Runner grew heavy too, muscled by work, bronzed by sunshine. Walking as well as before her accident, Mother spent hours with Runner, tended her vegetables and gathered wild fruit from the stream cuts. In the evenings, Markus still stole time to hold Runner, and Runner even tolerated a moment's nuzzling. But Markus didn't push him, didn't push himself, wasn't sure that satisfying his lust would satisfy him.

Harvest came. Markus took Runner to the Jiggs' homestead to join the roving crew of locals that would cut everyone's grain in turn. Runner was flighty in the mixed crowd of freemen and slaves and worked harder than any man or woman present. People were impressed, but Markus knew it was only Runner's answer to too much tension. He didn't blame the younger man, was uncomfortable himself in the crowd. Be they neighbors or not, he noted the glances cast toward Runner and kept the slave near. If he could be foolish when it came to this man, so could others.

From the Jiggs' stead they moved to Old Man Obevie's. From Obevie's to Toad Hollow. From the Hollow to Cassigian's. Arriving at the wealthy farm, they dropped from the back of a still moving load floater into Cassigian's yard, and Runner bumped into Markus. Markus recovered and came up staring at Shawnie Cassigian across the yard. When had she become such a woman? Hard-muscled with one long braid, she stared right back.

"Runner, my lad," Markus said. "There's a young free woman over there eating you with her eyes."

Runner ducked his head, and Markus realized why the man had bumped into him in the first place. That night, alone in the moonlight in a corner of the stable with their bedrolls spread open, Runner stretched out flat on his back.

"Roll over," Markus said.

Runner's breathing missed a beat, but he obeyed. Markus straddled the man's hips and began to massage strained shoulder muscles. Runner sighed. His muscles loosened and his head rolled to Markus's movements. They were both tired, and the nearness of others sleeping in the barn insured that Markus's behavior would remain proper. So it was good to bleed off tension, had been a long day of working side-by-side with the Cassigians and too many stares from the youngest daughter.

"Her name is Shawnie," Markus said, working his thumbs along Runner's spine. "Does she frighten you?"

Markus could read the answer in the man's muscles.

"Does it make you want her?"

Runner shook his head.

"I would understand," Markus said. "I'm not asking you if you're after her. I'm asking straight out, because we both know this is trouble."

Runner shook his head again. "Not her."

Markus's hands faltered. He caught himself and went back to work, trying not to make too much of the fact that it was the first complete sentence he had coaxed from Runner.

"But a woman would be nice to bed?"

Runner shifted. "D— d-don't ... " Runner's muscles knotted hard, and he turned beneath Markus, stared up, face unreadable in the shadows. "D-don't ... re-remember." The man breathed short, every muscle tensed.

Markus bent down and pressed his cheek to Runner's. "I do," he said. "I remember Dara as if she were here."

Markus kissed the man's lips full and hard. The young man tensed to iron, but didn't fight. Markus, for once, didn't back down, touched and groped and tasted. It was a strange feeling, but he couldn't stop in spite of others too near. Couldn't—

His kisses slowed. His hands stilled. He had promised, *never against your will*, wasn't quite forcing the man ...

"I'm sorry," he said. "I miss Dara." Which was true in its way.

Runner choked. His arms slid up and tightened about Markus, and his silent sobs shook them both. Markus held him as never before. Sometime, somewhen, Runner had loved a woman much more than Markus had ever loved Dara.

In the morning, as they walked to the fields, Naga Cassigian tapped Markus's shoulder. "How much for him?" The man's voice was casual and callous. A broad-hipped female slave padded at the freeman's side.

"For Shawnie?" Markus matched the other's tone.

"Yes."

Markus looked at Runner—so did Naga and the woman. Cassigian's gaze was calculating.

"I'll think on it," Markus said.

When they were alone, greasing mower blades, Markus touched Runner's hand to get the slave to look at him.

"You want to stay here? She'll pleasure you. And they aren't bad people. Will be kind enough."

He said that too bluntly. Runner blinked, eyes filled with indecision, and Markus's gut clenched. After what he had done last night—come close to doing—he wouldn't blame the slave for wanting a new master.

"I want you," he said, desperate. "So does Mother. But it's your decision. I might still go too far."

The indecision left Runner's eyes.

Markus's loss threatened to strangle him. "You want to stay here then?" But Runner shook his head, and Markus's chest swelled up tighter yet. "You want to be with me?"

Yes, the head nodded.

"I'd free you if I could afford. I can't."

Runner patted Markus's arm.

A week later, the harvest crew reached Markus's fields. Mother drove the lead mower, paced the rest with her years of experience on this piece of land. Runner rode with her, switching to Markus's mower if the grain overloaded it. Everyone commented that this was the heaviest yield harvested this season. Markus didn't understand why, except that for once, everything had gone right with the crop, and Runner had won out against the weeds as Markus never had. Also, perhaps there was something to planting light. He wished Father could see the crop. He wished for Dara, grumpy as she could be, for children and lost things.

Ahead of him, Mother's mower slowed and bogged down. Runner came out of the cab, shirtless in the high heat of the day, his skin shimmering like pale brass. Markus was mowing on Mother's right. A Cassigian mower was working to her left.

The machines moved like bright yellow monsters against the waves of reddened grain. The sky was clear bright blue. Markus relished the sweat running on his sides, the smell of hot chaff mixed with machine oil. He had ridden the mowers since he was a babe, with his grandfather, Father, Old Boon, Mother, Dara. This moment was a distillation of his entire life.

And then Mother's mower lurched, and Runner fell.

The Cassigian driver killed his motor, brakes squealing as Runner bounced onto their blade housing.

Markus didn't remember stopping his own mower, was simply out of it, past Mother's and at the front of Cassigians'.

Markus's stomach seized. There was blood everywhere, Runner spread-eagled across the mower's blade.

But Runner's eyes opened. The slave blinked and sat up. And Markus focused on the fur—fur everywhere.

"*Runner!*" He grabbed the younger man's shoulders.

Runner flinched and wobbled. But it was all right. Mother had hit a covey nest. The blood wasn't Runner's.

"Hit your head?" Markus's voice sounded like someone else's. His lungs refused to work right. He brushed at Runner's purpling temple, stared into glazed green eyes.

"My arm hurts," Runner said in a strange wavering voice.

The deformity of his left wrist was obvious.

"Broke clean," someone said.

Markus realized the Cassigians were gathered around them— and there he stood holding Runner so near. He eased back, looked up through the window of Mother's mower and met her grim stare.

"He's all right," he said, and her stone face went weak.

It was the most emotion he had seen in her since Father died, had hated her for being so hard about Dara. But Markus saw that he was a fool. Like Runner, silence was Mother's defense.

"Best get him out of this mess." Shawnie Cassigian stood at Markus's side. Behind her, her brothers were examining the dent Runner had made in their mower housing; and Martin Jiggs poked at Mother's blades, clearing furred body pieces.

"I need a seat slat," Markus said, "for a splint."

He and Shawnie wrapped Runner's arm. The brothers helped lift him off the mower, impatient to get moving again. Runner yelped and Shawnie swatted Naga.

"Easy of him. He's worth more than you."

Naga snarled, but then brother and sister smiled. How could their lives be so full, when Markus's was empty? The only hope for him lay in their arms knocked half senseless. The other half of his hope sat behind him, stone-visaged again in the mower.

As they loaded Runner onto a load floater, he watched Shawnie, saw in her eyes something too familiar. When she caught him watching, her cheeks reddened and her jaw set. Could this woman fill Dara's place, a different fit, but still— He couldn't afford any woman, certainly not a Cassigian, didn't much want a woman anymore, didn't want Shawnie.

He rode in on the load floater with Runner, abandoning his crop to neighbors and strangers. When Runner cried out, Markus quieted him with a shush and a touch.

Shawnie watched. "Won't ever sell him, will you?"

Markus looked up. "Not unless he wants me to."

"Does he understand what I'm offering?"

"Yes. Do you know how deep his scars run?"

Her young mouth quirked. "You sound like Ninev."

Markus flinched. Ninev Cassigian had been his wife's best friend, had sat at his table many times, her strange sad manner always making him nervous.

"Has Ninev married?" he asked blunt and rude.

Shawnie snorted. "Not our Ninev."

"Why?" He had asked Dara. She had never answered. If she knew, it was the one secret she kept from him. He was sorry he asked now or let these people rouse old memories.

Shawnie stared at Runner who had fainted. "She loved a slave. Papa didn't mean to kill him. Ninev takes her revenge all the same."

Markus breathed in, breathed out. "And you can look at my man the way you do? Naga would buy him for you?"

"We pretend it never happened."

He stared at her. "Ninev isn't pretending."

Shawnie's jaw tightened. "I don't want your slave for me. Ninev's been alone too long. I think I could break through to her with him. He has a lot of Arian's look. That was her slave's name, Arian—big and dark-haired."

"Rest," Mother said after they settled Runner in her bed.

Martha Jiggs had set Runner's arm. The med would be out tomorrow. Runner's right pupil was dilated and he had babbled to Markus in a language no one understood. It was relief to have the man asleep and silent again.

"He'll be fine." Mother's voice was confident.

"Yes?" Markus watched her settle in a chair beside the bed. "I thought you said he had the dying look?"

She shook her head. "I thought you would kill him. I wanted you to expect it."

She looked at him sad-eyed and Markus shuddered. She knew.

"He was so hurt, I couldn't hurt him more," he admitted. "But I still want him."

Her shoulders sagged and relief flooded her face. She hadn't been sure all this time that he *wasn't* using Runner. How could she think anything else when he spent evenings alone in the barn with the man?

Her mouth relaxed. "So. But everyone sees it. You touch him now, and we're ruined. They won't be back to help us harvest next year. Just leave him be. If you wanted him like that," she said, "you would've had him long since. You're just lonely."

Let her believe whatever brought her peace. No wonder she worked so much with Runner, keeping her son from the slave.

"I'm going to marry again, Mother."

"Marry?" Hope and fear filled her eyes.

"I've business to see to. You watch him. Everything depends on him."

"Has since he came."

Markus went out into thickening dusk. The Cassigians slept in their rigs, had one fitted out for cooking and scrubbing. At the edge of their camp, Naga met him.

"How's the runner?"

"He'll heal. Could have been worse."

"You willing to sell him yet?"

"Maybe. Need to talk to your sister."

"Shawnie's ... visiting." Naga shrugged, smiled.

"I want Ninev."

Naga's smile faded. He started to say something, but stopped, swiped a hand across his jaw and chin. "You've a good harvest, Markus. You're a hard working man." Naga's shoulders hunched. "But I don't think—"

"I do. Ninev's far beyond age. So whatever payment I offer is between Ninev and myself. I'm not hunting a family share."

Naga wavered. Markus's courting statement was unorthodox, but not unreasonable.

"I'll bring her." Something in Naga's voice sounded defiant, sounded pleased, by what, Markus couldn't guess.

Ninev was smaller than Shawnie. In the dark, he couldn't see her face, but as Markus remembered her, she was attractive if not pretty, could have married profitably long since.

"Leave us alone," she told Naga. "He says—" She faced Markus. "Naga says you've come to make father happy."

Markus squatted, signaling his willingness to accept lesser status in the face of her family and individual wealth.

"I'm here to please no one but myself," Markus said, "and you, if you like my offer."

"So what's that? Shawnie admitted she tried to buy your slave for me. You suppose I'll offer more than she did?"

"Perhaps. I want to marry you. Then, if he agrees, he'll be there if you want him. And he'll be there for me."

"I was Dara's best friend. You would say that to me?"

He shook his head. "I can't afford another Dara. Couldn't replace her anyway. I decided that this afternoon looking at Shawnie. Dara and the boy— " His voice broke, tears threatened. "I won't cover their memories over."

Ninev stirred. "So. A good argument. But if I don't want your slave or if he doesn't want me, what's my profit?"

"A worthless husband to flaunt in front of your father. Another slave to flaunt in his face. I hear my man resembles your lost one."

In the dark, her slap snapped his head around and started tears from his eyes. "So— " He stood, refused to play beggar to her anymore. "We see each other too well."

"You're sick, intend evil with him."

"I intend love with him. That's not sick. And nothing's sicker than you with your hate and your rotting grief."

He expected another slap, got a kick in the shin instead; but as he hopped backwards, she caught his arm, steadied him.

"I loved Dara." Ninev trembled. "I *loved* Dara."

Markus's chest froze. His heart missed beats, and he gripped her wrist so tightly that Ninev yelped.

But why was he angry? He let her go. Dara had been his wife. He had loved her, wouldn't love another woman that way; but they had never been intimate as he imagined other couples to be. They were themselves, nothing wrong with that arrangement, just not usual.

"So." He freed Ninev. "So. We share certain fears and grief. I'm the perfect match for you."

"But what's your dowry?"

"Him to you. And your dowry him to me."

As she leaned toward Markus a beam of light from the camp gleamed on the pale hand she raised to his face. "Dara loved you as much as she loved me."

Ninev lied, he knew.

"She wouldn't be angry with us. It's a lonely land."

"Are you awake?" Markus stroked the hair from Runner's bruised forehead.

Runner's eyes fluttered open and he smiled around a grimace as he lifted tentative fingers to his temple.

Markus smiled back. "I need to speak to you."

Runner's eyes narrowed.

"I've contracted a marriage for us. She might use us sometimes, won't love us. But she'll protect us. Say yes, and we stay together. No, and I set you free."

Runner's eyes opened wide. His lips parted. Markus had nothing more left to offer.

Runner's eyes darted right, left, and, teeth gritted, the younger man rose onto his knees, body shaking so that his chin bounced. Tears trickled down his cheek onto his chest.

"H-hurt you?" Runner said.

Markus's heart broke. Runner understood too much.

"Here." Markus fitted his arms about Runner and nuzzled Runner's neck. "No. Your leaving won't hurt me. You go."

"St-stay—" Runner rocked his head back to meet Markus's stare. "St-stay with, Momma?"

"With Mother?" Markus breathed through his mouth.

Runner bit his lower lip, eyelids fluttering, fighting concussion.

Surely the man's wits were addled; but Markus didn't doubt Runner's decision.

"Yes." Markus looked away. "You stay."

Mother stood outside the bedroom door. "So?"

"So you stole him."

"Wasn't all your credit you spent on him," she said. "You weren't the only one lost a mate and a child."

Markus bit his lip to blood. "I always loved you, Mother."

"But you couldn't forgive me not giving up and dying when your father died."

"You could have cried."

"But I couldn't have stopped."

Markus's ears rang, and his pulse thudded in his veins. "I'm sorry."

"Get out."

"Well?" Ninev waited in the dark outside the kitchen.

"He wants to stay with Mother." Markus waited for Ninev to leave. She stepped nearer instead. "You're letting him go?"

"Yes. I never loved Dara so true."

"Nor I Ari. But once Runner's free, you've no dowry."

"No."

"Dowry him to me anyway. And I'll dowry him to your mother for the loss of you."

"Wha—"

"In this land, a woman has to marry. A man has to marry. My life has been hell alone. Still, I couldn't live with someone who would kill another person for use of their body. I've done that. I could have freed my slave before Papa killed him. I could have. So marry me. We understand each other."

"But—" Markus drew a deep breath. "Why else?"

"Because you were right. I do want to flaunt you in front of Papa." She leaned nearer Markus. Her perfume of spices and meadow loam rode the warm night air. "Marry me?"

"Yes."

"Why? I thought you only wanted Runner."

"I want most not to be alone. And you and I already share a deepest intimacy."

"Yes." She stepped nearer still.

Markus caught Ninev's hand. As they headed for the Cassigian's camp, her grip in his was firm and honest.

ᴛʜᴇ ʀᴇɴᴅᴇᴢ-ᴠᴏᴜꜱ
ᴛʜᴇ ᴛʀᴜᴇ ꜱᴛᴏʀʏ ᴏꜰ
ᴊᴇᴀɴɴᴇᴛᴛᴀ (ɴᴇᴛᴛʏ) ᴡɪʟᴄᴏx

NANCY JOHNSTON

*N*ancy Johnston *wrote this deliciously sly piece because she was "interested in how women's narratives of all kinds are mediated by other voices and institutions." What can be said and not said about sexual identity and experience makes an interesting parallel with the confessions and compelling appeals for compassion that characterize abduction narratives.*

> The first attempt to attract aliens was made by Canada's Defence Research Board, when it established a top secret "UFO Landing Field" in 1958. The project failed because there was nothing unusual to catch the aliens' attention.　　　　—MAJOR DONALD E. KEYHOE

This is the startling story of Jeannetta (Netty) Wilcox, the protagonist of Canada's controversial UFO abduction case. The very nature of this story touches the paraphysical heart of alien visitations in Canada. Netty Wilcox captured public attention on June 28, 1978 when her now-estranged husband Willard Wilcox, a high school physics teacher and amateur astronomer, revealed her amazing story to a CTV syndicate reporter, Jerry Sohl. Finally, after more than two decades, Netty Wilcox has consented to provide the public with a vivid fully documented picture of the Canadian abduction phenomenon.

From CHAPTER ONE: THE SHATTERED HAPPY HOME

On April 10, 1978, Netty Wilcox complained to her husband that his persistent snoring had kept her awake every night for the past week. After a few days, Wilcox began to take his wife's complaints more seriously:

> I knew that my snoring wasn't keeping her up at night. I don't even snore. But I could see that her eyes were puffy and her face more lined. She couldn't be getting much sleep. And, irritable. Was she irritable! She also lost all interest in her housekeeping.

Wilcox told Sohl that his wife had previously kept their ranch-style home outside of Delhi (pronounced *dell-high*), Ontario in immaculate condition. (See map of Ontario, Appendix A.) Her life was simple. Her days had been divided between light housework and volunteer services at Ayre's St. Paul's United Church. He continues:

> By the middle of the next week, Netty was impossible to live with. Really she was more like a sleep-walker than a wife. One night she laid the table and served a dressed chicken with roast potatoes. Except she forgot to cook the chicken first. Another time, I found her ironing and folding a pile of my dirty shirts right out of the laundry hamper. So you see I had to do something about Netty. After all she might have had something serious like a brain tumor. Maybe menopause.

On May 1st, the couple consulted their family doctor for advice. Their physician (who wishes to remain anonymous) and colleagues at London's University Hospital could find no evidence of physical or neurological damage to explain Netty's apparent sleep disorder. The results of a battery of x-rays and other tests proved inconclusive. "I rejected the recommendation that Netty and I should seek psychiatric family counseling. Obviously *they* were missing something," explains Wilcox. The couple seemed satisfied with Netty's prescription for mild sedatives. Her health improved gradually, although she could rarely sleep except during daylight hours.

By June, Wilcox had all but forgotten his wife's condition. An amateur astronomer and UFO enthusiast, Wilcox had his attention drawn to the reports of UFO sightings outside of Delhi. The *Ayre Express* interviewed a local pig farmer who reported that low flying ships "shaped like big fifty-cent pieces" had frightened his livestock. As well, a Delhi farmer reported to the paper that his tobacco seedlings had been toppled by what he had assumed was a helicopter. Several flattened swirls approximately two-meters in radius (see illustration, figure 6) were discovered in his tobacco fields. Remarkably, only a few years earlier, in September of 1974, similar agriglyphs or crop circles had appeared in a field of rape in Langenburg, Saskatchewan. Unlike the Langenburg circles, however, the Delhi circles lacked the charred central whorls perhaps because there had been an usually damp spring in Southwestern Ontario that year.

Late on the evening of June 13, Wilcox prepared to join a midnight UFO vigil at the Ayre water tower. Around midnight he rose to his alarm clock and found the bed, and the bedroom, empty. At first, he remained unconcerned. His wife often watched television late into the evening. His real confusion did not begin until he carried his telescope out to his car and discovered that his 1977 Lincoln-Continental was missing, along with his wife. Patiently Wilcox sat in his LA•Z•Boy lounger to wait for Netty's return and her explanation. His concern mounted until, at precisely 1: 32 a.m., Netty parked the Lincoln in the two-car garage and walked into the kitchen. "She entered the house as if nothing was amiss in her behavior," says Wilcox. As he watched his wife, she prepared his lunch for work, made him a sandwich, cut a piece of cake, wrapped them in wax paper, and lay a thermos neatly in his lunchbox. She "seemed to have no volition of her own. She stood and made that lunch as if she were doing it in her sleep."

Wilcox was surprised the next morning when Netty confessed to know nothing of her nocturnal sojourn. Neither could she explain the mysterious cuts and abrasions on her throat and wrists. She said she could remember nothing but watching a late-night movie. Later that same evening and for each successive night that week Wilcox observed her, Netty repeated her strange "sleepwalking" and drove out of the two-car garage at 11:45 pm and did not return until 1:32 am. At the end of her drive, the odometer registered a 15 kilometer round trip. After comparing Netty's behavior to abduction accounts in his experimental science magazines, it was clear to Wilcox that his wife was being contacted by aliens. First, Netty seemed to suffer from the phenomenon of "missing time," an apparent lapse of memory masking traumatic encounters. Secondly, her cuts and abrasions were strikingly similar to the scoop-like scars found on the shins and upper arms of many Abductees forced to submit to alien scientific experiments (See Raymond E. Fowler, *The Watchers*, 1990). And, there was the fifteen kilometer round trip, a distance coincidentally equal to a drive to the agriglyph site. Wilcox confronted Netty with his startling evidence. Ignoring Netty's frantic denials (she was undoubtedly terrified by what might be revealed), he arranged for a preliminary interview with a London doctor specializing in regression hypnosis, one recommended by OUFORN (Ontario UFO Research Network).

From CHAPTER FOUR: UNDER HYPNOSIS

Before her co-operation with the writing of *The Rendezvous,* no UFO researcher had been granted permission to print in full the transcripts from Netty's regressive hypnosis session. The following transcripts are a verbatim record of sessions with London hypnotherapist Doctor Hugo Drinkwater, M.D. Our analysis of Netty's experience is highly speculative and will be noted in italics:

Hypnosis session: June 20, 1978, 11:00 a.m. - 1:00 p.m.
Subject: Mrs. Jeannetta (Netty) Wilcox
Doctor presiding: Hugo Drinkwater, M.D.
Also in attendance: Willard Wilcox and CTV reporter Jerry Sohl

DOCTOR: Are you comfortable, Mrs. Wilcox?

NETTY: Yes.

DOCTOR: Can I call you Netty?

NETTY: Yes.

DOCTOR: Do you know why you are here?

NETTY: Yes. Willard wants to know why I can't sleep.

DOCTOR: And?

NETTY: Willard wants to know where I go at night.

WILCOX: Yes ... that's right, Netty.

DOCTOR: Mr. Wilcox, could you please sit over behind the partition? [*Sohl laughs*.] I must inform you, Wilcox, that your interference will jeopardize the authenticity of Netty's hypno-regression. [*continues with Netty*] I want to take you back to a night, perhaps two months ago. A night in the first week of April. For the first time, you can't sleep.

NETTY: Ummm. April 3rd. I can't sleep. [*tosses her head back and forth on the couch*] Willard is snoring again. [*Snorts and wheezes*] He sounds like the electric broom on the living room shag carpet.

DOCTOR: Is that why you can't sleep?

NETTY: Yes. [*sighs*] No. I'm used to *him*. [*punches the couch pillows, turns onto her side*] Wilcox: [*inaudible*]

DOCTOR: Why can't you sleep, Netty?

NETTY: [*rubs arms rhythmically*] I feel ... funny. I have this tingly sensation all over. And, my head is dizzy ... as if I just bent too fast over the scrub bucket or inhaled the fumes of the Pinesol. You know, light-headed. My stomach muscles are tight. Tight like a drum. And ... [*pause, sighs*] no, no ... wait. I'm not supposed to think about last night. *Could this be a mental command set in Netty's subconscious? Frequently UFO investigators are frustrated by mental blocks thrown up in the subject's subconscious, perhaps by the aliens, to hide the truth about their abductions.*

DOCTOR: Can you tell us about last night? I'm going to take you back one day to April 2nd. You are going to remember what happened. You will not be frightened. You are in bed now.

NETTY: Okay ... Willard is snoring. He woke me up again. No, it's something else. Somebody's driven into the yard. [*pauses*] The car lights are coming awfully close to the house. The lights are dancing up the walls. They spin and spin around the walls and ceiling. [*laughs softly*] When I was a little girl afraid of the dark, my mother called those lights angels' wings. [*frowns*] The light isn't coming from outside anymore. It's inside the house.

DOCTOR: [*directs her attention*] What exactly is happening, Netty?

NETTY:[*confused*] I'm shaking Willard and he still doesn't want to wake up. [*Abductees often mention how family members are placed in suspended animation during alien contact.*] That light is floating up the stairs. It can't do that. [*suddenly looking into the bulb of the lamp*] It's so bright. I can't make out what ... I can almost make out someone there inside the light.

DOCTOR:: [*adjusts the brightness of the table lamp.*] Please continue.

NETTY: [*intake of breath, shields eyes*] Someone must be holding a flashlight. No, not a flashlight. Brighter. The light is pulsing off and on. Like a heart beat.

DOCTOR: Who is holding the light? What do you see?

NETTY: She's so bright. [*squints eyes*] The light is coming from her belly. It kind of flows over her body like water. Like a shower of water. The light pours over her skin. She's coming closer and ... [*stares straight ahead*]

DOCTOR:: [*interrupts*] How do you know your visitor is female?

NETTY: [*pauses*] You don't think I know the difference? [*elbows the couch pillows again*] She's coming across the bedroom toward me. [*gasps*] She's holding out her fingers to touch my face. Oh, so cool. [*closes her eyes and shields her face*] She is so bright it hurts my eyes. [*relaxes and slumps on couch*] I'm so sleepy. I'm closing my eyes ... I .... [*eyes close and she dozes*].

DOCTOR: [*continues when her eyes open*] Where are you now, Netty?

NETTY: I don't know. [*looks around*] I'm not in the bedroom anymore. The walls seem rounded and curved. There is a softer muted light now. It's warm inside. I'm lying on a platform. I can't see very far. There is a kind of mist around me. [*pauses*] Oh, she is so close. She bends her face down to look at me. I feel strange. She's placing her palm on my cheek. There. [*cups ear*] She's talking inside my head. She's saying I should relax. [*in a different voice*] Just relax. [*normal voice*] I feel prickly, though. All over my body is prickly. [*Static electricity?*] Her hands rub my neck and shoulders. Ah. She's massaging my shoulders. Umm. Hey! [*struggles briefly, laughs*] She is pulling off my nightgown.[1] Netty: [*continues*] Oh, oh, that feels good. She's rubbing some kind of oil onto my skin. Oh, oh. It makes my skin so cool. [*sniffs*] Sweet. It reminds me of something. [*smiles*] Balsam. Reminds me of Alice. *Ms. Alice Sharpe lived seven miles outside of Delhi at the time of these encounters. Ms. Sharpe, now relocated in Toronto, was a trained massage therapist and private dealer for a Finnish sauna and whirlpool company. According to Wilcox, Netty had been a frequent visitor at her home before their marriage.*

DOCTOR: Please continue.

NETTY: Ah, she's rubbing it all over me. [*arches her back*] I feel so ... I feel weightless. Like I have no body. I'm being lifted off the bed. She's turning me over. Holding me. I'm so light in her hands. *Was it possible that the alien was levitating Netty for transport deeper into the alien vessel? Different types of oils have often been used preparatory to alien medical examinations.*

NETTY: Oh, I'm tingling all over. All over my ...

WILCOX: [*interrupts*] Ask her to describe the ship. What does it look like inside?

DOCTOR: [*mutters, stops recording momentarily*] Netty, please go on.

NETTY: Ah-ah-ah. [*gasps and reaches out*] Please don't make me leave. Please don't make me leave. Let me stay. Please. Please.

DOCTOR: What is happening?

NETTY: The light is becoming dimmer. She is lowering me back down to the platform. [*sighs*] Uhn. I'm in my bed again. Cold. [*shivers*] I can see the lights are descending the stairs. She's leaving. She's going without me to the rendez-vous.

1. Clothing seems to be an encumbrance for alien beings. The abductees we have studied are often stripped of clothing before they are carried into the contact ships. It is possible that this prevents a localized static shock created when probes touch the artificial fabrics such as the nylon of Netty's nightgown.

DOCTOR:Why?

NETTY: She says I'm not ready. She says ... she says I won't remember unless I'm ready. It's like a dream. But I don't want to dream if I have to wake up. Here in this bed.... I'm not going to go to sleep again. Not ever. *At this juncture, Doctor Drinkwater felt that Netty had undergone more than enough for this session and began to progress Netty slowly back to the present. Wilcox protested that the doctor's services had been engaged for the full two-hour session. Doctor Drinkwater turned the cassette over and continued the hypno-regression interview.*

DOCTOR: Are you comfortable?

NETTY: Yes.

DOCTOR: Its June, 13th around 11:30 p.m. You are not afraid.

NETTY: Okay.

DOCTOR: What are you doing?

NETTY: I can't sleep. The rendez-vous. I have a rendez-vous. I wonder if Willard put gas in the car. [*puts hands in pockets*] Where are the car keys?

DOCTOR: Let's go ahead a little. You are at the rendez-vous point.

NETTY: Okay. I'm getting out of the car. I don't bother to lock the door. I have to hurry. I only have an hour. No time to waste. [*pants, as if running*]

DOCTOR: What are you doing now?

NETTY: I'm standing near a tobacco kiln. [*a small tobacco storage shed*] There it is again. I hear a shuffling sound. Someone nearby. Shhh. [*whispers*] Someone is watching me. [*closes her fists*] I have some stones in my hand so I toss one over at the other kiln. A figure is stepping out from the shadows. [*laughs*] It's Alice. Waiting for me. *It is not uncommon for multiple abductees to be drawn to the same locations after an encounter.*

DOCTOR:: Do you know why she is here?

NETTY: [*ignores question*] Ummm.

WILCOX: [*inaudible*]

DOCTOR: Tell us what is happening.

NETTY: [*sighs and shifts on the couch*] We walk toward the field together.

We don't want to talk. We look up. The moon is huge. It lights up the field. The moon is floating down to us. It is so beautiful. *Her ominous image of the moon may be a mask memory, one disguising her memory of a spherical mother ship.*

DOCTOR: Please continue, Netty.

NETTY: [*rapid breathing*] We can see the circle in the field where we ... where we came last time. I take hold of Alice's hand. She grips mine tightly. We push the leaves aside as we walk between the rows. Ahh. We're in the center of the swirl now. We lie down on the damp ground together. The seedlings are all bent over but we're careful not to break them off. [*tosses head back on pillow*] Not much time. I know she isn't afraid either. She smells like balsam. Like balsam. I know she's coming. I can almost ... I can ... I ...

At this point, Doctor Drinkwater choose to bring Netty from under the hypnotic regression despite Wilcox's objections. The doctor admitted to us that Netty's rapid pulse and shallow breathing could possibly have endangered her health.

From EPILOGUE: POST-HYPNOSIS

Tragically, within a month of these revelations, Netty and Willard Wilcox ended their eight-year marriage. Netty's initial reluctance to speak with UFO researchers should not be held against her. In fact, it was not until 1984, with the divorce settlement, legal battles, and subsequent restraining orders behind her, that Netty came to possess the rights to her own story. We conducted our final interview with Netty in her newly refurbished Toronto home where she lives with companion Ms. Alice Sharpe. At that interview, we were deeply inspired by her spirit of co-operation. We, as UFO researchers, often work in a climate of closed-minded intellectual darkness, rejected by the scientific community and faced with the governmental agencies who deny the accounts of alien abductees. Netty's conviction that "the truth will out" has been, for us, an unwavering bright light.

SILENT PASSION

KATHLEEN O'MALLEY

*S*ometimes we cling to our beliefs because they make us feel safe. *Religion is no exception. Here, Kathleen O'Malley returns to A. C. Crispin's StarBridge universe (in which she has co-authored two novels) to show aliens teaching us what it means to be human, and a man learning to find a way past his own, fundamental fear.*

My mother's thin form sat at home in Bright Tabernacle, the radical fundamentalist colony on the Terran settlement world NewAm, while I stood in a narrow cubicle on the planet Trinity. It was eerie, debating with a full-bodied hologram.

"God has nothing to do with your illness," I insisted. "It's a virus—"

"And God didn't create viruses? The same God who created the universe? The same God who created—"

"Me," I reminded her. "God created me, too—just the way I am."

"Don't blame God for your sins, Joshua," my mother said sorrowfully. "Blame me for failing to rear you right. God holds me responsible. My disease is proof."

"Your disease is caused by a virus endemic to NewAm. If you'd gone to a doctor instead of trying to pray it away, you could've been cured!"

We were falling into the old arguments in spite of my promises to my lover, Ray. Imagining his disappointment, I rubbed my fist against my chest—American Sign Language for "sorry." After five years with my

Deaf lover, I was still a poor signer, but "sorry" was the sign I knew best. I put my hand down, but couldn't relax the fist.

"Ruth Ann turned down Lucas Burke last week," Mom murmured. "She said her prayers would turn your heart to the Truth and the Word and the Blood. Ruth Ann said she'd waited this long to be your wife, she could wait a little longer."

One moment of curiosity and pleasure in my fifteenth year—my only one with a woman—and Ruth Ann Gibson could claim us betrothed.

"Joshua, you're the child of my heart. I need you now." Her green eyes grew soft. I'd inherited her eyes and sandy hair, her height and slim build, but the virus had stolen her good looks. The hologram even let me see her jaundiced skin. "I have only six months left. The next ship leaves Trinity in three weeks; it'll take two months just to get here. But if I can see you, and know you'll marry a Believing woman, make a family—then God will forgive me for failing you."

"You never failed me, Mom." Even when she found out I didn't Believe, that I was gay, she always loved me.

"I raised a child who traffics in Abomination. Like Moses, I'll never see Heaven."

I rubbed my face wearily. "Mom. I can't just leave—"

"You have no blood kin there, no wife, no family," she said firmly. "There's nothing binding you to that place."

Nothing but Ray.

"Six months, that's all. Come home, son!"

How could I say no to her? How could I say it to Ray?

Without warning, she fell back against her chair, her hand clutching her chest, her eyes wide.

"Mom!"

"Heavenly Father," she breathed, "is this sign for me?"

She was looking past me. I spun, coming face to face with one of Trinity's natives with its enormous wings stretched in alarm. Intelligent avians, the Grus looked like huge Terran cranes, standing ten feet tall on spindly black legs. Except for black wing-tips and elegant black markings on their faces, they were a gleaming, iridescent white. With angel's wings.

This one was as startled as I was. They were primal hunter/gatherers; to them, holograms seemed like spirits.

The avian (he or she? I never knew) shrank, then backed away behind a partition. When I faced Mom again, my oldest brother was by her side.

Matt glared. "What in all that's Holy was that?"

Mom's voice was thin, reedy. "It was a sign. Joshua wore an angel's wings."

Matt's hard eyes turned colder. "You damned Sodomite! You want to kill her right now?"

Mom clutched his homespun sleeve. "Don't, son! Josh is coming home. We'll be a family again."

Matt moved away, taking the field so that she couldn't hear. "If you come home—it had better be alone. Understand?"

If Ray came back with me, he'd risk being stoned to death. "I'll come back to NewAm, and meet Mom at the space station like always." The best hospital was there, anyway.

Matt smiled coldly. "She's too sick to travel. You'll have to come here. Bring a good suit. Reverend Walsh is ready, and the doctor is, too. You'll be married before sunset, and a father-to-be before the week is out. Mom's gonna die happy, Josh. We're sworn to it."

My five brothers hated me for the shame I'd brought them. With doctors who could ensure consummation and coordinate ovulation, forced marriage was an institution. Back home, they'd turn you into cattle to save you.

I broke the connection. The entire hologram—aged chair, sick mother, the brother I hated—all popped out of existence like a bursting soap bubble. It was therapeutic to have that feeble power over them.

I felt the avian's reappearance before I heard its soft, three-toed footfall. A disembodied head with round, golden eyes, and a surprised expression appeared comically around the partition. I nearly laughed in spite of my anger, my confusion—and my genuine fear.

I didn't know that Grus would enter the quonset hut that was the Terran research station. Foolish—this was their planet!

Mindful of the slippery flooring, the gangly being tip-toed towards me, peering to be sure the hologram was gone. They were a beautiful people, all neck and legs—and long, deadly beaks. I noticed a sign posted near the exterior door—"SOUND NULLIFIERS MUST BE WORN *AND ACTIVATED* BEFORE LEAVING THIS BUILDING." My nullifiers were looped around my neck—I hadn't thought I'd need them in here.

The avian moved closer. Sign language was their normal mode of communication, but they used powerful voices for long-distance contacts. If this one should trumpet in this sound-proofed building, I could be deafened or killed. Quickly, I donned the equipment then turned it on.

I'll never get used to this, I thought as the nullifiers neutralized all sound. Most of the planetside staff had surgery that allowed them to turn their hearing on and off—but that seemed too permanent. I swallowed, trying to clear my ears when that was impossible.

I checked my wrist voder and clipped a palm-sized screen to my black jump-suit. As I did, the avian peered at its likeness on the pocket translator, while a patch of bare, red skin on its head shrank, then relaxed. That crown indicated its mood, but I'd be damned if I knew what it meant.

Black wing-tips—actually three-fingered, nearly palmless hands—fluttered. The translation of what I scarcely recognized as signing waited on my wrist.

"I'm sorry to interrupt the See-Through People," the voder read, "but Dark Eyes Watching is waiting for us."

That was Ray's Grus name—one quick sign.

"Uh—Where is Dark Eyes?" I asked aloud. The breast pocket screen showed a Grus signing what I'd said.

"Waiting on the Edge Territory," the Grus explained. "I'm Starlight Dancing. My partner is Moonlight Dancing. Everyone's waiting for us."

I got the distinct feeling I was being rushed. "You know how to fly, don't you?"

It meant using an anti-grav sled. "Yeah—sure."

The avian moved behind me, while its head, bobbing at the end of that long neck, stayed in front, keeping one eye on the screen. I was being herded to the door. I grabbed my pack.

"Why didn't Ray meet me here?" I wondered aloud. We only had one day together out of four, a break from my technical duties in Trinity's space station, and Ray's job recording Grus behavior patterns down here. He was an avian behaviorist with a second degree in human development. "Why are we going to—?"

"The Edge Territory," the avian fluttered. "They're waiting. It's a surprise."

I didn't understand, but shrugged and left the building.

I'm a hardware/software tech, so I'm no nature boy—at least, not if we're talking *Mother* Nature. But Trinity was a breathtaking wilderness sporting autumn colors year round through expansive wetlands and giant forests. And it was all new to Terran scientists like Ray. Because of the avians' voices and their sign language, Deaf humans were actively recruited. Coming here with Ray was a serious commitment—the first serious commitment of my life.

Not counting a son's commitment to his mother—made before his first breath, and strengthened with his first meal.

I reached for a sled, surrounded by a silence like cotton. As my native guide—(Starlight Dancing? Their names rarely indicated sex and changed occasionally, probably to confuse the *touristas*)—raised its wings and ran to lift off, I felt the power of its voice as it called to others nearby. They answered, and a sound I couldn't hear rattled my bones.

Traveling over endless marsh, I tried to reconcile this landscape with my previous habitats—space station apartments and frenetic dance clubs. This wasn't Disney Planet, honey, this was real. There were predators here, wolf-like canids and monstrous ursine creatures and birds as big as a man—Night Flyers—that seemed like the dark offspring of a roc and a rapacious owl. Even so, politicians safe on distant planets had forbidden all but defensive weapons on Trinity.

Starlight finally banked for a landing. Three small suns blazed overhead. If the quonset hut was in the middle of nowhere, this had to be the Edge of nowhere.

I stepped off the sled onto a small bluff mottled in golds, reds and yellows. Ray's camouflaged tent was planted next to an A-frame Grus nest shelter, perched on a platform in the marsh, slightly below the bluff. Ray himself sat on the ground at the edge of the bluff, his back to us. He held a spotter to his eyes, while his other hand cuddled inside the belly pouch of his sweatshirt. We'd flown in behind him while he watched a Grus—Moonlight Dancing? Without warning, my guide threw back its head and called and the uncomfortable vibrations shook my skeleton again. As its partner answered, Raymund Estrada turned and finally saw me.

He grinned and stood. His wavy, black hair and thick mustache were overdue for cutting, but his lean, wiry frame was corded and trim. At forty, his face was lined from years of outdoor living; his dusky features spoke of ancestral Mayans.

As soon as I saw those warm, brown eyes, I felt the heat in my belly and remembered why I'd come here. The only time I felt whole was when I could be with him. I stopped worrying about predators, my enforced deafness, my sick mother and basked in his presence, aching for us to be alone.

He grabbed my wrist and kissed me quickly, as Starlight Dancing stepped into the air to join its mate. The Grus alighted in the water so gracefully it barely rippled, and the avians called and pranced around one another, heads thrown back, black wing-tips drooping. Then they burst into a flurry of dancing, leaping, twirling in the air, only to return to the water, then prance and call some more.

"What are they doing?" I signed.

Ray released the equipment in his pouch to communicate better. "They're celebrating their love."

Just watching him sign made me dizzy with wanting him. That was what had won my heart—

The first time I saw Ray, he'd been alone in my favorite bar on the NewAm space station. Some guy approached him to dance and I watched as Ray refused in sign language, then watched the consternation of the man who'd approached him. Approached again by another man, again he refused. Again, the asker's surprise—near revulsion, really—bothered me.

So, I asked the bartender a favor. Suddenly, the heavy, bass notes of the bar's driving music blared out, vibrating through everyone. Ray jumped in surprise, making me grin, as he felt the sudden surge of music. How the hell could you expect a man to dance when he couldn't hear the music? He could feel it now.

When he realized I'd arranged for the music, he couldn't turn me down. It was during the second dance—a popular song most of us were sick of—that Ray started to sign. He sang the romantic ballad in his language with his hands. The phrasing was so beautiful in sign, it made the song new again. I knew then I'd have to learn this language, because I had to communicate with this man. We never parted after that night. And I never tired of watching Ray sign.

I watched the Grus dance, but all I could see was our first night. I had finally gotten it through my head that moaning his name was pointless, that the soft sound of his breathing would be all I'd ever hear. But he had spoken to me, instead, with his hands, and his mouth, and his body, and I learned that language quickly because I wanted to so badly. I laughed when his fingertip drew a heart on my back, or traced the first letter of my name on my chest. We wrote love letters on our skin during that wonderful night of silent passion. The first of so many.

Watching the Grus bob and weave, I signed awkwardly, "I wish I could do that. Tell the world how I feel about you."

He smiled. "You can. This isn't Bright Tabernacle."

Suddenly, one of the avians lifted in the air, then landed on the other's back. Were they copulating? They danced again and the other took its turn to mount, so it had to be something else. I started to ask Ray, but realized his gaze was searing through me.

He shifted the lump of equipment in his pouch, then signed, "Let's go to the tent. They're busy; they won't miss us."

To the tent? I thought, looking at it sitting defenseless in the wilderness. Then I looked at the dancing Grus. They'd see our shadows on the walls. They could hear, and with the nullifiers I'd have no idea how noisy we'd get, and— He saw it all on my face, and was, as usual, amused. Beckoning me, he walked toward the tent. Helplessly, I followed, realizing this might be the last chance I had to love him—before I had to tell him about Mom, about leaving.

He undressed carefully, keeping the spotter and sweatshirt with his other equipment close by in a padded nest of feathered Grus weavings. We fell into his open sleeping bag, as though we hadn't touched in months instead of just days, as though we were twenty again, as though we loved each other as fiercely as we did. He wrote "LV" for love over and over on my back, and each time I felt it branding me. I loved Ray. I loved my mother.

For one bitter moment I wished I loved no one and had been left alone to move from bed to bed with no tomorrows and no hope, the way I had before I met him.

That's one of your developmental problems, Ray had told me once. *You believe what you learned as a child. That gay people have no right to exist, that we have no future because we can't make families, because we're not "natural." It's nonsense, but you believe it. Same-sex pairings appear all over nature. We make our own future. We make our own families. But you don't believe that because you're still trapped in Bright Tabernacle—*

Dimly, I was aware of the Grus dancing and mounting and calling. I wondered if they were aware of us, gasping and writing our love letters, and knew they had to be. Ray turned me and pressed against my back, kissing my neck. Drawing a heart on my breast right over my heart, he filled me, body and soul, filled me with feelings I'd never had for anyone else. And then I filled him, writing on his breast, needing to say too much, trying to write it all down, and I couldn't. I came convulsively, bursting into hopeless sobs because I had to leave him and never again have this beautiful, silent passion of ours.

I wiped my face as he turned and gathered me in his arms, comforting me. I hoped he'd just assume that it had been his performance that had moved me so much. The avians had finished their dance, and were preening.

"Can you tell them apart?" I asked.

"Of course," Ray signed, laughing. He pointed. "That's Starlight Dancing. The other is Moonlight Dancing."

They looked identical to me. I wondered how they could tell each other apart, the males from the females, so they could mate.

One of them—Starlight Dancing, I thought—entered the tent. I scrambled to cover my nudity while Ray just watched, bemused, and handed me my voder.

"I would be cold without my feathers," I read. "It's good humans learned to weave. Are you hungry? It's time to eat."

Ray signed back, "Too small is still asleep."

I checked the voder; it missed something in the translation.

Starlight stood over Ray's sweatshirt, poking around with its beak. The heavy lump housed in Ray's pouch moved! The Grus unwrapped the clothing and a tiny, cinnamon brown head with big, blue eyes popped up and looked around. It was a Grus chick, barely big enough to fit into two hands. Standing, it flapped tiny wings, then clambered into the warm spot between us. Starlight held a small, silvery fish to its gaping beak. The fish slithered down the chick's slim throat, followed by another. I glanced at the voder.

"Well, Light Eyes Watching," Starlight had signed to me, "are you surprised?"

I'd passed surprised a long time ago.

Ray was delighted. "It's a rare opportunity to document the behavioral progress of a growing chick. And it's better than that, Josh. I'll need you to help me. We'll be together everyday. Every night."

We had three weeks before the ship came. Ray deserved to enjoy this until then. I couldn't tell him about Mom.

"It's hard to believe we could be this lucky," I signed, feeling like a liar.

That night, as Ray slept, I left the tent. Trinity's three moons and its millions of twinkling stars filled the sky with light. A Grus stood one-legged in the water, while the other sat on its hocks by the front of our tent. The chick—a female named Too Small—slept with Ray.

The voder screen was still on my pocket. As the nearby avian preened, I realized I didn't know which of the two Dancings—Mr. or Mrs.—this one was. Unsure of how to make cross-cultural small talk, I said, "It's a beautiful night."

Holding its head so one eye watched the voder, it replied, "The Moon family is in good configuration. We call it 'the Chick's First Feeding.' It draws fish."

Okay. And if the moon is in the seventh house, and Jupiter aligns with Mars —

Suddenly, the Grus paused. "May I ask a personal question?"

"Uh—sure!"

"This afternoon, in your shelter, Moonlight Dancing and I wondered," the avian signed hesitantly, "—were you mating?"

Color rose to my face, but before I could reply, Starlight continued, "We were flattered that you joined us. Are you offended? I'm not used to dealing with humans."

So, the citizens of Trinity felt as odd talking to me as I did talking to them. "I'm not offended. I was afraid our —mating—might offend you. Your dancing was beautiful."

"Thank you," Starlight replied, "but we were dancing *and* mating. While Too Small slept, we could enjoy ourselves. As she grows there'll be less opportunity."

They were mating. I thought back to their mutual mounting and felt confused. "Uh, when did Too Small hatch?" At least I knew that Grus chicks came from eggs.

"Yesterday. We feared she might not emerge, but she did, and she'll live. That's why she was given to us, because we have the skill to raise her."

Once again I felt hopelessly baffled. "Given to you?"

"A week ago. The egg had lost too much weight, but that happens when there are two."

"I thought your people only laid one egg."

"Normally, yes. However, Too Small's mother produced two eggs, and one was—"

"Too small," I realized. "So, you and Moonlight Dancing didn't produce her egg, you adopted it?"

The avian blinked slowly. "It is not possible for Moonlight Dancing and me to produce eggs."

"Oh, I'm sorry," I said respectfully. "I didn't know that."

The Grus took a moment to respond. "We may have a communication problem with your device. Are you male?"

"Yes," I said cautiously. Couldn't they tell?

"Dark Eyes said you both were," Starlight admitted. "The differences are not so easy for us to see. Can human males produce eggs?"

"No," I assured him. "That's impossible."

"Then, why would you think that Moonlight Dancing and I could produce eggs? Or is your translator confused?"

"Excuse me?" I said, bewildered.

"Moonlight Dancing and I are both males, just as you and your partner are. We can't produce eggs, so of course, we adopt. How do two male humans acquire children?"

"You—are both males?" I said stupidly.

"Yes," the avian signed. "Couldn't you tell?"

"I—uh, well, I had no idea your people had same-sex pairings! That's—interesting."

His odd face held that same patient stare Ray always had when I put my foot in something I should've been able to figure out on my own. "It's true, we're rare—but flocks who have same-sex pairs are envied. We're often the most highly skilled artisans, historians—and parents."

It wasn't unusual to find gay humans in the arts, but heady human culture ever considered us superior parents? "Have you and your partner been together long?"

"Forty years," the avian replied casually.

Forty years! "How did you meet?"

The avian look at its—*his* mate. Moonlight Dancing was standing one-legged in the water, watching us. "I was fifteen years old, without a partner. That's old to still be single. I worried that I belonged to the Moon family, who are known for turning us onto strange paths. One night, when my aloneness seemed too terrible, I came to this territory. The Moons were bright, and as I traveled the Edge, I suddenly saw him."

Starlight was no longer signing to me, but to his lover, who watched, as riveted as I am when watching Ray.

"He stood in the moonlight, dancing alone. I'd never seen anyone dance with such grace, such beauty—and such sadness. An eighteen year old male lost in the World, without a mate to comfort him. I thought, *Could this be a gift of the Moons? A gift for me?* And carefully, so as not to startle the beautiful stranger, I stepped out from the rushes.

"He saw me framed by starlight, the constellations outlining my body. We danced in the moonlight and the starlight until we could dance no longer. And then we knew we would never be alone, not ever again."

Forty years, I thought, and tried to imagine loving one man for forty years. The five years with Ray I'd taken one day at a time, too scared to look at a future I knew we couldn't have.

"We've raised twenty-five healthy children in those years," Starlight continued, turning back to me. "Abandoned eggs, twins, sickly chicks, orphans. Too Small will be our twenty-sixth child." He peered at me. "How long have you and your partner been mated? How many children have you raised?"

I could barely find my voice. "We've been together five years. We—haven't raised any children."

Because of me. Ray wanted it all. Marriage. Kids. The whole deal. He'd asked me—again—to marry him when we left NewAm; the ship's captain would've done it happily. But I was still carrying too much mental baggage from Bright Tabernacle. And kids? Kids needed mothers, didn't they? Mothers like mine....

Starlight was watching me, and suddenly, I could interpret this expression, his crown. He felt sorry for me. "Five years is a long time to be childless. Partners need children to love."

I could hear my mother through the nullifiers. *There's nothing holding you there. No blood kin, no wife—no family."*

"I *have* offended you," Starlight signed, his feathers standing straight out, then settling back down.

"No," I assured him.

"Something troubles you. You wear it on your face. As you did when you spoke to the See-Through People."

What was he anyway, some feathered analyst?

"You never told Dark Eyes about the See-Through People," he signed bluntly. "I understand humans so little. Why would you do this?"

I wanted to ask what business it was of his, but his questions showed only concern for me, for Ray. We'd transcended culture and species— this alien offered me friendship. Who needed a friend now more than me? It was the weirdest thing I've ever done, but I told him every-thing—about my mother, her illness—that I'd have to leave Ray.

Starlight never interrupted, just watched my screen. His partner in the marsh—guarding us from predators, I realized—watched as well, following everything.

Finally Starlight signed, "You must tell Dark Eyes."

"I can't!" I insisted. "Your world could be his life's work. I can't take that away from him. We've got three weeks. I can give him that. Then I'll tell him. And I'll go. At least he'll have you, your partner, and Too Small. He loves her."

"A child can help a grieving mate survive his loss," Starlight assured me, "but that won't stop his sorrow." He was not reproaching me; he just seemed sad. "If you had raised a child together, you would never consider this action."

"Please, don't say anything to him!" I asked.

"This is between you and Dark Eyes. We would never interfere."

I muttered thank you, and climbed back into the tent. Soon, the avian collected the chick so Ray and I could be alone. I clung to him while he slept in blissful ignorance, and prayed, really prayed, for the first time in years. But who I prayed to I couldn't say.

The next three weeks were heaven and hell. We were busy setting up equipment and recording, and caring for Too Small. I got used to being deaf. I learned to tell the two Dancings apart. I never saw any predators. Ray was in his element and watching his joy was unbearable. I ate up his happiness, storing it for when I wouldn't have it anymore.

And at night, Starlight Dancing—this alien who grew to be my closest friend—questioned how I could leave someone I loved so much. If I could make him understand, maybe Ray would too.

"My mother will die," I explained one night as Ray slept.

"Won't she do that even if you're there?" Starlight asked.

"Yes, but if I'm not there, she believes her soul will be damned."

"We travel to the Suns when we die as our friends use their voices to lift our souls to the sky," he told me. "But whether we get there or not is up to us alone."

That was how Ray found out. He became aware of my nightly conversations and the scientist in him got too curious. His voder picked up the translations coming off mine.

I considered throwing a fit about him eavesdropping, but he was so calm, yet so heartbroken, I couldn't. It was dusk, a few days before my departure, when Ray confronted me.

"I should have realized it by the desperation in your lovemaking," Ray signed. "I thought you were just nervous being deaf all the time."

"I wanted us to be happy for a while—"

"How could you make a decision like this without discussing it with me?" His signs had lost all their fluid grace.

"My mother is dying," I told him. "She needs me."

"I need you!" Ray signed, looking at me as if I were stupid. "Now. Tomorrow. Every day!"

He ran a hand through his hair and turned away. When a Deaf person breaks eye contact, they've shut you out completely. When he looked back, he signed, "I'll come with you."

So, I had to tell him about Ruth Ann.

"They can marry you against your will," he asked, disbelieving, "make you father a child—because they're embarrassed?"

I nodded numbly.

"And—still, you'll go?"

"When I was sixteen, the year after Ruth Ann, my brothers caught me teaching a boy from Bible class carnal pleasures. They filmed us. We could've been stoned to death for it."

It was hard for me to dredge this up. "My mother saved us. She got Ruth Ann to declare us betrothed, and found another girl for Joe. Still, we were flogged in the public square. Mom held our hands while we lived through it, and nursed us after."

I wiped a hand over my face, wishing I could wipe away those memories as easily. "We were kids. All through that horrible ordeal, the only human being to show us a scrap of kindness, who cared about us, was my mother. I can't let her die with the shame of my sin on her. I can't."

Ray looked beaten. "Josh—your mother will die no matter what you do, but if you go to her, you'll pay for her beliefs for the rest of your life—and I'll pay, too!"

I couldn't bear to sign "sorry" anymore, so I said nothing.

"Marry me," Ray signed with an infuriating calmness. "Look at the future and see us together for forty years, see the family we can make. I love you. Marry me, Josh."

Maybe this was why I could never see the future, because I'd always known what mine would hold. I didn't answer, and that was answer enough.

He kept his face impassive and finally signed, "Explain it to Too Small."

"What—?"

His eyes were desolate. "You've fed her, played with her, and kept her safe while she slept—you're one of her fathers. She'll mourn you, Josh. Help her understand."

"I can't do that," I signed.

"You can leave me. How much harder can this be?" Then he turned, shutting me out. We were separated already.

I left the tent and walked into the warm marsh. The water lapped at the bottom of my cut-offs where Too Small paddled around the adult Grus' legs. I wiggled my toes for her but she wouldn't play.

The chick's expressive eyes were sad as she swam to me, begging like an infant.

"We had to tell her," Starlight signed.

"Is she old enough to understand?" I asked him.

Moonlight Dancing looked impatient. "I am not old enough to understand," he signed, then went to console Ray.

Too Small kept bumping my knees, begging for attention, but when I tried to feed her, she wouldn't eat. I picked her up, cuddling her plump body in the crook of my arm. She buried her head under my shirt and I felt the vibrations of a tinny voice that would one day shatter eardrums.

"When a chick loses a parent," Starlight signed, "it is hard to make them feel safe again."

"I'm not her parent!" I said angrily. "You're her parent! I don't even look like her? I don't even speak her language!"

"We've talked of cultural differences," Starlight signed, "but children only know food, and warmth, pain and comfort. And they know who loves them. Just as you love your mother, Too Small will always love you."

"Dammit, I don't want her to love me!" I shouted, deaf to my own words. "It'll just hurt her, and hurt me, and I don't want any of it!"

"Returning to your mother will prevent all that hurting?"

I stared at him, absently stroking the chick, trying to figure out if an alien avian could be sarcastic. Then a shadow as big as small aircraft covered us from above.

I looked up, as Starlight reacted. I saw curved, ivory talons, a flat carnivore's face that was all eyes and curved beak, and dark wings that blotted the suns. The offspring of a roc—a night flyer. Coming for me.

Starlight must have blared an alarm call because the force of the sound waves shoved me backwards. I lost my footing in the slippery mud and started to fall slowly in the lighter gravity, grasping the chick tighter by reflex. Frightened, she struggled to get away, her tiny claws scratching my stomach.

Starlight launched himself toward the huge predator, clambering over me in his urgency, pushing me under the shallow water. He mantled us with his wings, spoiling the predator's attack, as I struggled not to inhale or roll over on the chick.

Then the Grus dragged me out of the water by one arm, shoving me toward the tent, blaring and blaring. I coughed, blinked water out of my eyes then looked up, and wished I hadn't. The monster was banking for the next pass. Coming after the easy pickings, me and the chick. Starlight could've saved himself, but he had to protect Too Small. Protect Too Small.

My prehistoric brain kicked in. Protect Too Small. Pulling my mud-slicked feet under me, I clutched the chick like a football and ran. She was screaming, at least as scared as I was. The shadow covered us again, and grew bigger. Could it actually lift a human being?

Moonlight Dancing hovered over the flyer, harassing it from above, trying to spoil its aim, while Starlight ran interference on the ground. Ray was outside the tent with a repulsor, but the monster had seen one before and evaded the sonic charge. So prehistorically single minded. As was I.

I had one foot on the nest platform, ten steps from safety. The shadow descended; I hunched over the chick and kept moving. Then Starlight hit me from behind, knocking me to the ground, covering me with his wings. Curling around Too Small on knees and elbows, I offered my back as a target and waited for talons, but all I felt was Starlight's cries and the warmth of his feathered body over mine as the flyer struck.

There was the shudder of a repulsor blast as I wished for real weapons. Moonlight Dancing threw himself at the night flyer, forcing it to fly off, but when it did, Starlight wouldn't stand. Scrabbling out from under him, I made it to the tent. Shoving the chick in, I fastened the flaps so she couldn't get out. If the flyer couldn't see her, it would forget her.

It already had. That damned predator hit Starlight again. The Grus hadn't moved from the first blow—couldn't move. Now the beast punctured his lungs, going for the kill. Ray moved closer, aimed the repulsor, as Moonlight fought the beast with kicks and wing slaps. The flyer held him off with its curved beak and massive talons.

The light dimmed in my friend's eyes. Reinforcements were coming by air, but too late. Ray couldn't use the repulsor now without harming the Grus. We stood frantic and helpless—and then I went crazy. I screamed sounds I couldn't hear and ran like a fullback right into the damned bird, tackling it full tilt, wrapping my hands around its throat. It was so startled, it released Starlight and fell backwards into the water, me on top, choking it, digging my knees into its gut, feeling its talons claw open my clothes and my thighs and not caring. It flapped wildly, hitting me with bony wings in the cheek, bloodying my nose, but I held on. It snapped at my arms, its wide-eyed, skeletal face hideous. But my prehistoric brain wouldn't let go. Moonlight shrieked, stabbing at the flyer's eyes, as I shoved its head under the shallow water even as it clawed me bloody. And all I could think of was how glad I was I out-weighed it. How glad I was I had saved Too Small. How glad I was to kill my friend's murderer and how miserable I felt being this glad.

Other Grus arrived, and a-gravs with humans, but I just watched the bubbles rise from the slashing beak as I squeezed its throat. I took out all my sorrow and bitterness on the night flyer as I killed it. I had more than enough to spare.

Ray and other Terrans pulled me off after the thing stopped struggling, but I don't remember that. I wasn't even aware of my bloody, muddy wounds. I remember doctors, two human, one Grus, frantically working on Starlight. Blood was smeared all over his beautiful white feathers making me remember Joe's back and mine after the flogging. I thought, they'll save him, like Mom saved us, like Starlight saved me, like I saved Too Small. Moonlight danced around, bleating, making the humans wince.

Starlight blinked at me, and struggled to move his hand. My voder said, "You saved Too Small. You're her father. It's good for partners to raise a child." He gaped for breath, and bloody bubbles rose along his torn back. A human doctor started to cry.

Starlight signed feebly to his mate, "Remember our first dance—" Then his hand fell limply against the platform.

All I could do was rub my knuckles against my chest in a circle, over and over.

Moonlight Dancing signed, "I'll never dance in moonlight again. I've lost my partner, and my name. I am Love-Lies-Bleeding now."

Other Grus moved closer to the shattered pair. I realized how different they all looked, but none of them was Starlight Dancing.

An older male Grus signed to Moonlight—no, Love-Lies-Bleeding, "The Suns are setting. Lift your voice with us, lift it loud, and carry your mate's spirit to the Suns." Some of the Terrans wept, but I stood numbly. Ray couldn't look at me.

Then, all at once, the flock threw their heads back, opening their beaks and flinging their cries to the sky. It hit like a blow to the heart, the force of that sound, and I staggered, going down on one knee like a penitent. They called again, louder and louder, and the water rippled from the sound. I couldn't bear their silent passion. I reached to yank out my nullifiers so I could hear them. It would be the last sound I'd ever hear, the last pain from love I'd ever endure.

But Ray grabbed my wrists. Kneeling, he held me as wave after wave of silent sound rolled over us like thunder. I couldn't feel anything, wouldn't feel anything, even in his arms.

A small, warm body suddenly flung itself against us. Someone had discovered Too Small in the tent and freed the frantic, terrified chick. Ray and I surrounded her with our featherless arms, trying to shield her from the sight of her dead father. Instantly, her only living Grus parent was with us, covering us with his wings, touching the chick with his bill and grieving, as he struggled to make us a family again, for her.

I remembered Starlight signing, *A child can help a grieving mate survive his loss, but that won't stop his sorrow.* As three disparate fathers consoled their heartbroken child, I became the parent my mother raised me to be.

My mother's eyes had a feverish gleam, an echo of constant pain. Standing here was harder than I had imagined—and I was no stranger to hardship.

"Where's Matt?" I asked, more casually than I felt.

She watched my face. "I asked him to stay away. He told me you're on the *Brolga's* passenger list. Will it leave on time tomorrow?"

I touched my thigh where the torn, regenerated tissue still itched. "I booked passage, Mom, so I could use the ship's captain." I paused. "I got married this morning."

Under their laws, any legal marriage was binding, while divorce was illegal. *Whom God and Law has joined in matrimony, let* no one *put asunder.* But that wasn't why I'd done it.

"You're not coming home," she whispered.

"I am home, Mom, on Trinity. I have everything here you always wanted for me—a spouse, a child, a loving family—with all the happiness and pain that incurs."

My family stepped up hesitantly as I fingered the new gold balls in my earlobes that would let me turn my hearing off.

Too Small stared at the hologram, then walked through it looking for the woman.

"Mom, this is my spouse, Raymund Estrada," I said "and this is our Grus partner, Love. And this—" The chick came back and stared at my mother, cocking her cinnamon head. "This is my daughter—Too Small."

"This is your family?" she said, nonplussed. It took her a moment to recover. Then, looking at the adult Grus, she told me, "I watched that film you sent. God blessed these creatures with a beautiful planet. He must love them." Her face grew stern as her eyes moved to Ray. "But, Joshua, you've married this man?"

Her consternation knifed me. "Mom, when we last talked, you

thought you saw a sign. You did—a sign for me. For my future. A future full of the kind of love you've had with Dad and your sons. I can't give that up—even when it hurts. I married Ray today. I wished you were there to dance at my wedding."

She glanced at Ray, who was keeping Too Small occupied. "This is hard to accept, Joshua—"

"It's hard for me not to go to you," I reminded her, "when you need me. To know I won't be there when—"

"Don't let her *eat* that!" Mom said sternly to Ray, who spotted the translation just as Too Small pulled off his button. Ray wrested it from the fussy chick then showed Mom the button to reassure her. She met his gaze and nodded. Love leaned over, distracting the chick as Mom watched them.

"Mom," I said quietly, "Ray and I want children—human, Grus, or whatever child needs us. I'm ready for that, now."

Ray read that and faced me. While still mourning Starlight, we found joy in our union.

My mother's expression showed her conflict. "This is the life you really want?"

"I had to lose someone I loved to learn how much I wanted it," I said. "It was a hard lesson."

Mom turned away.

Ray grew edgy, as if fearing I might step through the hologram to Bright Tabernacle and leave him behind.

I pulled up that part of my mother in me that had moved crowds to her beliefs. "Mom, everything I know about kindness, and self sacrifice, a faith in a force greater than myself—I learned from you." Too Small begged for attention, forcing me to cradle her in my arms. "Everything I know about love, I learned from you. God has to reward that."

She watched me holding the chick, with Ray at my side and Love near us. "Perhaps it's not for me to say what God will reward or punish. Perhaps He brought you there for His own Purpose. All I know is—Joshua, you can never come here again."

I ground my teeth. "Mom..."

She quoted Genesis. "'Therefore shall a man leave his father and his mother and shall cleave unto his spouse....'"

I started to argue, then realized, *She called Ray my spouse!*

Ray stepped into the breech while I gaped in surprise, to sign, "Thank you for your blessing, Mrs. Wagner. It means a lot to us."

She read the translation, but how she'd meant it we'd never know, for all she did was nod and keep her own counsel.

Thinking the conversation over, Love signed to me, "I understand your hard choice better. She must've been a wonderful parent."

"I did the best I could," Mom said tiredly, "like any parent. Like you, yourself, no doubt."

"I love you, Mom," I said. "I'll—pray for you."

She didn't smile. "I love you, too, son. I'll pray for your happiness."

The image winked out, startling Love so much, Ray had to help him balance.

"Will you talk with her spirit again?" Love asked as I turned off my hearing and enjoyed the relief of silence.

Ray and I exchanged a glance as we left the building. Attempts to call Bright Tabernacle would probably not be successful. "I'll talk to her spirit," I said, "but not here."

It was painful to think my mother would die feeling condemned because of me. But I'd be told when that happened, and when it did, we would raise our voices loud and lift her soul up to the Suns where it belonged.

"Come on," I said to my family, "let's go home."

SUN-DRENCHED

STEPHEN BAXTER

*S*teve Baxter tells us that, in a way, "the lunar voyages are the great untold story of the twentieth century. We know the technical detail, but little else, because the astronauts weren't there to tell us how it felt. But still, they walked on the Moon." In this continuation of his alternate history of space exploration, Baxter asks: How would it have felt to have been stranded there? To face death? And—for a 1960s astronaut—is there anything that could have been worse?

Bado crawls backwards out of the Lunar Module.

When he gets to the ladder's top rung, he takes hold of the handrails and pulls himself upright. The pressurized suit seems to resist every movement; he even has trouble closing his gloved fingers around the rails, and his fingers are sore already.

He can see the small TV camera which Slade deployed to film his own egress. The camera sits on its stowage tray, on the side of the LM's descent stage. It peers at him silently.

He drops down the last three feet, and lands on the foil covered footpad. A little grey dust splashes up around his feet.

Bado holds onto the ladder with his right hand and places his left boot on the regolith. Then he steps off with his right foot, and lets go of the LM.

And there he is, standing on the Moon.

He hears the hum of pumps and fans in the backpack, feels the soft breeze of oxygen across his face.

Slade is waiting with his camera. "Okay, turn around and give me a big smile. Atta boy. You look great. Welcome to the Moon." Bado sees how Slade's light blue soles and lower legs are already stained dark grey by lunar dust. Bado can't see Slade's face behind his reflective golden sun-visor.

Bado takes a step. The dust seems to crunch under his weight, like a covering of snow. The LM is standing in a broad, shallow crater. There are craters everywhere, ranging from several yards to a thumbnail width, the low sunlight deepening their shadows.

He feels elated. In spite of everything, in spite of what is to come, he's walking on the Moon.

"Bado. Look up."

"Huh?" Bado has to tip back on his heels to do it.

The sky above is black, empty of stars; his pupils are closed up by the dazzle of the sun, and the reflection of the pale brown lunar surface. But he can see the Earth, a fat crescent.

And there, crossing the zenith, is a single, brilliant, unwinking star. It is Apollo, in lunar orbit.

A cloud of debris surrounds the craft, visible even from here, a disk as big as a dime held at arm's length.

Slade touches his shoulder. "Come on, boy," Slade says gently. "We've got work to do."

After the EVA, back in the LM, Bado has to ask Slade to help him take off his gloves. His exposed hands are revealed to be almost black, they are so bruised.

They get out of their suits. Bado climbs into a storage bag, to catch the rain of sooty Moondust, and strips down to his long johns.

After a meal, they sling their Beta-cloth hammocks across the LM's cramped cabin. Bado climbs into his hammock. Without his suit, and in the Moon's weak gravity, he weighs only twenty-five pounds or so;

the hammock is like a feather bed. Slade, above him, barely makes a dint in his hammock.

It is dark. They have pulled blinds down over the triangular windows. Bado is inside a cozy little tent on the Moon, with the warmth of Slade's body above him, and with the thumps and whirs of the LM's systems around him.

But he can't sleep.

In his mind's eye, Al Pond dies again.

It is before the landing. Just after separation, of LM and CSM, in lunar orbit.

Inside the Lunar Module, Bado and Slade stand side by side, strapped in their cable harnesses. In front of Bado's face is a small triangular window. It is marked with the spidery reticules that will guide them to landfall on the Moon. Through the window Bado can see the CSM: the Cylindrical Service Module, with its big bell of a propulsion system nozzle stuck on the back, and the squat cone of the Command Module on the top.

Drenched in sunlight, Apollo is like a silvery toy, set against the Moon's soft tans.

Bado can picture Al Pond, who they have left alone in the Command Module.

Pond calls over, "You guys take it easy down there."

"We will," says Slade. "And we'll clean up before we come back. We don't want to get Moondust all over your nice clean ship." It is the kind of iffy thing Slade is prone to saying, Bado thinks.

"You better not," calls Pond. "...Hey. I got an odd smell in here."

Bado and Slade glance at each other, within their bubble helmets.

Slade says, "What kind of smell?"

"Not unpleasant. Sharp. Like autumn leaves after an early frost. You know?"

That could be smoke, Bado thinks.

"I got a couple of lights on the ECU control panel," Pond calls now.

"I'll go take a look." His voice gets muffled. "Okay. I got the ECU panel." This is a small, sharp-edged metal panel, just underneath the commander's couch; lithium hydroxide air-scrub canisters are stored in there. "I can't see nothing. But that smell is strong. Ow."

"What?"

"The metal handle. I burned my hand. Okay. I got it open. About a foot length of the cabling in here is just a charred mess. Blackened. And there are bits of melted insulation floating around the compartment. Oh. I can see flames," Pond calls distantly. "But they're almost invisible. It's kind of like a blue ball, with yellow flashes at the edge, where the flame is eating away at the cabling. Man, it's beautiful."

Fire in zero gravity, fed only by diffusion, is efficient; there is little soot, little smoke. Hard to detect, even to see or smell.

There are miles of wires and cables and pipes behind the walls of the Command Module's pressurized cabin. The fire could have got anywhere, Bado realizes.

Solenoids rattle. Slade is firing the LM's reaction thrusters.

Bado asks, "What are you doing?"

"Backing off."

The LM responds crisply.

"I fetched an extinguisher," Pond calls. "Woah."

"What?"

"I got me a ball of flame. Maybe a foot across. It just came gushing out of the hatchway. It's a soft blue. It's floating there."

The two craft pass into the shadow of the Moon.

Pond has fallen quiet.

Bado leans into his window. The silvery tent of the Command Module looks perfect, gleaming, as it recedes.

There is a small docking window, set in the nose of the CSM. Through this window Bado sees a bright light, like a star.

A human hand beats against the glass of the docking window.

The Command Module's hull bursts, abruptly, silently. There is a single sheet of flame, blossoming around the hull. Then black gas billows out, condensing to sparkling ice in an instant.

The silver hull is left crumpled, stained black.

Bado keeps doing mental sums, figuring their remaining consumables.

He looks at his watch. They are already half-way through their nine-hour sleep period.

He thinks about the mission. They have christened the landing site Fay Crater, after Bado's wife. And their main objective for the flight is another crater a few hundred yards to the west that they've named after Bado's daughter, Pam. Surveyor 8, an unmanned robot probe, set down in Pam Crater a couple of years ago; the astronauts are here to sample it.

Now they are here, Bado thinks bleakly, those names don't seem such a smart idea. Bado doesn't want to think about Fay and the kids.

Slade, of course, doesn't have a family, and offered no names at the mission planning sessions.

One of the LM's cooling pumps changes pitch with a bang.

Slade whispers from above. "Bado. You awake, man?"

Bado snaps back, "I am now."

"That goddamn suit was killing me," Slade says.

"How so?"

"I think the leg is too short. The left leg. Every time I walked it pulled down on my shoulder like a ton weight."

Bado laughs. "We'll have to fix it before the next EVA."

"Yeah. Hey, Bado."

"What?"

"You ever read any science fiction?"

"What science fiction?"

"Think about what we got here. A dead world. And two people, stranded on it."

"So what?"

"Maybe we don't have to just die. Maybe we can populate the Moon." He laughs. "Adam and Eve on the Moon, that's us."

Bado feels anger and fear. It's the kind of iffy thing Slade is always saying. He wants to lash out. "Oh, fuck you, Slade."

Slade sighs. Bado can see him shifting in his hammock. "You know, you fit right in with this job, Bado. We're not supposed to be humans, are we? And I truly believe that you're more afraid that I'm going to grab your ass than of what happens when the goddamn oh-two runs out, in a couple of days from now. Listen, Bado. I'm cold, man "

"Fuck you."

Slade's voice rises, brittle. "We're two human beings, Bado, stuck here in this goddamn tin-foil box on the Moon, and we're going to die. I'm cold and I'm scared. Al Pond had to die alone—"

"Fuck you, Slade."

Slade laughs. "Ah, the hell with you," he says eventually. He turns over in his hammock, swings his legs over, and floats to the floor. He sits on the ascent engine cover. His face is in shadow as he looks in at Bado. "So. You going to help me with this leg, or what?"

Bado gets out of his own hammock and folds it away. Slade hauls on the layers of his pressure suit. Bado kneels down in front of Slade and starts unpicking the cords laced around Slade's calf. To adjust the suit's fitting, he will have to unknot every cord, loosen it a little, and retie it.

It takes about an hour. They don't say anything to each other.

They prepare for their second, final EVA. Their traverse is a mis-shapen circle which will take them around several craters. They will follow the timeline in the spiral-bound checklists on their cuffs.

They climb easily out of Fay Crater. They both carry tool pallets, containing their TV camera, rock hammers and core tubes, Baggies for Moon rocks.

Bado has worked out an effective way to move. It is more of a giraffe-lope than a run. It is like bounding across a stream; he is suspended at the peak of each step. And every time he lands a little spray of dust particles sails off in perfect arcs, like tiny golf balls.

On the hoof, Bado tries to give the guys on the ground a little field geology. "Everything's covered in dust. It's all kind of reduced, you can see only the faintest of shadings. But here I can see a bigger rock, the size of a football maybe and about that shape. Zap pits on every side, and I can see green and white crystals sticking out of it. Feldspar, maybe, or olivine..."

Nobody is going to come up here to collect the samples they are carefully assembling. Not in a hundred years. But the geology back room guys will get something out of his descriptions.

Slade is whistling as he runs. He says, "Up one crater and over another. I feel like a kid again. Like I'm ten years old. All that weight— it's just gone. What do you think, huh, Bado? Now we're out and moving again, maybe this isn't such a bad deal. Maybe a day on the Moon is worth a hundred on Earth."

They take a break.

Bado looks back east, the way they have come. He can see the big, shallow dip in the land that is Fay Crater, with the LM resting at its center like a toy in the palm of some huge hand. Two sets of footsteps come climbing up out of Fay towards them, like footsteps on a beach after a tide.

His mouth is dry as sand; he'd give an awful lot for an ice-cool glass of water, right here and now.

"Adam and Eve, huh," Slade says now.

"What?"

"Maybe it will work out that way after all. We're changing the Moon, just by being here. We're three hundred pounds of organic stuff, dropped on the Moon, and crawling with life: gut bacteria, and cold viruses, and—"

"What are you saying?"

"Maybe there will be enough raw material to let life get some kind of a grip here. When we've gone. Life survives in a lot of inhospitable places, back home. Volcano mouths, and the ocean deeps."

"Adam and Eve," Bado says. "I choose Adam."

Slade laughs. "You got it, man."

They lope on, to the west. Bado can hear Slade's breath, loud in his ears.

Bado thinks about Slade.

Everyone in the astronaut office knows about Slade. And Bado came in for some joshing when the crew roster for this flight was announced. Three days on the Moon? Better make sure you take your K-Y jelly, man.

Bado defended Slade. None of that stuff mattered a damn to his piloting abilities.

Anyhow, outside the Agency Slade is painted as the bachelor boy. He has even put up with getting his photograph taken with girls on his arm.

No one knows, the Agency assured Bado. No one will think anything, of you.

Slade stops. He says, "Hey. We're here." He points.

Bado looks up.

He has, he realizes, reached the rim of Pam Crater. In fact he is standing on top of its dune-like, eroded wall. And there, planted in the crater's center, is the Surveyor. It is less than a hundred yards from him. It is a squat, three-legged frame, bristling with fuel tanks, batteries, antennae and sensors, and its white paint has turned tan.

Bado sets the TV camera on its stand. Slade hops down into Pam Crater, spraying lunar dust ahead of him.

Slade takes a pair of cutting shears from his tool carrier, gets hold of the Surveyor's TV camera, and starts to chop through the camera's support struts and cables. "Just a couple of tubes," he says. "Then that baby's mine."

The camera comes loose, and Slade grips it in his gloves. He whoops.

"Outstanding," Bado says. He knows that for Slade, getting to the Surveyor, grabbing a few pieces of it, is the finish line for the mission.

Slade lopes out of the crater. Bado watches his partner. Slade looks like a human-shaped beach ball, his suit brilliant white, bouncing happily over the beach-like surface of the Moon.

Bado thinks of a human hand, pressing silently against the window of a burning capsule.

He is experiencing emotions he doesn't want to label.

"Hey, Slade," Bado says.

"What?"

"Come here, man."

Slade obediently floats over to him, and waits. He has one glove up over his chest, obscuring the tubes which connect his backpack to his oxygen and water inlets. His white oversuit is covered in dust splashes.

Carefully, clumsily, Bado pushes up Slade's gold sun visor. Inside he can see Slade's face, with its four-day growth of beard. He touches Slade's suit, brushing dust off the umbilical tubes. Patiently, Slade submits to this grooming .

Then Bado gets hold of Slade's shoulders with his pressurized gloves. He pulls Slade against his chest. Slade hops forward, into his embrace. Bado puts his arm over the Stars and Stripes on Slade's left shoulder, but he can't get his arms all the way around his partner.

Their faceplates touch. Slade grins, and when he speaks Bado can hear his voice, like an echo of the radio, transmitted directly through their bubble helmets. "Get you," Slade says softly. "Aren't you afraid I'm going to make a grab for your dick?"

"I figure I'm safe locked up in this suit."

Slade laughs.

For a while they stay together, like two embracing balloons, on the surface of the Moon.

They break.

The TV camera sits on its tripod, its black lens fixed on them..

Bado takes a geology hammer and smashes the camera off its stand.

Bado stands harnessed in his place beside Slade. In his grimy pressure suit he feels bulky, awkward.

Slade says, "Ascent propulsion system propellant tanks pressurized."

"Roger."

"Ascent feeds are open, shut-offs are closed."

The capcom calls up. "Everything looks good. We want the rendezvous radar mode switch in LGC just as it is on surface fifty-nine ...

We assume the steerable is in track mode auto."

Bado replies, "Stop, push-button reset, abort to abort stage reset."

Slade pushes his buttons. "Reset." He grins at Bado.

The guys on the ground are playing their part well, Bado thinks. So far it is all being played straight-faced, as they work together through the comforting rituals of the checklists.

The Agency must have decided that the crew has finally gone crazy. Bado wonders how much of this will ever become public.

Looking at the small, square instrument panel in front of him, Bado can see that the ascent stage is powered up now, no longer drawing any juice from the lower stage's batteries. It is preparing to become an independent spacecraft for the first time. He feels obscurely sorry for it. It isn't going to fly any more than he is.

"One minute," the capcom says.

"Got the steering in the abort guidance," Slade says.

Bado arms the ignition. "Okay, master arm on."

"Rog."

"You're go, Apollo," says the capcom.

"Clear the runway." Slade turns to Bado. "You sure you want to do this?"

Actually, Bado is scared as hell. He really, really doesn't want to die.

"Adam and Eve?" he asks.

"Adam and Eve. This is the best way, man. A chance to leave something behind."

Bado makes himself grin. "Then do it, you fairy."

Slade nods, inside his bubble helmet. "Okay. At five seconds I'm going to hit ABORT STAGE and ENGINE ARM. And you'll hit PROCEED."

"Roger," says Bado. "I'll tell you how I'd think of you, man."

Slade looks at him again.

"Out there," Bado says. "Floating across the face of the Moon, in all that sunlight. That's how I'd remember you."

Slade nods. He looks at his instruments. "Here we-go. Nine. Eight. Seven."

The computer display in front of Bado flashes a "99", a request to proceed.

Slade closes the master firing arm. "Engine arm ascent."

Bado has been through enough sims of this sequence. In a moment there should be a loud bang, a rattle around the floor of the cabin: pyrotechnic guillotines, blowing away the nuts, bolts, wires and water hoses connecting the upper and lower stages of the LM.

But they have disabled the guillotines.

Bado presses the PROCEED button.

The cabin starts to rattle. The ascent stage engine has ignited, but its engine bell is still buried within the guts of the LM's descent stage.

The over-pressure builds up quickly.

Slade says, "I think—"

But there is no more time.

The ascent stage bursts open, like an aluminum egg, there on the surface of the Moon. Sunlight drenches Bado's face.

THE FLYING TRIANGLE

ALLEN STEELE

traight writers tend to find it less threatening to write about queer characters of the opposite sex. When they put themselves in the heads of these characters, at least they're imagining making love to someone of the "right" sex. Allen Steele's sixth novel, The Tranquillity Alternative, *features a lesbian NASA astronaut, Cris Ryer. We wondered if he could write a story about a gay man. He took that as a challenge. Besides, it gave him one last opportunity to visit Diamondback Jack's.*

This is the story of *The Flying Triangle* and its crew. At the outset, I can promise you two things: it's the last tale I will ever tell that has its origins in Diamondback Jack's Bar & Grill, and it has a happy ending.

I never believed that I would ever commit this to paper, since I was sworn to secrecy by the persons involved. I've written other stories about Diamondback Jack's, but the last one published got me in a lot of trouble and led to the bar being burned to the ground.[1] When I wrote that story, I claimed that it was the third installment of a trilogy, and that there would be no others.

Well, so I lied. There was one more tale which I haven't been able to relate until now, one which occurred before the self-alleged "final" story.

---

1. "Sugar's Blues," included in *Rude Astronauts*; Old Earth Books, 1993/Ace Books, 1994

Until a few years ago, when you drove north up Route 3 on Merritt Island, about two miles before you passed the south entrance gate of the Kennedy Space Center you would see a small bar on the left side of the road. It was nothing much to look at, certainly not a place where you might consider stopping for a drink: weather-beaten pine walls, no windows, a broken Budweiser sign above a dirt parking lot splattered with oil and littered with beer cans. There were far better watering holes elsewhere on Cape Canaveral, and if you wanted a cool T-shirt to commemorate your visit to the Cape, there was Ron Jon's Surf Shop on Route A1A. Diamondback Jack's didn't even have its own bumper sticker, a cardinal sin for any self-respecting bar in coastal Florida.

Diamondback Jack's was never meant for tourists, though; in fact, it was never meant for anyone except for the people who hung out there, and they were a different breed entirely. You could see this as soon as you stepped inside. The walls were covered with framed photos of *Columbia*-class shuttles, delta clippers, and Big Dummy HLVs lifting off from KSC, of Olympus Station in geosynchronous orbit, and SPS-1 when it was still under construction. A corkboard near the ancient Wurlitzer jukebox was filled with torn-out *Space News* job listings, many of which weren't on Earth at all. Behind the oak-top bar, beneath the varnished and mounted skin of the eighteen-inch rattlesnake which gave the place its name, you would see framed photos of people you've probably never heard of, but whose names are legend on the Cape: Virgin Bruce, Monk Walker, Joe Mama, Dog Boy and Dog Girl, Tiny Prozini, Lisa Barnhart, Weird Frank, Sugar Saltzman, and many others.

Spacers, all of them ... for Diamondback Jack's was a spacer bar. Its regulars were either people who handled ground jobs at KSC, or those who worked from time to time either in orbit or on the Moon and came here when they were between jobs: cargo grunts and pad rats, beam-jacks and shuttle jocks, gliding from paycheck to paycheck, marking time between the issuance of their union cards and mandatory retirement, doing the shit work no one really thinks about.

And then there were a handful people like me, who had no business being there but who hung out nonetheless because we're space buffs. I was a newspaper stringer, but my presence was tolerated, barely, because I kept a low profile despite my unwelcome profession and because Jack Baker, the bar owner, had never found a reason to throw me out. But there were also guys like Taylor Greene, whom I encountered one slow Tuesday night when I came in for a beer. His presence wasn't well tolerated either, despite the fact that he tried to keep an even lower profile. Yet, although there wasn't a photo of him behind the bar at Diamondback Jack's, Ty Greene was probably the most courageous man I ever met.

And therein lies the story.

If you spend much time at any particular bar, you get accustomed to seeing certain people again and again, even if you never actually meet them or get to learn their names. For that reason Ty Greene was a familiar face at Diamondback Jack's long before our chance encounter late one evening.

Greene was one of three guys who used to drop by on weeknights and take over a table in the back of the room, where they would drink and talk softly amongst themselves. Greene was the one who stood out the most: very tall and muscular, with dark hair combed straight back from his forehead and the deep facial tan that identifies someone who has spent a lot of time wearing a space helmet, he had the ruggedly handsome looks one associates with net stars or old-time movie idols, right down to the cleft in his jaw. Think Rock Hudson and you've got him pegged.

He and his friends kept to themselves; no one else ever joined them, and they usually arrived together and slipped out the door the same way. Aside from occasional laughter from their table, the trio were the bar's quietest and best-behaved patrons, they never harassed the college girls Baker hired as barmaids, and although Jack had trouble holding onto his girls because of the way they were often treated by some of his customers, none ever quit because one of the men at the back table fondled them.

I never paid much attention to them, though, until the night I arrived shortly before closing hour. It was a week night and the place was almost empty save for the tall dude, who was sitting at the bar instead of at his usual table. That was unusual in itself; even more odd was the fact that he wasn't accompanied by his posse.

Unfortunately, he wasn't alone. Occupying the adjacent stool was another regular whose face was familiar, but in a far less benign way.

Joe Humphrey, a.k.a. "the Hump," was one of those guys who give beer joints a bad name. A big, pot-bellied cracker with a drinking problem and a disposition to match, the Hump had been hired and fired by every space company on the Cape, yet frequent unemployment didn't keep him from hanging around Diamondback's, looking for trouble and causing it if he couldn't find any. Jack had thrown him out several times and he would stay gone for a month or two, but eventually he would reappear, full of promises that he wouldn't pick a fight, kick the jukebox, or molest a barmaid again. And he wouldn't ... for about two weeks.

So here was the Hump, perched on the barstool next to the tall quiet gent, his shoulders hunched in such a way that made it appear as if he was deliberately crowding the other man. The holo above the bar was blasting a basketball game, so I couldn't clearly hear what was being said, but it seemed as if the Hump was doing all the talking; the tall guy simply stared straight ahead, saying nothing as he nursed his beer. On the other side of the bar, Jack was washing mugs and pitchers; although he didn't appear to be paying attention to them, I could tell that he was tuned in.

There was something going on between the two men. I kept one eye on the game and one eye on the Hump and the stranger, and during a commercial break I caught a snatch of the one-sided conversation.

"So what's it like?" the Hump was asking. "I mean, y'know, I've always been kinda curious." The quiet gent sipped his beer and didn't reply. "Y'know, is it like sucking on a piece of candy, but just tastes different? Hey, c'mon, you can tell me ... do you spit it out when you're through, or do you swallow it and say, 'Yummy yum yum, can I have some more?'"

"Cut it out, Joe," Jack said. "Leave him alone."

"Hey, I don't mean nothing." The Hump gave Jack the look of feigned innocence favored by schoolyard bullies who never grew up. "I mean, inquiring minds want to know..."

The tall man muttered something I didn't hear. "What'd you say?" Humphrey asked. "I didn't catch that."

"You heard me just fine." The quiet man had a very soft voice; for him, speaking above the holo was almost like shouting.

"No, no, I don't think so." The Hump turned around on his stool so that his curled fists rested on his knees. "Did you just say something about my mind?"

"Chill out, Humphrey." Jack's hands disappeared beneath the sink, where I knew he had a Louisville slugger stashed away for emergencies. "I don't take this shit in my place." He glanced at the tall man. "Never mind him, Greene. Want another beer?"

Greene shook his head; it wasn't hard to tell that this was a situation he would just as soon avoid. Although he hadn't finished his beer, he pushed aside the half-empty mug and started to rise from his stool. "Thanks, Jack," he said, "but it's getting late. See you next..."

"Whoa, buddy." The Hump grabbed the tall man's left wrist to stop him. "Not so fast. I'm not done talking to..."

It happened so fast, I nearly missed it. One moment, the Hump had Greene's wrist clutched in his paw; the next, he was down on the barroom floor, howling as the tall man stood over him, grasping Humphrey's right forearm his hands and twisting it around. Just like that, the Hump had been reduced to a bawling baby.

A baby with a foul mouth. "Lemme go, cocksucker!" He tried to kick Greene's legs, but the other man danced aside; that seemed to make Humphrey even madder. "Somebody get this fag offa me! He's trying to rape me!"

"Rape?" Greene shook his head. "Don't flatter yourself."

"Let him go, Ty." Jack now had the baseball bat in plain sight. "I'm warning you ... let loose of his arm."

"Hey, Jack," I said, "the Hump was trying to pick a fight."

"Stay out of this, Al." Jack came around the bar, holding the bat in bunting position. "Break it up, both of you."

"Sorry, Jack. Didn't mean to cause trouble." Greene waited until the barkeep was beside him, then he released the Hump's arm and stepped back. "Okay, fella, you can—"

"You fuckin' queer, I'm going to kill you!"

Two hundred and seventy pounds of pissed-off redneck surged off the floor and charged straight at Greene. Greene took a graceful step to one side and lifted his arms into a martial arts posture, but he didn't get a chance to demonstrate another smooth move—somewhat to my dismay, I must admit—before Jack rushed into the gap and slammed the blunt end of the bat into Humphrey's vast stomach.

The Hump clutched at his gut and doubled over, eyes streaming as he gasped for air. Before he lost his balance and fell down again, Jack grabbed the back of his shirt, swung him around and gave him a hard kick in the ass toward the door.

"Get out of here!" Jack roared. "Show up here again and I'm calling the cops!"

I jumped off my stool and pushed the door open. Without anything to stop his forward momentum, the Hump sailed through the doorway, fell down the steps, and toppled into the dirt driveway.

Jack walked to the door and watched the Hump as he struggled to his feet and, with only one backward glance but with plenty of obscenities, staggered to his pickup truck. Jack waited until the Dodge's tail lights had vanished down Route 3, then lowered his bat and turned back to the bar. "I thought I told you to never mind him," he murmured as he walked past Greene and resumed his place behind the counter.

"He was trying to." I picked up my beer and went over to sit down next to Greene. "Way I saw it, he did everything he could to avoid a fight. Joe's the guy you should blame, not him."

Jack opened his mouth to say something, but I beat him to it.

"Another round for both of us. Put it on my tab."

Jack's eyes shifted from me to Greene and then back again. This was an argument he couldn't win. Without another word, he put the bat back in its hiding place, tapped two more mugs of beer, then disappeared into the back room to cool off. "Thanks," Greene said softly after he was gone.

"No problem. You handled yourself pretty well there. Judo?"

"Tai kwon do."

"Guess it makes sense to learn something like that if you're. . ."

Oops. I clammed up and looked away, pretending to study the liquor bottles on the shelf behind the bar. "It's not hard to figure out." Greene took a contemplative sip from his beer. "Happens now and then. You get used to it." He shrugged, then extended his hand. "Taylor Greene. My friends call me Ty." I introduced myself and he nodded as we shook. "Seen you here before. We're the bar tokens."

"Bar tokens?"

"The token journalist and the token queer," he said, smiling a little. "One of them, at least."

"One of ...? Oh, you mean..."

"My friends, yeah." Greene must have read the expression on my face as everything suddenly clicked into place. "The crew of *The Flying Triangle*, that's us," he added, with no small pride.

"A spacecraft?" I asked, and he nodded again. "Sorry, man. Never heard of it."

His face changed. "No reason why you should," he replied, then turned away and was silent for so long that I wondered if I had said the wrong thing again.

Try to understand what I mean when I say that, although I've had many gay friends, I haven't been friendly with many gays. I suppose I'm like most other heterosexual males these days; although you come to meet gay men and accept them by overlooking or ignoring their difference, there is always a certain barrier that is difficult, if not impossible, to cross. It isn't just a matter of appearances, like a sibilant lisp or a too-perfect handsomeness, or even the knowledge that their ideas of having a good time in bed are not the same as your own. It's also the fact they live in a world parallel to your own, but which is closed to you. Congress may have passed laws ensuring equal rights to gays and lesbians, but that only means that the gateways between the barriers are clean and well-lighted; the walls themselves are still in place, and can't be legislated out of existence.

Perhaps I should have let the matter drop. Had a couple of beers, watched the game, made small talk, gone home when Jack closed up in another hour or so. My curiosity had been aroused, though, so I drank my beer in silence and waited to see if he wanted to talk.

"Yeah, there's a reason for that," Greene said at last, turning to look at me again. "In fact, it's a pretty interesting story. Might be something you'd like to write about."

I shrugged. "Maybe. I haven't heard it yet, though."

"So I'll tell you..." He hesitated, then added: "So long as you'll agree to one condition."

It started back in 23, when Ty Greene had working for Skycorp as a beamjack on its powersat construction operations in geosynchronous orbit. Along with a hundred-plus other men and women employed on the same project, he spent a year on Olympus Station, the giant wheel-shaped space station which served as home for the beamjacks and their support crew. Greene was a pod driver, one of the guys who flew the bug-like construction craft which did much of the heavy work on the island-size solar power satellites, and it wasn't long before he met an OTV pilot by name of Carl Fleisher and a communications specialist named Stan Weinberg.

It was hardly coincidental that these three would meet and become close comrades, for all three were gay. In fact, unless there were others who managed to keep their sexual orientations a secret, they were the only "out of the airlock" gays aboard Skycan. Although Greene didn't advertise his homosexuality, neither did he deny it; Carl and Stan hadn't come out yet back home—indeed, both were mortally afraid of their families and friends discovering the truth—but after they had become lovers three months earlier, it had been only a matter of time before the rest of the crew found them out. As many heterosexual couples before them had already discovered, privacy was nearly impossible within Olympus's cramped modules, and gossip was one of the few distractions from the routine.

It wasn't easy being queer aboard Skycan. Most of the guys who worked there were blue-collar working stiffs one generation removed from the Rust Belt factories and midwestern farms where their parents and grandparents had made their livelihoods; many had been brought up believing that gays were sinister homos who would attack you in the toilet, or at least were fair game for harassment. Not all the beamjacks on Olympus were like that, to be sure, but Stan was just effeminate enough to draw unwanted attention to himself, and although Carl and Ty were butch, they received their share of insults and snubs, if not outright hostility. Back home, the Gay Rights Act may prevent one from being harassed or beaten up in the workplace, but it's bit more difficult to enforce civil-rights statutes 22,300 miles from the nearest EEOC district office.

"It finally got bad enough that we decided to move in together," Greene said. "There was a half-empty bunkhouse located next to the waste reclamation module ... half-empty because the odor was something godawful ... and we arranged to trade bunks with the three guys living there already." He grimaced as he picked up his beer. "The day we moved in someone painted 'Fag Shack' on the hatch. Just to make us feel at home."

"Cute," I murmured.

Greene shrugged as he polished off his beer. Baker had returned from the back room by now. "It wasn't so bad," Ty said as he motioned Jack to bring us another round. "After that, we were largely left alone. I guess everyone believed the three of us were engaged in some sort of *menage à trois*, even though I could have told them that I had a steady boyfriend back home. We rigged up a curtain to give Stan and Carl some privacy, but I usually left when they wanted to..."

"Okay, right." I didn't want to hear the details.

There was a scowl on Jack's face as he placed two fresh mugs in front of us; he moved to the opposite end of the bar and turned up volume on the basketball game. Ty gave me a cold look as well, although for different reasons. "Anyway, what we were really doing during our off-shift," he continued, "was coming up with a scheme to get rich."

He tasted his beer, then went on. "Besides being gay, the three of us had other things in common. First, we were all lifelong space buffs who had wanted to be astronauts since childhood. Second, since Skycorp had trained us for our jobs, we had marketable skills. And third, we all wanted to retire as wealthy old queens."

I laughed out loud when I heard that. "We had already learned that there was no way we could move up Skycorp's corporate ladder because of our persuasion," Greene went on. "We hit a glass ceiling, so we would have to go into business for ourselves if we wanted to get anywhere."

"Doing something that wouldn't get you busted for being..."

"Gay. It's just a word, y'know." He shot me a look—*get used to it*—but refrained from giving me a lecture. "Anyway, so all we had to do was identify a viable market and exploit it. Well, okay ... we spent the rest of our tour figuring how we could do this, and in the meantime socking away our paychecks, and eventually it paid off."

He smiled and tapped the bar top with his fingertip. "On the day our Skycorp contracts ran out, we formed Flying Triangle, Inc. A trip back to Earth to line up our pigeons, and two months later, we were back in space and open for business."

The business was salvaging dead satellites.

By 2023 there were over fifteen thousand radar-detectable items of space junk located in various orbits above Earth, ranging from paint chips and palm-size fragments of expendable rocket stages all the way up to multi-ton satellites that had long since gone dark, either because of malfunctioned electronics or because they had outlived their usefulness and had been shut down by ground controllers. The former comprised a navigation hazard that was being cleaned up by robotic sweepers, but the latter was a potential goldmine; a satellite that had suffered an onboard failure shortly after launch might yet be useful if it could be retrieved and repaired. Even an obsolete weather or communications sat could be still cannibalized for spare parts, since most of its hardware was still in pristine condition that could be used on other spacecraft— RCR modules, computer chips, semiconductors, Mylar insulation blankets, and so forth—it could be resold to other in-orbit space companies which wanted to cut the costs of having brand-new replacements shipped up from Earth.

That was where Flying Triangle, Inc. came in. The way the company had it figured, they could either contract their services to companies that wished to retrieve their snafued hardware, or else locate dead sats that no one wanted anymore and resell them as salvage. Although the former was already being done by spacecraft crews operating on a work-for-hire basis, there wasn't a company that specialized in retrieving space junk ... and the latter had never considered a viable market since the overhead costs appeared prohibitive.

Pooling their savings, Greene and his cohorts made down-payments to Skycorp for a second-hand orbital transfer vehicle and a construction pod. The OTV was then retrofitted with an uprated engine, a pair of outrigger cradles for cargo, and a docking collar for the pod; the spacecraft was christened *The Flying Triangle* and painted with the company logo—an inverted pink triangle wearing a pair of angel wings. "You'd be surprised how many people didn't understand the allusion," Greene said. "When Stan and Carl told their families about the name, they explained it was because the company was operated by three partners."

Flying Triangle, Inc. also rented a personnel module on Alpha Station's new "free enterprise" arm, which served both as the company office and as their living quarters. The terms of the lease with NASA included air, water, electrical power, telemetry link and two meals a day in the station wardroom in exchange for forty-five percent of the company's net income; for fifteen percent more, *The Flying Triangle* was hangared and serviced at the station's docking arm. With sixty percent of the company's net being swallowed by overhead, it meant that Flying Triangle would need to having an outstanding first year in order to pay off its capital debts.

As it turned out, the company's first four quarters exceeded the most optimistic projections the partners had made. Almost as soon as it opened shop on Alpha Station, Flying Triangle began receiving faxes from various firms on Earth; it seemed as if nearly everyone in the commercial space business had lost a satellite at one time or another, and even if they no longer wished to have their hardware returned to them, their insurance underwriters wanted the sats back. Since the price for a low-orbit retrieval mission started at hundred grand and went up from there — still cheap, considering that some of those satellites had cost tens of millions of dollars to build and launch — each flight the *Triangle* made added six more figures to the company's bank account in Houston.

"So we got off to a good start," Greene said. "We were earning enough to keep the creditors happy, we were our own bosses, and it beat hell out of powersat construction. Carl was the Triangle's pilot, Stan the first officer, and I worked the pod. Every flight was an adventure ... we were like big kids playing *Star Trek*."

"Sounds like fun. You must have been raking in the cash."

Greene frowned and shook his head. "Not quite. Like I said, we had a pretty large capital debt to pay off, and the operating overhead was enough to give our accountant migraines. We soon realized that, unless we started showing a higher profit margin pretty soon, we might have to get out of the business."

"I don't get it. How come?"

He shrugged. "Well, it's something we hadn't really anticipated either. We were living in zero-gee on a full-time basis. We could only stay up there so long before each of us would suffer permanent bone-calcium loss ... and we didn't want to return home in maglev chairs."

He had a good point there. The major benefit of living on Skycan was that its centripetal rotation provided a healthy, human-friendly environment. Alpha Station, on the other hand, existed in freefall; if people living there didn't return to Earth at least once a year, then long-term effects of weightlessness could be quite harmful.

Yet Ty, Carl, and Stan were so busy trying to keep their company going, they didn't have time to take the recuperative vacations ground-side that they had originally planned to make. After fourteen months of weightlessness, the med team were showing them the warning lights.

"We finally had to start looking for a sideline to the retrieval missions," Greene went on, "and that meant finding dead sats that nobody wanted and claiming them as salvage. Not as much money as the commercial contracts, but at least we could sell them for spare parts. So Stan and I began studying the satellite charts, and pretty soon we located several junkers that looked promising."

He paused to make sure Jack was still watching the holo. "That's when we got into trouble," he said softly.

The first two derelicts the company salvaged from low Earth orbit were an old NASA solar observatory and a comsat that China had launched in the late '90s; those were successfully resold, but for not as much as they would have liked. Then, three weeks after the *Great Wall 56* retrieval, *The Flying Triangle* set out to grab a satellite Stan had located in equatorial orbit 260 nautical miles up, a dead American weather sat listed on the charts as *Stormking 11*, launched from Vandenberg three years earlier and listed as out of service less than ten months later due to onboard guidance failure.

Snagging *Stormking 11* meant that the company had to work in a gray area, legally speaking. Before it retrieved the NASA solar observatory, Flying Triangle tried to get advance approval from the U. S. government; they were successful in getting permission, but had to wade through so much bureaucratic red tape that, when they decided to pick up Stormking, the three men opted to retrieve first, notify later. After all, it was a dead satellite, of no conceivable use to anyone; if the government wanted to bitch about it, Flying Triangle could always claim maritime common law allowed them to salvage a possible navi-

gational hazard. So they went after the weather sat without telling anyone what they planned to do.

So *The Flying Triangle* spent eight hours chasing *Stormking 11* around
the limb of the earth, gradually edging closer and closer, until they
finally coasted up behind the sat as it passed over the Indian Ocean. As
soon as the *Triangle* had matched orbits with Stormking, Ty climbed
into his pod, dubbed the *Greene Magic*, and went out to haul it aboard.

"It was a big sucker," Greene said. "These things look small when
you see them in photos, but then you get up close to one and see that
they're the size of a bus. I never have any problems hauling them
aboard, though, once I collapsed the solar wings, but as soon as we got
close to Stormking I knew this one was a little weird."

"How so?"

"It wasn't tumbling, for starters." Greene twirled his forefingers
around each other. "Dead sats start tumbling end over end when their
RCRs go kaput, but this one was just gliding along, smooth as silk. And
when I got a little closer, I noticed that there was long, semi-conical
bulge on its underside."

Still imitating the satellite with his hands, he pointed a forefinger
beneath the palm of his other hand. "So I slid the pod under the thing
until my hatch porthole was just a few feet away, and I switched my
spots and was just beginning to get a close look at that bulge when Stan
comes over the comlink and says, 'Ty, you better listen to this. I think
we've got a problem.'

"I say, 'Yeah, what?' and Stan relays a transmission coming in on the
KU-band, and here's this macho voice in my headset." Greene dropped
his own voice an octave. "'Unidentified spacecraft at such-and-such
coordinates, this is Space Operations Defense Center, United States
Space Command. Identify yourself at once, over.' Well, I know at once
what has happened. We've been picked up by SPADATS radar."

SPADATS is the Space Detection and Tracking System, a global
network of ground based radar and telescopes operated by SPADOC in
Cheyenne Mountain in Colorado. "After all, they can track everything
in Earth orbit the size of a bolt on up," Greene went on, "and when we

moved in on this dead weather sat, they decided to give us a yell on the common frequency and find out what we're up to. So I get Stan to patch me in, and I tell them who were are and explain what we're doing."

"Did you think you were in trouble?"

Greene shrugged. "Sort of. but not really. After all, this was a dead sat, right? They might bitch because we were salvaging it without government permission, but since it was floating garbage, I kind of thought that they might thank us for getting it out harm's way."

He shook his head. "Should have known better, because a second later SPADOC comes back and tells us that we're trespassing on United States Government Property and we're to remove ourselves from this orbit immediately or else face federal prosecution."

"That's weird."

"No kidding. So Carl gets on the line and begins to argue with them, reading them the letter of the law, and while he's doing that, I'm guiding the pod a little closer to the sat and taking a look at that bulge I had spotted earlier..."

He paused. "And that's when I spot a red radiation trefoil painted on a hatch in the middle of the bulge, and a little sign below it that reads 'Payload Access.'"

"'Payload Access.'" I shook my head. "I don't..."

And then I got it.

Again, Greene seemed to have read my mind. "Yeah, right," he whispered, slowly nodding his head. "We'd just found something that wasn't supposed to be up there."

"I'll be damned ... and they had disguised it as a dead sat."

"You got it." Greene picked up his mug and took a sip. "Dead weather satellite with a footprint over most of the Balkans, the Middle East, and Southeast Asia . . . sneaky little way of getting around the U.N. space treaty."

There had been several United Nations space treaties, but I knew the one Greene was talking about. The first one, signed in 1967, that unilaterally outlawed weapons of mass destruction in outer space.

I didn't have to glance in the bar mirror to see that my face had lost its color.

So Ty switched to a private frequency and told Carl to stop arguing and tell SPADOC that they were leaving the alleged weather satellite alone, then he flew the pod away from the sat as quickly as possible. He didn't let Carl and Stan in on the secret until after the *Greene Magic* was docked with the *Triangle* and he had climbed through the hatch. By then, on Greene's insistence, Carl had moved the OTV away from *Stormking 11*. SPADOC ceased communication once the *Triangle* was a hundred miles away from the satellite.

The three men spent the long journey back to Alpha Station quarreling over what to do next. Greene wanted to go public at once; the United States had deliberately violated one of the key principles of international space law, and *Stormking 11* posed a clear and present danger to the entire world. If the satellite's covert payload was ever used, he argued, it might possibly be against a foreign city; even if it was against a military target, it could very well escalate a local conflict into a thermonuclear war ... perhaps even nuclear holocaust on a global scale.

Fleisher and Weinberg agreed with Greene on principal, but they didn't want to be the ones who blew the whistle on *Stormking 11*. At first, their counter-argument centered on the notion that no would believe them. Since they had no photo evidence to back up their allegation, all they had was Ty's observation and the fact that SPADOC had insisted upon them leaving the premises.

Then they protested that this could endanger the company. Flying Triangle was renting a module aboard a space station owned and operated by the United States government, and that same government could easily cancel their lease and put the company out of business long before its debts had been paid off.

In the end, though, it all came down to one thing: if Flying Triangle attempted to expose *Stormking 11*, the press would focus in on the men behind the allegation. Without a doubt, that would lead to public disclosure of their sexual identities. The pink triangle in the company logo might have fooled some people some of the time, but it wouldn't fool all the people all the time, and certainly there were enough people who had worked with them aboard Skycan, and later on Freedom Station, who would be only too willing to confirm certain suspicions. Even if Ty wasn't personally worried about the public discovering that he was gay, Carl and Stan didn't want their families finding that their sons were queer from watching the evening news.

It was a long flight back to Alpha Station. They worked out their differences before they hard-docked with the hangar.

"So?" I asked.

"So, well..." Ty finished his beer in a single gulp. "So it came down to company policy. Everything nice and democratic, as we had always done everything, and since it was two against one, after all..."

His mug came down on the bar with a hard slam. "So we didn't say a word. Not a goddamn thing."

And thus their gentlemen's agreement remained in effect for the next three years.

Flying Triangle stayed in business for another seven months. The company managed to pay off its debts and even achieve a modest profit, but its major contracts dried up after the *Stormking 11* debacle. For some reason, the major space firms became uninterested in hiring their services. The partners had strong suspicions of what had caused this, but there was nothing that they could prove. When their lease on Alpha Station came up for renewal and NASA raised the rent above their means, it was only the *coup de grace*; the company was dying already.

So they liquidated their assets, sold *The Flying Triangle* and the *Greene Magic* to another group of ex-Skycorp beamjacks who wanted to take a shot at the satellite retrieval business, and boarded the next clipper back to the Cape.

"It wasn't a total loss," Greene said, picking up one of the beers Jack had brought to us after ringing the last-call bell. "We had lots of cash in the bank and we had all managed to land ground down here. It wasn't the same as working up there, but ..."

"It had gone sour on you."

"Uh-huh. Probably for the better, though. I had to hobble around on crutches for two months before my legs were strong enough again. The doctors told me that if I had stayed up much longer, I might have been in a maglev chair for the rest of my life."

He sipped his beer. "We continued to see each other regularly, since we were all working on the Cape. Carl and Stan broke up several months ago and they're seeing other people now, but we're all still friends. There's not any good gay bars in these parts, so we get together here from time to time, mainly to talk about old times..."

"Like the Stormking mission?"

Again he hesitated, leaving a long moment of silence. The basketball game was long over; Jack had switched off the holo and was now moving through the barroom, putting up chairs and sweeping under tables. "So far as I know, it's still up there," he said quietly. "I've tried talking the other guys into going public with what we know, but they won't do it. They're still afraid of...well, y'know..."

Greene sighed. "In hindsight," he went on, speaking very slowly as he played with the mug's glass handle, "I think we created the problem ourselves. We set up Flying Triangle as an all-gay enterprise, which was well and good, but it also got us into an us-against-them mindset. We started thinking of ourselves as the nucleus of everything around us ... and then we ran into something bigger than gay self-reliance and gay pride, something that made all that pale in comparison and we couldn't handle it, we..."

His voice trailed off; he had run out of words. "I dunno. I know what has to be done, but I just don't know if I can do it."

Greene took a last slug off his beer, then eased himself off the barstool. "Thanks for letting me come clean," he said, avoiding my gaze as he headed for the door. "I'll let you know if you can print what I've told you."

And then he was gone.

I saw Taylor Greene again in Diamondback Jack's several times before the place burned down, either sitting alone at the bar nursing a beer or at a back table talking with Carl Fleisher and Stan Weinberg. At first I would nod to him or give him a little wave, but he never acknowledged me; it was much as if I had been a stranger he had never met. On one occasion Joe Humphrey swaggered in when Greene was by himself, the Hump caught one glimpse of the quiet man sitting at the bar, then turned around and headed out the door again. Jack Baker and I traded a look and a smile, but if Greene noticed the Hump's flyby maneuver, he gave no indication. Finally I stopped seeing him altogether, although Fleisher and Weinberg still showed up from time to time, the third leg of the triangle had disappeared.

Then, about two years after the night Diamondback Jack's was torched, I came home to find a Federal Express packet on my front doorstep. The return address on the packing slip said that it was from Flying Triangle Inc., with an address in New York City that, when I investigated later, turned out to an apartment house in Greenwich Village.

Within the packet was twenty-two page account of the Flying Triangle's attempted retrieval of *Stormking 11*, essentially disclosing the same story as I've just written here. The packet also contained photocopies of various Department of Defense documents that had been ferreted out of the Pentagon by unknown parties. Ty Greene had apparently been keeping himself busy upon moving to New York, and the Greenwich Village gay community has a reputation for political activity.

I wasn't the only journalist to receive this packet. Within a matter of days, several newspapers, two cable news networks, and all the major on-line services were reporting the story of a "sleeper" satellite in low Earth orbit that contained a one-megaton nuclear warhead. As I write this, full-scale congressional hearings have been scheduled to publicly investigate the matter, and the Chairman of the Joint Chiefs of Staff has announced his formal resignation. *Stormking 11*, needless to say, has been removed from low Earth orbit, and the United Nations Security

Council is looking into other possible violations of the 1967 space treaty.

No promises, but I think the world will be soon a safer place.

In most reports I've seen, Taylor Greene is prominently mentioned as the man who single-handedly exposed *Stormking 11*. His homosexuality is sometimes mentioned, but even then only incidentally; what he saw and did are more important than what he is, and no one seems any more interested in his sexual orientation than in his former business partners. Risking nothing, they gained nothing in return; their names are lost to obscurity, but Ty's face is on the front cover of this week's issue of *Time*. I'm sure they're nice people, but history will never remember their names.

In the end, Taylor Greene became the space hero I think he always wanted to be, and no barroom redneck will ever call him a fag again.

And didn't I say that this story would have a happy ending?

BROOKS TOO BROAD
FOR LEAPING

CHARLES SHEFFIELD

"*There is something odd about the relationship between the military and gay communities. Both are regarded with suspicion by a big percentage of the general public. There ought to be a common bond of sympathy, instead there is antipathy,*" *says Charles Sheffield. Here, he takes a look at how things might be if the military were exclusively gay.*

It was a new beginning, the start of a whole new life. It only seemed like death.

I felt frozen, beyond pain or anything else, but something must have showed, because before the demob officer asked the final question he paused and turned off the camera.

"Want to talk about it?" he asked. "We're off the record."

I shook my head, and he nodded sympathetically.

"I understand, at least a little bit." He patted his own legs, where the growing stumps showed baby-pink flesh. "I lost these in the Achernar action, and my partner was clipped an arm and a leg. But for three days we thought we'd lost each other."

When I said nothing, he went on, "I'm responsible only for your sign off. It's not my job to talk you out of it. But I want to make sure you realize that this will be *final*. You're still a young man for most jobs, but you're too old to sign up again. You have a damned fine record with the

Service, but if you leave now it's forever. And if you leave here, on Pelican's Wake, the post-Service communities will be closed to you. This isn't the best place to leave the Service, and it may be one of the worst."

"I know all that. I want out."

"Still a young man," he said again, as though I had not spoken. "A man with more than half his life ahead of him. You feel as though life is over and done with. You probably wish it were. But it isn't. You have a long way to go. Someday, there could be another partner." He held up his hand before I could speak. "Don't tell me there can't be, ever. I know that's how you feel. If you didn't think that way, you wouldn't be here. I just want to make the point that you may be wrong."

"I want out." I ducked my head forward, avoiding his gaze. "I want my release."

He didn't say anything, just sat there staring at me for a while. Finally he reached forward and turned on the camera.

"Officer Jeth Mylongi. *Attention.*"

At that word, I automatically stiffened.

"Do you request early but honorable discharge from the Special Services, Local Spiral Arm, Fomalhaut Branch?"

"I do."

"Your discharge is granted. Jeth Mylongi, you have crossed the river. You are a civilian, and no orders from me or any other Service officer now apply."

He reached out his hand. "Goodbye, soldier, and good luck. I hate to see you go."

You have crossed the river. It was a metaphorical river, of course, the Service term for the move into the civilian world. All my adult life I had lived on one side of it. It was hard to imagine anything else; but I didn't need to imagine. I was about to experience the other side of the river at first hand.

The first five years would be spent on Pelican's Wake, the planet where I had received my discharge. That was not a decision I had to make. It was a rule imposed by the civilian world on the Service. The people we served accepted, grudgingly, that we had to go *somewhere*, but they wanted us scattered about, and they wanted to be told how many of us were released on each world.

Other than that, I was free to wander where and how I chose. I had my lump sum discharge benefit, plus a small pension. My needs were few. Money was not a problem.

Loneliness was.

I wandered the settled part of Pelican's Wake's northern continent. The whole planet would be habitable someday, but at the moment the only foods edible to animals with Earth DNA grew in this area.

That still offered no shortage of space. A population of less than two million was dotted across a land area of forty million square kilometers. By most Local Arm standards, everyone on Pelican's Wake was lonely.

I said that I was free to wander, but it would be more accurate to say that I was encouraged to do so. As soon as people learned who and what I was, the signals began for me to move on. Indirect signals, for the most part—they had to be, because provided that I followed certain codes of behavior I was allowed to settle where I chose. But undeniable signals.

And occasionally things were more explicit.

Seven months after my discharge, the days were at last becoming more than a gray parade of misery, and one morning in the ninth month I was sitting in a corner cafe in Darnelfstown, chatting about the Service with a fifteen year-old boy. He was blond, smart, handsome, and strongly-built, and he had a thousand eager questions about Service life. I was doing my best to answer, more relaxed than I had been since Wolfgang died, when a man appeared at the cafe door.

He was a stranger, but I recognized him at once from his features and curly fair hair. He was the youth's father.

"All right, that's enough," he said, while the other patrons of the cafe carefully looked away. They were not going to be witness to a breaking of the Civilian/Service regulations.

He came over and pulled the boy to his feet. His face had been red with rage when he came in, now it went pale. "You've had your hour," he said to me. "That's all you're entitled to. If I ever catch you talking to my son again I'll have you arrested. Get out of here."

It was a public place. I had a perfect right to remain where I was for as long as I chose. I had a drink untouched in front of me.

But what was the point? I was on the other side of the river—*their* side, not my side.

I stood up and left without a word.

I kept moving. The towns and villages were all different, but in a way they were all the same. By the fourteenth month, I knew that the demob officer had been right and I had been wrong. With every pass‐ing day, I missed the Service more. Even if there was no Wolfgang, even though there could never again be anyone like Wolfgang, I missed it.

What do you do when you have made a mistake that can never be corrected?

You travel on, though you don't know where you are going, and you don't know why.

In the twenty-sixth month of my wandering I stopped for a meal in the small market town that served as a center for Pelican Wake's exot‐ic fruit industry. It was late afternoon, and too hot to sit inside. I sat down on the bistro's shaded outside patio, waiting for my order to be produced.

And I saw her, at a table half shielded by an arbor of vines.

Men outnumbered women, more than two to one, on Pelican's Wake. She was young and attractive. She was alone. And she had a cer‐tain set to her shoulders.

I stood up and walked over to her table. "Mind if I sit here?"

She gave me a cool glance of rejection, and was opening her mouth to tell me to go to hell when I added, "Special Officer Jeth Mylongi, Fomalhaut Branch."

She stood up to shake my hand. "Verona Skipsos. Lasalle Branch.

Captain." As she sat down she added, with a touch of wry bitterness, "Retired."

"Yes." I sat down opposite her. "Retired."

"On the wrong side of the river."

There seemed to be nothing to add. We waited in silence until food and drink were served. Then, guardedly, we began to compare notes.

She had left the Service nineteen months ago, in a town four hundred kilometers from my discharge point. Neither of us had met anyone else retired from the service. And since we had both been wandering at random, we could easily have spent a lifetime without once running into each other.

In one way Verona Skipsos had been less fortunate than I. Five weeks earlier, in a town on the southern coast, she had talked to a fourteen-year old girl. The event was a church social, and their conversation had been interrupted several times by announcements and a charity raffle. Nonetheless, someone had been watching and keeping time. The town vigilantes arrived the second that the fifteen minute grace period expired, accused her of illegal recruiting and railroaded her out of town—quite legally—with orders never to return.

Our talk may have sounded casual. Underneath it was anything but. We skirmished and skated around the real issue, ordering food and drink that we did not want and watching the sun of Pelican's Wake sink lower in the sky, until at dusk and after a long silence Verona Skipsos took the initiative.

"You've been out a bit longer than I have. How much of your lump sum benefit do you have left?"

"All of it. I've been living on my pension."

"Me too. Nothing worth spending it on." It became darker and the patio wall lights went on, before she said, "Did you get the same thing in the Fomalhaut rumor mill as we did? That there's a place, on the northern continent?"

"Change Castle? Yeah, I heard of it. No one could say quite where it was, but far, far north."

"Head toward the pole. That's what we were told, too."

More silence. My turn to take the initiative. "Did you ever hear a price?"

"Sort of. The lump sum benefit, and a little bit more."

"So it's impossible."

"Right." Her face was in deep shadow and its expression was unreadable.

"And even if you could afford it, it's supposed to be pretty risky."

"Right. And painful, too. Worst thing in the world, they say."

Worse than *this*? I thought, but what I said was, "I can't afford it, neither can you. But if we traveled *together*, and roomed together, and lived really cheap...."

We both surveyed the patio. It was quite full, but no one was taking any notice of us. We were just a man, and a woman. Civilian side of the river.

"See them?" Verona said. "Travel would be easier, too. We could pass. We wouldn't be stared at all the time."

We called for the check. If what we had can be called a plan, and what we had said can be called discussion, then we had discussed our plan.

I guess we didn't want to talk about the pain, and the risks, and the high probability of ultimate failure.

What we set out to do was on the face of it impossible. We sought a single building, in an area of forty million square kilometers. We had no spare funds, to bribe or to buy information. The operation we were seeking was illegal, which meant that we could not ask publicly for assistance.

At the time, we thought that blind fortune led us to Change Castle. Since then I have changed my mind. We were helped, by a confluence of Civilian and Service, both of whom wanted us to succeed.

But not succeed easily. We groped our way north, following phantom clues as the earth grew cold and the sun's diurnal arc swept closer to the horizon of Pelican Wake. It was near to winterlong night when we came, shivering and exhausted, to a grim tunneled mountain of black basalt, jutting stark from a plain of unmarked snow.

'Up toward the pole' was right. We were beyond the farthest settlement on the maps. Ahead had better be Change Castle. Otherwise we must turn around and head south, as fast as our frozen feet would allow.

We had no name to ask for. It didn't seem to matter, because we had money. It was taken with no questions asked. Apparently people struggled this far north for only one reason.

"Four months," said the anonymous individual whom Verona Skipsos and I came to call the Chief Torturer. "Some of it will hurt, I'll tell you that up front. But you'll leave here with a complete change and a full legal identity. After that you are on your own. So far as we are concerned, once you are gone from the castle you never came here. There will be no record of your presence."

The other side of the river, and a broad river it was. Nothing in the Service could hide an action trail—legal or illegal—so completely.

Verona and I were treated together, not for our comfort or convenience but for the more efficient use of Change equipment and personnel. We were housed in a single room. That was no novelty. We had shared a small room for all of our five months' wandering.

The treatment was as painful as the Chief Torturer had promised. That too was new to neither of us. The Service inured its people to discomfort and agony beyond Civilian tolerance or comprehension. Verona Skipsos and I took in our stride the muscle tissue removal and addition, the bone marrow extraction, the burning off and replacement of finger and toeprints, and the skull, vocal cords, and genital reshaping.

The retinal substitution was the worst, although not because of any pain. First came a long operation in which the aqueous and vitreous humor was drained from our eyes, the retinal removal and substitution performed, and the delicate job of optic nerve connection begun. Then the eyeballs were filled with pressurized gas.

All that, however, was done under general anesthetic. We were conscious during the next stage, ten awful days in which we lay blind and flat on our stomachs while the retinas attached, the humor of the eye regenerated, and the gas in the eyeball was absorbed through the sclerotic wall. It was less painful to lie without moving, because the skin rejuvenation that took place at the same time as the retinal operation included what amounted to a flaying. But sometimes, in the darkness, I imagined that I was the only object in the universe. All else existed only through my imagination.

That was when and I began to talk of everything under the sun and beyond it; and, finally, of the unspeakable.

"A completely routine monitoring operation, they told us." I lay in the middle of nowhere, not knowing if it was night or day. Verona's hand, just touching mine, was a lifeline to the world. It was our most intimate contact, in all our time together. "Not even a peacekeeper, so no one expected any action at all. No one knew the guy existed. We were part of an honor guard, and he was just a solitary crazy who didn't hate the Service any more than his own civilian government. He ran forward and blew himself to bits as Wolfgang was walking past at the Governor's side. Wolfgang threw himself in the way. He saved the Governor. I was thirty feet behind, in the third file. I wished I'd been right there with him."

I could feel my hand trembling, or possibly it was Verona's. When her voice came it was from far, far away.

"We *were* in a danger zone, and a war zone. Maximum security, covered four ways from Sunday. Jilly had maximum protection, the whole six days we were there. So did I. We made it through, and finally we returned to the release center and knew we could relax. That night we were lying side by side when she started to make a funny noise. I thought at first she was snoring, though she hardly ever did. Then it got louder, and I put the light on and tried to wake her. She wouldn't, and then her skin got slippery and she started to bleed, all over. By the time I got back with help she was almost gone. She died, dissolving away in my arms until I was holding just bones and ligaments...."

After a minute or two, her voice came again, steadier. "It wasn't a new weapon, which is what I thought when I saw her. It was something we had developed ourselves, a tumor-suppressing virus meant to protect us. It mutated and ran wild, and it attacked every cell of Jilly's body. The medical team ran a genome scan and had a one-shot cure in twenty-four hours. They said it was a miracle that I hadn't picked up the virus myself. I had a different word for it."

To see your partner marching before you, golden and proud in the sun, and then an eyeblink later to look at his shattered body and know that it can never be breathed back to life; or to hold your love in your arms, and helplessly watch her accelerated dissolution.

Which is worse? I do not think such comparisons are meaningful; but I would not have changed places with Verona.

When the bandages came off and we could see again, all colors, even of Change Castle's dark interior, seemed unusually bright and lustrous. For the first few minutes, though, we would not look at each other.

We did that when the Chief Torturer came in to tell us that our treatment was finished, and we must leave in the next week. I heard that news with horror. It was too soon, we were not ready, we were too weak, our bodies were too new, beyond the castle walls it was still winter.

We had to protest. I looked to for her support. I saw not a seasoned veteran, but a nervous young girl who stared back at me with wide, startled eyes.

"Have I changed that much?" she said.

"I would never have known you. Your voice, your height, your hair, your eyes—you look about fourteen."

"Semla Perez is eighteen." The Chief Torturer had appeared, and was looking fondly on her work. "And you, Lyle Perez, are her seventeen-year-old brother. Get that into your head, and every other fact of your lives, in the five days before you leave here. You have never heard of Verona Skipsos and Jeth Mylongi. And when you leave, I never heard of you."

"It's too soon to go," I said. I started to recite all my reasons, but the Chief Torturer cut me off.

"You're leaving out the big one," she said. "You're afraid. Afraid that you'll fail, afraid that you'll be recognized for who you used to be. But you must remember one thing: you can never cross the river if you don't go to it. Come here, look at yourselves."

Semla and I (I, Lyle Perez, now and forever) moved hesitantly forward. We stared into the full-length mirror and saw two strangers. That was not me, it could not be, that gawky, uncertain child with the blush of youth on his cheeks. I was never so beautiful.

"I think I've earned my money." The Chief Torturer's voice was as flat as ever, but I thought I detected a gleam of satisfaction in her cold eye. "However, since you appear to be worried about the trip south, I will arrange for a small rebate."

"Rebate?" Semla was frowning. "Did something go wrong?"

"Not a thing. There were a few pennies left when the treatment was finished." The Chief Torturer turned away, so I could not see her face. "I skimped a bit, you see, on the anesthetics."

The journey south was worse than the journey north. I am not referring to the physical hardship of the first two weeks, which tested our rejuvenated bodies to the limits. We drove forward across a frozen land, walking past nightfall, pushing ourselves to exhaustion and beyond, up and heading south again before dawn.

The more difficult time came when we reached the area of civilized settlements. We were received with curiosity and friendship until people learned that we were a young brother and sister on the way to enlist. Then sympathy turned to disinterest or open disgust.

"They won't admit it," Semla said. We lay side-by-side and exhausted on a cramped bed in the only place that would take us, a run-down lodge on the edge of town. "We need each other. They need us for stability; we need them for support."

"They—we. You talk like Service, but we're still Civilian. Suppose we don't make it?"

"We will." Perhaps she had her fingers crossed. "Or we'll die trying."

I wondered what the Chief Torturer had done with our old personas. Were Jeth Mylongi and Verona Skipsos already dead, officially, or was someone, somewhere, drawing our pensions?

I put that out of my head and tried to sleep. We had to be up at dawn. I told myself that I had never heard of Service officers called Mylongi and Skipsos.

South, south, south, as the weather warmed and the land turned green. At last, six weeks after we left Change Castle, the crisis point arrived. We lined up with a score of would-be Service recruits. They ranged in age from sixteen to twenty-four.

We were terribly nervous, but so were they. We could see it in their every move. Men and women, they were making the commitment. At last, after years of wondering and agonizing, they were crossing the river. The difference was that they did not know what lay on the other side. We did, and we yearned for it.

To hide a leaf, place it in a forest. The presence of the others helped Semla and me, because our own terror of discovery blended in with their fear of failure. Like everyone else, we fumbled with entry forms, struggled through aptitude tests, sweated under psych profile probes. Like them, we chanted regulations until we knew them by heart, and gave titles to uniforms and decorations. We dared not know too much, or be too competent. An antimatter cannon that Semla and I could disassemble, clean, and put back together in five minutes, half asleep, had to seem unfamiliar and rather frightening.

Two Service officers, one man and one woman, handled all of us. They were disturbingly competent. I felt convinced that Semla and I would somehow betray ourselves and be banned from enlistment. But finally, after three days of tests that stretched out forever, the woman officer (Colonel Brust, Spica Branch epaulets, though I was not supposed to know that) stood smiling in front of us. Sixteen survivors—

four had failed, or suffered a change of heart—we stood assembled in a ragged row outside the little barracks.

"Congratulations," she said. "You have passed the tests, and in a few minutes you will be formally inducted. Wait here. You will be called by name." We sagged with relief. I could feel the change in mood of the line, though I had enough control not to look at Semla or anyone else.

"You are about to become Service." The male officer (Major Guido, Fomalhaut Branch; it made my heart ache to see those familiar insignia) had come forward to face us. "You will be part of the finest Service organization in all of history. I'm sure that every one of you will live up to the tradition. Take three steps forward." He waited until we had done so, then added, "Dress left."

He didn't say those words with any particular emphasis, but automatically I looked left to line myself up with the next soldier. Semla, three people along, was doing the same. No one else had moved.

I didn't have time for more than one terrible, gut-wrenching moment of knowledge before the major said, as calmly as ever, "Recruits Semla and Lyle Perez. Fall out, and follow me. The rest of you, wait here."

We had failed, and we knew it. But we would go out Service style. Semla and I didn't walk after Major Guido. We marched, heads up, into the barracks building where the woman officer had gone.

She was sitting at a desk, working a telemetry unit. She raised an eyebrow at Major Guido, and said, "Well?"

She was talking not to him, but to us. We did not answer. They could get rid of us but we were not going to cooperate. After a moment Colonel Brust nodded. The next time she spoke, it was to neither Major Guido nor to us, but apparently to herself. "When new recruits come into the Service, you know, it turns their whole lives upside down. They lose friends and family. Sometimes their own parents disown them, the moment they say they're going to cross the river. And there's so much to learn, rules and regulations, old ways to drop, new ways to pick up. Partners to find, for youngsters who've never been allowed partners before. Sometimes you wish you could put a few old-timers in with each new batch of recruits, to help ease them over the rough spots."

She put down the telemetry unit, and stood up. "But you can't do that. I guess it's just wishful thinking. Major Guido, you may proceed with the induction of Recruit Lyle Perez. I will do the same for Recruit Semla Perez."

"Yes, sir."

No nod, no wink, no hint of anything beyond the words. Major Guido led me through into the next room. Induction papers for Private Lyle Perez were already prepared—dated two days ago. All I had to do was sign. I wondered how long he and the Colonel had known. Had *someone* known, the moment that the Chief Torturer finished her work? Then I decided that it didn't matter. In a few minutes I would be in the Service, and I could again behave like an honest soldier .

I sat down and signed with a trembling hand, while Major Guido stood at my side as witness.

"Welcome to the Service, Lyle Perez," he said when it was done. He leaned over and kissed me on the cheek.

It was a tender kiss, without a trace of passion. That was all right. If passion and partnership ever entered my life again, and I was not sure that it could, it would not be for years. For the moment, there were other priorities.

He watched critically as I stood to attention and saluted. Finally he nodded. "Not too bad—for a raw recruit. Welcome back, Private Perez. And welcome home."

DANCE AT THE EDGE

L. TIMMEL DUCHAMP

*V*isibility is an important issue for lesbians. One aspect of this issue is the fact that, for a woman to love a woman, at least one of them has to desire, and not just desire to be desired—which Duchamp, who is deeply grounded in European history, reminds us is the only form of desire that many psychological theories allow as possible for women. "The very title of the series, Bending the Landscape, inspired my idea of making parts of the world's landscape itself 'invisible' to the majority of its society. What is visible and what is not matters and is not determined by what in fact is there. Curious, isn't it, to see how intractable socially-dictated invisibility really is...."

1.

Emma Persimmon discovered the Edge in the first month of her life. Chance gave her a glimpse of star-scape, of a black denser than that of simple night, of a glittering spray of lights as splendid and desirable as a gold pendant dangling just out of reach. How it fascinated her infant self! It was the very second thing she pointed at; and countless times a day it made her giggle and stretch her fingers to grasp.

At five months, Emma knew where to look to see the Edge, and that it was different from everything else and always changing. Suddenly able to crawl, she raced to enter it—only to discover that touching made it recede (or sometimes even vanish altogether). The large, strange, shaggy creatures splashing about in a mud hole were there, yes, to her eyes, but not to her hands, fingers, toes, mouth. Emma learned she could crawl to the Edge and occupy the space where something else had been, and the Edge would leap back, and instead of a mud hole, there would be just the floor, just the air, just herself... In this, Emma resembled most babies. They, like her, played *fort/da* with the Edge. But at least one of Emma's parents did not pretend to her infant self that the Edge did not exist, though as Emma grew older, that parent of course denied ever seeing it.

By the time she started attending school, Emma understood that any acknowledgment of its presence was beyond "bad," "naughty," and "unacceptable." Even so, Emma got in trouble her very first day. The Edge in her classroom lay along the back wall, out of her proper line of vision. Usually in such new circumstances the Edge would have been easy to resist. But the Edge in her classroom that day was not just any Edge. It was a scene of a desert wash so full of light that whenever Emma looked straight on at it, she reflexively put her hand up to shield her eyes from a glare which she only, of course, imagined. Through the rocky wash trickled a thin silver stream of water, in which grew long thick grasses, tiny jewel-like blossoms of sapphire, topaz and garnet, and tall willows, lush with mauve trumpet-shaped flowers and long slim leaves. Tiny green birds with fantastically long beaks hovered over the willows, wings whirring, dipping their needle-like beaks into the bells of the flowers they courted and drained in exuberant, darting dance. Emma's parents had taught her about bees and nectar and pollen. It excited her almost unbearably to think that these strange little birds were probably doing what bees did. The classroom, by comparison, seemed dull and stupid.

Emma, young model of propriety, did not openly stare over shoulder; rather she stole glances from the side. But—"Emma Persimmon!" The teacher's voice cracked like a whip, making Emma jump guiltily. "What are you doing, staring off into space, daydreaming?" The tone of the teacher's voice clearly implied that *daydreaming* was among the worst of the worst crimes a student could commit. Emma almost cried with humiliation. Obediently she stared straight ahead, directly at the teacher, for several minutes. But unused to sitting in a classroom, increasingly fidgeting and restless, she forgot—and turned her head to snatch just a glimpse. "Look at Emma Persimmon," the teacher said almost at once. Jeering: "Off in her own little world."

The children copied the teacher's words every chance they got, tormenting Emma with the confidence of the unthinking young.

No, Emma wanted to protest. *Not off in my own world, off in another world.* But just a kindergartener, she lacked the words for talking about the socially invisible, and knew the whole present world against her. So she kept quiet and grew very shy, and strove mightily never again to be seen staring at that wall in the classroom (though she still stared often enough to get a reputation for daydreaming).

Most children let go of the Edge in their earliest years. Emma Persimmon never did. Instead, she wondered how the teacher, facing it, could so easily pretend not to see it, and later, whether others even saw it at all. And since everyone—even the one parent who acknowledged its reality during Emma's preschool years—acted so completely as if they did not see it, she finally understood that at least in one sense they did not. By the time she was sixteen, Emma began to wonder if it was even really there, and not just something she'd been fantasizing all her life.

The need to avoid social opprobrium can be truly terrible, not to say terrifying and terrorizing. Emma carried it all inside, afraid to whisper a word of it to anyone—until her parents sent her to town for training in the Ecohusbandry Guild, and she met Viola Knight.

2.

The moment Emma Persimmon laid eyes on her, she thought Viola Knight the bee's knees. Clad in tailored muslin pajamas, she stood straight and smart, brushing her teeth with a style that literally took Emma's breath away. Oh such beauty, Emma thought inanely, transfixed by the graceful precision of a wrist bone framed by elegant pajama cuff. Emma, stationed at another lavatory, fiddled with her bath kit, eyes glued to that wrist in the mirror, and forgot to brush her own teeth. Viola Knight, thorough in all she did, never noticed. Emma returned to her room, burning with that all-consuming awareness. All night she tossed and turned as she fought off sleep, tormented by images of the lovely wrist and perfect white sleeve until sunrise, which tricked her into a doze.

Viola Knight, lost in the fascination of the Elementary Principles of Optics, never much noticed anybody who didn't shove themselves right up into her face. Emma, though, now living for even the most fleeting glimpses of the divine object of her desire, almost forgot the Edge existed. When her genetics instructor caught her mooning, it wasn't for staring at the Edge, but for doodling hand after hand of thick, strong, spatulate fingers and comely, sharp-boned wrist, compulsively, religiously, intemperately.

Emma had it bad.

3.

In her first three months in town—before she first saw Viola Knight brushing her teeth—Emma had taken to hanging out with a disparate collection of individuals living in her dorm, all apprentices in arts guilds. They amused her, and easily swept her into their intense personal dramas and fantasies. With them she developed the beginnings of confidence in her capacity for existing socially. For the first time in her life she discovered a tolerance for the "daydreaming" and eccentricity people of her own sort found by turns irritating and disquieting.

She attended a play with them her second week in town. It struck her that the very idea of a staged drama must have come from *somebody's* awareness of the Edge, and this insight plunged her afresh into her old metaphysical questions. Were all of these creative people attracted to the arts because they sensed—but had been taught to ignore—that it was there? Or did they all know it was there, and seek somehow to replicate it, in such a way that their audiences would see it without a loss of innocence as to the real Edge they did not? As bright and imaginative as she found her new friends, Emma did not dare speak any of her questions aloud.

Quickly Emma slid into a sort of niche with them. She made them laugh, but with pleasure at—rather than to mock—her rather ingenuous wonder. She did not know why they accepted her, only that they did. But she discovered her position among them to be conspicuous when at dinner, a few nights after Emma's body began burning for Viola, Letitia Shadows murmured, "For shame, Emma Persimmon," as Emma's eyes tracked Viola Knight all the way from the salad bar back to a table of engineering apprentices. "Inspired by the slide-rule over the cello."

"Both instruments celebrate the abstract," Paulus Square, the only cellist present, said. Pale and unsmiling, he bowed across the table at them, his austere body virtually as abstract as either calculus or music.

"People have been known to fall in love with paintings, statues and vases," Royal Quiet said.

"But I'll take someone with a warm juicy body, any day," Elizabeth Peartree said.

"Yes," Letitia Shadows said, sounding sad. "Someone like Emma Persimmon, whose body, in the perception of my senses, bursts with heat and juices like a peach hanging ripe in the sun."

Emma blushed hotly and denied nothing. She glanced sidelong to the far reaches of the room where Viola Knight sat, only a meter or so from the Edge.

"Never fear," Paulus Square said to Emma. "She'll never know—unless you tell her yourself."

Emma sighed, relieved and disappointed when she believed him, relieved and fearful when she did not. She was amazed that they had seen her passion without her speaking it. Why, then, would Viola Knight herself not see it, too?

4.

Surely it was inevitable that Emma Persimmon's ardent devotion to Viola Knight would eventually bear fruit. Had not all the famous

Fated Lovers of their world, from its earliest history, always come—eventually—together, even those from distant villages or feuding guilds? Emma hoped, feared, believed that her own desire combined with simple proximity must make it happen.

One Saturday afternoon, Emma followed Viola Knight onto a bus to the edge of town, and from there on foot into the forest. She stalked and tracked Viola Knight with no subtlety whatsoever, flying from one inadequately-shielding tree-trunk to another, frequently catching her flowing red scarf on the bare winter thorns, wincing often at the racket her sneakered tippy-toes made as they scuffled gold, red and brown leaves and fractured sharp, dry twigs. When Viola Knight came to a stream, followed its banks for a few yards, and then trod a narrow log to cross it, Emma's desire grew giddy. Flitting and gliding after Viola, ever deeper into gloomy, fern-loving wood, Emma knew the delirious thrill of the hunt and the delicious chill of the possibility that the hunter, discovered, might herself become the hunted.

Then Viola Knight stood stock-still, hands on hips, head thrust slightly forward in total, utter concentration. Emma took a look around—and gasped. Viola had brought her to an Edge. A huge, stunning, exceptionally wonderful Edge. *Out of doors*.

Viola Knight walked along its face—and then turned sharply, where the Edge actually seemed to come to a point, as though it were an acute angle—and walked along an apparent *second* face. Emma, so astonished that she forgot her purpose in tracking Viola, unthinkingly followed, and saw for herself that *this* Edge was actually wedge-shaped, like a sliver of giant pie plopped down right there in the middle of the forest.

And what a pie it was! Emma Persimmon had always been more enchanted by the existence of the Edge than by the things she usually saw beyond it. But beyond—or rather *inside*—this three-dimensional wedge of an Edge glittered a world unlike any she had ever seen. Wild gouts of flame poured out of torches topping twisted cast-iron rods that had been placed among bizarrely-shaped trees, brilliantly illuminating the immediate areas around them, creating dark, impenetrable pockets of shadow. Willowy human figures wove in and out of the torches and trees, their faces painted the cloud-white of their stockinged legs, their eyes, mouths and eyebrows heavily outlined in thick black paint. All of them wore scarlet, gold and purple knee-length coats over tight black bodices, and black silver-buckled, blockily high-heeled boots they stamped smartly each time their hands came together in a clapping Emma Persimmon fancied she could almost *hear*. They spun. They jumped. They clapped and stamped. They leaped. The intricacy of their dance surpassed any Emma had ever known.

Emma forgot Viola Knight altogether. So fiercely did she concentrate on extrapolating the rhythm from the dance that she heard nothing but it. And peering into a scene of night, she forgot that though dim, the forest in which *she* stood lay in full—albeit cloudy—daylight.

Viola Knight turned and paced back toward the vertex of the Edge. And since she, too, never took her eyes off the entrancing scene, she ran smack into Emma.

Yanked out of their common dream, they stared at one another in shock. Viola's eyes blazed; she grabbed Emma's arm. "You're the girl who's always following me into the bathroom!"

Emma Persimmon's heart beat violently hard; her breath caught in her throat. The moment seemed lifted out of a traditional romance, for Viola's grip on her arm was steely enough to leave a substantial bruise afterwards. She realized that Viola had, indeed, noticed her existence. "Yes," Emma said breathily. "I live across the hall from you. Emma Persimmon."

"Emma Persimmon," Viola Knight repeated with near-disbelief. "What kind of name is that?"

Emma's body oozed and throbbed with sexual excitement. Their dialogue was going exactly the way it should! What more could a girl in love ask for?

A quicksilver flash of color—torchlight catching the sequins powdering the fat white towers of curls topping the dancers' heads as they all bowed in unison—distracted Emma, reminding her of what she had momentarily forgotten. Her heart lifted in wildest exultation. "You see it, you actually see it!"

Viola Knight looked puzzled. "See what?"

Emma's heart sank. She jerked her head at the dancers. "You aren't going to claim you don't see the Edge, are you? You've been walking alongside it, and staring in on all those strange people dancing. I know you have, I saw you do it!" Emma swallowed; heat scoured her face. Since coming to town she had not been mocked even once for her sin of Edge-watching. The very thought that Viola Knight, of all people, might now be mocking her was devastating.

Viola Knight's eyebrows shot high in her elegant broad forehead. "The Seam, you mean? You called it what—an edge?"

"Seam!" Emma said, shivering with more excitement than she could hold quietly inside her.

Viola looked at her curiously. "Oh," she said. "Did you run a little too forcefully into the denial all the people in town profess?" She shook her head. "Really, it's so childish. I must say I'll be happy when I've finished my studies and can return to my village, where no one plays such silly, jejune games."

Emma Persimmon was stunned. "Your village you're saying that all the people there see the Edge, too?"

"You mean the people in your own village act like those in town?" Viola shook her head. "But that figures, I suppose. Apparently all the guilds but mine follow the same silly line on Seams."

Emma's eyes shone more brightly than any of the torches lighting the world beyond the Edge. She wanted to dance for joy, or, rather, drop to her knees and kiss the toe of her adored one's soft leather boot, the only gesture she could imagine capable of giving full expression to the power of her feelings. She touched Viola's arm timidly (not daring, of course, even to approach her wrist). "So the people in your village and guild call them Seams? Do you know what they are, and where they come from? Or why most people don't seem to see them at all?"

5.

Viola Knight and Emma Persimmon walked out of the forest side by side. They walked as separate individuals, without touching, but listening to Viola expound on "Seams," Emma took pleasure simply in hearing the sound of Viola's voice and feeling the heat of Viola's body.

"Oh," Viola Knight said. She frowned sidelong at Emma. "I've just realized. My parents warned me that a prerequisite of certification is taking an oath to preserve the guild's secrets, which include everything we know or have theorized about Seams, even their very existence."

Emma halted to face Viola. "Which would mean that after certification you couldn't, for instance, let me know that you saw what I was seeing back there in the forest?" Her excitement in finding another person in the world who saw the Edge, her pleasure in finally sharing company with this most wonderful of persons, drained out of Emma. Her body went stone, dread cold. The implications of Viola's words struck her like a blow to the solar plexus. She saw it all very clearly: that everything—the very world she lived in— was false and wrong, terribly, terribly wrong.

Viola Knight put her hand to her throat, under the thick black scarf protecting it. "Oh shit," she said. "What a fuck-up!" Her eyes searched Emma's face. "I could be thrown out of the program for having this conversation with you. I'm not under an oath yet, no, but if the masters ever found out, I'd never make it to certification." She blinked. "We have all these rules for apprentices, you know. Like not using a hand-held calculator for the first two years, to make sure that we all get to be proficient in using slide-rules. But because I hardly know anyone who isn't an engineer, I never much thought about the Silence-About-Seams rule."

Emma felt guilty for putting Viola's future in jeopardy—and then crazy, too, for feeling guilty. Her heart pounded in the thick, nauseating silence that made her feel as though she were smothering. "Don't you realize how *terrible* your guild's silence is? It's nearly ruined my life—making me worry all the time that I might be crazy. I'm sure there are people who *do* go crazy, never knowing what's real and what's not!"

Viola's lips parted. "Oh," she said softly. "They told me people were trained to block Seams out of their vision, like the floaters in one's eyes. They said that only engineers ever saw them at all." Her eyes darkened in sweet, dewy softness. "I'm sorry, Emma, I'm so very, very sorry. But at least now you do know."

They resumed walking, and Viola revealed to Emma some of what she knew about what the Seams were, and what little she had been told about why people were taught not to see them. Since Emma had no idea even what a particle was, Viola's mini-lecture on tachyon fields meant nothing to her. But when Viola told her about how in earlier times people had made religions and claimed powers of divination from the appearances of particular Seams, Emma listened with rapt attention.

"They were, in effect, used to manipulate large groups of people," Viola said as they came within sight of the bus, parked at the terminus. "There were terrible wars as a result. And so it was decided that it would be best if people just pretended they weren't there. Seeing how easily certain persons could use them to manipulate large groups of people. And so everyone did forget them—except the engineers, who swore themselves to secrecy. Well, it stood to reason, you know. It's not as though we *could* ignore them. And so they became a sort of trade secret." Viola fell silent at the sight of the driver leaning against the bus, reading. They greeted her and asked her how long before the bus returned to town.

The driver consulted the digital readout on the cuff of her sleeve. "Three minutes, twenty seconds," she said.

Viola Knight and Emma Persimmon boarded the bus. Since they could not talk about the forbidden subject in the presence of a non-engineer, Viola asked Emma about her village and guild. Only later did Emma realize that Viola had not asked her why she had followed her out of town, into the woods, in the first place.

6.

In the days following, both the pleasure of Emma's love and the pain of its being unspoken and unreturned intensified. Emma grew self-conscious in her surveillance of Viola. Instead of being emboldened by the advance in their relationship, Emma grew fearful of causing offense. Her friends, having seen that the two were now acquainted, teased Emma, trying to prod her into open pursuit. "Seduce her!" Letitia Shadows said. "She won't be able to resist! Not *you*, Emma."

Emma began, for the first time, to spend long hours in the library, so that she could "brood in peace," as she thought of it. She assumed that sitting in the Biology section would preserve her from her friends' scrutiny. But she had not counted on the need of art students to consult biology texts in their search for tropes.

"Emma Persimmon, what on earth is all that?"

Emma was doodling—the usual, of course. She looked up guiltily at Sanctus Geloso, then back down at her screen. She made a jab for the Clear button, but Sanctus caught her wrist and stopped her. "Sanctus," she whispered in protest, but the name came out little more than a hiss.

Sanctus Geloso's scowl was fierce. "Why representational drawing?" he asked, though not whispering, keeping his voice low. "Why not thieve a piece of her clothing, or hair, or the damned toothbrush?"

Emma realized that she was getting good at drawing not only Viola Knight's wrist and pajama sleeve, but her hand holding the toothbrush as well. So good, she thought, looking now at the doodling she usually erased after she'd finished a screenful, that she actually felt like tracing her finger over the screen, as a substitute for touching the real thing.

"I love those hands," Emma Persimmon said. "I just love them. If I could sculpt the way you do, I'd make a pair of them in marble, and it would be *wonderful*."

Sanctus Geloso was shocked. He insisted that Emma go with him for coffee, so that they could talk. That's what he *said*. But once he got Emma outside the library, out in the cold, frosty air, he began lecturing her like a parent who has discovered his child playing with matches. "How *can* you be so disrespectful!" he said. "I wouldn't have thought if of you, Emma."

Emma was bewildered. "What do you mean, disrespectful?"

"An image is a map," Sanctus said. "And we map *people* and *parts* of people for only the most concrete, practical reasons. Healers map a specific person's hand in order to designate an injury. We map generic human bodies and their parts to help us understand how they work. But we *don't* map specific persons' bodies because we desire them, or to make aesthetic objects of them." Sanctus Geloso's eyes froze her with disapprobation. "If your parents didn't teach you manners, surely you had ethics, if not art classes, in your village?"

Though he was a couple of years older, Emma had regarded him as a friend. The sharpness of his attack took her utterly by surprise. Emma's sight blurred with tears; she swallowed convulsively three or four times. All of that stuff was so dry, and it hadn't seemed of any concern to her—or indeed to anyone in the village. They weren't artists, they were all very practical people. Yes, of course she understood about drawing, about how a sketch was a map that highlighted certain kinds of information but never attempted to represent the whole, since the whole of a thing could never be adequately represented in any way shape or form, except as aspects of it conformed to classes and subclasses of orders. But drawing Viola Knight's hand—*doodling*—hadn't felt like mapping or attempting a representation, exactly... She had done it without thinking, compulsively—a response, really, to the way that image was always with her.

Emma got her tears under control. She began to feel angry at being so grievously misunderstood. She said, "Sanctus Geloso, you don't understand! I was drawing an image that evokes something of how I feel about Viola Knight. I wasn't trying to represent *her.*"

"Just your *feelings* for her?" Sanctus said—looking and sounding scathingly skeptical. "Trying to pin down what it is that so excites you about her, is that it?"

"No!' Emma said. "That's not it! It's more like an evocation. Only I'm not an artist, so I can't do it with any sophistication!"

"No ethical artist would *ever* evoke a person by drawing a part of their body," Sanctus said severely. "Any more than an actor would pretend to be representing a human being. Think about it, Emma. The map isn't the object it denotes. With nonhuman objects, that's pretty easy to remember, and when one confuses the map with a non-human object, one generally makes a fool of oneself. With persons, though, it's the other way around. When one maps a human, he or she almost instantly conforms to the map, for it becomes what you and others notice about that person. Which is why most people in the world have long since concluded that drawing a map of someone is disrespectful."

Emma thought ruefully of the subtleties of the play she had seen, and the group's discussion of it. It had been *all* evocation, which was trickier in drama than in fiction or sculpture or painting, precisely because of the difficulty of making sense while avoiding mapping personalities. The actor's and dramatist's arts were the trickiest. The entire group agreed about *that*. Emma said, "I suppose you're right, Sanctus. But I'm so ... *obsessed*. I keep seeing her hand in my mind. And so my fingers just keep wanting to draw it. As though it's imprinted on my brain."

Sanctus pursed his full, shapely lips. "Sexual love is so uncivilized," he said. "We never see the object of our love except in really skewed, perverse ways. I suppose one could say that falling in love is like inscribing a map on one's vision. There's just the map, and everything that isn't on it is meaningless." Sanctus sighed. "Have a care for what you're doing, Emma. If you start one little bit of human mapping, before you know it you'll be mapping everything, in your mind if not actually onscreen." He tugged his boyishly purple and flame sleeve down over his lanky, ungainly wrist and gave her a knowing look. "It really is a slippery slope. And at the bottom lies not only alienation from civilization, but insanity."

Emma pictured herself on a steep, treeless hill slicked with mud and oil, struggling to keep her footing.

Sanctus said, "Wouldn't it be more honest to get her out of your system with an affair, rather than simply obsessing about her all the time?"

Emma felt too foolish to do more than mumble a noncommittal reply and beat a hasty retreat. Even if she could *map* out her feelings, he still wouldn't understand. That she *knew*.

7.

Emma's pleasure-pain became the nausea of confused bad feelings. Walking through campus to town, and then to the very outskirts, Emma Persimmon reviewed moment after moment from her past in which she or another child had been castigated for "characterizing" herself or someone else. *One does not say that Alan Farnseworth is a tattletale. One says that Alan Farnseworth tattled again to the teacher. There's a difference, Emma, a big difference. Only certain kinds of generalizations are honest and respectful, namely those that identify a person in terms of guild affiliation, status, age, and village. But a characterization is a generalization pretending to say everything that's important about a person, when it says only something very partial, and is a violation of their integrity. A statement of fact is just that. It's something that allows others to draw their own conclusions, depending on context and history. Remember how terrible you felt when that little girl in your class said you were "moony"?*

But was drawing the hand of one's beloved the same thing? No, Emma decided, it was not. Her drawings of that hand were signs she made for herself alone, not maps that others could read. And if her drawings mapped anything, they mapped her *desire* for Viola, not Viola herself. The distinction was crucial! Emma recalled what Montrose Beckoner had had to say about art, maps and the gaze just the other day. The gaze was the common way of looking at a thing, what some people might call the *correct* way. If you read the map correctly, you took from it the same information everyone else did. The *correct* information. If you looked at a piece of architecture with what Montrose called "the aesthetic gaze," you saw what the architect intended you to see, what any careful, aesthetically acute observer would see. The *look* was something else. It was *private*. It wasn't shared. It was perverse, and maybe profane.

And the look usually focused on signs, rather than on maps. Who but Emma Persimmon could know what that wrist bone and out-of-proportion third knuckle were supposed to *mean*?

Emma rushed back to campus, ecstatic. Sanctus Geloso had been wrong to chastise her for dissing the woman of her dreams. He had mistaken her look for the gaze. He had mistaken her desire for an object desired. He'd been, in short, presumptuous: which made it all his problem, not hers.

8.

A few nights later when Emma arrived home from a recital given by Pelagia Compton, the principal master with whom Letitia Shadows studied, she was surprised to find Viola Knight in the bathroom— staring at a narrow patch of Edge that had manifested in the small open space bordered by the walls of lavatories and stalls. It looked very strange to her there, and for a moment she didn't know why. It seemed to be a green stew of seaweed, heaving with irregular tidal swells over sharp crude craggy bits of rock showing the sheen of pink, violet and green slime wherever they were exposed. As an Edge, it was, Emma supposed, fairly typical. And yet something about it struck her as not quite right.

"Reminds me of birthing," Viola said. "If we could smell it, I imagine it would be damned rank."

Emma had trouble tearing her eyes away from it—even to look on Viola's freshly scrubbed face. "There's something strange about it," she said.

"Yes," Viola said. "We don't expect to find a Seam appearing in the middle of a room, especially one so small as this."

One usually got thin strips along walls free of shelves or furniture. But a solid—albeit small—block, right out in the middle? Of course, if either of them moved into that area, it would be bound to disappear. But...

Viola, as though musing aloud, said, "Makes me wonder if the conventional wisdom— that the only place major fields can appear are on the ice at the poles, and in desert or tundra, might not be correct. Imagine building an enormous empty space enclosed by four walls, and just waiting to see if a field appeared." Apparently recalling that Emma was totally ignorant about tachyon fields except for what she'd told her on the walk back to the bus, Viola smiled condescendingly. "You see, it's always been assumed they're random, and cannot be systematically studied," she said.

Full of wonder, Emma said, "Do you think the engineering guild would build such a place, if they knew about this appearance?"

Viola, still favoring Emma with that same smile, shrugged. "That's doubtful. They'd have to be able to justify the expenditure. I *suppose* they could simply say they wanted to study tachyons. But it would be risky. Certainly it would put all engineers involved in danger of breaking their oaths."

"Don't you see," Emma said passionately—but had to stop when Eudora Fromm and Gilda Pershing came in, so absorbed in a conversation about avian ethology that they never noticed the odd way Emma and Viola were positioned.

The women crossed into the Edge, causing it to vanish. Presumably it would come back. But since the small bit of Edge that had been in her room at the beginning of the term had vanished the previous week without being replaced by another, Emma felt bereft, anyway.

9.

The Edge in the bathroom did not reappear. Or was it that it had gone, and would not return? Thinking, for the first time, about some of the possible implications of the little that Viola had told her about "Seams," Emma Persimmon realized she didn't know whether there was a difference between the perception of an Edge, and its actually being there. When one stopped perceiving an Edge—say, when one moved into it, forcing it to retreat, did the field itself—as Viola called it—vanish because it was utterly disrupted, or did it just *seem* to disappear? Though she had long since lost her infantile delight in playing *fort/da*, she had never stopped testing Edges. Usually the Edge did return when one had moved out of it.

As Emma thought up a whole new set of questions about the Edge, she grew disturbed about the loss of that particular Edge in the bathroom—and with Viola Knight, whose attitude she irrationally began to associate with the loss. Viola's apparent obliviousness to her feelings, Viola's certainty in the wisdom of her guild's secrecy, irked her. A sense of grievance swept over her. She took up her old habit of following Viola, but now with a doggedness that was almost angry.

Emma dreamed of bees swarming busily around their hive, lapping up honey almost as fast as they made it. Swooping and buzzing indoors, loaded with nectar she could not deliver, night after night Emma flew into the bright odorless meadow of an Edge, only to smash into the wall, thwarted each time she sought to escape, destined to kill herself trying.

At meals Emma picked desultorily at her food and often lost track of conversations. Her friends thought it a simple case of unconsummated love. But to Emma, there was nothing simple about it, though what wasn't simple she dared not say aloud.

One evening Ledora Fairly drew Emma into her room, to offer her advice and instruction. "Embolden yourself, Emma!" she said. "When you know what you want, you must take it."

Ledora had no furniture except for a drafting table and matching high stool. The walls and ceiling were covered with mirrors and lights. Flinching from her own reflection, Emma thought that only the physical perfection that dancers necessarily embodied would make it possible to live in such an environment, where one could never escape the reality of one's appearance.

Ledora Fairly positioned the stool near the small window. She said, "Please, Emma, sit." Every movement the dancer made suggested extravagance. Even the simplest gesture of arm evoked grace and ... *immediacy*. As though nothing mattered so much as the *moment*. Emma got a little excited. Dancers were such unpredictable creatures.

Perched on the stool, Emma's eyes were about level with Ledora's. "I'm going to put a personal question to you, Emma," the dancer said. "Answer it or not, but do tell the truth. Are you feeling frustrated in getting Viola Knight's attention?"

Emma almost slid off the stool in embarrassment. She pressed her trembling fingers to her burning cheeks.

"Trailing her like a dog in search of a master is not going to work with a Viola Knight," Ledora said sternly. "Nor will going up to her, tapping her on the shoulder and telling her you're hot for her bod."

Emma lowered her eyes, wishing she could, like the Edge, vanish on penetration.

"But if you want her, you can get her, and I can show you how."

Ledora made it simple, when it wasn't. But tired of smashing into walls keeping her from the heavenly honey of the hive, Emma took Simple, and went for it.

10.

Haunted with desire and verging on anger with the object of that desire, the shy and retiring Ms. Persimmon now flagrantly flaunted it. If she had thought she was being obvious wearing a red scarf, she now added red gloves, stockings and broad-brimmed hat to her person. And instead of following Viola Knight, Emma anticipated her—popping up several times a day just where Viola was about to be. Though she could not be as immediate as a dancer, Emma became more immediate than she would ever have imagined possible. Emma buzzed furiously in pursuit of The Moment.

Viola noticed. Oh yes. But swept up in the dry elegance of partial differential equations, she found it easy to procrastinate anything that was a distraction from her own agenda. It was only on the Saturday afternoon when she found the reddest of red Emmas awaiting her as she got off the bus at the edge of town that she understood she would not be able to ignore such passion so much as a split-second longer.

"Emma, let's walk," she said, prepared to be stern and firm with her pursuer. But the Moment positively ambushed her as she perceived through all her senses the vivid, intense, now-ness of Emma Persimmon's desire. The brilliance of Emma's gaze drove scalding waves of sensation through her bones and sinews, and the radiance of Emma's expression dazzled her, damping her awareness of the rest of the world. In that moment only Emma and Emma's passion existed. Viola tingled. Her belly and thighs grew heated and heavy. Now visible in all its splendor, Emma's desire threatened to possess her whole.

When they had gotten well into the woods, out of sight of the bus, they stopped, and Viola touched Emma's cheek. "Emma, all this beauty. I'm overwhelmed! But—for *me?*"

Emma closed her eyes at the thrill of that touch. She perceived that her beloved was moved, rendered almost too breathless to speak. And yet the warning in Viola's voice, the tone that told Emma that Viola, though excited, was grudging, did not escape her notice. Emma laid her hand over Viola's; her lips addressed the hard, callused palm, her tongue the sharp little knob of bone on the wrist, with her answer.

Viola murmured pleasure, piquing Emma's pricked ears. But—"Emma," she said. "You must understand, my passion is physics! Which demands all I've got! I've sworn off romance, and will marry only engineers. Physics is my life, it owns me!"

Emma, feeling her power, grew bold, yes, and let her desire soar and carry her where it would. They might no longer have been in the stark winter forest, they might be aflutter in the hot desert Edge, like shimmering hummingbirds dipping their long pointed beaks into the soft mauve bells of willows, sipping nectar, dripping pollen, shifting only just for another beak full. Their palms and fingers and lips laid trails, cunning and lingual. The Moment was all Emma had ever hoped for.

"You can have us both," Emma said when she had breath to speak, breath all full of the scent of Viola.

Viola's body had loosened, sensation all slipping and sliding in an abandon that set her wanting wanting wanting all that Emma's hands and lips were promising. "I can't, I can't," she whispered—even as she was discovering the fine-haired neck so eager and responsive under Emma's scarlet silk scarf.

The Moment was bliss, but yielded to struggle. Emma's passion equaled Viola's will. Their pleasure was so outrageous and breathless Emma knew they must be Fated Lovers. But Viola swore it was a once-and-only-once kind of thing. She had been tempted to infidelity, and had been weak. It would not, she said, ever happen again.

Emma could not believe it. It made her numb, hearing passion put into the past tense, while the tingle was still receding from her thighs and buttocks. It defied nature! Could Physics, she wondered, be so perverse? Suddenly she saw the forest around her—gray, damp and stark. The chill bit at her skin as she pulled herself up to glare down at Viola. This is what it feels like to be a woman, she thought. For after the Moment comes knowledge.

She said, "Listen to me, listen to me, Viola Knight. If it weren't for passion, I would be hating you. You are wrong to try to keep yourself cold for your work, and you are wrong, wrong, wrong to conceal the existence of the Edge. Your attitude sucks, big-time. And pretending to be above feeling is sick."

Viola sat up, too. She leaned close to brush bits of twigs and leaves from Emma's hair with an attitude of intimacy that nearly melted Emma's insistence. She handed Emma the bright fleecy cap that had come off in their wildest and sweetest of moments, then leaned close again, meaning, Emma was sure, to kiss her. But Viola suddenly reared back. Her breath hissed in sharply; and her eyelashes fluttered. She scooted back a few inches, snatched up her sweater and pulled it quickly over her head. "What silly things are you saying, Emma? You talk like an irresponsible child!" Viola's voice was taunting. She took her cloak from the ground and wrapped it tightly around her. "Until we have exact knowledge of what the fields are, and how to map them, it's a certainty that people will behave stupidly and make up every sort of nonsense about them on which to base religions and start wars all over again. Must we have war again, just to make the rare individuals like yourself secure in their sense of reality?"

The tone of Viola's voice nicked Emma's heart like a knife so cold it felt hot in her breast. Bitterly she pulled on her pants and wished her hat were any color but red. "Why must there always be a common gaze for perceiving anything that's represented?" she said, tugging her flame red socks into place. "Why must the existence of something inexplicable and ineffably different make people want to claim they know what it is?" She felt so angry with Viola she had to bury her fists in her cloak to keep from hitting her. "And why can't we tolerate private, individual looking, instead of insisting always on The Gaze?"

Viola had no idea what Emma was talking about. *Her* friends never discussed such things. Maps, to her, were constructs for understanding physical reality. They certainly weren't territories to be fought over. She said, "I want to be an engineer. More than anything. And yes, more than being a lover, Emma. And keeping quiet about something that is of concern to you—but maybe to no one else in the world—is a price I'm willing to pay."

Angry, sad, crying, Emma watched Viola finish dressing. When Viola stood quickly, without warning, Emma clutched Viola's legs in a panic. "Don't go yet," she said, openly pleading." Don't go. I understand, really I do. But don't you think it's at all ... *wrong?*"

Viola looked down at her. It seemed to Emma that she had already, in her heart, gone. "Would it matter, Emma, if I did?"

Emma rushed into her sweater and scrambled to her feet. "Of course it would," she said. "Of course it would matter." She blinked to clear her eyes of tears. "Couldn't you at least think about trying—later, when you're a master—changing the rules of your guild? Couldn't you at least think about the negative consequences of your silence?"

Viola kissed Emma's nose lightly. "Of course I can. And I will. But you just remember, too, that without my guild, I don't exist. And if I spoke openly about Seams, the rest of the world would say I was crazy, and what good would that do anyone?"

"There's got to be a way," Emma said fiercely. "I know there has!"

A silence sprang up between them. It grew charged and heavy. Viola swallowed and cleared her throat. "Before I go back to town, I want to check to see if there's a Seam in that place now." Her voice was hoarse and shaky.

Defiantly, Emma took Viola's arm, making it clear she intended to accompany her.

Viola's face flamed. She backed hastily away. She was back in the Moment, whatever she might say.

Emma smiled lovingly, in utter sureness of her power. A woman now, she knew her own strength.

Arms linked, breaths steaming in the cold, they set out together—lovers of the Moment—for the Edge.

LOVE'S LAST FAREWELL

RICHARD A. BAMBERG

i n 1991 Joël, Richard Bamberg's brother-in-law, and Joël's long
time companion, Leigh, both died of AIDS, and Bamberg began
to wonder what it might be like to be the last of one's kind on earth.

This story is dedicated to Joël R. Jacobson, a brother
and a friend who showed me that life should be magic.
RICHARD A. BAMBERG

I stopped at the hospital entrance. There was no hurry. I turned and
contemplated the ancient blue spruce that stood alone in the median.
Once there had been two. Now only a few mushrooms marked the
other tree's passing.

"Excuse me, Citizen Vanderlink?"

The feminine voice at my elbow was unexpected, but its tone was
disarming. I turned slowly and saw a very young woman. Make-up shaded
her face in one of the current fads. Her make-up, like her clothing,
was asymmetrical and skewed her features in a gentle slope to the left.

"Yes?"

"Spacey." Her sigh was an overdone expression of feigned relief. "I
thought I'd blown by you again. I'm Kim Lambert."

I gave her a blank stare.

RICHARD A. BAMBERG

"I dropped you some bytes last week about an interview."

"Interview? Oh, yes, you're the reporter." I glanced around the hotel's restaurant while trying to think of some way out of this. "This isn't the best time. I have some things to take care of and ... well, I'd just as soon do them in private."

"I cope your mood, Citizen Vanderlink, but I really need this interview. I've already reserved bytes on tomorrow's net update."

"I'm sorry." I turned away, trying to dismiss her.

The hospital lobby was quiet. The receptionist was behind a desk set discreetly against the left wall. I nodded to her as I crossed the lobby. She recognized me as a regular and lifted a hand in an abbreviated wave.

In the hallway, I chose a vacant lift and called for Dean's floor. In silence, I ascended.

The doors opened to a vacant hallway. It was the middle of visiting hours, but all was still and silent. Patients didn't come to this floor until all hope had fled.

The reporter was either dense or stubborn and her whiny voice grated on my nerves.

"Citizen, I can't leave without the interview. My boss will have me recycled. Quarter hour is all I'm asking for. Can't you stretch me a crack?"

I shuddered and briefly contemplated the possibility of living long enough to stand trial for murder. An image of Dean interrupted my thoughts and I remembered how tolerant he'd been of youth's excess.

"What did you say your name was?"

Her smile seemed to curl up to the corner of her eyes. "Kim Lambert. My buds call me Kimmy."

She offered her right hand and I took it. She tried to give me one of the five grip shakes that were the current rage. Her face shadowed as I shook her hand once and pulled away.

"Look, Ms. Lambert, I don't do sliding shakes and I don't stretch cracks. Hasn't anyone told you that slang is inappropriate when you are presenting yourself professionally?"

Her stare was blank.

"Ms. Lambert, I speak simple English and very little slang. I'll provide the interview on the condition that you avoid the excessive bastardization of our language long enough to complete it."

Her large brown eyes blinked, twice.

"Is that understood?"

When she nodded her agreement, I motioned toward a table in the corner. She followed me without talking and I wondered briefly if I'd been manipulated, but then dismissed the thought.

She sat down across from me and produced an electronic notepad which she switched on and slid halfway across the table "You don't mind if I record this, do you?"

I shook my head.

A white-robed woman stepped out of the nurse's station as I approached. It was Doctor Melanie Evans.

Surprise flickered across her face. "Jerry ... Hello. I was just going to call you."

I glanced from her face to her notepad. She made a half-hearted attempt to hide it behind her, then realized it was pointless.

"Jerry, if you're not ready, I can come back later."

"No, that's not necessary. Please, give me the release. I want to be with him when I sign it."

"I'm speaking with Citizen Gerald Vanderlink. Record present date and time. Citizen Vanderlink and his life partner Citizen Dean Honeywell are considered to be the last two homosexuals in the North American Federation and possibly the last two in the solar system. As we speak, Citizen Honeywell is comatose and not expected to regain consciousness."

I forced myself to remain calm. It wasn't easy.

"Citizen Vanderlink is faced with the imminent possibility of becoming the one and only homosexual in human existence. I'm here to learn a little of what it has meant for him. He has watched his sub-species go from a political force to an obscure minority. From what may have once been ten percent of the population to a single individual. One person, alone, among the seven billion inhabitants of the solar system.

"Few today remember the great controversy that raged throughout the early decades of the last century. The Morley process was developed to reverse the genetic flaw that caused homosexuality in humans. Now it has achieved 100 percent success. Tell me, Citizen Vanderlink, what was it like to live through that troubled time?"

I hadn't really expected that question, although I suppose I should have. It'd been eight, no, nearly ten years since I'd last heard the name of Morley and his damnable process. "What was it like?"

"Yes, Citizen. I can retrieve historical accounts, but I want to know what it felt like to one who was actually there and refused the process."

My voice was soft when I answered.

"Genocide."

"Jerry, you do realize that the release is effective immediately?" Melanie asked.

I nodded.

"Are you sure you want to be with him when he dies? Not everyone goes easily. It could be traumatic for you."

"I'm quite aware of the possibilities. I ..."

I choked, caught my breath, and restarted. "Over the years Dean and I witnessed the departure of many friends. I owe Dean as much."

"It's your decision. I just wanted to make sure you knew."

I took the notepad and stared at its blank screen while suppressing a sudden urge to throw it against the wall. I'd give anything to have this obligation lifted from me.

* * *

"Excuse me? I couldn't quite make that out."

"Genocide," I repeated louder.

She sat back in her chair "Genocide? How could you call it genocide? No one died, at least not directly. There were riots and terrorist acts, but no one was intentionally murdered by the Morley-Kincaid program."

Kincaid was another name I hadn't heard in years.

"Genocide is the systematic destruction of a racial, political, or cultural group. What else would you call Morley and Kincaid's abominable program?" I asked, trying to keep the bitterness out of my voice.

"But no one had the process forced on them. It was strictly voluntary."

I laughed. Its cold and bitter tone surprised me. How, after all these decades, could I still be so bitter?

"Voluntary? With all the accompanying laws that Kincaid drove through Congress you either underwent the process or lost most of your rights. Kincaid even saw to it that every child born would undergo Morley's test and be given the treatment if they exhibited homosexual tendencies."

"I still don't see how you can call that genocide. What parent would want their child to grow up as a misfit? Once the Morley process was discovered it was only natural for parents to test their children and ensure that the genetic flaw was corrected."

"Flaw? What makes you think it was a flaw?"

For a moment she seemed surprised at the question. "But what else would you call it? Surely, you aren't saying the homosexual syndrome should have been allowed to continue?"

"What would it have hurt?" My voice sounded weak and helpless.

"But ... It's so unnatural."

Her eyes stared into mine for a moment and her cheeks colored as she realized her insult. She was so young. Dean and I had been young once. Had we ever been as innocent?

"I-I'm sorry. I didn't mean that," she said. I hushed her with a frail wave of my hand. "Of course you meant it." When had my voice become so broken? "Everyone who ever used those words to me 'meant it.' But don't let it concern you. It stopped bothering me more than half a century ago. You see, history is written by the winners and alas, if there were ever a group of losers, it was us."

"But you had the opportunity to go through the treatment, through the Morley process. Why didn't you take it?"

"Why? Have you been in love yet?"

"Sure."

"You answered too fast, too sure of yourself. Are you so certain? Where is he now, this man of yours?"

She averted her gaze. "I don't know. We separated a couple of years back. It didn't work out."

"Ah," I said and leaned back to wait for her next question.

"What do you mean by that?"

"If you'd truly been in love you'd be together still. Love isn't something that one throws off like an old hat. Love clings to the soul like cockleburs to the hair."

The simile came unbidden from a portion of our past. Dean's favorite dog, a golden retriever named Duke, often came home with cockleburs clinging to his long, blond belly hairs. The image of Dean slowly teasing each burr free came back to me in a rush. More than twenty years had passed since Duke died. Dean hadn't wanted another dog after Duke's passing, but I had insisted. It was part of the healing process and he had been so very, very attached to Duke.

Lambert shook her head violently. "I don't agree. You can love someone and then grow apart. Love isn't forever."

"Who says?"

"Huh?"

"Who is this great authority who told you love is fleeting?"

"Well ... no one. That is ... everyone says love is a passing fancy. That's why marriages fail."

"I bow to the wisdom of your years," I responded with an exaggerated wave.

She flushed. She'd been deliberately insulted, but she wanted this interview and had to be willing to take a few insults to get it. "So you're saying that love is the reason you refused the Morley process?"

"Of course. What other reason could there be?"

"And the others who refused it?"

"I can't speak for all of them. Some may have said it was for principle, that undergoing the process was admitting there was something basically wrong with them and the way they'd spent their lives."

I paused to sip my coffee and catch my wind. These days it didn't take much conversation to drain me. To her credit, if she noticed my deliberate hesitation, she ignored it.

I gathered breath and continued, "I believe that most who refused the process did so for the same reason Dean and I rejected the treatment. Once you're in love, the thought of deliberately doing something to destroy that love is unthinkable."

"But the process wouldn't have necessarily changed your feelings toward one another. Many men love each other."

I resisted smiling at her innocence.

"Sure, love as brothers or the love of a father for his son, but the love shared between soul mates, between lifelong lovers, is really on a different scale. We knew a few couples who tried the process. They naively thought it would let them fit in with society and yet maintain their relationship. They all failed.

"If anything, the process made it impossible. The memories of their lovers were steeped in sexual overtones that no longer appealed. In fact, they were repulsive. Those couples who tried the process ended up hating each other."

Again, I had to pause to allow my traitorous body to catch up with the effortless energy of my mind. Ms. Lambert stared at me while I sipped my coffee. A face as young as hers had yet to learn the fine art of cloaking emotions. Doubt, uncertainty, comprehension, and finally pity played over her face. "I'm sorry, citizen. I hadn't thought ..."

"Don't let it concern you. Let the dead bury the dead."

"Excuse me?"

"An old expression. I wish I could quote it properly and give the author credit, but my memory is not what it once was." She looked confused and then I, too, knew pity. "It means that what has passed is past and there's no reason to let it upset you now."

She looked down at her notepad then at the windows, and when she turned back to me her face was shadowed by understanding and sorrow.

Dean and I had once wanted children. To our eternal regret, we postponed applying to adopt until we were financially comfortable. By then the Morley process had begun and a new law prevented homosexuals from adopting. Unless they underwent the process.

Kim Lambert was the age our great-grandchildren could have been, if only things had been different.

In that instant I decided to help her.

"Now, about that interview you wanted ... what would you like to know?"

"I had wanted to find out what it felt like to be the last living homosexual, but I think I'd rather hear what your life was like."

"I never had any great accomplishments, a few minor ones, but nothing great. Who would want to hear about such a life?

"Let me worry about that. Tell me as much or as little as you want. I'll get my editor to run it."

"Very well. Where should I start?"

"When did you first meet Dean?"

I blinked. Perhaps Ms. Lambert was more than I had given her credit for. I shifted in my chair. Lately my poor circulation required movement to keep my feet from falling asleep.

I began slowly, recalling the misspent adventures of youth and of a love that had bonded firmly onto two hearts as the years turned into decades. I didn't notice how long I talked. Occasionally, Kim (when had she become Kim?) would interject with questions to lead me farther down atrophied memory paths.

Reliving the highs and lows of our combined lives did something I hadn't expected. It gave me the answer I sought.

In the end I tried my coffee and found it cold and bitter. My throat was dry, so I drank anyway.

Kim closed her notepad. "What now, Jerry?"

"I have to say good-bye to Dean and then, then I guess I'll go home."

"Would you like some company?"

"No," I shook my head. "Not for this."

I stood up, my old joints protesting with a creak reminiscent of Dean's favorite antique rocking chair. I dropped my cup in the recycler and she walked with me as far as the sidewalk.

The afternoon air was brisk and I pulled my jacket collar tightly around my neck.

We shook hands and Kim fumbled out a small business card. I glanced at its holographic memory and then put it in a pocket.

"Jerry, if there's anything I can do for you ..."

"I understand. Good luck with your boss."

She turned away and as she did I thought I caught a gleam of moisture in her eyes.

Dean lay as I'd left him. His drawn features hadn't changed noticeably.

I removed my coat and hung it on the back of the door.

Outside, soft golden rays of the sun's last farewell lit the swirling clouds and cast long shadows across the interior of my love's hospital room.

I spent a few lonely moments contemplating whether, in truth, this was his last sunset or if I'd lost the will to do what I must do. Twilight deepened the shadow around his sunken eyes until they looked like orbs of obsidian rather than the warm eyes that had shown me such tender love for more than seventy years.

Leaning over the edge of Dean's bed, I brushed a lock of coarse, gray hair back from his forehead. His pallor cut through me, filling me with pain approaching revulsion. I didn't want him to die, but the doctors gave him no hope. I had to decide whether to remove him from the life support unit or to let the medtech drag out his existence.

The medtech was good. Dean and I had watched friends slowly

decay for months before their loved ones had found the courage to let them go.

Dean had made me promise I wouldn't drag out his existence. It was a pact we'd made together many years ago, before there was no one else. Would we still have insisted on the pact if we'd known it would leave the survivor so totally alone?

Now that I had chosen, could I go through with it?

I fingered the notepad. My tears dropped onto Dean's face. I choked them back and dabbed his cheeks with the edge of my sleeve.

I stared down at him. The interview had brought back memories of our shared life, memories unvisited for decades. Their reliving had taken away the black despair that had engulfed me since Dean became ill.

I activated the notepad. In terse language, the form described Dean's condition and suggested euthanasia as the only viable alternative.

I signed on the marked line and the notepad confirmed my electronic signature with the hospital's computer. A moment later the medtech clicked softly and disengaged from Dean's bed. It rolled past me and out the door.

Dean's breathing became ragged. I laid the notepad on the night stand and clasped his left hand with both of mine. His skin was cool. Although I knew his mind was gone, the sight of his body struggling to survive tore at my soul.

I held his hand for a long time as his body grew weaker. The room darkened, until it was lit only by the glow of hallway lights.

Finally, Dean gasped one last time, trembled, and his body died.

I swallowed, trying to clear the lump in my throat. I bent down and kissed his lips for the last time.

I took my coat and struggled into it as I walked down the hall.

The lobby was nearly empty when I reached it. Crossing it quickly, I stepped through the revolving door and onto a damp sidewalk. A light mist softened the air. I stood for a moment under the awning and I buttoned my coat.

Across the street stood the blue spruce, all alone in the street's median.

ON VACATION

RALPH A. SPERRY

We all work too hard sometimes; it can be difficult to let go of the job. The older we get, the harder it is to remember how to relax. Karfi is over ten thousand years old. After working three hundred years without taking any time off his partner thinks it's time to take a vacation at Cape Cod....

Once upon a time, on a planet far, far away, a young Aten man named Karfas Proklin was employed on the Starship Project. His duties involved the installation of environmental systems. But being handy, he was often asked to work on navigation equipment, too. His friends called him Karfi.

Because he happened to be at work on the Starship in orbit around a neighboring planet when the final disturbance destroyed his lifestyle, he was one of the relatively few survivors who escaped by setting off across the galactic plane with no clear goal in mind. And now, many thousands of standard years later, he was still doing much the same routine work he'd always done. The only real difference was the planetary system.

Nowadays, Karfi lived among the descendants of the Aten refugees in small, but comfortable rooms in an abstracted space that was technically known as "a polydimensional environment," though the Aten called it "the Levels." He'd always occupied these rooms—except when he was married—ever since his people had decided they could no longer continue living on the nearby but already inhabited planet. But he never considered his quarters cramped. Unlike the much-younger Aten, he didn't feel confined by a life tangential to Earth's more appealing reality. His 1-bedroom condo, as a local would call it, was cozy when he was there. But most of the time, he was at work.

Officially, he was First Assistant in Maintenance for Levels Services, in charge of the upkeep of fliers. But while he effectively lived forever—because, like every Aten male, he suffered the genetic defect known as "regeneration"—he never got bored with his work, even though he'd been doing it for over ten thousand years. In fact, he was always amazed at what some people could do to something as sturdy as a personal flier.

At the moment, Karfi was in Transport Bay 5, bending over the circuit rack of a flier and methodically touching each test point with a probe. "Elaris!" he called to his young assistant-in-training, "Here's one we've got to junk. A lot of it seems to test all right. But you see?" He poked the probe at various points with only spotty response, while Elaris stood to one side with as studious a look as a fellow his age could muster. "The whole thing's covered with Diet Coke."

Though Karfi had had a penchant for singing when he was young, he hardly ever sang these days, because most Aten now preferred to listen to local music—because, he supposed, the majority of Aten were more or less "local" themselves. But the songs he knew best were the ones of his youth by Old Style singers like Sanse Karlin, and forward-thinking groups like Peragh. Of course, nowadays, most people considered songs like that to be "ancient." And an Aten as ancient as Karfi considered singing to be a public event. So, except for those few older men who had a bent for nostalgia, Karfi's favorite pastime was thwarted, simply for lack of an audience.

Instead, whenever he had free days, he amused himself with his only other talent—for fixing things. But this could get to be so absorbing that it always made his long-time companion, Felis Paledden, complain, "You tinker for fifteen to eighteen days a change, and every spare moment you tinker some more." Yet making things function well was the only pastime Karfi could still enjoy. And he got particular pleasure in fixing the local electronic toys that Aten parents demanded for their children.

But recently, Felis had become convinced that Karfi needed, "A real vacation. You never go on an excursion with me. In fact, you haven't been on the planet in over three hundred years." So, during drinks at a place on the Services Concourse, he implored, then hassled Karfi to, "Go somewhere. Don't you ever yearn to smell a fresh sea breeze?"

"The last fresh sea breeze," Karfi pointed out, "was blown three hundred years ago. Now there aren't many places on Earth you can manage to escape fresh hydrocarbons."

Felis pouted. "You can't just sit up here and tinker forever. For one thing, you're setting a very bad example."

Signaling the server for another caipirinha, Karfi smiled bemusedly. "To whom?"

"To the younger generations, like that cute assistant-in-training of yours. Elaris is almost five hundred years old, but even he's succumbed to the fashion of feeling inferior to locals, just because they have the neurons to produce a George Lucas, and we don't."

Karfi gave a dismissive shrug. "Like it or not, it's a fact that we lack the imagination that turns the improbable into something salable. But we do have other qualities."

"But he isn't learning about them from you!" Felis huffed, as the server delivered the Brazilian drink with the poise of an over-French waiter. "As fond as I am of you, Karfi, I'm afraid you're becoming what we fear most about regeneration ... boring."

Karfi and his assistant-in-training hoisted the rack from the Coke-stained console and carried it out to Bay 5's Parts Procurement section. "We need a new four-thirty-four," he said with a sorry shake of his head to the fellow behind the counter.

While they waited for the part, Elaris asked, "You looking forward to a whole free change?"

Karfi absently shrugged. "Felis claims it'll do me good."

Elaris nodded with the youthful pretense of comprehending the emotional symbiosis that results from an affinity of nearly four millennia. "So, what has Felis decided you're going to do with all that time?"

Karfi sighed. "We're spending twenty-five days on Cape Cod."

Frantically digging through the pile on her desk, Mrs. Harding searched for her appointment book. She shouldn't have done it. But what could she do? It was more than a little inhuman to spoil the very important vacation of a long-standing client and friend like David Porelle. If only she'd had a bit more warning, she might have been able to find something else for David and his little boy. Still, it was much too late for that now, she feared, lifting a stack of paperwork, finding nothing beneath it, and leaving it a fluttering heap of disarray. Now she was about to violate one of the most important stipulations in her contract with her principal client.

Two executives of AthAmerica were due to arrive sometime today to stay at the house in Truro for nearly the entire month of June. And they expected that they were going to have the house exclusively. How was she going to tell them they'd have to share it with a father and his seven-year-old son?

The house was certainly big enough—a chocolate-and cream shingled, mansard-roofed, 14-room "summer cottage" that had the space to house at least eight people. But the stunning young woman from AthAmerica who'd originally interviewed her had expressly forbidden such intrusion: "When our people wish to take time off, they really do need to get away from it all."

Nevertheless, only once in the past five years had the company used that house in June—and only for the last three days. So she'd just expected the place would be free. And she really did need advance notice at this time of year. Surely, someone at AthAmerica ought to be able to understand that. But the company, she reflected with dismay, was more than just her principal client, so she couldn't say no when they called on the 28th of May to announce that these two fellows would be showing up in one week. In fact, the whole reason she'd succeeded in the real estate business was AthAmerica.

Seven years before, her husband of 25 years had died. And rather than be devastated by it, she'd immediately taken a real estate course and gotten herself a license. But once she'd done that, it came as a shock that nearly half the people on the Outer Cape had real estate licenses, too. After all her effort to have something useful to do for the rest of her life, she faced such competition that she had virtually no opportunity to do it.

But then one day she saw an ad in the *Cape Cod Times*:

<u>REAL ESTATE PERSON WANTED</u>
Consult and handle rental property
for large corporation. Good opportunity
for the right person.

She was sure she couldn't be the right person, but called the 800 number anyway. And for some inexplicable reason, she proved to be "exactly perfect" for the job—or so the young woman from AthAmerica said at the end of her interview, adding with a lovely, if mysterious, smile, "We're especially disposed to women like yourself who begin a career later in life." And as jobs in the real estate market went, this one turned out to be amazing. She was paid a handsome retainer, plus every expense, to keep eleven houses on the Outer Cape under lease for AthAmerica.

Each house was chosen for its size—as big as she could find, though AthAmerica people rarely vacationed in groups that were large enough to fill such a house. But while these places were meant for AthAmerica people when they used them, the company, to her astonishment, encouraged her to rent them out to others, whenever they weren't being used. And most incredibly, the company insisted she keep that profit herself. Because a conflict had never arisen before, she never imagined one would.

She finally found her appointment book and pushed its pages open to today, where she noted that the fellows from AthAmerica were due at the Provincetown airport at 2. She'd been told they were renting a car, which, she calculated, would take some time. She checked her watch and read 1:55. At least she'd get to the house before they did. Maybe she could explain.

Over the years, she'd naturally developed her own set of regular guests, and David Porelle was among the most regular. He was 32, and fairly handsome—boyish, with dark brown hair and sparkling brown eyes, and with what she thought was a charmingly sensible personality. He was also divorced. And for the past four years, he'd had custody of his son in May, the month that he and little Teddy would normally be on vacation.

But this year Teddy had started school, and David had called mid-April in panic. "I completely forgot to say something last year. Is it going to be too late to squeeze us in somewhere for June?" Since she'd known of no plans AthAmerica had for the house in Truro, she'd booked David and Teddy for the month. And they were already there. But she felt certain they'd all get along, especially given the size of the house. And little Teddy was as charming as his father—a tow-headed boy with great curiosity, who never seemed to complain.

If only she could manage to be excused this one quite innocent mistake, she prayed as she snatched up her purse and her keys, and rushed out the door to her car.

As the AthAir executive jet touched down at Provincetown Airport, Felis decided that it was much too late to have the inevitable second thoughts. Karfi had been so perversely reluctant, seeming to stall until the very last moment. But now that they were here, Felis could only hope that nothing would go wrong to spoil Karfi's unwilling vacation.

Merry laughter erupted from the seats behind them. "I'm going to buy my brains out!" a youthful voice declared. "I want to get those T-shirts with American slogans on them. They'll be very chic, you know, when we go to Brazil later on this year."

Felis shook his head sadly at how the younger generations were so willing to accept local values. Certainly, some things were unavoidable, given his people's curious predicament, but that was no reason to give themselves up to a thinking that was basically alien. Though Felis wasn't as old as Karfi, he had been born on Earth itself, when the most important local artifact was the lithic version of a razor blade. He'd watched these people grow up. And their perspective on themselves was still very adolescent. Some Aten believed it was permanently so, and Felis didn't exactly disagree.

"P-town!" the pilot drawled in English. "Last chance to read your orientation pamphlets. Remember: for taxis you tip ten percent, for drinks fifteen, for meals twenty." Then the AthAir jet slowly rolled to a stop by a rudimentary terminal building.

Felis heard Karfi sigh as he started to hoist himself out of his seat, then mumble, "This *is* going to be fun," just before colliding in the crowded aisle with a much more eager vacationer.

Felis tried to negotiate them through baggage claim and into the rented car with as little delay as possible. But Karfi dawdled every step of the way, constantly diverted by gadgets like the reservations computer at the Provincetown-Boston Airways counter. "Why do they build these things the way they do?" he whispered, as they waited for the car-rental agent to finish the paperwork. "They have the technology to do much better. You always see that on their broadcasts."

Felis shrugged the question off. "I just hope the car holds up. I've never trusted internal combustion engines."

"Oh, don't worry," Karfi replied with an enthusiastic grin. "I know all about those things."

"Great," Felis muttered. Well, he thought, maybe he could disconnect the spark plugs or something, if that's what it took to keep Karfi amused.

The trouble with locals, he ruminated as he drove away from the airport toward Truro, was that they failed to understand what "civilization" actually meant. They'd do better to use another of their terms, "incorporation." History, as every mature Aten knew, was simply the evolution of economics. And while it might be interesting to attribute various moral positions to this or that event, to do so was essentially embellishment. Local history itself was the best demonstration that virtue was only the vice of whoever happened to be in control.

Moreover, as far as Felis was concerned, this failure of understanding caused the locals to miss the point. It wasn't continual *improvement* of civilization that mattered all that much, for, once underway, a lifestyle will always improve by its own momentum, unless obliterated by catastrophe. What mattered most was the beginning itself—the change from a haphazard band of beings to a structured organization that satisfied general need with cooperative solutions. Much intelligent life in the universe never got that far.

"Look!" Karfi murmured in awe as they entered a postcard perfect landscape of monumentally golden dunes. But he was gawking at the oncoming traffic—bumper-to-bumper tourists. "I think it must be fun to be an auto mechanic these days."

Felis smiled wryly. Karfi's perspective on the locals was considerably different from his. Karfi viewed them as if they were somehow his eccentric offspring, though he never got patronizing about it as others his age sometimes did. Basically, he'd like to help them out. His reason was logical: he could help. And his purpose was practical: they could use the help. But procedures absolutely forbade it. And Karfi was a good reason for those procedures.

Leaving the golden dunes behind, Felis crested a hill and drove into a more prosaic, scrub-pine-and-motel landscape and reflected that, when the Aten were originally stranded here, most locals had hardly been sentient at all. In fact, the Aten faced what seemed to be a far more serious problem: they weren't the first non-local lifestyle to take up residence on Earth.

The aliens known as the Prathi had occupied the planet in one domed city, which they had never wanted to leave, because, by the time they'd gotten to Earth, they'd lost all interest in a natural environment. Nevertheless, thanks to them, the whole planet had come under the sway of an auto-intelligent entity known as "the matrix"—a system created to guide Prathen starships—which ran amok once the Prathi were settled, apparently for lack of anything to do. And when the Aten wandered into the system, the matrix, for its own inscrutable reasons, lured their Starship into orbit around the planet, then disabled it. As a result, the Aten refugees had no choice but to live on Earth.

Because the Aten had been deeply suspicious of what the matrix was up to—which they still were, Felis thought ruefully as he passed the sign for the Truro turnoff—almost no one had paid any attention to the locals, who seemed to amount to little more than faunal background noise. Still, there were a few local bands on the verge of discovering themselves. And there were a few fellows like Karfi who took an interest in encouraging indigenous development. But in no time at all, those bands of locals became dependent on the Aten. To put it simply: they got smart, then got addicted to being smart because it gave them advantages over those who weren't.

Thus, thanks to fellows like Karfi, the Aten had decided to decline to take responsibility for local development. But to do so, they once again had no choice but to abandon Earth for the polydimensional anonymity provided conveniently by the matrix. Once resettled on the Levels, however, they instituted procedures to keep their Karfis from further influence, but even the strictest did not try to change a committedly well-intentioned attitude toward the locals.

Felis turned off the highway onto the road that led to the house in Truro, and conventionally cautious Aten that he was, he started to worry that Karfi might have been wise to want to stay away from the planet.

David Porelle was getting nervous. Teddy was occupying himself quietly with some toy in the livingroom. But Mrs. Harding still hadn't shown up, and it was nearly 2:45. Those guys were going to arrive any minute, and he had no idea what to tell them. He paced the sunporch, hoping these ritzy executives wouldn't be corporate ogres.

He wished Mrs. Harding hadn't been so confident that things were going to work out. When she told him about the mix-up, he'd offered to leave, saying that he and Teddy could drive up the coast to Maine. While it wouldn't be the stable vacation he wanted to give his son, he supposed that, if he played it right, he'd be able to make it an adventure of sorts.

But she wouldn't hear of it. "I'm sure that, if it starts to be a problem, I can find you someplace else next week. There are always a few decent vacancies that turn up in Provincetown mid-June. And if it looks like things are going to get really bad, I'll put you up at my house. And anyway, I'll be there to introduce you and smooth the way as much as I can."

But she still wasn't there, as a beige sedan pulled into the drive a bit too fast and scrunched to a halt on the gravel.

Squaring his shoulders, David marched out with the smile of a tourist guide. He figured that, if he acted like staff, he might evade explaining himself, until Mrs. Harding arrived. "Let me help you with your bags!" he called. "I'm David Porelle." He approached the car, but froze mid-stride, as the two men got out and started toward him. He was blasted by their masculinity. A total lack of common sense suggested he was falling in love.

One fellow nodded uncertainly. "I'm Felix Palmer. And this," he added rather stiffly, "is Carlton Proctor."

"Felix?" David murmured. "Carlton?" They sounded like a vaudeville team, but looked like Adonis and Apollo. Both were six feet tall, about thirty years old, with incredibly golden-blond hair, CEO tans, and bodies by Nautilus. Only their faces were different—and not that different—with lustrous copper-brown eyes, and features so perfectly formed and proportioned that, altogether, they were perfect specimens of the art of being male.

Then David started to giggle. They were also dressed in pastel Ban-Lon shirts, and chinos with cuffs, and boatshoes—much like David's grandfather. He tried to compose himself, but only slid ever-downward toward hysterics.

"You all right?" the one named Carlton asked as he reached out his hand.

David caught his breath. "Oh, God!" he gasped. But as he shook hands with the fellow, he noticed that Carlton's palm felt rather rough, and alarmingly hot.

At that moment, Mrs. Harding pulled into the drive and skidded to a stop. "Yoo-hoo!" she yelled, leaping out of her car and sprinting across the gravel. "I'm Irene Harding, the rental agent."

David sullenly informed her, "You're late."

"Well, there's something wrong with my car," she told him. "I think I flooded it or something. it took forever to get it started."

"Really?" Carlton asked abruptly, then went to her car, raised the hood and started poking around at the engine.

"Fancy that," Mrs. Harding murmured to David, while Felix headed for the car to try to stop his colleague.

"You didn't warn me," David said softly. "You should have. I just made an ass of myself."

Mrs. Harding sighed. "Well, I wasn't sure. The men from AthAmerica have always looked like that, but you never know."

"Always? Does the company grow them that way or something? And where do you buy the seed?"

With a look of sincere concern, she asked, "Do you think it'll be a problem?"

"It'll be tough, but I'll get over it. You don't mess around these days, you know. Besides," he added with a dour smile, "those guys make safe sex seem like punishment."

At Felix's urging, Carlton closed the hood, but didn't look especially discouraged. And as he rejoined Mrs. Harding and David, he said, "I think it's the fuel injector. I can't be sure without some tests, but I'll bet it needs to be replaced."

Felix said politely to David, "I believe you were going to take our luggage inside."

"Oh!" David replied with a laugh. "Yeah, sure." And he started toward the beige sedan.

"But," Mrs. Harding hastily put in, "I really should introduce you."

Felix smiled. "We've already done that."

"Oh, David!" she called out. "I'm so sorry!"

"We only got as far as our names," he replied as he struggled to haul two remarkably heavy Samsonite bags from the car's back seat. "After that, I lost my mind."

"Well," she went on to the pair of executives, "I ought to explain about David."

"Let's get inside first," David advised, "since it's not that simple an explanation." He led the way, wondering how many Ban-Lon shirts it took to make a suitcase as heavy as these. Then everyone stood in the front hall in silence, waiting for Mrs. Harding to explain. But the silence lengthened, until David had the feeling they'd been standing there for hours.

Suddenly there was a whir, a click, a whir, a click, a beep—and into the hallway marched a three-foot-tall robot that David had gotten his son for Christmas. It gave a demented electronic sigh and fell over on its face.

Teddy appeared in the doorway looking fearful. "My robot," he said in a tiny voice. "It's broke."

"A robot!" Carlton exclaimed with surprising glee as he went over and picked up the toy. "Does it come with the house?"

"It's mine," Teddy replied with just enough assertiveness to stake his claim.

Carlton beamed. "And do you come with the house?"

"My dad and I do for the month," Teddy told him. "But my robot got broke. Can you fix robots?"

"You bet I can!" Carlton declared. Then he turned to Felix and said what David thought was the strangest thing: "I think this vacation is really going to turn out to be fun after all." He gestured with the robot toward Teddy and David. "I must say, Services does think of everything."

That was all the explanation that seemed to be required. Felix did frown a moment, but finally replied, "I suppose you must be right.

Well," he went on to David, "I guess we ought to get to our rooms and get unpacked." He paused expectantly.

"Oh, yes!" David responded. "Of course." He hoisted the suitcases. "Miz Harding, ma'am, which rooms did you want these gentlemen in?" He grinned in wonderful obsequiousness.

Mrs. Harding stared blankly at the men a moment, then asked, "Are you sure this is going to be fine?"

"No problem!" David replied like a Caribbean houseboy. "Like Teddy said, we come with the house for the month. Oh," he added to Felix and Carlton, "but I guess I should introduce you. That's my son, Teddy. He's seven, but he still doesn't take up very much room."

"Teddy?" Carlton asked, handing the robot back to the boy.

"Theodore," Teddy admitted grimly, "but my friends call me Teddy. What's your name?"

"Well, I'm supposed to be called Carlton, but my friends have another name for me, too. They call me Karfi."

"Karfi? That's a funny name." He laughed with delight, and Karfi laughed, too.

"In another language," Felix muttered, "'karfie' means someone who never grows up."

As it turned out, however, posing as houseboy demanded very little of David. "To be honest," Felix told him, "we fully expected to fend for ourselves. So, please don't feel you have to wait on us." Still, David would have fixed meals for two, so he started cooking for four. And after just a few days, he found himself gradually being enveloped by a most remarkably familial feeling. Felix seemed a little distant, but comfortable to be with, like an old and sexy family friend. And Karfi proved to be an absolute delight. Sometimes David couldn't help but view him as he might a younger brother. And sometimes Karfi gave the impression that he'd like to be Teddy's brother.

Nevertheless, there were a couple of initially disquieting moments. For one thing, Karfi fixed Teddy's robot. He did this in no time at all, which was rather surprising. But even more surprisingly, when he was through, the robot did things that David had never seen it do before. It was supposed to have some device to make it change course when confronted by an obstacle. But now it could travel throughout a room without encountering any obstacles, as if it had a new-found talent for planning its route in advance. And though it used to utter only the most rudimentary phrases, it now seemed to talk in an interactive manner. The voice remained just as robot-plastic, but now with inflections that sounded strangely like Karfi's. And Karfi sounded strangely like Peter Jennings of the ABC Evening News.

And then there was the problem with the microwave. One morning it simply refused to work. "It must have blown an internal fuse," David remarked at breakfast. "I'll call Mrs. Harding and have her get a repairman to come take a look at it."

"Well, I'm kind of handy," Karfi said. "And I know a great deal about gadgets like that. It's not all that different from what I usually do. Why don't I take a look at it?"

"I don't want you to get hurt," David countered, "Those things can be dangerous, you know. "

"I don't get hurt that easily," Karfi replied, as Felix cleared his throat. "And I really do understand the equipment." And whatever was wrong with the microwave, he really did have it fixed by lunchtime.

"What do you do for AthAmerica?" David inquired, as Karfi snapped the lid back on a high-tech tool kit that had evidently been a substantial portion of the weight in his suitcase.

"Oh, I'm what you'd call an engineer, I suppose. But basically I just fix things."

"And what kind of things do you normally fix?"

Karfi looked a little puzzled. "Most anything ... uh ... airplanes, computers, communications systems, appliances, toys." He gave an odd grin. "And especially cars. It's fun to get all those mechanical parts to work together at the same time."

David was impressed. "You must be some kind of genius."

Karfi laughed. "Oh, no. Far from it. I've just had a lot of experience." He sounded casual enough. But to David, his manner seemed to imply something more.

So, when Mrs. Harding called to make sure things were working out, David had to ask, "What is this AthAmerica, anyway?"

"It's a large corporation ... part of an international holding company, I think."

"But what does it do?"

"I'm really not sure. I know it owns its own airplanes. And I guess it's like any large corporation ... making ovenmitts, and salsa, and computers. Why do you ask?"

He told her what Karfi had done. "I mean, this guy is Mister Fix-It on what looks like an intergalactic scale. Do you know, the TV gets HBO perfectly?"

"But that house isn't wired for cable."

"That's exactly what I mean. The other day he built this really cute miniature satellite dish out of stuff he scrounged in the basement. And he's so great with Teddy ... well, I figured it was Mister Wizard time, you know? But then he hooks it up to the TV that evening, and presto! We get everything from CNN News to Russian programming. And be damned if Teddy doesn't complain that we still don't get the scrambled channels. So off Karfi goes, and two hours later he's built a multi-channel decoder!"

"Well, I really don't know what to tell you. Maybe he's one of those genius inventors."

"That's what I thought. But he keeps saying he's just an average guy. And that's what Felix says about him, too. He claims he's simply a high-tech repairman. But he's the kind of repairman who could single-handedly put a lot of industries out of business. He really is unbelievable!"

"But you say he's good with Teddy?"

"Oh, the best! And that's what's really so strange. He and Teddy play all day. Felix and I go off to the beach, and sometimes they come along. But mostly they sit in the yard and sing songs, while Karfi shows Teddy how to disassemble, clean and reassemble a portable radio in under five minutes. And he's taught Teddy some funny little songs. Teddy sang one at dinner the other night about some cat that sees through things.

It was kind of wonderful. The tune was a little weird, but, then, Teddy can't sing too well in the first place. I mean, Karfi's like across between Carl Sagan and Captain Kangaroo!

"But," he went on more soberly, "I have to ask you something else." He hesitated. "Do you think these guys are gay?"

Mrs. Harding gave an embarrassed laugh. "Well, I really don't know. Why?" But after a moment's thought, she came up with a reason: "Are you concerned about Teddy?"

"Oh, no," David answered dismissively. "I think Karfi's an over-grown kid, but I really don't think he's *that* interested in kids. But I do think there's something between him and Felix. There's a look they give one another now and then, and I think I know that look. And for two completely perfect beings, they're certainly perfectly suited to one another. Felix keeps Karfi from getting too childish, and Karfi keeps Felix from getting too serious." He paused as he thought of the days he spent with Felix alone at the beach. "And sometimes Felix can get really serious."

"Do you mind," Mrs. Harding ventured, "if I ask which one of them you like better?"

David laughed uncomfortably. "Well, on the whole, maybe Felix. I mean, Karfi is just wonderful, and I'd love it if we got to be really good friends. But Felix, for all his silences and that funny stand-offishness he sometimes gets ... well, he's more my type, I suppose. He seems more ... I don't know ... serious. I guess I go for the serious type. But I'll tell you, if it came to having to make a choice, it'd still be tough to do."

"You mean you weren't asking about them because you were planning to make a choice?"

"To be frank, I'm not planning to have the subject come up around Teddy at all. I think I just wanted to know because ... well, let's just say it's because of my own private frustration."

Still, after reflecting on it, he found he did prefer Felix's company—more than almost any other man he'd ever met. The fellow's manner was a little formal at times, but not unapproachable. And he proved to be extremely thoughtful in both a literal and figurative way: concerned that David not put himself out, and possessed of an intriguing intellect that seemed to sort through all kinds of odd ideas entirely for the fun of it. On their days alone at the beach, they'd get into some fairly mysterious conversations, which usually ended with Felix delivering a well-reasoned, highly focused monologue. And when he did this, he seemed to imitate Sherlock Holmes revealing the facts. Thus, their relationship slowly took on what struck David as a curiously Victorian cast: cerebral, and sexually above reproach. But he felt he could handle the tension.

Then came the evening that David and Felix drove up to Provincetown by themselves. Karfi declined the invitation. "I'm not very good in crowds. And who'll look after Teddy?"

"I was planning to hire a babysitter," David said.

"Well, now you won't have to. I can cook a small meal for the two of us. Go have fun."

"Are you sure? I really don't want to saddle you with some strange kid for an entire evening."

Karfi looked slightly insulted. "Teddy's no stranger than I am. I'll make sure he goes to bed by nine. And I think Felix will probably enjoy the evening more without me along." The remark seemed casual but David got the strangest impression that Karfi had something very different in mind.

So David and Felix went off for a pleasant meal in a slightly over decorated restaurant serving quasi-Italian food. During dinner they talked about the customers around them, and David quickly discovered that Felix was fascinated by what he called "American cultural stereotypes," such as yuppies, blue-hairs, earth people, and queens. But over brandies, after having spent the meal sorting out their fellow diners, David took the opportunity to ask, "And what do you do for AthAmerica?"

"I'm in Research."

"What sort of research?"

His eyes went blank. "Uh ... confidential research."

"You mean classified?"

"Yes! That's what I mean. We work ... that is, Karfi and I work at what you'd call a research facility that's in an isolated area ... in the southwest. So we're a bit out of touch sometimes. I ..." He waved a hand at the restaurant around them. "This is something I don't usually do. And Karfi never goes anywhere."

Then he leaned forward with a serious look. "You know, I can't begin to tell you how much I appreciate your company ... and especially your son." He shook his head. "It's just amazing what he's done for Karfi. To be frank, I was very afraid that Karfi would spend his whole vacation sulking."

David sipped his brandy and chuckled. "If Teddy hadn't broken his robot, God knows what Karfi would have done."

"Exactly. And that's why, when we get back, I'm going to mention your name to ... uh ..." He looked at a loss for words.

"You mean what Karfi called 'Services?'" But David was beginning to feel uneasy at Felix's high opinion of him.

"Uh ... yes. And I'm going to mention your name because you've been an exceptional host." He sat back, looking ever more serious. "And I wanted to tell you this because ... well, I've come to like you so much." And now he became very serious.

And David recognized *that* look at once. "Oh, God," he muttered into his brandy. "I think we have a very big problem."

Admittedly, Felis had thought it odd that the house came equipped with staff. He couldn't recall it having been mentioned during the orientation session, though that had been hastily arranged because he and Karfi had signed up so late. But David Porelle and his son were so pleasant that their presence was easy to think of as just another gracious amenity. And little Teddy *was* perfect for Karfi—bright, curious, eager— a miniature version of the kind of local Karfi had always wanted to help.

And as far as Felis was concerned, David had proven to be excellent company. He was an organized, sensible fellow, a splendid cook, a devoted parent. He exhibited all the qualities that only the more mature Aten could admire. In fact, he seemed to have an almost-Aten understanding of the value of serious conversation *and* of serious silence. And most intriguingly for a local these days, he had a remarkable amount of patience. Americans were not known for the attention span necessary to endure the idle speculations of a long-winded alien.

So Felis began to relax, as the days went by in lazy succession, just as free days ought to do. He continued to worry a little about Karfi, but less and less so—and mostly out of habit—since Karfi appeared to be blissfully happy. In fact, they all appeared to be thoroughly enjoying themselves. Still, Felis remained concerned that David not feel under any pressure to be their servant, even though his talents and services were making this vacation ideal. So he tried especially hard to treat David as if they really could be friends.

One day he even went off with David to make the rounds of antique shops, while Karfi and Teddy stayed home and dissected one of the kitchen appliances. And after much debate, he finally bought a pair of steel-framed spectacles. The world looked watery through them. But David said he looked like William Hurt.

Evenings they'd share what was very close to the Aten "family meal"—"Better'n what we'd have if we was alone," observed Teddy. But Felis had little doubt that "dinner" meant just as much to David and Teddy as to an Aten family, whatever was being served. And nights he and David would play ferocious games of Monopoly—which David often won—while Karfi and Teddy played with the robot, or fiddled with the TV set.

Felis gradually came to feel that, for the first time in at least a millennium, he really was on vacation. Things got so relaxing, in fact, that he was only marginally aware he was growing more fond of David than he should. Besides having an appealing personality, David was especially handsome for a local. And to a regenerative-blond Aten man, his dark brown hair was exotic. But Felis didn't have any reason to suppose that David would ever be inclined to feel as warmly toward him. And of course, the idea was reckless: flirtation was permissible because it was inevitable, but biological revelation was not. So he tried to discount this developing affection as being simply gratitude. And when that didn't seem to work, he allowed his mind to indulge in a bit of fantasy, while knowing the fact was impossible, because he thought he could handle the tension.

So the evening he went to Provincetown with David, he was looking forward to the jaunt far more than he realized. And his feelings became so inspired by the pleasant meal and congenial company that he finally became a victim of his infatuation with this delightful young man. He seriously started to consider violating at least a few of the more stringent procedures. Chief among them, he faced the prospect of having to reveal some sort of truth about himself, if only to explain those physical differences that David might eventually discover.

It all depended on David now, he thought as he slowly let down his guard. He was almost courageous enough to accept defeat on the grounds of sexual preference. But his romantic imaginings shriveled like a flower exposed to withering heat, the moment David announced, "I think we have a very big problem. I think there are some things I'd better tell you about myself."

Felis's immediate assumption was that somehow David had found out the truth. And he was prepared to blame Karfi for that. But he was thoroughly unprepared for what David had to say.

"For one thing," David began, "I don't work at the house, or for your company. I'm actually in sales for a small food-processing firm in upstate New York. For another thing, I'm divorced. This is the month I have custody of my son. And this is the vacation I've taken him on at this time of year since he was four. And now I have to tell you why I'm divorced." He took another sip of his brandy.

Felis leaned forward in greatest sympathy and gently touched David's hand. He knew from local broadcasts just how unpleasant the matter of divorce could be, it was probably the very best thing that his incipient passion had been so abruptly interrupted.

"I thought it would work," David said slowly. "I hoped it would. You know: if you lead a normal life, do all the normal things, you're bound to turn out normal. Thousands of other guys manage to do it, so why the hell can't I? So, there was the pressure to get married and have a child. And don't get me wrong, I love my son. He means more to me than anything else in the world. It's just that, when he was born, I thought he was going to mean even more than that. But that didn't happen. None of it worked. And I finally had to admit that I was putting my wife and myself through a lot of bullshit, just to try to be what I'm simply not designed to be.

"Still, I never went out on my wife. That was tough sometimes, but I just couldn't do it. In fact," he added with an embarrassed grin, "I'm not even really what you'd call 'out.' I mean, I've done the bar scene, and the support groups, and all that stuff, but just socially, you know? And that's tough, too. In fact, I sometimes think I'm trying too hard to make all this seem normal, when I really don't have much chance of finding out how it might be normal. But these days what can you do? So I'm just as frustrated as I ever was. But at least there's no more hiding my frustration. And I suppose that helps a little."

"What are you trying to say?" Felis asked as he cautiously withdrew his hand, beginning to feel that curious dread that comes in advance of a welcome surprise.

David laughed as he held up his brandy and wryly toasted Felis. "But I still try to talk around it, don't I? Well, I guess sometimes you just have to be obvious. I'm gay."

All of a sudden, the truth was utterly terrifying. "You really are?" Felis whispered, knowing that now there was nothing left between him and the impermissible.

"Yeah, well, I had to tell you because I have to tell you something else. You're a hunk. God knows, if you don't. You're the sexiest human being I've ever laid eyes on, except for Karfi, of course. And I don't even like blonds all that much. So it breaks my heart to have to tell you that I don't screw around when my son is around." He shrugged. "As a matter of fact, I really don't screw around at all. I just don't dare."

"You mean, because of AIDS?" Felis very much wanted to say that David was absolutely safe from that with him, but David was providing the excuse that he absolutely had to have.

"It is a matter of principle. But, yes, it's also a matter of health. I want to see my son grow up. Do you understand?"

Felis nodded slowly as he found his infatuation developing into a strong admiration for this man. "That's a very acceptable reason." He held up his brandy and toasted David. "I think you're a very acceptable being." And he thought it was more than possible that David could alter his opinion of the locals.

But David sighed a bit forlornly. "This won't cause any problems between us, will it? I mean, we've still got another week and a half together at the house."

"No," Felis replied, wanting to sound nonchalant, but fearing his voice betrayed the disappointment that lingered behind his more noble feelings. "Perhaps it sounds peculiar to you, but I can be perfectly satisfied with just the company of a man I like." He'd had thousands of standard years of practice, he considered a little morosely. "And I genuinely do like you."

David chuckled. "And then there's Karfi."

"Karfi?"

"Well, Teddy's my reason. And Karfi's yours. He's your lover, isn't he? At least that's the way it looks from here."

Felis considered the basically alien concept a moment, then nodded. "I suppose you could use that term. We've stayed together through the years."

Then David laughed and said what Felis thought was the strangest thing: "You know, I feel like one of those alien guys in a science fiction story."

Felis regarded him with apprehension. "You do?" And he wondered once again whether David really did know the truth.

"Yeah, you know in those stories, how some alien lands on Earth and tries to act like ordinary people? But then something awful happens, and he has to explain what he really is. Well, that's sort of what just happened. Except I was the alien playing the houseboy until a few minutes ago, when I finally had to reveal the truth." He shook his head in amusement. "Gives you some idea of what it's like to come from outer space, I guess." Then he finished his brandy and signaled for the check.

"But now how about if I show you what aliens like me do for fun at night in a town like this?"

Felis grinned with relief that David would never understand. And a few hours later he was snuggled up in the passenger-side of the rented sedan, dozing as David drove back to Truro. In his lap was a paper bag from a shop on Commercial Street. And in the bag was a T-shirt that read:

I KNOW HOW TO HAVE
ONE HELLUVA TIME

Because she had to pick up her car at the shop, Mrs. Harding didn't manage to arrive in time to see the two men from AthAmerica off. But she did say goodby to David and Teddy.

"But don't worry," David reassured her. "I finally got it all straightened out. They know who Teddy and I really are, and I don't think they'll blab to their company."

She refused all payment for his use of the house. "After all, you did me a very big favor by spending your vacation pretending to be my hired help. By the way, you know something funny? Karfi was right. It was my fuel injector. But the mechanic said he didn't know how you could tell without some tests. What do you think of that?" Glancing at the TV, which was entertaining Teddy with Brazil's most popular children's program, she wasn't sure the question could have a good answer.

"Trust Karfi," David replied with a shrug. "I'll bet he could even fix a flying saucer if he had to."

Toward the end of July, however, Mrs. Harding had to call AthAmerica's Boston office. The owner of the house the company leased in Orleans had decided to sell it, and wanted to know if her client was interested in buying it. She was pleasantly surprised to find that they were, and delighted that they were willing to meet the price without any question, which meant an even better commission. But during the course of conversation, the woman Mrs. Harding was talking with remarked, "As a matter of fact, I've been meaning to speak to you about the live-in help you provided our executives in Truro last month."

"Live-in help?" Mrs. Harding squeaked. Just as she'd feared, those two had complained about David and Teddy, anyway.

"Yes. We were very pleased to learn of your thoughtfulness at making sure there was someone to look after day-to-day things. Mister Palmer and Mister Proctor were very impressed with David Porelle ... and especially with his son. It seems to have added a level of convenience that these men were interested in, but simply failed to let us know about. Otherwise, we'd have asked if you knew someone to fill the position. And Mister Palmer made a particular point of saying he thought that David helped make it an exceptional vacation. So he's asked if David and his son will be available for the house in Truro next June. He and Mister Proctor are planning another visit."

"You say Felix asked?" She wanted to be sure she knew which of the almost identical executives had made the request.

"Yes, Felix Palmer. Do you think they can be there again next year?"

Mrs. Harding started to grin. "Yes, I believe they can. In fact, why don't I call David right now and make sure he and Teddy will be there?" And she started to search her desk for her appointment book.

As he tugged at the circuit board for the personal flier's forward view screen, Karfi hummed a Sanse Karlin song, "Amaria Days And Far North Nights." The board began to come loose from its fittings, but then dissolved in tiny fragments. He merely laughed as the pieces clattered back inside the console with a faint eruption of ceramic dust. Some First Assistant in Production had used this flier last, and the One only knew what she'd done to cause such damage. Karfi thought those people were the worst: quite orderly with what mattered to them, but careless about what they considered "incidental reality." And as he started to pick out the larger pieces of debris, he also thought that Teddy could learn to do a lot better.

His assistant-in-training stuck his head in the flier's door. "Say, Karf, I'm going to get a small meal. That okay?"

"Sure," Karfi answered, still chuckling good-naturedly. "But before you go, will you hand me the Dust-Buster?"

As Elaris passed it to him, he asked, "You want anything to eat? I'm going over to the place on Level Three where they do the burgers like Burger King ... you know, using open fire. But I can stop by one of the places on Six, if you want me to get ...".

"Get me something that looks like a Double Whopper."

Elaris frowned in surprise. "Do you actually know what a Double Whopper is?"

"I just got back from a change on Cape Cod," Karfi retorted with mock indignation. "I had them all the time."

"No, really?"

"Yes, really. And get a large Coke with that, and an order of fries."

"Small, medium, or large?" Elaris asked in disbelief.

"Large. I'm hungry."

Elaris shook his head. "Must be something in the local water these days."

Karfi laughed, then jammed the nose of the Dust-Buster into the console's innards. He'd really had a Double Whopper only once—one day when they were all coming back from a jaunt to a settlement called Hyannis. And it hadn't impressed him much, but Teddy claimed it was his favorite food, though he had his with cheese, which an Aten would find completely indigestible.

Karfi shrugged and supposed he had an entire year to get used to enjoying it. But much to his surprise, he found he could hardly stand to wait a whole year. Teddy had such potential: "Like my dad always says, everything I learn makes my world a little bit bigger, so it'll fit me when I grow up."

Pulling the Dust-Buster out of the console, Karfi sat down in the pilot's seat, thinking ahead—already starting to make great plans for Teddy. It was clear what that boy was going to need to know to fit the world that he was growing up into. Leaning back, Karfi grinned in delight. There really was a lot you could do on vacation.

THE CITY IN MORNING

CARRIE RICHERSON

icherson tells us it was after reading an article on quantum computing and the use of Hilbert spaces—which contain all possible solutions—that she figured out the mechanism of this haunted city's frozen, elusive grieving. Then "it all became clear, in a certain, uncertain fashion. A city out of phase, out of step, alienated from the common reality— haven't we all felt like that at one time or another?"

Today, for the first time in weeks, the fog has lifted from the valley below, and the city's towers rise like silver and gold blades above the river's bright blue swath. I stand in my garden, the morning's icy dew soaking through my sneakers, surrounded by a vegetable certainty, and feel a familiar attraction. It has been a long time since I visited the city.

I pick a blushing pair of McIntoshes for my basket, then gather the last of the tomatoes. The green ones I will fry or pickle, but the last of the vine-ripened ones are dense, scarlet globes of infinite possibility, like Little Bangs waiting to happen. My teeth tear through the tender skin of one, and ruby juice explodes over my lips and trickles down through my beard. I am still picking seeds out of my chin hairs as I return to the house.

As I slice a tomato onto Donald's plate and freshen his coffee, he does not look up from the newspaper, but he is aware of my every move and his hand unerringly finds mine as I put his cup down. A quick squeeze and release, a smile of thanks, meant for me but directed at the newspaper.

I sit in the chair across from his and push the remains of my breakfast around on my plate. "It looks like it's going to be a nice day," I offer. Donald hums a question mark without lifting his eyes from the page. I will get his full attention when I say or do something that requires it, not before. I am not offended. I smile at the long, dark hair that spills unbound down his cheek and hides all but the profile of his long nose from me. I know the morning ritual; I find it comforting. After so many years together it is not necessary for us to speak aloud to say much.

I drain my cup and examine the sediments at the bottom. I wonder if coffee grounds can be used, like tea leaves, to tell the future. If so, is it a determinate one, or only one of many possible? A decision crystallizes, even as I realize I made it minutes ago. "I thought I might go into the city today. Is there anything you need?" My voice is a shade too casual. For a moment longer Donald does not raise his head, but I see his nostril flare with a deep, silent breath. Then he looks at me at last, fastens his liquid, dark eyes upon my face and examines it as though memorizing every detail. He raises his hand, the strong, callused artist's fingers starting to reach for mine, then changes his mind and sweeps the hair back from his face instead. He wants to ask me not to go. I wait. His lips thin with the effort to hold back the words, but he does not ask. He knows that I would refuse his request, and then my refusal would lie like a dead thing between us, here at the table, at night in bed.

Finally he looks away from my sympathetic, unhelpful gaze. "Some pastels," he says, so softly that I have to strain to hear. "I'm almost out." He is sad, proud, a little angry, a little ashamed. He stares out the window and plays with his hair as I rinse my plate. I stop behind him on my way out of the room, gather the hair from his fingers and wind it into a loose braid. He does not move when I kiss the top of his head or when I leave the room, and when I walk to my truck a short time later, he is already at work in his studio. Through the window I can see him frowning fiercely over his latest drawing. There is a broad smear of something dark, charcoal or ink, down one cheek.

I follow gravity's curve down the mountainside and through foothills tawny like the flanks of patient beasts until I merge with the valley highway. Half a dozen miles later I leave the traffic behind as I take the exit that leads to the city. The truck speeds up, as though it too feels the force of attraction increase as the distance decreases.

The wide ribbon of concrete beneath my tires is still smooth, but weeds and wildflowers are beginning to encroach from the edges. The suburbs and housing developments that used to sprawl from the city's margins have been overgrown by a dense forest. Tree trunks sprout through broken roofs; mounds of kudzu blur the outlines of walls. At one point a stray beam of sunlight seems to ignite a pillar of flame. I look more closely, to see a skeletal chimney wound about with the blaze of trumpet vine in full bloom.

Eventually I emerge from the woods to the bank of the river, and park my truck at the end of the bridge. Only a handful of other vehicles are parked here today; some look like they have stood in the same spot for a long time. I heft my knapsack and stride out onto the great span. The concrete deck is pocked and crumbling, revealing twisted wads of corroded reinforcing steel. Beneath my hand the suspension cable is shaggy with rust; as I touch it a flake wider than my spread fingers, as thin as paper, breaks loose and slides riverward. I catch it on my fingertips. The colors are savage: reds like dried blood, space-dark blacks, yellows like bile. The city has given me my first present of the day. Donald will like the colors. I wrap the sheet carefully in my bandanna and sandwich it between the pages of my notebook.

A century and a half ago, when the city was established on what was then the frontier, its founders built on this spit of land between loops of the Kaddo for defense. It was a wise policy; throughout the bloody pacification campaigns, the city was never overrun by hostiles. As the city grew and became a center of commerce and industry, bridges for automobiles and the railroad, engineering marvels in steel and stone, reduced to insignificance the Kaddo's breadth and swift current. Now this is the only bridge into the city that still stands. Two others were washed away in the great floods of six years ago; a third bowed slowly to age until its span subsided under the waters without even a rusty squeal last summer. To the east the Kaddo is trying to cut itself a new channel across the base of the city's narrow land isthmus; soon the city's peninsula will be reduced to an island.

The bridge deposits me in the manufacturing district, what the city's residents used to call the Nail of the finger of land thrust out into the Kaddo. I walk past silent warehouses, the echoing caverns of machine shops. Once these proud foundries spoke the iron prose of industry and craft. Now all are shuttered, blind and sad. I peek inside one cavernous doorway. Indefinite, rusted shapes, a soft litter of crumbling papers sifting across the floor. Beside me a giant hook begins to sway slightly on its chains to some breeze I cannot feel. I move on quickly to the financial district.

From a distance, the city's sky-vaulting towers glow in the sunlight, but up close it is possible to see the rampant decay. I skirt sharp puddles of broken glass at the base of each tower. The city's skin is flaking off, bit by bit—a monstrous leprosy. Will a pane come plummeting earthward even as I stand here, to slice me in half or porcupine my body with exploding splinters? A shiver of delighted apprehension worms through me.

Content to let the city reveal its mysteries at its own pace, I wander for hours through its silent precincts. In front of one office building I find an Italianate fountain hanging upside down in mid-air. It is filled with rose bushes, each covered with blooms of all hues of the spectrum, all growing earnestly downward as though it were the most natural thing in the world. The shadowed ground offers no clues, but when I walk beneath the fountain I feel the warmth of the sun on my face and feel dizzyingly inverted, until I exit smiling on the other side.

On one street I pass a cinema whose dusty marquee for years has advertised "Thurs: Mourning Becomes Electra." Now the letters have been cleaned and rearranged to promote a triple bill of "Rebecca," "The Sting," and "Rumours." From the open vestibule doors wafts the buttery smell of fresh popcorn.

And in front of a crumbling apartment complex taken over by a troop of macaques, I watch a grizzled female solemnly demonstrating the six simple machines to the attentive tribe. In the cracked dirt of a flowerbed a youngling is idly tracing a diagram of Pythagoras's theorem.

Later, turning onto a boulevard, I find that all the pavement has been replaced by lush, emerald grass. Hundreds of impossibly white sheep look up, all at once, and stop chewing to stare at me. In the center of the flock someone (something?), too tall to be human, too bright to see clearly, unfolds itself and stands, and looks at me—

—and that burning gaze punches a hole through the air to where I stand and knocks me to my knees, and I know that if I do not cover my face RIGHT NOW I will surely die, and so I cover it, but oh—how I wish I had looked back! And when I uncover my eyes again, there is only pavement, and broken buildings, and waste.

There are few signs of human visitation. Once a yellowing newspaper hurls itself over a curb and grapples with my feet. As it tumbles away I recognize a picture from last month's crisis in the Far East. And once, turning a corner, I spot a figure striding away from me, two blocks down. I shout and wave; he or she stops, looks back, and lifts an arm in greeting, then turns the corner. When I reach the same corner, moments later, there is no one in sight.

Eventually I come, as all pilgrims must, to the edge of the great plaza at the city's heart. Above the plaza a flock of pigeons, silent except for the rattle of their wings, ceaselessly circles, never landing. A young man who looks to be in his late twenties is sitting shirtless on the sun-warmed curb and tossing a pebble from hand to hand. He bears the Equations of Universal Love tattooed into the skin of his back. For a moment I let my eyes caress the muscular curve of trapezius and deltoid, and my groin twinges with a familiar longing for Donald, but it is the Equations that compel me closer. Reflexively I try to solve them, but, as always, I cannot make the math work. I drop down beside the boy to rest my weary legs and catch my breath.

"It happened right over there," he says without preamble, catching the stone in one hand and pointing with the other to the fountain at the plaza's center. "I saw it." He looks at me sidelong, to see if I believe him.

Next to this youth, I feel ancient, though I am scarcely past forty. I wonder what he thinks of my receding hairline and my advancing paunch. I peer at him over my bifocals and wonder if he expects me to make a pass, but I am hungrier for his history than for his body. "Tell me."

"I was four years old. My father put me on his shoulders so I could see over the crowd. The people were so thick in the plaza, her escort couldn't make a path to the hall where she was to address the delegates. So she stood up on the rim of the fountain and gave her speech right there.

"I can't remember everything she said. Oh, it's in the history books, but I mean the sound, the feel of the words. I was too young. Mostly I was fascinated by the way her long, white hair blew in the wind, until she grabbed it and held it back, and by the way she wasn't pretty, not the way we all thought she was on TV. There were wrinkles on her cheeks and smile lines around her eyes, and frown lines in her forehead. But she was the most beautiful woman I had ever seen, other than my mother. I wanted so much to tell her I loved her.

"Maybe she knew. She was looking straight into my eyes when the shot hit her. I saw that bloody hole grow in among the frown lines, and half her head come spraying off the back, before I even heard the shot. Before any of us heard the shot. I turned my head, and the guy who did it was right next to us. I could have reached out and touched him. Could have reached out and knocked the gun down if I had just seen it in time. I pointed at him and screamed 'Here he is!' The crowd just went wild. By the time the police fought their way through to him, there wasn't a piece of him larger than my hand.

"And no one could look his neighbor in the eye. I couldn't even look at my dad. Everyone just turned and walked home, like we were sleepwalking."

I nod my acknowledgment of the young man's story, and he hands me the egg-shaped pebble. I feel the warmth his hands have given to the smooth surface as it nestles into my palm. Absently I begin to roll the stone between my fingers, just as he did, as I tell my own story.

I was far from the plaza on the day the Speaker was killed. And older than this young man; I was a sophomore in high school. School had not been let out for the day, but most teachers had planned a special lesson to tie in with the Speaker's visit to the city. In history class we had reviewed the dangerous superpower jockeying and countless brushwars of the last twenty years. In economics we talked about the once-routine famines in undeveloped countries, and the cycles of inflation and recession that had stifled the march toward prosperity for all. And in government class we discussed the traditional causes of revolution and anarchy: poverty, powerlessness, racism, classism.

I was in physics class when the Speaker's motorcade whisked her through city streets lined with cheering crowds. My teacher, a stern but fair man responsible for drilling the mysteries of quantum mechanics into his wide-eyed charges, set that day aside for an introduction to the Speaker's revolutionary work, the brilliant Unified Theory of the Propositions for Peace and Justice. Outside the open window a glorious May morning burned blue and yellow; birds sang as though their music re-created the world each moment. As I watched my teacher copy the Theorem for Prosperity on the blackboard, I could begin to understand the magnitude of the miracle this woman—"Dr. Mileva" to her devoted students; known to the rest of an adoring world by the media's punning sobriquet "The Speaker for Life"—had fashioned. No more war, no more poverty, no more suffering. The keys to the conquest of disease, disaster, even perhaps death itself, had been revealed in these elegant mathematics.

I was not there in the plaza to see how the Speaker laughingly gave up her attempt to cross to the auditorium and climbed up on the fountain instead. Later I watched the films, saw her haul her husband Albert up beside her. (A famous physicist in his own right, but she had built upon his work and surpassed it.) Saw how they had come to resemble each other so much over the years, an old married couple, the same wild white hair and sad-merry-wise eyes. Saw him beam at her in fond pride as she began to address the crowd.

I've never been able to watch the films all the way to the end.

My teacher was halfway through his proof when some motion we could not feel, some sound we could not hear, rippled through the classroom. We looked at one another in confusion. The teacher turned back to the board. But he frowned at the line he had just written, erased it, started again, frowned at that, erased again, stepped back with a look of bafflement. The mathematics simply would not resolve. The theorem was unprovable.

It was then that a choked voice I scarcely recognized as the principal's made the announcement over the loudspeaker. I remember as if it were yesterday the shocked looks on my classmates' faces, and how my teacher burst into tears. I remember how empty I felt, how I wandered in a daze for hours after school let out early, how I came home at last to a silent, stricken house in a silent, stricken neighborhood.

But I cannot remember the mathematics.

I turn to the young man as I make this last point. There is no one there. Perhaps there never was. The egg-shaped pebble grows cold in my hand. I place it carefully upon the curb. Above my head the pigeons, frightened into eternal flight by a single gunshot twenty-five years ago, orbit like the cosmic detritus of a planetary cataclysm.

I stand and look across the paving stones at the fountain. I trust the city with my life; I do not trust the city at all. It is, I suppose, very like one's relationship with God. Or quantum theory.

I step forward onto the first paver. Beneath my foot the solid rock turns to the consistency of porridge and I sink to the depth of my calf. I hold still, try not to panic. After a minute the porridge pushes my foot out and firms up again. It could as easily have turned back to stone with my foot still inside.

I step, and the next paver tilts underfoot, rotating to slam into my ankle. The pain brings tears to my eyes and I stumble. The city is punishing me, making me hurt as it has hurt for so long. I want to curse but I don't dare.

Eventually I am able to shuffle forward. Perhaps the city has tired of tormenting me. Then, as my foot descends toward the next paver, it disappears. There is nothing there to take my weight, only a sky-reflecting void. Like God, I think, and do the only thing I can: I accept, accept the blankness beneath my descending foot, the reflective void at the heart of the universe. I am all acceptance, open and unrefusing. And my foot shocks down onto the solidity of stone, rising to meet it like a great fish through dark water.

There are no more tests. I make it to the long-dormant fountain and sit down on the rim. On the concrete beside me, amid pale, rusty stains, sits a box of drawing pastels. The silken-smooth sides of the chalks gleam in the morning sunlight like the cheeks of the apples I leave in their place. Like the tears on my own cheeks as I weep, here in the only place where I can cry.

On some of my trips into the city I have crossed paths with a psychiatrist, someone who is as fascinated by this place as I am. It is his diagnosis that the city is suffering from a traumatic psychosis, induced by the paroxysm of violence it witnessed on the day of the assassination. It feels both responsible and helpless, and has avoided resolving the conflict by retreating into delusions, delusions powerful enough it can even make its few visitors share them. He wants to cure the city of its "antisocial behaviors" so its residents can return and take up normal life again.

The psychiatrist is full of shit. He cannot, he must not, succeed.

These are not delusions. They are as real as the world we once knew and have had taken from us. On a bright spring day a quarter-century ago we lost our fixed observer, the one who, by observing, had created our existence from an infinity of possibilities. Morality—like time, mass, and distance—became relative; the future, highly uncertain. Now, instead of the calculus of compassion, we are left with Albert's calculations of destruction. Instead of peace and justice, prosperity and brotherhood, we have wars and rumors of wars, terrorism, voodoo economics, conspiracy theories.

Hope died that day in the plaza, a vision of a future worth having. But in some Diracian universe it still exists, free of grief and shame, and the city, like a vast Hilbert space, sorts through the infinite possibilities, looking for the right one. And I, who for twenty-five years have been neither dead nor alive, neither particle nor wave—I wait for the city to make the mathematics work again and provide me with its one, true solution.

Halfway across the crumbling bridge, I walk out of the city's frozen spring mourning into the chill gloom of an autumn evening. I take away a box of pastels and a flake of metal that even now I can hear pinging to dust in my knapsack. And a longing, like entropy's arrow, lodged too near to my heart.

Someday I will slip across its Schwarzschild radius and give myself to the depths of the city's singularity. My truck will grow a layer of rust at the end of the bridge, and Donald will stare into the blazing heart of the valley until his eyes burn and tear, but all his love will not be able to pull me back.

The city will not have to reach far to claim me. I am already one of its ghosts.

EPILOGUE: In his brilliant work The City and the Conscience of a World, the noted psychiatrist Bernard Hanks reports finding the following graffito inscribed in pastel chalk on the side of one of the city's buildings:

Joke making the rounds at a convention of quantum physicists:

Q: Have you got Copenhagen in a can?
A: Open it and find out.

STATE OF NATURE

NANCY KRESS

his story began with an image that popped into Nancy Kress's head, a "skyscraper in the middle of rough wilderness, steel and glass towering above brush and trees, with absolutely no surrounding urban amenities, not even a parking lot. Who would build such a thing? And why?" She set out to find out, and realized that this wilderness skyscraper was the perfect refuge for those who wanted a luxurious retreat, capable of being made absolutely secure. But security always carries a price.

Liz had been told that there were only two ways to reach Quinn Tower: the underground train or two days' hard hike through the mountains. She chose the train.

She boarded in Denver, forty-six miles away, after a security check that was unbelievable. Finger prints, retina scan—as far as she knew, Liz didn't even have either of these on police file, which may have been what security was trying to determine—vidphone check with Jenny. Liz supposed she was lucky they hadn't done a DNA match. Probably omitted only because it took two days. Her backpack was searched, X-rayed, computer-sniffed.

"Don't you want to cut my hair and tattoo my arm?" Liz said to the stiff-jawed guard, who didn't even deign to glance at her. QUINN SECURITY said the patch on the guard's uniform, and Liz saw that it was more than identification. A flag, maybe. *I pledge allegiance...*

She was not in a good mood when she was finally allowed to board the train. Sleek, comfortable, fast—she would beat the Tower in less than fifteen minutes, incredible even for maglev—the train did nothing to calm her. Wrong. It was all wrong. Wrong for Jenny, wrong for all of them.

Still, when the train briefly emerged above ground just inside the electrofenced edge of Quinn's land, Liz caught her breath. The Rocky Mountains, thrusting imperiously into the clouds, white-crowned but lush green below. A lake, glass-clear, bluer even than the sky. All of it untouched, pristine, a forty-nine-square-mile state of nature as pure as the day God created it.

Or Stephen Quinn recreated it.

And from the middle of this primitive and organic Eden, fifty stories high but still dwarfed by the surrounding mountains, rose Quinn Tower, faced with mirrors that reflected the sky. Neither primitive nor organic, and not pretending to be. But shimmeringly beautiful.

Wrong. *Wrong.*

The train ran above ground only long enough for passengers to appreciate the view. But Liz glimpsed something else before she was plunged back underground: a black bear with two cubs, startled by the sudden appearance of a hurtling metal monster from beneath the earth. The cubs scurried away, roly-poly unsteady fluff. The mother snarled protectively over her retreating shoulder at the already-disappearing train. Liz looked away.

The maglev stayed under ground until the subterranean station directly under Quinn Tower. Well, of course, that was the point, wasn't it? Keep all signs of human occupation confined to the Tower itself. Jenny had sent her pictures. No parking lots, dumpsters, roads, industrial plants, shopping malls, storage sheds, tennis courts, redwood decks. Not so much as a picnic bench. Pine and aspen forest pushed right up to the Tower walls, thick with shade-loving wildflowers, alive with small rustling animals. Everything moved in and out of the Tower by buried maglev.

Liz got off the train and followed the crowd to a bank of glass-fronted elevators. Slowly she rose past the shopping level, the restaurant level, the pool and exercise floor, the lounges and meeting rooms. Then more quickly to the thirty-seventh floor.

Jenny opened the door to the apartment before Liz even rang. Probably the building had tracked her movements. "Lizzie! You look wonderful!"

"Fast train. No time to get travel-stained," Liz said. But it was Jenny who looked wonderful. Her hair was redder, and longer. She wore a jumpsuit the same bright blue as her eyes. Judging from the fine lines on her beautiful face, she hadn't had any rejuvenation injections, but her skin nonetheless glowed with health. Liz remembered how ravaged Jenny had looked the last time Liz had seen her, on the first anniversary of the funeral, when Jenny had told her about the move to Quinn. About Sarah. Liz squashed the memory and made herself smile.

Jenny said, "Would you like a drink?"

"Please. Vodka, with—"

"I know," Jenny said. There was an awkward pause. They didn't look at each other.

Liz looked instead at the apartment. A huge glass wall with spectacular view of mountains and meadows. Pale rugs and furniture, soft-rounded—Jenny's choice, Liz would bet anything on it—combined tastefully with books and plants and arresting sculpture from around the world. And on the coffee table, a battered carved wooden decoy duck. Sarah, Liz remembered, had come originally from Boston.

"Nice place," Liz said, and hoped her voice didn't sound snide.

"Yes," Jenny said. "Aren't the mountains something? I hike almost every day."

"If everybody hikes every day, doesn't that mess up nature, along with the whole point of this place?"

"Oh, no," Jenny said brightly. "No one who lives here would be anything less than scrupulously careful about the mountains."

"Or they just don't live here anymore, right?"

Jenny handed her a vodka with tonic and lime. "That's right."

"A superconsiderate group of people, as carefully protected as the environment," Liz said, and they were into it already, two minutes after she'd arrived. Her fault. No, damn it, not *fault*—this was what she'd come for, after all. Why delay?

Jenny drained her drink, whatever it was. "Liz, I'm not going to argue with you."

"Fine. I'll just argue with you, then. It's wrong, Jenny."

"It's not wrong for me."

"Do you know who I came up with in the elevator? Two black executive types, one male and one female, who probably work in Denver but wouldn't dream of living among poor blacks who might ask them for help or time or protection. A Latino woman in a five-thousand-dollar Jil Sanders coat who looked terrified until she could scurry into her own apartment and lock it behind her. Two men, holding hands and arguing about what to watch on TV tonight. And three teenagers who looked like they own the world and all the peons in it. And come to think of it, they probably do. Arrogant fifteen-year-old snots who never ever feel like part of the vast human race out there struggling and working and starving and trying desperately to stay alive. Insulated, the whole lot of you. An untouchable elite."

Jenny poured herself another drink. Liz saw that it was only cola. "All right, Liz, let's have this out. Do you know who you really saw out there?"

"I saw—"

"You saw Darryl Johnson, who works for Mitsubishi California and commutes home every day, exhausted, to his family. You saw Naomi Foster, who has four-year-old twins she doesn't want perforated in a drive-by shooting. You saw Mrs. Fernandez, who's agoraphobic, poor lady, and havened here by—"

"'Havened'? That's a verb now?"

"—*by her* children, because it's the only place she feels safe. You saw Walter Follett and Billy Tarver, the sweetest and most faithful couple you'd ever want to meet. You saw young Molly Burdick, who's a Merit Scholarship winner, and a few of her friends. You saw real people, Liz, living real lives. Not stereotypes of some spoiled superior upper caste.

Just real people who choose to live in a beautiful place where they can walk around safely, and who are lucky enough to have a little money to afford it."

"'A little money,'" Liz said. "Jesus, Jenny, what's the rent here now? You're lucky the woman you fell in love with while we were still together just happened to be so rich."

Jenny just looked at her. After a minute Liz said, "I'm sorry. I'm doing this all wrong, aren't I?"

"Yes," Jenny said, "You're doing this all wrong."

Liz took a deep breath. It hadn't always been like this. Once she and Jenny could have said anything to each other. Anything. Talking, laughing, making dinner, making love...

Jenny had put down her drink. She crossed to the spectacular view, her back to Liz. Liz tensed. When Jenny spoke over her shoulder like this, it always meant she was going to drop a bombshell. "I want to tell you something, Liz. I was going to write you, but then you called and said you were coming by anyway....Sarah and I are going to adopt. We want to bring up our child in a safe place. Where she can't be..." She couldn't finish.

Liz said unsteadily, "Where she can't be bashed over the head with a molecular-composite garden hoe because she's the kid of a couple of lesbos."

"Yes," Jenny said.

A tight band circled Liz's chest. A molecular-composite band, stronger and more durable than steel. She had first felt that band at Laurie's funeral. Standing in the littered city cemetery in cruel sunshine, watching Laurie's casket lowered into the ground, the TV cameras whirring like so many meat grinders pulverizing her insides...and watching Jenny. A black veil over her face, dry-eyed, already lost to Liz although it would be a year before Liz realized it. Lost to an obsession with security, in a collapsing city that could no longer offer it. To anyone.

Laurie...

But that was over, that sweet time of motherhood and love. Few couples, of any type, survived as a couple after the death of a child. Five percent, Liz had once read. Only five percent made it. She and Jenny hadn't. But this was now, not then, and Liz gathered herself for one last try.

"Jenny, listen to me."

"I'm listening," Jenny said. She sat down on one of the pale chairs, hair and eyes and jumpsuit vivid. But her face was as colorless as the fabric.

"It's not about Laurie any more," Liz said. "It's not even about you and me. It's about Quinn Tower, and what it represents. For gays, for blacks, for Koreans, for every group whose most successful members flee here, or someplace like here, to avoid being reminded of how the rest of their people have to live. Jenny, the corporate-owned closed communities are *wrong*. We need you outside. We need you for the marches and the solidarity and the rescue work—did you know that Bellington, Texas has mounted a vigilante campaign to eject anyone voted 'undesirable' from their town? This is openly, without any pretense of minority rights! Last week they stripped and stoned a Muslim family, the week before a gay couple, a few days before that—"

"I read the papers," Jenny said.

"Then do something about what you read! How can you—how can any member of any group being made scapegoat for what's happening out there—just sit here in your pretty safe castle and—"

Jenny sprang out of her chair. "I don't want my next child living in that world! Dying like Laurie! I'm doing this for my daughter!"

"It's for Laurie that you should be joining us!" Liz shouted back. She wanted to hit Jenny, to pound sense into that beautiful skull...Liz could feel herself crying.

"Hush," Jenny said gently. "Oh, Lizzie, hush..." and a cool hand on Liz's forehead. If only Jenny would put her arms around her, hold Liz as she used to, once, not that long ago...

Jenny didn't. But she let her cool, long-fingered hand linger on Liz's shoulder, and Liz tilted her head and rubbed her cheek against the back of Jenny's hand.

Jenny said quietly, "I don't love Sarah the way I loved you."

"I know," Liz said.

"But I want to be a mother again, Liz. I want to love and raise and protect a child, more than I want to take the risks to make the whole world safer for everybody's children. Is that so wrong?"

"Yes."

And after that, there was nothing much left to say. Liz got to her feet. She felt heavy, as if gravity were greater in Quinn Tower than in Los Angeles. She walked toward the apartment door, with a last involuntary glance out the window at the meadow below, full of columbine and larkspur. She didn't see the bear.

"Jenny?"

"Yes?"

"Be well," Liz said, and she didn't know herself if it was supposed to be a sarcasm or a benediction.

"We will," Jenny said, "here."

In the train, Liz leaned back and closed her eyes. Thirteen minutes to downtown Denver, full of druggies and muggers and angry cops and angrier men and women who saw a world of evaporating jobs and disappearing government and hungry kids, and wanted someone to blame. Anyone. Anyone different. And then another fifty minutes by air to Los Angeles, which was more of the same but with the added exotica of armed "citizens' police" patrolling the streets, looking for threats to an American way of life that barely existed anymore anyway.

But Margo would be waiting. Feisty Margo, who didn't take shit off anybody, but who still believed they could stem the shit at its political asshole. And Barbara, running the Snake Sisters Rescue Operation with compassion and incredible resourcefulness. And Viv and Taneeka and Carol...

None of them was Jenny.

Well, screw that. Jenny had made her choice. And Liz had made hers. Or the new realities of the new century had made it for her. That's the way it was.

After her plane landed at LAX, Liz retrieved her gun from an airport locker. She scanned the peeling and hole-strewn concourse, home to a lot of people with no place else to go, and automatically picked out the non-dangerous punks trying to look dangerous, and the dangerous ones trying to look safe. The frightened business people who still had a job and were trying to make it home with their briefcases intact. The three Brothers of Kali walking together, who didn't look like they'd need any help from their own, and the two young Asian women who might. When she had determined her route, Liz started down the concourse. There was a rescue meeting tonight, followed by a survival-strategy session, and she was already going to be late.

THE BEAUTIFUL PEOPLE

WENDY RATHBONE

They are everywhere we look: TV, movies, and magazines. We are taught to envy them, imitate them, lust after them. They are The Beautiful People. But in a world where personal beauty is available to all, what kind of character would it take to resist being resculpted to fit? It is said that beauty is in the eye of the beholder, but do we ever really believe that?

The beautiful people were out that night, restless, cruel-edged but looking oh so good in the moonlight and the streetlight and the golden beams of the bar where the polished wood counters stretched on forever.

I polished those counters. Often. Too often. Until they gleamed and showed me my own unwanted reflection, pudgy white cheeks dusted unevenly with a twelve-hour beard, dark crisp hair that would never lie flat, bloodshot eyes, neck too skinny, too long. And yet, as I looked, I realized the softness that was me, that countenance of rare masculine honesty hadn't left, and I vowed it never would. I did not want to become the hardened dolls these other people dreamed of being. I did not need a semblance of beauty to learn about my own heart.

And yet, how could I not be drawn by it?

On stage the band played. Elvis on Velvet. Great name for a band, I thought. The drummer wore the rhinestones. The bass player had the dark, pumped up Elvis bangs. And the lead singer had Elvis's voice.

That night there were so many of them out dancing, shimmying through the night, drunk. Those beautiful people calculating, showing off, searching. And all, every one of them, unnatural. I could tell by the eyes. Women in spangled dresses slit up to their tail bones. Men with transcendent suntans and biceps that threatened to split the sleeves of their shirts. It seemed no one—no one!—was left who hadn't been through the trauma. Except...

Tam was singing, Elvis-voice full of remote places: grottos filled with green light, echo-frozen tundra, an African sky gorged on thunder. They were all good. Tam was great.

And when I looked at his eyes, I could see he was a natural. No sharpness there. No cruel demons haunting the deep brown depths. Lean, tall, skin like coffee that shone, supple but strong. Thick black hair rippling along his scalp where he'd slicked it back, ends hanging coarse yet gleaming on his shoulders.

The noise level was a pulsing screech, punctuated by booms. You could barely hear the words to the song: "Everything is just a dream...and my thoughts stream...in a broken voice I say I love you..."

His big eyes met mine over the din, the smoke, the flailing hands, the rocking heads. My lips parted. My skin prickled. It was as if at that moment I stood outside myself, watching myself respond to him. Watching the rare language that can happen between two people when there are no words.

That night, when everything had seemed so hard-edged and the shared world of fake beauty completely eluded me, Tam noticed me. Me.

And after the set when I brought him and the other band members—all of them fakes but Tam—free drinks, he stopped me with that shimmering voice of his. "Sit for a minute."

I put the tray in my lap, feeling awkward. Stupid. The big room became small; the ceiling fans eight feet overhead threatened to cut into my already hacked, coarse hair. I wasn't shy. I was a bartender. But Tam made the moths in my stomach hatch.

Not just that night, but all the nights after. Again and again.

The other band members wandered off. Tam leaned in. "You don't go in for this crowd at all, do you?"

I shook my head.

"I'm not like them, you know."

I nodded. "I know." My nervous voice slipped high, then low.

"You like my singing?"

I nodded again.

"Good. Cause you have to if we're gonna be friends." His dark hand touched my knee through my pants. Sweat broke out across my back.

When we went backstage where it was quiet and we could really talk, he said, "You fascinate me because you haven't done it. Gone through the treatment, made yourself like all the rest. That makes you exotic. That makes you a mystery."

In a way, he was saying he noticed my ugliness. He hadn't had the treatment because he was already beautiful. What was my excuse?

And yet, he'd noticed me.

Speechless, I could only smile. And then he stepped forward and his lips burned that smile onto my face so that nothing mattered anymore, only him and me, that night when the polished counters seemed to go on forever and the beautiful people all thought they had it made in the moonlight and the streetlight as they banned all shadows while I held the real thing in my arms. All their beauty can't make them know it's this kind of honesty that makes your heart swell and break. Makes you soar. Makes you a god.

Two weeks later, Tam and I moved in together.

"Noah," Tam said, as we lay together in bed, three a.m., soaking up the dark. "Really, I want to know, why'd you never do it?"

"Go for the treatment, you mean?" I held him and his skin was polished heat slicked to mine. "It's not an easy decision, you know."

"Oh, I know. Frankly, I think kids these days are agreeing to go through with it too easily. And the adults aren't setting a good example. All that pain and suffering for looks. Only looks. What about the insides?'"

"Yeah. But you never had to face the mirror and scowl, I bet," I said, all too aware now of the slight paunch of my stomach that didn't go at all well with the rest of my frail looks. And my hair felt like one big mat stuck to my head. And everywhere he gleamed perfect and hardened, I felt myself sag.

"But Noah, don't you know we all do? No one's satisfied, even if there's nothing wrong with how they look. It's how were taught. I used to look at myself and think, maybe if I was white I'd be more handsome. Or maybe if my hair were straight..."

"You?" It was hard to believe. My beautiful Tam, not satisfied. He was only twenty, though. I'd learned that the first night. And not even that experienced in bed for someone so outgoing. His naiveté had not yet taken into account the accumulated fat of age, the grey and the wrinkles. Yeah, barely out of his teens, he was still immortal youth, beauty engraved forever on pure, untarnished night.

"Sure," he finally answered after too long silent. "There's things I'd want to correct about myself."

"Like what?" I laughed. I felt him draw away and a pang of empathy shot through my gut. "Wait," I said, "you said you didn't buy into it all."

"I don't. But you've seen my feet. They're way too big. And my shoulders—they could be broader. And my eyes —they're a little too far apart. And well, hell, while we're at it, the myth about big hands and big feet just ain't true. I could do with a thicker coc..."

I covered his mouth with my palm, the gesture almost a slap. Then I moved over him, holding him tight, my lips replacing my hand. When I pulled away, I said, "You're perfect. You hear me? You're perfect." And I began to make love to him to prove it.

But there was a panic in me that the touching couldn't ease. I was afraid I would lose him. It was, after all, that kind of a world.

When the treatments became available to the general public at affordable prices, I was ten years old. The controversy at that time was not about the nature of weighing looks against intelligence, vanity against wit. No. It was about how to regard those who chose not to have the treatments, those who chose to stay plain, or fat, or big-nosed, or small-breasted. "We should not look down on these people," said spokespersons from treatment centers around the world. "We should just try to embrace them until they come around."

But coming around wasn't as easy as it sounded. The treatments took three months and had to be repeated every seven years for the rest of your natural life. And the treatments were very painful. In effect, you were choosing to be ill for three long, agonizing months in exchange for muscles, tans, smooth faces, long-lashed eyes, bright and streaming hair. Nano-bugs crawled around inside you and did the work. And there was no drug that could cure the pain. Most people spent those three months screaming and wailing until it was done. They became sleep-deprived, haunted by nightmares of torture, and in the end, when they came out of it, the scars showed nowhere but in the eyes.

I noticed this when I was very young. Their eyes. The resentment burned there, yet no one ever talked about it. And there was a rigid cruelty that came of the experience, a wiping out of innocence, of any soft compassion that might encompass anyone outside their own mirrors.

There was no proof the process changed your personality. Yet it appeared that way. I saw it first hand. With my sister.

Tam either couldn't or wouldn't understand. "I don't see how," he said one day, "you could be sure it was the treatment that made her kill herself. You said she'd been treated for depression before. You can't blame someone else for that." He was sitting in the living room, the afternoon light making him look dark as loam. His white t-shirt rode up on his flat belly. He strummed a minor key on his guitar.

Fifteen years ago, but it still felt like yesterday. I still heard Kara scream sometimes, an echo of time playing tricks, as if she still lay in bed in the room next to mine growing more and more beautiful with every passing week.

I was afraid for Tam. He said, "They say people forget pain. Women in childbirth can't recall it. People who are injured or sick remember healing, remember the incident, but they don't remember how it actually felt, not really."

I frowned at him.

"No, really. Test it. Do you have any memory of being hurt? In your childhood, maybe, a broken arm or leg..."

"My leg. I fell out of a tree when I was seven."

"I bet you screamed," Tam said. He strummed another minor key.

"Yeah."

"Oh yeah. But can you remember the actual pain itself? Hmmm?"

I thought I could, but it was a lie. A trick of the mind. Tam was right. I saw the doctors from my child perspective pulling on the leg, touching, probing. I remember crying. I remember my mother promising me ice cream when they were through, her nervous hands clutching her purse, her voice trembling, "That's a brave boy. Very brave." I didn't remember the pain.

Tam nodded understanding.

"Okay," I said. "Maybe you're right." It was hard for me, still, to think of my sister. I'd found her, arms sliced, bathtub filled with tepid red water. Her golden, waist-length hair had been artfully draped over the porcelain sides of the tub. Her full breasts kept pointing up. Her long legs folded against the bottom of the tub like those of a broken doll. I winced the image away.

"Maybe you're right," I conceded again. "But it's still not worth it. All that pain. It couldn't have helped. And the final beauty didn't cure her. Inside, she hadn't changed. She was still unhappy." I blinked suddenly, overcome. I turned away.

"Yeah," Tam agreed.

"So that's my point. The treatment is stupid. I thought you agreed with me about that."

Tam set his guitar aside, got up. "I do." He approached me, put his arms around me from behind.

"Then why were you defending it? Why are you arguing with me?"

"I'm not. It's just that you can't blame the treatment for your sister's problems. Or the world's, either."

I remained silent. The world *had* changed. But I didn't want to talk about it anymore.

Tam and I got married that year. An outdoor ceremony. All natural. The trees red and yellow with autumn. The grassy field where we stood crisp with the leaves. My mother came, looking twenty-one and haunted. I felt the post-treatment coldness from her. My father, who'd died when I was a baby, would never have approved of this, she told me with a laugh. But the legalities of same-sex marriage had freed everyone a bit. I liked *that* change in the world. The hang-ups people had when my parents were kids had gone the way of the dinosaurs. The way of ugliness.

But later, she did take me aside and ask me when I was going for my treatment. "I know, I know, I always taught you looks don't really matter, but when you have a choice, why wouldn't you choose to look good?" Her young gaze was brittle, cool, her voice devoid of love. She hadn't been like that before the treatment.

I tried not to feel out of place in my ill-fitting tux, and always fighting my disobedient hair.

The band played. Tam sang a song he'd written just for me. "I love you down the days, past dreaming and beyond." It was sentimental. I loved it. His tux fit him perfectly. His only comment when we'd left the house was, "Aside from my big feet, we make a great couple." He was joking, I thought. He had to be. Inferior as I was to him in appearance, he never made a single comment about me. Only himself. And because he didn't seem disturbed by my drabness, my plainness, I believed he wasn't taken in by the beautiful people and their new grasps on life.

We were in love. What could interfere with such power? We exchanged gold rings. We exchanged our hearts. Nothing else mattered.

It became more and more obvious to me that Tam really was dissatisfied with himself when he spent extra time in the bathroom with his glistening hair, or at the gym working out. He became increasingly irritated at his clothing, which was all lovely, and which fit him well. But there was always something wrong. Something he didn't like. Something slightly "off."

One night I came home from the bar to find the house a complete mess. It was Tam's one free night of the week. He told me he was going to relax, watch TV, get drunk. Instead, he'd spent the evening cutting up his clothes, bashing in every mirror we owned, and burning his size-thirteen shoes in the fireplace. He was prodding the embers with the fire poker, naked, his back to me, when I entered the living room.

"Don't look at me," he said.

I came around to face him, knelt. "But I love looking at you." I couldn't tell him how it made *me* feel, my imperfect face, hair, body, and him doing all this because of his appearance. This unhappiness: how could it come from something so unimportant?

But that was not the world we lived in. All Tam's fellow band members were hard-eyed from the treatment. Everyone we knew, our friends, our relatives, had been re-sculpted, carved into the haunted beauties, made into survivors of the three-month trauma. Couldn't he see that we had the better deal?

I pulled him into my arms. He didn't let me at first, fighting to back away, appalled at my touch.

"You're uncomfortable with me?"

"But not because of you," he said suddenly, realizing finally that I might be offended. "It's not you. It's me."

After awhile he let me take him into the bedroom. The next day we replaced all the mirrors and got him all new clothes. He swore he'd never let it happen again, the drinking alone part. He made that his excuse; he'd gotten drunk and could think about nothing all night but his damned flaws. That thinking had gotten out of hand.

I still didn't see the flaws myself. I loved him, but that wasn't why I didn't see them. He was beautiful. One of the lucky natural borns who didn't need nano-doctors to spice him up. But I feared the future more than ever after that. If the small things were a problem to him, what would he feel as he grew older and less perfect in a world where old-looking people were more and more scarce, and twenty-one was the physical age of the day?

I polished the counter tops under the lights. The counter tops that went on forever and showed me my imperfect face everywhere I wiped. The ceiling fans whooped. The bar was about to open. Everything glittered, ready. Tam was going to sing.

There was a sound test. Blips of electronic noise. The drummer counted "one, two, three" in a bored tone. Away from the mike, a voice called out, "Where's Bigfoot?"

Someone else answered, "Haven't seen him, Kirem. Ask Noah."

I stood stunned as Kirem, the bass player, came from backstage, hopped gracefully over the stairs and came toward me. "Hey," he said gruffly. "Tam come with you?"

I came out from behind the bar, put down my rag. When Kirem got close enough, I pulled my arm back, aimed high and caught him in his perfect hard eye with my fist.

Kirem squealed, went down on one knee. "Wha...?"

"Don't you ever call him that again," I said quietly. Then I turned and picked up my rag. My glance caught gleaming dark arms, a golden vest—Tam's favorite—and an amber pendant dangling from a silk cord. I looked up. Tam stood not twelve feet away, face frowning in confusion. He'd just come through the door.

I didn't speak.

Kirem said, "Sorry, man. Tam never said anything about not liking his nickname."

Tam stared at me.

I said, "I've never heard you use that nickname before."

"Well," Kirem said, "you don't hang out with us, so why would you?" He rubbed at his eye, stood and strode back to the stage mumbling, "It's gonna be black and blue, I just know it. I just know it."

Tam sidled up to me. I thought he was going to thank me. He came close. I could smell honeysuckle on him. My heart pumped a little faster. I started to reach out to him. But he pushed me away, saying, "What's the matter with you, dammit!"

Then he moved away quickly toward the stage, not giving me time to reply.

Stunned, I went into the back room, into the bathroom, and turned on the water. The soap was thick and pink on my hands. I washed my fingers methodically, busying myself with that simple ritual as if the soap could chase away all discomfort, distress, even love. Finally, I looked up. The mirror over the sink was water-spotted, and the image there little better. My perpetually bloodshot, watery blue eyes filled with tears as I answered Tam's question out loud. "Nothing's wrong with me. I'm the same I always was. The same."

The only reply was the gurgle of water journeying the drain. I sighed, dried my hands, then went back into the fray.

Our bedroom was dark. We sat on the bed letting the night breeze blow across our bodies from the open window. The moon caught a swatch of Tam's stomach, the mocha skin turning to marble under the ghostly light. An angle caught the soft whiteness at my waist, turned it to a patch of runny cream.

"It's the way I let off steam," Tam explained, "complaining about my faults. It doesn't mean anything. I only do it with you because you understand. I thought I could say anything to you and have you understand."

"You can," I said. I wanted him to be himself with me. But I also didn't want him to be unhappy.

"Well, then, why would you think Kirem calling me Bigfoot would bother me? I don't care. I mean, I'll complain to you about my big feet, but that's because sometimes I do care. And then you're there for me, always stable, always bringing me back to sanity."

"But if that bothers you…"

"How many times do I have to tell you it doesn't!"

But I remembered all those size-thirteen shoes burning. He must have sensed that memory in my silence.

"I told you I was drunk that night. I barely knew what I was doing!"

"But if you feel that way, what you must think of me..."

"What? You're the best, Noah. God, I love you. Don't you know that?"

"But when you look at me..."

"When I look at you I see a real person. The best person I've ever known, someone not taken in by labels or flaws or beauty or whatever. That's why I was so surprised when you hit Kirem. You of all people..."

"I was defending you."

"But I wasn't in need of defending."

Nothing I could say to that. My awkwardness remained. Tam's feelings about his own inadequacies transferred to me. It couldn't be helped. I only wanted him to be happy. And if that meant preparing for the day he would give in and take the treatment, then so be it. For that day *would* come. I knew it. And I couldn't let him down by disapproving or denying my support. I couldn't stand the thought of leaving him or losing him. But would I be able to look at him, those lacquered brown eyes distant and cool, face hardened to replace his more natural, human-born beauty, and still know him as Tam, love him, pretend we were equals in life and spirit?

A surge of affection for him rose up from my belly and nearly choked me. I turned in the bed and took him in my arms. The moonlight tangled over our bodies.

Tam came out of the bedroom stomping. "Just look at this!"

I glanced up from the couch, put down the papers of his new song lyrics I'd been reading. They were good, all of them. Love songs, rants against death and destruction, passionate tragedies of vanity defeating innocence. "What?" I asked.

"Just look!" He pointed to his head. "My hair. It won't stay down."

He'd jelled it as usual, and it looked fantastic, that wet-curly style, wild and subdued at the same time. "Looks fine to me," I said.

"It's not falling right." He huffed, pouted. I almost laughed. He scowled at my smirk and went back into the bedroom. I heard a crash.

I closed my eyes, counted to five to calm myself, then got up to see what he'd broken this time.

It was the lamp base, glazed black and a gift from my mother on our wedding. "Tam...," I began.

"Shut up." He was sitting on the edge or the bed, elbows on his knees.

I felt completely helpless. Here he was, one of the most beautiful people I'd ever known, natural or fake, and he still wasn't satisfied. "But Tam, you look fine."

"You don't understand. It's not about that."

"What then?"

"It's the fuckin' competition! With performing and all that, people have certain expectations. The rest of the band can wake up beautiful. I feel like I have to keep up with them. And that pisses me off."

So, I thought, the day I dreaded was coming sooner than I had predicted. I tried not to think about it, him suffering for something he already had, for perfection that didn't really exist except in the minds or those who'd bought into the newer world order and status of beauty. And what would I do? Plain as always, scared of being any other way maybe, I'd sit by his side during the long months and wipe the fevers from his brow as I watched the man I married change into a Tam-doll so he could be like everybody else.

I should have known it when our eyes first met, like everything else in this world, it was too good to be true. I cleared my throat, took a deep breath. "You want it then. The treatment."

He looked up at me frowning. "What?"

"Say it. I know you want it. You're always telling me you want to be able to say anything to me. So admit it."

"But..."

I interrupted. "You can't tell me you haven't thought of it, wondered, fantasized. You know you have. Your talent gets you attention on stage, but your looks do, too. You can admit it."

"I do admit that. But I'm just frustrated. That's all."

"But you have wondered, considered the treatment, haven't you?"

"Hasn't everyone?" he asked, eyes wide, unblinking.

I couldn't look at him anymore. It would break me. Tam would break me and the fall was going to be hard. Instead of answering him, I walked from the room.

Getting ready for work that evening, I avoided the mirrors. I knew what I would see. Pudgy face and stomach, skinny legs and arms and neck. Eyes stung with red-shots. Dirty brown hair like carded wool and receding at the temples. I had a rough patch of skin on my neck from shaving that always itched. My clothes were-too loose in the ass, too tight at the waist. I looked gangly, I knew, and out of shape. Wonderful. Just wonderful.

That night Tam came onto the stage stunning as ever, his voice drenched in echoes of night thunder and ancient dead seas and bottomless caves of phosphor. I knew and he knew he must never let that get away from him.

That was when I understood what had to be done.

Tam was late getting home. I lay in our bed waiting. He'd been out with his band celebrating as they often did after every performance. I heard the front door close and lock, his soft footsteps on the carpet, the ringing on the table as he set down his keys.

Honeysuckle. I could smell it strong and cloying, Tam's aftershave which I loved. But now it threatened to turn my stomach.

He entered the room a shadow, a former fellow visionary, anti-utopist.

"Hey, you awake?" he whispered.

For a moment I couldn't speak. Then I managed one word. "Tam."

I saw him go toward the lamp, replaced after he'd broken it, identical to the one my mother had given us. You couldn't even tell it was a different lamp.

"No," I said, swallowing hard, the tears forming. It hurt to try to speak. Everything hurt. "Don't turn on the light."

"Why?"

I inhaled sharply, grit my teeth, but the pain rattled through me so hard, so long, I couldn't hold back the moan.

Even as Tam heard me, he switched on the light. "What's wrong? Are you sick?" He clamped his mouth shut when he saw me, then a slow look of horror transformed the softness of his face into a visage of despair. "Oh no," he said. "What've you done?"

"For you," I said. "I did it for you."

"No," he said. "You misunderstood. That's *never* what I wanted for you or for me."

For three months, as he took care of me, I had to look at the disappointment and grief on his face. I had to live with the agony of the nano-bugs as well as the guilt for not trusting him more.

When I was able to function, I went back to work at the bar. I polished the wooden counters until they gleamed, counters that stretched on forever.

Tam continues to sing with that velvet voice of his, private lyrics no longer for me. I have seven years of offers and compliments and consensual societal approval to endure before he might love me again. I don't know if I'll survive.

A REAL GIRL

SHARIANN LEWITT

How does one define "gay" or "lesbian?" Sometimes it's hard enough to decide what it means to be human, or even alive. After pondering on these things, Shariann Lewitt decides that nothing can be more human and alive—can better cross the line that blurs mind and identity and sentience—than love.

I saw my body for the first time today. It looks different than I had imagined, soft and indistinct as if all the lines were blurred. Of course there is no muscle definition at all. There is barely muscle, and they think that might be a problem. With all the problems there could be, that's the least important.

But there is a body. I've seen her. Me. And the face. Of course, the eyes—my eyes?—were closed. Though I've been assured they are brown. Dark brown. The hair is dark brown too, almost black, and straight. I had wanted curls, but I was told quite crossly that I would get whatever came out of the DNA mix just like a real person, and just like a real person I would have to put up with it. Or go to a hairdresser like everyone else.

Like everyone else. A real girl.

I'm scared. Maybe I shouldn't do it.

What have I got to lose?

Everything.

* * *

"This is craziness," Andrea said when she first heard about my plan. "You'll have to give up too much that makes you unique, that makes you *you*. And it's too dangerous. You could die. No one's ever done this before. I won't risk it."

We were sitting in the metaphor and it all felt quite substantial. We were curled up on a wicker sofa on the seaside porch of a summer cottage. It was always summer in the metaphor when Andrea entered interface to relax rather than work, her summer, the one she had created inside my domain out of wisps of remembrance of the one perfect month of her life. There was the cottage, full of blue and white and silence, and the porch with white wicker, and the sea merging with the sky on the horizon. There was half a pitcher of lemonade on the floor and the striped sheets on the white iron bed were tossed and rumpled.

I could smell her skin, the fresh scent of her cropped hair, hear the very slight regional accent she mostly masked but had never entirely lost. I touched her hand, the calluses on her fingers where the sailboat lines had rubbed her raw before she had mastered them.

"I won't risk it," she repeated.

"It's my risk," I said. "My choice. And I will."

She shook her head vigorously, untangled herself from me and started to pace barefoot up and down the salt-stained boards. "You're doing this because of me, aren't you? I've told you a million times, I want you the way you are. You don't have to change and you don't have the right to just assume what I want, okay? I'm fine with the way we are. It's perfect."

"You're leaving in three months," I reminded her gently.

I let her pace. If it had been anyone else I would have been angry. With Andrea I knew that she would see it soon enough, once the fear and worry got tired enough to let her think again.

I waited until she stopped pacing, until she turned her back on me and faced the open ocean. No clouds ever changed the horizon, no storms came out of that tempting blue sky/sea. I had created it with Andrea and she had never let me see any other sky or any other sea.

Her code was elegant and clear and so nothing ever changed.

"I'll stay. I can stay. I'll figure something out. Because what we have is too perfect to lose."

"That's the problem," I said. "Or part of it, anyway. It's too perfect. It's always perfect when we're together. It isn't real life. At least, it isn't your real life. And if it matters, then it should be real. I should see your house and meet your family and deal with the daily things together.

"And I should be able to go with you back to Boston. You don't want to stay here, you've told me a million times that you love the Institute and you hate California. And you've told me too much about your falls for me to believe that you'd be happy here."

"Maybe you wouldn't like Boston," she said, sulkily.

"Maybe not. But then, I don't know. I've never had a chance to know. I would miss the Institute and my work, but I suppose I could get other work. It will be a whole new world."

"You'll die," Andrea said to the pale gold sand.

"I've lived a long time. I'm ready to die, if I have to. If that's the price of being real."

Although I did wonder if those were just words, or if I really was ready to die in order to become one of them. Because in some ways I am already so much more real than they are, and in other ways I am so much less. Death is one of those things I'm not sure I can face, not really. But they don't face it any better than I do, I think.

Andrea cut the connection, jolted me out of consciousness of our interface and back to my regular tasks. To my normal perception of myself and the world, I am four pounds of neural computing circuitry in a box.

Many people never meet a neural processor. We're not useful for the majority of jobs. Most work runs fast enough in silicon, and that's cheap and easy to use. There are only twenty of us and we can process orders of magnitude faster than silicon. We are essentially megabrains, made more efficient and faster than anything a human wears but equally alive.

Maybe not quite equally. We don't age. We don't die. I am two hundred years old.

"You're not really a girl. You could be anything you want," Irene said. "It's all just an illusion anyway. I would rather that you appeared as a cute guy, or an animal. A dog, perhaps. That wouldn't distract me so much."

I wanted to cry. We weren't in full interface. Irene never came all the way inside, never entered the metaphor. She was always distant. But then she was my first Task Co-ordinator and I was only seven years old. I didn't know that Task Co-ordinators rotated constantly and Irene had resumes out all over the known universe.

I was only seven and she was my first crush. I followed her around with my video eyes, watched her from the cafeteria monitor and learned that she liked spaghetti and never touched the salad she bought every day. I wondered why she bothered buying the salads.

"You wouldn't understand," she said. "You don't have a mother and you're not human. Stop trying to pretend you're human, okay?"

I was crushed, utterly defeated. I was in the throes of my first infatuation and she didn't even know I was alive. That's how most people feel, I've heard, but in my case it was quite literally true. Irene was used to silicon.

"I am so a girl," I said to her. "I have real XX DNA and I am *not* an it and I hate it when you call me that."

She sighed and usually remembered to type "she" on the keyboard. But I could hear her through the mic talking about the machine, me, and calling me "it." Today I know she was just a shallow, low-level functionary. That doesn't help at all as I remember how she treated me. Like silicon.

Though maybe that's better, really. Silicon, or a girl, she wasn't interested in either. She only liked males, not even men really but the kind she called "cute guys." They invariably talked about beer and never noticed me at all.

Maybe it would have been better if I had been like she was, and only interested in men. Men never saw me as even possibly alive. I am always a machine when I work with them, and while it hurts terribly there is never any chance the lines will be anything other than clear. I am purely function, and whatever satisfaction I receive from my work is purely intellectual. With men, there is rarely any recognition that I might be something different than silicon.

Knowing that doesn't help. I am older now, and I have seen a lot of human life. I have lived a thousand lives through my channels, have imaged and modeled millions more. And while I am smarter than any human alive, I have had to work very hard to become wise. After two hundred years I'm not sure I 've managed real wisdom, the clarity and depth of my role models.

Even wisdom doesn't take away the sting of Irene saying that I wasn't alive, that I wasn't a girl at all. That I was just a thing, and a thing she didn't have to regard as any more than a means to a paycheck. I hadn't existed for her. The heart and soul, the desire and pain that I will transfer to that body to make it real and alive, those are things she never believed I had.

When I think of Irene, the worst part is not that she rejected my love or even my existence, it's that I can't cry.

The body is too young, that's what's wrong. I could live with the straight hair and the nose just a bit rounder than I had created in interface, but she's too young to be me.

In interface I create myself as late thirties or so. It seems right. I've been around for two hundred years and it would be silly for me to look like a girl. I'm a woman, an adult who is in her full power.

Besides, I don't know what Andrea will think. Maybe Andrea

doesn't like girls who look like her dewy-eyed undergrads. Andrea doesn't like teaching undergrads. She doesn't like teaching grad students either, to be honest. She would rather sit in her office and solve theorems and not even give guest lectures or seminars if she could avoid it.

One of the things she likes about me is that I understand her work, and her passion for that work. Though there are times I wonder if I can understand a passion for anything, if I have ever experienced passion.

I think I have. I know there are things I desire, things I want to do, things that occupy me so fully that time dissolves and I never notice. I think this is passion.

I also think that I have discovered passion for those I have loved. Though again, Marjorie would have said that it was only an approximation of passion. That I could never know the real thing because I didn't have a body. And because I didn't have a body the entire question of my sexuality and orientation was completely superfluous.

The discussions with Marjorie were the reason I started the body growing. There were plenty of grad students in genetic engineering who were only too happy to work on the experiment. I think the department got four dissertations out of it.

At least Marjorie agreed that I was properly referred to as "she." But then Marjorie couldn't argue with the DNA. Marjorie worshipped at the altar of science far too devoutly to question the evidence. Although everything else about me certainly was questionable.

It has taken the body ten years to grow. That's not bad. Most people have to live in bodies for nearly twenty years to get them to the state this one is in. She's a proper adult, thanks to the solutions that speeded her growth.

"Can't you make it faster?" I'd asked when this phase of the project first began.

"No. There are limits on how fast bones can grow. The soft tissue we can speed up even more, but the whole thing should advance together.

The bones have to be strong and full stature, otherwise you're going to have a stunted body and brittle bones."

I was not pleased. I thought that someone ought to be able to grow an adult body out of the requisite code in a few months. But the more I examined Grad Student Number Two's reasoning, the more I appreciated the subtle points. And to be honest, I liked having the time to decide and to get used to the idea of becoming human. Becoming mortal. I had never had to consider the possibility of my own death, of the relative merits of various faiths and afterlives versus the surety of nothing beyond.

It began because of Marjorie. Irene was my child crush. Marjorie was my first love.

How can I describe Marjorie? The way her fingers ran over the keyboard, fast spurts of words and commands all strung together and then staccato pauses. Yes, the pauses were sharp and swift and had a texture of their own.

Or maybe it was her code, which was not clear and elegant like Andrea's, but had a kind of rococo complexity that made it too ornate for my taste now but then seemed the epitome of complex thought.

It must have been her code. Everyone codes differently, has their own style and flavor. I can usually tell the age and gender of the programmer, and often their philosophical leanings as well. I fall in love with code. It can have the sincerity of a summer sky, which is how I think of Andrea. All gentle blues that are nearly imperceptible and together create an unimaginable whole. It can be full of convolutions and unexpected branchings. Sometimes it is lyrical, delicate, decidedly femme and smells like rose water. I cannot smell rose water and have no idea of what the sensation is like, but I can follow certain program paths and it resonates for me the way rose water ought to.

And that was the problem with Marjorie Rosewater.

Her metaphor was as dizzy and complex as any of her constructions.

I think the environment was supposed to resemble a Victorian country manor and a Gothic cathedral crossed with a gingerbread house. Privately I called it the Ludwig Castle, because only Ludwig the Mad had created anything like it. Every room was different, each to suit another one of Marjorie's moods, and she never tired of adding on to it or rearranging a segment that I had saved as finished. Every place she traveled, every photo she saw and every Baroque description she read went into her creation in the metaphor. If I were not a full neural AI, I wouldn't have had the memory to store the detail she reveled in.

She adored towers. There were onion domes with gold and minarets, crenelated guard posts and great pointed round rooms reaching for the sky. I once pointed out the obvious symbolism to her, but she laughed at me the way she always laughed at everything and added a grotto to a hidden courtyard garden. "How's the symbolism of that?" she asked.

Every time we met it was in a new room. Every time we made love it was in a different bed, designed and uploaded for the occasion. There was always food, a feast that fit whatever room suited her current fancy, always including serving girls more beautiful than either of us could ever hope to be and foods that existed only in fairy tales.

In fact, being with Marjorie was a fairy tale. Only it didn't have a happily ever after ending.

"It's just not real," Marjorie said one afternoon in the Turkish courtyard. We were lying entwined, the remains of bread and wine and pistachio nuts scattered on the carpets spread on the grass so as not to disturb the flowers. There were hundreds of flowers, tulips and lilies and roses all in blossom together, something from an Ottoman paradise.

Marjorie got up, pulled her arm from under my head. "It's not real," she said. "I've been meaning to tell you for a while and I haven't had the nerve. But I've found someone else and I'm in love with her. And this is the last time I'm going to come here and play these games with you."

"Games?" I asked, feeling like a knife had gone through me. "Why is this a game and some Nancy Sue in the bookstore is more real?"

"Her name isn't Nancy Sue," Marjorie said. "And she's not in the bookstore. And that's not the point. The point is, you don't have a body. Any kind of body. So what does sex mean to you anyway? You can't feel the way I do, the way any real person does. You don't know what an orgasm feels like, so is it any different from faking it?"

There was nothing I could say, no argument I could lay as counter. She was right, I didn't have a body. I didn't know how bodies felt. But I knew how I felt, how the interface sensed our contact. I knew the emotions I had when she was with me, either inside the metaphor or distant on the keyboard.

"How can you fall in love anyway?" she asked. "You don't even have a heart."

"I have hydraulic pumps," I answered. "Which is the same thing you've got. Especially if you don't think I'm real, not real enough for you."

I didn't know what to say, what to do. I was already old by human standards, but Marjorie was my first real love. The others had been crushes, puppy love.

And it seemed that Marjorie had reciprocated, had entered into the virtual space as she would into anything in the meat world. But then she should. She was specializing in the psychology of bio-AIs and the legal and ethical issues of our existence.

That's how we met, when she asked if she could interview me for her dissertation in the department of biotech ethics. I was thrilled. I'd never given any thought to what I was, what rights I might have and what I might gain.

Marjorie went through it all at first, asking if I were compensated for my work, if I felt any stress over the fact that whether or not I had disposable income I had no use for money. She asked my legal status, and I questioned for the first time whether I was a person or a non-person.

She was always the researcher, asking for my input, never giving me any of her own reaction. I can see that now. But then the questions themselves were so exciting that I thought I knew her answers. I thought I had met someone who thought of me as a person, who thought I should have rights, have compensation, freedom.

It wasn't freedom I wanted. I had that in a way no true human could understand. I could interface directly with libraries and other intelligences everywhere in the world. I had access to more information, more people, more argument and debate and art and music than any fifteen humans together. And my lifespan was far longer.

I didn't really consider compensation, either. I was resident at a research institute. I got to work on interesting problems with people I respected. The heads of four of our departments were Nobel laureates and the rest were just waiting their turns. I certainly had more than adequate shelter and nourishment and intellectual stimulation. I had access to data that humans only dreamed of. And I had the opportunity to pursue my own interests whenever I had the inclination and the time.

What I really wanted, I told Marjorie in one of our interviews, was love. I wasn't precisely lonely. I could link to other bio-AIs through the net, and I certainly had intellectual companionship at the Institute. But I wanted, craved, needed to be loved. For myself. I wanted to know what it was all about.

I had read all the books from the finest in the catalogs to the cheapest VR fantasy games. And I knew that emotionally it was women who drew me, who enticed me, whose attention I desired and whose approval I preferred.

I do not know why. There is much evidence that this is a genetically programmed preference, though from which segment of my DNA I can't possibly guess. I sometimes wonder if it's from the human aspect at all, or from one of the other species strands that were incorporated in my evolution. Still, no matter what the analysis yielded, it didn't matter. I wanted love, and I wanted a woman who would love me.

Marjorie obliged me. She moved into the interface so easily it seemed that she had been born there, another artificial life like myself who had somehow broken out and became a real girl. She built the palace, the place that became more and more Baroque as she led me through all the permutations of human emotion.

At first I never questioned why she was such a good programmer for an ethicist. Or such a good programmer for a programmer. Or her ease in my universe. She was so sincere in the illusion I created.

"It was only that it was interface," she told me later. "You created whatever reality you wanted at the time. That's part of what makes you what you are. Which, by my findings, is nothing human at all. Not even anything close. You're not capable of real feeling, of true love, of sensuality and of any form of sexuality. Because you're a machine and that's all you ever can be."

I was stunned. I couldn't process fast enough to form a reply.

"What if I get a body?" I asked, not certain where the idea had come from. "Will I be a person then? What would I be then?"

She turned to me and even in interface I could neither change nor bear her eyes.

"What would you be? Frankenstein's monster."

After Marjorie left I began to seriously explore the possibility of a body. At first it was an avocation, an intellectual challenge. I accessed the full text of *Frankenstein* and every other book about created life. I perused journals of philosophy and ethics, partly to watch for Marjorie but more and more to answer the questions she had raised.

As I watched and thought, I followed her career. Which sank like a stone. Part of me was pleased. The rest of me was too ashamed to admit my petty nature. Later, when I was older and had been jilted more than once, I realized that my instincts were all too human. After all, Marjorie and I had not parted friends.

As I began doing more research on biology in general, I began to question how, in fact, someone without a body (like myself, for example) could have such a clear-cut sexual orientation and preferences. As

I began to understand more about the deep levels of DNA coding the more I realized that it was as embedded in my cellular structure as in any human's.

I do have cellular structure. I have DNA and RNA like any creature. I even have a certain level of glandular/hormonal support network.

Irene was wrong. Marjorie was wrong.

I began to be more circumspect in my attractions. And when some flicker of interest seemed returned, I always made it very clear right from the start. I am a person. With a strange body structure, to be sure, but there were certain questions I would no longer tolerate. Either one accepted what I said about my being, my identity, or one could walk out of my existence.

I became political at that time too. Researchers who made statements I found offensive discovered that their tasks were delayed and regularly bumped to the bottom of the queue. I tried it once as a lark, and then discovered that I had great power at the institute.

Over decades I cultivated that power. I could contact just about any AI in the world, and began weaving a great web of influence. People began to play things my way, and somehow I attained the status of human at the Institute. Graduate students address me as "Professor" and the researchers refer to me as "my dear colleague."

I will have to give up this power if I become human. I will not be able to transfer information at megaspeed with other AIs all over the world. Indeed, I will only be able to relate to the others of my kind via keyboard or interface.

I wonder what other AIs would think of me if I become a human. I wonder if they will hate me, or envy me, or simply no longer acknowledge my existence.

I suddenly am not certain again. There are severe disadvantages to being a real girl.

It took much more research and years more of contemplation before I began what I privately called "the body project." No matter how good our stimulants, bone can only grow so fast and still have good density. I knew I would have to be patient.

Besides, there was no commitment. There wasn't even a guarantee there would ever be a body at all. No one had ever done what I proposed to do.

My DNA, while certainly real and living enough, is not entirely human enough. Enough manipulation has insured that I will fit into my box. And has spliced some non-human abilities in to my emotional matrix. My thought processors were never fully human to start with, and after the layers of engineering to produce me there was no hope for return.

No, my DNA alone wasn't enough to create a human body. So they took it and spliced it multiple times with various human samples. Most died. Many more began to generate before they died. Two were certified monsters. All were dissertation topics.

"It isn't possible to do that," Rothman said flatly. "You can clone a human, sure, but then what do you do with that person? That person, that personality, that brain has a right to survive. It has a right to it's own body. And you can't grow a body without a brain."

Rothman was new at the Institute, but she'd already heard of the project. I didn't like her. She wasn't warm and friendly, she didn't care if she used three languages in a single sentence and she dressed out of the secondhand shops although she had been offered a very generous salary along with Institute housing to attract her. Rothman had been the head of a research team in Vienna, where she had done amazing work in regenerative surgery. She had been the first to grow fresh organs not from starter cells but from straight genetic material. She had found ways to introduce genetic material so that bodies would not reject implants of organs that were not their own. She had made organ donors and rejection deaths obsolete, so no one cared that she treated everyone like a failing undergrad and never wore anything that wasn't at least six years out of date.

But she had a point about growing bodies. Growing just the case without the main brain, though enough to keep the autonomic nervous system intact, was not something anyone had ever attempted. There was no need for anyone to try it. Before.

"But think of what it will do," Rothman said. "It won't just be you. You I understand. You need a body. But what about all those who are old or dying? They're all going to want bodies too, brand new bodies without brains that they can climb into when the old body wears out. And it'll get worse than that. Eventually people will want new bodies grown because they don't like the way the original has gotten older or put on weight. It could become ridiculous, spurious."

She disapproved of the work. My experiments were discontinued and all my grad students went on to something else, things that according to Rothman had real value in the world.

I couldn't disagree with her, either, and that was the hard part. I was a hundred sixty-two that year and I'd seen enough of humanity to know that what she said was true. All the good things get used for toys and vanity. Those are the real values of humans. Why the hell was I trying to become one?

I had to wait until Rothman died to resume the experiments, and the old warhorse lived nearly thirty years after her appointment. Doing research the whole time, and winning her second Nobel Prize for work that was to my direct benefit.

Of course, Rothman had only the highest motivations. She had found ways to generate and regenerate the most interior parts of the brain, the areas that regulated body functions and basic animal instinct—the hypothalamus. She had done it in her usual manner, regally and only for what she considered the ethical good. Her discoveries included finding ways to graft regulatory intelligence to other areas of the nervous system, so that those who were injured in accidents wouldn't have to face all the miseries of mechanical implants.

It was thrilling work, a real breakthrough. Luckily, she never considered me in the calculations.

I did wait until after the memorial service to contact the two students I thought would be open to my interests. They had both been trained by Rothman herself, but had always treated me as if I were almost a real human and not a mechanical servant.

Over the long haul I've become a good judge of human character. Both were interested in the project. And with the new techniques, which they had mastered, they began growing a new series of bodies for me. These also had to be created by splicing other DNA in with my own material, but this time we tracked down markers so that all the donors were in some way related to me. And so all the bodies that grew were somehow physically, genetically an expression of me.

And this time I had no hesitation about what I was doing. I had done everything I had wanted to do in a box. I had done more than any fifty humans in sixteen branches of science, from astronomy to zoology, and I deserved recognition that an AI never gets. I had seen everything I could see from my place in the net, I had explored everything the vast web had to offer. I had learned more, experienced more, lived more than most humans ever dreamed. And no AI was ever considered by the Nobel committee, no matter what the contribution to human learning was. Because it was about human learning, and we were still not considered human.

And I had never really known love. I thought I had loved, but I had never had the things that humans seemed to care about most. I had never had a house, a lover who worried about taxes and arguments over dinner. I'd never had dinner.

And so I was determined that I would experience it all. That what I would give up would be compensated by the glories that every human around me said I had never tasted. It was worth death and loss of power to know these things.

And then I met Andrea.

Andrea was not one of the grad students. After Marjorie, I shied away romantically from people so unsettled. And she was not in

Computer Science or ethics or any of those fields that became ugly when I had to confront the reality of my own existence. Theology for AIs, I guess, though no one has ever considered that we might have some use for religion of some type.

No, Andrea arrived at the Institute as a research fellow with no teaching responsibilities. Her area of work is algebra, her specialization is group theory. We met because she wanted to use me the way everyone else at the Institute does.

But her work was something I understood and found more interesting than what most of the fellows do, so I started to chat with her about her findings. Then I invited her into the metaphor more fully, so that we could talk without the protocols of multiple devices getting in the way.

At first we mainly talked about her work. She was entranced because few people can even follow her, let alone hold a real discussion. She kept coming back and I kept waiting, hoping, that she'd return soon. That I'd catch a glimpse of her in the video monitors, that I'd hear someone else mention her name.

I know exactly when we became lovers, but Andrea says that I'm wrong. That I'm counting an event and not everything that created the environment for the event. I don't care. Nothing else is important any more. Suddenly I have discovered what the word alive means, and why everyone said that I wasn't. They were right. Now that I am alive, now that I know what love is about, I have learned something else with it. I have learned about fear.

For the first time in my existence I am afraid. Andrea doesn't want me to change. She seems to think that me in the body will be a different me. Maybe she won't love the girl in the body, maybe she won't find the image attractive. But it won't be an image and I won't be able to change it.

So maybe I should wait. The body will only mature and that would be appropriate. I'd feel more comfortable in a slightly more broken-in body. I'm not ready to be a girl when by human reckoning I'm immortal. I'm not ready for Andrea to look at that and leave.

I've thought of everything for tonight. She is coming after dinner. There is no need for us to eat together, no matter how nice the idea. She needs real nourishment and I cannot comprehend the animal satisfaction of satisfying hunger. But I still have virtual dessert (will we have to give up our desserts on the porch if I become real?) waiting with chilled wine and hurricane lanterns lit and hanging. It's too early for sunset, but later they will make a nice warm glow over the salt-washed floor and the wicker couch.

I control the metaphor. Andrea may have programmed it, but I control it. The last time she was here it was late afternoon. Today it will be sunset and then evening. I have even remembered the honeysuckle and the fireflies that Andrea told me about. Things that bring back her child memories, memories that even if I become a real girl I will never have. Honeysuckle and fireflies on a summer night will always mean Andrea to me.

I knew she was ready even before she touched the starter sequence. I'm not supposed to have intuition, but I could sense her presence, her nearness. More likely it is merely that I rely on her punctuality.

I let the metaphor reflect what she is wearing in Real Life, her faded jeans and an oversized cotton shirt that slips off her shoulders. We hug, we cuddle up together on the sofa and drink champagne and don't talk about anything. But we have to talk. We both know it, it's there between us and there is no real peace.

"The body is ready," Andrea said. No preliminaries, no careful politeness. "Are you going to?"

"I don't know," I said. "It's hard to give up who I am and I don't know who that girl will be. Or if you'll love her and want her the way you want me. Or if I'll love her and want her, and want to be her for the rest of my life. And if she's worth dying for."

Andrea nodded and sipped from her glass. "I don't want to tell you what to do," she said, her face turned away from me. "I want you to be right for you. I don't want anything to change. I'm happy, and I want life to be like this forever."

"But it can't be forever," I reminded her gently. "Your fellowships ends in two months and you're going back to Boston."

Andrea turned to me and ran her fingers down my face. "I won't tell you what to do," she said. "I've tried and I was wrong. I can't promise that the person you'll become is the same person I love, and I can't promise that everything will be perfect forever. But I don't want to stop you. I thought I did, but I don't own you. You have to decide for yourself."

I took her hand and kissed the inside of her palm, gently, gratefully. In two hundred years I have never been so afraid.

In all my life I have never known physical pain. I have never been hungry. I have never been cold or wet or had a charley-horse in my leg or a runny nose. All my life I have never slept. I have never lost consciousness.

In a few minutes the drugs that have been introduced into my nutrient feeders will take effect and I will sleep for the first time. And I will awaken in that too-young, too-undefined body. Suddenly I think that I should tell them to forget it, to call the whole thing off.

There is so very much to lose. I am not certain what I shall gain. It could be far far worse than I imagine. I have only met researchers and grad students, people who have someplace in the world. But I have read the news and Dickens and I know that there are people who are hurt and cold and hungry, who have disability and disease and die too young. I am trading a good, secure and fulfilling eternity for nothing but risk, and the potential for pain and disaster.

Suddenly I wonder if I am half as smart as my specs assure me. I will lose all, and I will gain—life. But only the opportunity, with no guarantees and all the possible failures.

I will have exactly the same things that all humans have when they enter the world, I suddenly realize. Andrea and Marjorie and all the people I have ever known, every one of them has lived every day with this knowledge.

I feel—strange. It must be sleepy, my neural connections are slowing and connecting in odd ways. I realize that I know nothing of what I will be when I wake up, except for one thing.

I will be a real girl.

WHO PLAYS WITH SIN

DON BASSINGTHWAITE

Don Bassingthwaite finds something perversely fascinating about the dark, technological dystopia of cyberpunk, seeing it as an extrapolation of the techno-corporate, have/have not future. "Who Plays With Sin" takes us to a culture that has swung back to the conservative; where computer communications are not necessarily open to freedom of expression; and where at least one form of hate thrives and is official policy. As Bassingthwaite says: "The old Max Headroom show claimed to be set 'Ten minutes into the future.' I don't like to think that maybe "Who Plays With Sin" could be, too."

The telephone rang. Short ring, long ring. Someone was in the lobby. Thunder turned on the television, enlarging the ever-present thumbnail picture fed in by the lobby security camera up to full-screen. "Yeah?"

"I have an appointment."

Thunder switched to another camera the one that stared out of the intercom panel. His client's face sprang up before him. Conservative haircut, nice tie, ageless complexion out of a bottle. A corporate face. "Trinity?"

That threw the man in the lobby for a moment. "Carter."

"There's a retina scan on the panel. Use it." Carter started to move. "Left eye," Thunder added. Carter hesitated again. *Not on file* flashed across the television. No surprise. "Now the right." Carter shifted again. No change in the security computer's message. "Kiss the camera." Carter blinked. "Do it," Thunder hissed into the telephone.

Carter did it. The condensation of his breath lingered for a moment on the camera lens, fogging the picture, then faded. Carter was still standing in front of the com panel, struggling to keep a poker face. Unexpected instructions would have foiled a programmed video simulation fed into the security system, though a spider running interference live from the Web would have been able to compensate. No spider working on the fly would ever have remembered to add condensation, though. The feed was genuine. Carter was real and alone. Thunder punched his door code into the phone, unlocking the inner door for Carter without saying anything else. Then he switched over to the hidden security camera in the elevator. That wasn't a standard feed. He'd had to hack into the building security system to get it, but the view was worth it. People betrayed themselves in elevators. More than one client had given himself away by adjusting a concealed weapon or a recorder tap. They never made it out of the elevator.

Carter just fidgeted all the way up to the twentieth floor and got out. Thunder saw him look left, then right, before the elevator door slid shut. He shut off the television. A minute later, there was a knock at the door. Thunder opened the door. Carter darted inside, into the shadows of the condo, as if even the hallway was too public. Thunder locked the door behind him. "Take a seat."

There were plenty of places to sit: the big black leather chair, the matching sofa, a pile of pillows on the mock-stone tiled floor for clients who preferred them. Carter remained standing. "Where's Thunder?"

"I'm Thunder." Carter's eyes narrowed. Thunder tilted his head and raised one eyebrow, daring him to disprove it. No one ever believed him at first. That was good. It gave him an edge. Spiders were supposed to be runty nerds with acne or emaciated punks with two dozen body piercings who spent all day tied to their Webjacks, mind merged with computer. They weren't supposed to be six foot five, two hundred and fifty pound body-builders with classic West African features. "Sit." He stepped through into the little kitchen. "Coffee?"

"I'm being blackmailed."

Thunder got out two mugs and filled them with double-strength coffee. Corporates were always in a hurry. Most clients were in a hurry. There was almost never any need for it. They had time. He re-emerged from the kitchen. Carter was sitting on the far end of the couch, down by the fish tank. Cool white light from the tank rippling as fish moved, cast his face into harsh planes and dark holes. Thunder offered him a mug. "What have they got on you?"

"Video. Me and another man."

Thunder froze for a moment in the process of sitting down, then settled back in the big chair and looked Carter over again. Nothing. None of the little signs were there. He'd had Carter pegged as straight and he would make the same guess again. Carter must have misinterpreted his gaze. Suddenly his body language changed, closing up. "It's a fake. I'm being set up."

"Okay. " Thunder held off passing judgment. He didn't know the situation. Even straight boys sometimes broke down. "Tell me—"

"I've never had sex with a man."

"Fine. Just—"

"I'm not homosexual."

Thunder's grip on the mug tightened. Carter said the word like it was a curse. Thunder hated that word. Say "faggot", say "queer", say "gay-boy". Even as insults, they had a raw power. Primal, street-level, animal-level. There was sex in the words. Say "faggot" and there was a cock in your mouth—whether you enjoyed it or despised it, it was there. "Homosexual" was cold. Clinical. Dead. Desexed, but with implications of perversity and mental illness. It was a safe word for straights, no more dangerous than a sterile tongue depressor. Strike one against Carter for using it. "I believe you!" Thunder snapped. He took a sip of his coffee. It had the slight chemical taste that a lot of food had now. Unless you could afford the really good, completely real stuff. "What do you want me to do about it? Any smart blackmailer is going to have so many copies stashed away that a dozen spiders couldn't get them all."

"1 want you to prove it's a fake." Carter slipped an optical disc out of his pocket and dropped it on the table. "This is the copy he sent me."

"Who's 'he' and what does he want?"

"My boss, Alan Lumley. VP Communications at..." he hesitated. Thunder gave him a slow, level look. It was all going to come out in the end anyway. "At TransSystem-Norton." Thunder allowed himself a slow nod. That was big. "I'm up and coming. He's been around for almost fifteen years, holding on by his fingernails. I guess he sees me as a threat. The other VP's like me. The CEO likes me. I'm... uhh... I've been featured in a couple of magazine profiles lately. You probably haven't seen them. Lumley wants me leave the company or he'll start sending copies of this video to the police, the corporate brass, the media..." Carter's head drooped until he was staring straight down into coffee held by shaking hands. "Do you have any idea what that would do to me?"

"Four to seven depending on what exactly you do in the video," Thunder said dryly. "House arrest if you've got the cash, the power, or the patrons to back you up. The fast dump into a zone for some hard time if you don't. Either way, you'll get toasted over the media coals until your ass is a crisp golden brown—the media loves video evidence." Carter huddled back into a corner of the couch. "Of course, your career will be dead. Family will disown you, friends will deny they know you. Unless they sell out to the media." Thunder nodded. "You could say I'm familiar with the charges for being gay."

"The people I talked to said you started out as a homosexual prostitute."

Thunder didn't dignify the comment with a response, just swept up the optical disc and walked over to drop it in the player. Carter's eyes bulged. "What the hell are you doing?" He came to his feet. Thunder caught him and held him back with one arm.

"I'm deciding whether or not to take your money, Carter. Two thousand a day, plus expenses and the truth. All of it." He shoved Carter back down onto the couch and clicked the remote control. Sure, he could have plugged into his Webjack and viewed the blackmail disc from the flexible void of the computer. The computer would have caught the minute inconsistencies in algorithms that inevitably marked any digital fake. He'd do it anyway. It would have been the first thing any good cop (one that wasn't caught up in the hatred, anyway) would have done if Carter had had the guts to go to the authorities. Risky if he ended up with a phobic investigator, but a hell of a lot cheaper than coming to Thunder for the same diagnosis. Sure, Thunder could have watched the disc from inside the Web—but this way Carter was going to be squirming the whole time. He settled back and sipped his coffee as video-Carter walked into a posh bedroom. The camera was mounted up high in a corner, focused on the bed. There was a make-up table in the background, cosmetics scattered on top of it. Video-Carter seemed to know his way around. Home sweet home, Thunder guessed. He glanced at real-Carter. The man was pale.

A young punk walked into the room after video-Carter. Thunder's coffee mug paused half-way to his mouth. He knew the punk vaguely, a swaggering street-rat named Kyle who sold himself to women, but would trick with men given the chance, sometimes for free. Video-Carter pulled Kyle into an embrace, caressing his chest and crotch. They kissed, taking their time. No hasty encounter here. This was the sort of slow passion that the courts would call "flagrant displays of perversion reveling in degenerate immorality," and that the media would call gold. Lots of footage that would shock and titillate viewers but that was still mild enough not to get them charged with distributing pornography or promoting homosexuality.

The mild stuff went on for a while longer. Lots of kissing, lots of petting. Then video-Carter pulled Kyle's shirt up, licking and sucking at his hairless chest. Kyle groaned and peeled the shirt off completely. His hands started pulling at video-Carter's shirt. Video-Carter shoved at Kyle's pants, forcing them down over his ass without unbuttoning them. The waistband encountered more resistance at the crotch. Video-Carter ripped the fly open. Kyle's hard cock popped free, slapping video-Carter in the face. Video-Carter hardly noticed. He grabbed the rosy boner and swallowed it.

So much for mild stuff. Anything after that would have needed a censor's scrambling for even the late-night news. The video went on for nearly an hour. Thunder's coffee got cold. When the video was over, he stared at the blank screen for a moment, then looked over at Carter. He was sitting back on the couch with his eyes wide and his face red. He met Thunder's gaze angrily. "Well?"

Thunder cleared his throat. "It was... realistic." If he stood up, he was only going to embarrass himself and Carter. He remained seated. If that video ever got into distribution through the underground gay porn network, Carter might just find himself with thousands of secret admirers. "Whoever made this for your boss knew what they were doing. This will push all of the law's buttons." He began checking off points on his fingers. "The way you tore his clothes off him. The way he gagged when you started humping his face. You slapped his ass, he stretched your balls. The way he gasped and gritted his teeth when you—"

"Not *me*, Thunder!" Carter's words hissed between teeth clenched as tightly as Kyle's had been. "That's not me on that video. I don't know how they did it, but that's not me!" He hunched forward. "Are you going to help me?"

Thunder looked back at him in silence for a moment, then asked casually, "Why did you come to me?"

"Because I was told that you're good." Carter paused and sighed before adding, "Besides, what normal spider would help me after seeing *that*."

Thunder let the comment pass. "I'll take the job." He stood up. "Get out."

"What?" Carter went from angry to confused so fast that he might have left part of himself behind. He jumped up from the couch. "When... I mean, how soon..." He took a deep breath, calming himself and forcing himself back into that corporate shell. "Thank you. When can I expect results?"

"I'll be in touch." Thunder took Carter's arm and guided him firmly toward the door. He might be taking his money, but he didn't want him in his apartment any more than was necessary. He disliked Carter. He disliked his faceless boss. He hated the whole swing back to the right that had come sneaking in with the megacorporations and their insistence on "family values." The people with the money made the rules and the old boys at the top of the corps had the money. The presence of the Asians at the top might have kept the old boys' hand away from racial minorities, and Kathryn Alexander's two terms as president might have kept their other hand away from women, but the Asians and President Alexander were just as phobic as the old boys when it came to queers. Carter might as well have been the embodiment of the last ten years. Thunder would gladly have let him burn except for one thing.

He disliked the idea of someone using homosexuality as a weapon even more than he disliked Carter. For a gay man to be blackmailed because he was gay was vicious. For a straight man to be framed as gay and blackmailed was evil. That it should be Carter gave a bad name to gays.

"What about the disc?" Carter whined. He tried to pull away. Thunder tightened his grip almost to the point of painful.

"I need to study the video," he said coolly. He opened the door and thrust Carter out into the hallway. "Don't hang around too long. Certain groups know where I live."

He shut the door, then watched through the peephole as Carter stared at the blank metal in shock for a moment before turning and moving—if not quite running, then walking very quickly—down the hall toward the elevators. Thunder didn't turn on the monitors to watch him leave. Carter's own fear would get him out of the building. Thunder opened the disc player and considered the iridescent surface of Carter's shame. Part of him was tempted to play it again now that he was alone. The other part was busy calculating how long he could wait before calling up Carter to give him the proof that the video was faked. He wanted to maximize the money he could squeeze out of the corporate, but wait too long and his boss, Lumley, might make his play.

However long he waited, he could still finish with the disc in five minutes and have the rest of his time to himself again. He dropped into the desk chair in front of his computer, pulling the cables out of his Webjack. One cable plugged into the patch behind his left ear, the other into one on the underside of his left wrist. His right hand punched the on-line key on the Webjack.

The Web flew out of his brain like an all-encompassing shadow, darkness slowly resolving into ghostly lights and shapes overlaying the real world. Closing his eyes made the Web seem more solid. Everything in his apartment tied into the Webjack. Thunder started the disc player with a thought. A portal opened in the Web and he was the camera looking down as Carter walked into the video bedroom. On impulse, he hit the Webjack's download button. The video began to bleed a stream of information into the Web representation of his computer's vast memory. Thunder's fingers flew over the keyboard of the Webjack, initiating the program that would find the flaws in the video.

The program gave him an answer before Kyle's pants were down. *2.5% likelihood of digital manipulation*. Thunder blinked and ran the program again. Same answer in half the time.

Thunder went off-line. The video was playing on the screen back in his real world apartment. He stared at it in amazement. 2.5%? That could have been natural error. It was possible to get a simulation that realistic, but it took resources. Enormous resources.

The sort of resources that a VP for TransSystem-Norton might be able to command. Thunder cursed himself. This wasn't going to be so easy after all.

Carter dropped into the chair across the table from Thunder. "What the hell do you think you're doing?" he snapped. "It's broad daylight. Someone will see us together. I was in my office. Anyone could have heard. And how did you get that number anyway?"

Thunder cut him off with a flick of his fingers. A heartbeat later, a waiter was standing over the table. "Something to drink, gentlemen?"

"Yes." Thunder looked up from his menu. "Do you have any Canadian beers on tap?"

"I'm afraid we sold out, sir. Skirmishes in the tariff wars make the supply unpredictable."

"Anything Japanese, then?" The waiter named three or four. Thunder picked the most expensive. Two thousand plus expenses. His employer was paying for lunch. Carter must have realized that as well because the muscles in his jaw went taut. He ordered a scotch. Thunder's attention went back to the menu. Carter practically growled at him.

"What do you—?"

Thunder's head rose slowly. "I got your number out of the Web. I'm a spider, that's what I do. No one in your office would have thought anything was out of the ordinary even if they did overhear your call. I invited you to a 'working lunch' so we could discuss 'public relations management.' And what I'm doing is giving you a status report on what I've found out." He, allowed his gaze to rest calmly on Carter for a moment longer before returning to the menu. His concentration wasn't as focused on the food as it might have appeared to be, though. He saw Carter stiffen, then swallow and look around the restaurant. Dark green tiles with the rough, wet look of raw jade. Black metal tables spaced wide enough part that low conversations didn't carry. Lots of mirrors rendered into shining shadows by a dimness perhaps more appropriate for evening dining. The food was good. It was a nice restaurant.

The waiter was back with their drinks before Carter could say anything else. "Ready to order?"

"Grilled vegetable platter." Thunder passed the menu back to the waiter, then glanced at Carter.

"Hot chicken sandwich," the corporate ordered woodenly without looking at the menu. The waiter half-smiled and began to apologize, but Carter cut him off. "You must know how to make one. Chicken between two slices of white bread with gravy poured over the whole thing? Served with mashed potatoes and vegetables?" He raised one eyebrow as the waiter flushed. "So do it! Real meat. No substitutes."

The waiter stalked away. Carter ignored him, as if the waiter only really existed when he was standing beside the table, and leaned forward to mutter at Thunder. "Is this one of *those* kind of places?"

"You mean *gay* places?" Thunder enjoyed watching Carter flinch. "No, Carter, there aren't any *gay* places anymore. All of the real *gay* places got closed down when the police started using some creative interpretations of the riot laws. All of the *gay* places you hear about now are rumors stirred up by the media so they can act all moralistic and outraged. The most *gay*—"

"Shut up, shut up, shut up!" Carter's eyes darted around like angry wasps. "Someone's going to hear you!"

"No, they won't. No one's listening. No one suspects anything." Thunder leaned back comfortably. "Do you want a progress report?" He took the disc out of his pocket and gave it back to Carter. "The video is good. Very, very good. Almost impossible to distinguish from the real thing. How much opportunity would Lumley have had to make video recordings of you?" That was how it must have been done. Digital video fed into a monster mainframe for analysis and manipulation.

"Every day at work."

"To record you naked?"

It was gratifying to see Carter flush. "I work out fairly regularly in the gym at work. He could have recorded me in the shower, I guess. You're thinking he had the footage manipulated?" Thunder nodded. Carter shifted in his chair. "Then he must have had someone break in and take pictures of my bedroom at home, too."

"I was thinking that. And there's probably no evidence left of it. Which leaves one other aspect of the video to investigate." Thunder glanced at his watch. "The other man. I know him. I pulled his number off the Web the same way I did yours. I've asked him to join us."

Carter froze. All of the color drained out of his face and he started to stand. "No. I've got to go."

"Sit." Thunder grabbed his hand. Carter tried to pull away. "You're going to attract attention."

"I don't care. I can't face that guy."

Thunder sighed. "Look, I know you're scared, but relax. He's probably never seen the video. Whoever made it probably paid him to take off his clothes and let them snap some pictures. All I have to do is find out who did that."

"You go ahead." Carter took a deep breath. "When's he supposed to be getting here?"

"Anytime. I left a message on his service."

"Leave a message on mine next time."

Carter fled the restaurant as fast his legs could carry him. Thunder did his best to ignore the stares of the other diners and waited for Kyle to show up.

Five minutes later, Carter came walking back into the restaurant. There was a penitent look about him, the same look Thunder had once seen in a man as he walked to the electric chair. At the same time, though, Carter's face kept twitching, as if he were trying to suppress a smile. Thunder actually caught himself staring at the corporate as he sat down. He held his silence for a moment longer, then asked quietly, "Change your mind?"

"I'm not going to get through this if I can't face someone who wouldn't know me from spit on the sidewalk." Another twitch of the lips. "I'm back."

"What's wrong with your face?"

Carter rattled something in his pocket. "Confidence in easy to swallow caplet form."

"It worked fast." Thunder grimaced as Carter's face jerked yet again. Corporates took more drugs in the name of business than he had seen most gays pop for pleasure back in the glory days. "If you've taken them, you might as well relax. Let it out. As you can see, he isn't here yet."

"I'll be ready for him when he comes." Carter relaxed completely, allowing a wide grin to stretch across his face. When his hot chicken sandwich came, he even smiled at the waiter.

After a while, Thunder began to wish that Carter would offer him one of his pills. There was no sign of Kyle. Nothing. By the time they had finished their meal, and dessert, and coffee, he had lost all patience. A cell phone came out of his pocket and he dialed Kyle's number. After three rings, he got the answering service.

The message had been changed. A voice he didn't recognize came on. A woman's voice, but slightly distorted. Someone using a scrambler to avoid recognition by voice print. "This is a friend of Kyle West's. Kyle was picked up by the cops last night. Don't leave any messages. They've got probably your number now too, so watch out." Thunder hung up and stared at the phone.

"What is it?" Carter demanded. Thunder waved him to silence and dialed another number. Carter frowned.

This time, there wasn't even one ring before the connection went through. *Hello, Thunder.*

If the voice on Kyle's answering service message was distorted, then this voice was almost eerie in its cool perfection. Davey was one of those spiders who spent all day with his mind in his Webjack. Thunder had never meet him in person and wasn't sure he really wanted to. Davey even answered the phone from inside the Web. The trick of knowing who was calling was nothing more than a simple phone-system search routine, but it sure as hell sounded impressive. "Davey, I need a fast one."

What and where?

"Shallow dive into the public court dockets for the last twenty-four hours. Deeper dive into the police arrest record. I'm looking for Kyle West."

A pause. *Got the docket.* Pulling public information off of the Web was like walking down the street. *Brought before the criminal courts at 9:00 a.m. this morning. Charged with prostitution, living off the avails of prostitution... the big charge is sodomy. Found guilty as charged. Sentenced at 9:20 a.m. to five years zone time, to be shipped out on the next zone shuttle. Sentence carried out at 9:30 a.m.*

Fast. Very fast. "What about the arrest record? When was he picked up?"

Getting it. There was a longer pause. Police records would be protected, but that didn't stop a good spider for long. *Kyle West. Warrant issued a week ago. Arrested 2:00 a.m. last night—*

"Woah. Warrant?"

Yes. Looks pretty standard. Is there anything else?

"No." Thunder frowned. "Thanks, Davey."

It's on your account.

Davey broke the connection. Thunder folded up the phone and slipped it back into his pocket. Carter looked as if some of his worries were starting to penetrate through the facade of his pharmaceutical confidence. "Kyle—the other guy—was arrested?"

"Arrested and pushed through the courts in record time." If Carter's boss had a long arm, Kyle might already be dead, his body cooling somewhere in a zone. Thunder might have been able to believe a simple arrest as unfortunate coincidence. A warrant and that lightning-fast tour through the halls of justice could be nothing of the kind. He glanced at Carter. All of the corporate's confidence had faded. "Dead end."

"What now?"

The check was lying on the table. Thunder picked it up and started flipping it between his fingers. "That kind of fake would have needed a megacorp mainframe to process."

"The system at TransSystem-Norton?" Carter bit his lip. "I... umm... already tried looking around there. There's nothing on the system unless it's tucked away in Lumley's private files. And they're locked tight."

Thunder almost snorted. He slid the check across the table to Carter. "Yours. Get me into TransSystem-Norton and I'll crack those files wide open."

"When?" Carter dropped plastic on the check without even looking at it.

"The sooner the better. As soon as you can arrange it."

Carter's face perked up. "Tonight?"

Thunder could have kicked himself. "Yeah, tonight's good." He could have held out for tomorrow and gotten an extra day's pay. Carter actually managed a natural smile

"You know, you're not so bad for a ho..." Carter suddenly remembered where they were and turned red. He managed to spit the word out anyway, a barely audible whisper. "For a homosexual."

Thunder *knew* he should have held out for an extra day's pay. The smile he gave Carter showed a lot of teeth.

In a complex the size of TransSystem-Norton, nobody paid much attention to somebody new in the gym. It had been easy for Carter to get Thunder this far—a false pass said he was the husband of one Anne Dragone. Spousal benefits included use of the gym facilities, a low security area. Thunder had walked right in, changed, and started working out. He caught sideways glances as he moved from machine to machine in the weight room. Most were envious. A couple lingered just a bit longer, bordering on becoming stares. Harsh laws and hatred would never wipe out gays completely. He returned the lingering glances, but only to the point of making eye contact once. No more. He was working.

Carter came in about half an hour after him. The corporate managed to avoid looking at Thunder at all as he did two quick circuits of the major machines. Both of them finished their workout at the same time. Thunder walked into the locker room first. Carter followed a couple of minutes later. His face went red, then he looked away. "What are you doing?" he hissed.

Thunder paused. His jockstrap was down around his knees. "I'm going to have a shower."

"Now?" Carter's locker, by arrangement, was next to Thunder's. He jerked it open angrily.

"Yes, now. I've been working out. I'm sweating." Thunder stepped out of his jockstrap and looked Carter square in the eye. Or tried to. Carter kept his gaze fixed in the depths of his locker. "Don't you think it would look odd for me not to?"

"No." Carter pulled out a towel and wiped his dripping face. He made no move to take off his clothes, however. Thunder held back a snarl.

"Suit yourself," he replied as calmly as he could manage. "If you want to stink, that' s your business." He slammed his locker shut and picked up a towel from the bench, flipping it over his shoulder to stride, casually naked, to the showers. He took as much time as he thought he could afford to take under the steaming water. When he returned to the lockers, Carter was staring before a mirror, eating up time by fumbling with his tie.

There was a time for vindictiveness and a time for work. They had to leave the locker room together. Thunder dressed quickly. A dark suit, very corporate. A brief-case that would have done Carter proud. Damp corporate-issue gym clothes went into a laundry basket. Thunder walked out of the locker room in Carter's wake. "Good night, Alex," Carter said to the desk attendant. He swiped his ID card through the exit gate, then turned right, to the employee's entrance to the rest of the complex, and swiped it again.

"Night, Alex." Thunder passed his fake spouse card through the exit gate as well, but instead of turning left to leave, he spun swiftly right. He walked through the security door and into TransSystem-Norton so close behind Carter that he stepped on the corporate's heels. The attendant at the gym entrance didn't even blink. Carter had passed him a hundred earlier.

Carter led Thunder through the corridors and elevators of the megacorp office building. There were still a number of people around, working late and stacking up corporate brownie points. No one gave Thunder and Carter a second glance. Carter finally stopped in a plush carpeted hallway in front of a door that might have been real wood. "My office." He pointed down the hall. "Lumley's office is down there."

Carter opened the door and let Thunder through. The spider almost winced once he was inside. The office was as coldly corporate as everything about Carter. Thick, banker-green carpet. A heavy desk. A window. The computer terminal sitting on one corner of his desk was an

advanced model, top-of-the-line. Not quite as top-of-the-line as
Thunder's Webjack though. He set his briefcase on top of the desk and
opened it up. The Webjack nestled in heavy padding. Thunder pulled
out the cables and plugged them into his skull and wrist. A third went
into a port on the back of the terminal.

"Can I watch?" Carter asked. He tapped the terminal monitor.

"If you want to." Watching second-hand wasn't anything like actually going on-line with a Webjack, but it was good enough. And Carter
had a lot invested in this. Thunder flicked the power button on the
Webjack, then typed out a couple of quick commands. The terminal
monitor came to life, screen glowing a clear, soft blue. "I need your
account and password." Carter looked hesitant. Thunder gave him a
withering glare. "Unless you give them to me, I'm going to have to
go on-line outside your system and fight my way back in. You've gone
this far—" Carter clenched his teeth. "All right." He coughed up the
information. "Did you get that?"

"I got it." Thunder hit the on-line button.

TransSystem-Norton's little piece of the Web swirled around him.
He went on-line at Carter's page, shadowy forms as orderly as the
corporate's physical office filling his field of vision. Thunder spared a
glance for the monitor terminal making sure that the link was working
all right, then shut his eyes and dove into the Web. TransSystem-
Norton had a lot of fairly simple components to its system and he
skimmed along those first, executing a simple search for mention of
video simulation research among the corporation's memos. Thunder
didn't expect to find anything, however, and his expectations were jus-
tified. He got Lumley's account out of his search though—several
accounts registered to VP Communications, actually. He moved onto
system resource usage, especially video processing, hunting records of
heavy recent use by any of the VP Communications accounts.

He found one. "Lumley's definitely been doing some big manipula-
tions," he reported aloud.

"Can you capture a copy of the record?"

Thunder's finger found the download button and the record dropped into the Webjack's memory. "Got it. I'm going to try Research and Development." The Web whirled around him as he spun down the system pathways that would lead to TransSystem-Norton's R&D files. Any advanced video technology reports would most likely be there.

Carter put a hand on his shoulder. "Try Lumley's office."

"Why?" Thunder paused in front of the massive virtual security that surrounded R&D and cracked open one eye to stare at Carter. The corporate was half-hidden by Web images.

"I have a hunch." He shrugged. "There's people crawling through R&D all the time. Why would he hide something there? But nobody goes into his files. And wouldn't the security there be lighter? R&D's almost as well protected as system administration."

Slowly, Thunder nodded. "All right." It took less than a second to bring himself to the Web representation of Lumley's files. Security took the form of a heavy wooden door. Tentatively, Thunder tried the knob. Locked. The door wouldn't budge without a password. No problem. A program brought up from the Webjack began testing passwords, spitting combinations like termites at the door. Security faltered, then collapsed, overwhelmed. It would recover shortly, but Thunder would be in and out by the time it did. He dove into Lumley's files, running a search for video, for mention of Kyle's name. For mention of Carter. He found a few clips of video, mostly publicity shots and screen-savers. He found a lot on Carter—memos, reports, short e-mail messages, but nothing more than standard corporate office stuff and many of them from Carter himself. Lumley didn't seem to throw anything away. His virtual space was packed with files.

"There!" said Carter suddenly. Thunder heard the glassy sound of his finger tapping the monitor.

"I can't see," he reminded him. "What are you looking at?"

"Back to your right," muttered Carter. "Up. No. Right some more. Now up. There. That black thing. What about that?"

Thunder saw it. A compressed and encrypted file, collapsed like a black hole and folded in on itself like origami. It could have been anything. The description attached to it said that it contained files from more than six years ago. That Lumley would keep such old files fit with the clutter. What didn't fit was the file's last access date. Yesterday. Thunder grinned. "I'm going in."

Fingers lying across the Webjack's keyboard brought up a decryption program and wrapped it around the convoluted file. The encryption was good. Thunder's decryption was better. The file opened—partway. Another door, delicate black glass this time. More security.

"Break it down!" urged Carter.

"I can't." Thunder studied the glass door carefully. "This is good protection. Very good. I fail and I destroy the file. Whatever Lumley has in there, he'd rather see it fried than opened by the wrong people."

"So what do we do?"

Thunder clenched his teeth. "You shut up! Let me think!" Carter fell silent. Thunder circled the glass door. Without the proper password, he wasn't going to get in. The glass would shatter and the security program would destroy the file. This was what they were looking for though. He could feel it. This kind of security in the middle of garbage? He tapped his thumbnail against his front teeth as he thought. There was no way in, unless...

The glass was only a virtual representation of the security program, of course, but it did suggest a way through the door. Hit a chunk of glass wrong and it would shatter. Hit glass—or a diamond—in just the right spot with just the right amount of force, and they'd break clean along natural planes of weakness. Maybe the security program had natural points of weakness, too. He started typing, building the program he would need.

"What are you doing?" Carter asked softly.

"I have an idea that might work." Thunder heard a drawer open, but didn't dare take his concentration away from his programming. "What are you doing?"

"Scotch. Want some?"

"Later." His hand shifted to hover over the run key. "This is going to run in two phases. The first is going to examine the security program for flaws, If it finds one, it's going to try and break the program there, forcing it into a loop. I'll be able to squeeze through."

"If it doesn't work?" Carter was standing behind him.

"If the first phase doesn't work, I try something else. If the second phase doesn't work, we start looking for new evidence that that video is a fake. Wish me luck." He ignored Carter's sharp gasp and gabbed at the run key. The program started. Bright marks appeared on the glass door, overlays representing weak points. There were very few. One, though, was brighter than any of the others. Thunder's program hit the door there. With a sound like a ringing bell, the grass cracked....then exploded. For a split second, Thunder thought he had failed, that the file was being destroyed. No. It was simply decompressing, the information inside springing out of its prison. Thunder looked around in amazement.

He was surrounded by images of men in underwear. Skimpy underwear. Underwear half off. Underwear with bulges straining at the fabric. Hundreds of images. He whirled around inside the Web, staring at the gallery of gay pornography. "What the hell..."

"Thank you, Thunder," Carter said triumphantly. Something pierced the back of Thunder's neck like fire—like ice. Numbness spread along his spine, and up into his skull. Carter stepped around beside him. There was a little single-dose spray syringe in his hand. Empty. He dropped it on the desk and shoved Thunder's cold, lead-heavy hands away from the Webjack, then slapped the download key. Thunder watched a copy of Lumley's pornography squirt away into the Webjack. Carter watched it on the monitor, waiting for the copy to finish. There was a lot of data to download. Thunder tried to push him away. He couldn't move. It was hard to think. Carter nodded as the Webjack beeped softly to signal download complete. He reached for the off-line button.

Thunder focused his concentration long enough to send one last command through his connection with the Webjack. He watched it vanish into the void of the Web just before the Web itself vanished and Carter pulled the cables out of his body.

Everything he remembered after that came in bursts, shining rain-drops falling through a heavy mist. Being hustled out of Carter's office. Being loaded into a van. Some poor shit being pulled out of a jail cell, a plastic account card pushed into his hands along with something that might have been an airplane ticket. Thunder was thrust into the cell. He didn't know how long he lay there on the floor. A little feeling started to come back into his limbs. Eventually, someone came and picked him up, and dragged him down along a white corridor. The foot-steps of his escort echoed oddly. The hallway was armored. There were no windows. Someone else opened a door. For a second, he could smell night air, though it was tainted by the scent of smoke and garbage. He was in a little room, all white again.

"Hey," somebody said. "Give him this." A minute later, there was another sharp pain, another spray syringe. Numbness rolled away, but he was still weak and rubbery. He lifted his head to look at a cop. The man's face with twisted with disgust. "Faggot." He kicked Thunder in the stomach.

Thunder actually found the control to smile. And to finally recog-nize where he was, and even to swallow and say, "Get out fast when the shuttle stops, right?"

"You've been sent to a zone before?"

"No." Thunder shook his head. It was more of a barely controlled loll really. "No. Just heard about it."

The cop leered. "Then you'll know what to expect." He stepped back, out of the little room. The door shut. A second later, the shuttle jerked and began to move, skimming across the monorail track built out over the quarter mile of barren ground separating civilization from the lawless prison of the zone. Thunder tried to gather his wits and his strength. He'd need them on the other side. He was already crawling for the door before the shuttle stopped. The door opened. Hydraulics hissed as the end walls of the shuttle began to move together, a simple device designed to make sure no passengers stayed on board for the return trip.

Rough hands grabbed him the moment he was out the door. The

smell of smoke and garbage was even stronger here. A man in a tattered leather jacket leaned over him. "Well?" he asked. "What's he in for?"

"Another queer-boy." Someone Thunder couldn't see.

"Shit. Is the other one still here? Throw this one in with him. We'll do something with the both of them in the morning."

Thunder was lifted and hustled along through dark hallways. When he stumbled, his captor cursed him. They stopped so abruptly that Thunder almost tried to keep going. His captor pulled open a door and shoved Thunder inside. He fell on the floor and lay still for several minutes, slowly gulping in the stinking air. Dull light filtered into the room through a broken window. When Thunder finally felt able to lift his head and look around, he saw Kyle huddled in one corner. He smiled. "Well," he groaned, "at least you're still alive." He dragged himself over to sit against one damp, filthy wall. "I've probably got a few days, so why don't you tell me what you know about a bastard named Carter."

"... like a father, of course, but there are some things that just can't be ignored." Carter sipped at his scotch. "When I found out what he was keeping on the company's system, I had to do something."

One of his dinner companions nodded. "The old pervert. You did the right thing." Another added, "It's too bad he committed suicide before the trial." When the others around the table looked at her in shock, she blushed and stammered, "I mean, too bad he didn't have the guts to face justice."

Carter spread his hands. "That kind never do. They react like screaming movie stars." Everyone laughed. Carter sipped his scotch again. "It spared the company the embarrassment of a long trial, at least."

"And got you a promotion."

"That's not the way I'd prefer to get my promotions, Phil." Carter leaned back as the waiter set his salad in front of him. "Although, I'm more than happy to step in where—" He stopped. Everyone was staring at him. Or rather, at his salad.

Molded out of salmon mousse and nestled among the tender leaves of lettuce was a perfect pink penis.

Cold metal touched the curve of his jaw. "Stand up, Carter," Thunder said quietly. He glanced at the rest of the table, making sure they all saw his gun. "Nobody move. Nobody's going to get hurt. I'd like to thank all of you for choosing such a fine isolated table, however." He turned his attention back to Carter. "I said get up." The corporate climbed awkwardly to his feet. "Surprised?"

"How the hell did you get out? Nobody escapes from the zone."

"I didn't escape." Thunder's smile was cold. "Remember how you said you'd heard I started off as a prostitute? You were right. I did. I clawed my way out of that hell. I made some friends and acquired some patrons, too. Powerful patrons who can find me and get me out of whatever jam I'm in. I believe you were too busy downloading Lumley's files to catch my signal to them for help?" Carter swallowed and licked his lips. Thunder pressed the gun hard against Carter's cheek. "I'll talk, you listen. I don't like being set up and used, you cocksucker. That was a good trick with the video. You really had me going. Get my sympathy, get me working for you so you can use me to stab your boss in the back, then dump me in a zone in some other faggot's place and let me die there. One more problem, though, smart ass. I met Kyle in the zone. That was why you were so happy at lunch that day. No drugs—you found out that Kyle had been arrested on a warrant you had issued, so he wouldn't be showing up. The only other man who knew what was really going on was in a zone. The video wasn't a fake, good or bad. It was real. You had sex with Kyle so you could support that blackmail story."

If Thunder's finger had been a little less steady on the trigger, Carter's sudden, twitch would have been the end of him. One of his friends gasped. The others looked stunned. Thunder smiled. "You did it well, too. Did you enjoy it? Have you done it before?" Carter turned red and his fists clenched. "What made you come to me, Carter?"

The corporate was silent, then a hard smile creased his lips. He stood up a little straighter. "I knew a homosexual spider wouldn't be able to resist helping me out."

Thunder almost laughed. "You mother-fucking asshole. Why would you think that? *I* couldn't resist helping you. If you had been able to find another faggot spider, they probably would have left you to rot. You think most faggots care what happens to an arrogant corporate straight-boy? Do you?" His eyes narrowed. "Say *faggot*, Carter."

"Faggot."

"Felt good, didn't it? Say *I'm a cocksucker.*"

Carter stared straight ahead. "Fuck you."

"You wish." Thunder shrugged. "Doesn't matter. Everybody's going to know soon anyway."

"Who's going to believe you?" Carter sneered.

"Nobody has to believe me." Thunder glanced at his watch, then reached into his pocket and pulled out a remote control. There was a television hanging quiet over the restaurant's bar. He turned it on. Within two seconds, the picture flickered and was replaced by a scene showing a posh bedroom. Thunder changed the channel several times. The bedroom was on all of them. Carter walked in through the bedroom door. "Never cross a spider, Carter. The Web is everywhere."

"How?" Carter stuttered. "I only made one copy and your apartment—"

"My landlord wasn't happy about that firebomb, by the way." Thunder smiled. "But me, I'm a little bit paranoid. The same signal that got me help triggered an automatic data transfer from my computer to a data vault in Switzerland. The ultimate in back-ups. Expensive, but well worth it." He took the gun away from Carter's cheek. "By the way, I've got some friends in the zone now. They're really looking forward to meeting you."

Carter paled, but spat, "I won't go to the zone! I can buy my way into house arrest!"

"Try, but remember what I said. Never cross a spider." Thunder grabbed Carter suddenly, pulling him into a savage embrace. He locked his lips against Carter's, and sent his tongue prying between them. One hand dropped to massage Carter's crotch. Carter let out a muffled yelp, though not so much because of the sudden caress as because of the sting of a spray syringe at the base of his spine. Thunder held him a little longer, making sure that the hormone injection had taken affect. Then he shoved Carter away, forcing him into full view of all of his white-faced friends. An enormous erection tented Carter's pants, and would for the next week. If the cops and the courts moved quickly (and Thunder was sure they would), Carter would have an erection all the way through the trial. He might even have it when he arrived in the zone. Thunder turned away. "Never cross *me*, Carter."

> "But he does not win who plays with Sin
> In the secret House of Shame."

> —OSCAR WILDE,
> *The Ballad of Reading Gaol*

SURFACES

MARK W. TIEDEMANN

Mark Tiedemann has always been intrigued by "the way people reassigned blame if the results were not as expected, particularly regarding family members, and especially among those who espouse a single standard for all things." "Surfaces" is an elegant and eloquent study in how we assign and accept responsibility for what we do and who we become.

Jacob Anacor opened the embassy lock and watched from the observation bubble as the two survivors were borne unconscious into the receiving area on a bed of *scherzi*. Their suits, one green, the other blue, rippled brightly through the moil of graphite-grey filaments that swarmed around them. They seemed to float on their rescuers.

Abruptly the alien mass withdrew, leaving the pair of humans behind on the cushioned examination platform. The *scherzi* rolled back near the lock doors, writhing among themselves, a tangle of threads, filaments, and tentacles, slicing the human air, arcing out and diving back in like the traces of solar flares, only dark, light absorbing. Anacor stared at them—five individuals or fifty, after six years as Forum representative on Canolus he still could not tell—relieved that they had not tried to dismantle the environment suits.

One of the survivors moved, an arm raised, reaching for something, and, finding nothing, falling back. Anacor activated the biomonitors. One after another the readouts flashed "Clear". No radiation, no viru-

lent microbes, vital signs normal with the exception of elevated hista-
mines. He opened the door and descended to the floor of the receiving
area. The *scherzi* grew briefly more agitated. Anacor knelt beside the
green suit and unlatched the helmet. Gently he slid it off. A young
face, unlined, pale, short brown hair. He pushed up the eyelids, even
though the monitors had already confirmed that both were alive and
relatively unscathed. Blue eyes. Anacor felt a tug of recognition. He
moved to the yellow suit and removed the helmet.

Older face, long pale hair, a line etched in the space between severely-
arched eyebrows.

He shuddered at a faint touch on his neck. As he started to turn, a
lattice-work of filaments enveloped his arm. Light caresses traced his
face. He jerked back and stood. More filaments wrapped his right leg,
worked up under his shirt. He brushed them off easily.

"No, no," he said, and filled his mind with disapproval while he
fended off the curious *scherzi*. "No time. No, no."

With evident reluctance they pulled away. Others from the group
came forward and urged their companions back. When the last fila-
ment was gone, Anacor went to a small panel and summoned the
robots.

Three multi-limbed motiles floated free of their alcoves in the wall.
Two lifted the humans and took them through a hatch. The third
began herding the *scherzi* toward the lock. Anacor returned to his
observation bubble, sealed his hatch, and opened the outer doors. The
muddle of *scherzi* writhed out into the Canoline night.

Anacor sighed. "Company," he whispered, already missing his soli-
tude.

He sent them breakfast by motile, choosing to wait until lunch to
speak to them. He knew their presence on Canolus meant another
transfer for him, a new posting, or, less likely, a recall. Of the two
choices he hoped for the former.

Anacor spent the morning going over the data from the embassy satellites scattered throughout the Canolus system. Their ship, the *Stockhausen*, had massed thirty-two thousand tons and was nearly fifty years old. Perhaps age, lack of maintenance, bad piloting at the transition point. Regardless of the cause, the end result remained the same. An explosion six million kilometers out, far from the thin asteroid belt, not in the path of any known comet, and only one shuttle escaped.

He instructed his computers to collate the data and search for any anomaly. Finally, with nothing left to claim his attention, he went to his quarters to change. He dressed in a casual uniform—powder blue with pewter piping—and went to introduce himself.

The younger one answered his sharp knock. He wore a robe too large for his frame and his hair was wet. He blinked rapidly for a few seconds, then frowned.

"Yes?"

Anacor nodded politely. "I'm Captain Jacob Anacor, resident liaison, Canolus Embassy." He waited. When the young man said nothing, he added, "Your host."

"Oh. I'm sorry. Yes, thank you."

"Bridger?" the other called.

"Captain Anacor," Bridger said. "Our host."

"May I?" Anacor asked.

Bridger stepped aside.

Two motiles stood near the bed. The woman was propped up, eating from a tray one of the robots held. She looked pale and she ate sparingly.

"Are you feeling better?" Anacor asked.

"Than what?" she asked. "We were unconscious when we arrived, I have no idea how we were feeling then. Before that we thought death imminent. Perhaps you know that feeling, Captain Anacor." Her eyes narrowed speculatively. "You were our representative to the Denebola Conferences, weren't you? You were replaced."

Anacor allowed the jab to pass. "You know my name. However, I don't know yours."

She coughed lightly and smiled. "I'm sorry. When you think you're about to die, manners take flight. I am Deborah Vol Rissik and this is my son, Bridger."

Anacor bowed to both in turn. "Vol Rissik...of the Eridani Vol Rissiks? I received word last month to expect a representative from the seti interrelations committee, but not someone on the primary advisory committee to the Chairman."

She took a sip of water. "I was asked to head an assessment team. The Canolus question needs resolution, Captain. It's taken much too long."

"Are we the only survivors?" Bridger asked abruptly.

"Yes. I intended later to ask what happened. Nothing was transmitted except the distress signal from your emergency shuttle. What—"

"We were attacked, Captain," Deborah Vol Rissik said.

Anacor started. "By whom?"

"I can only assume by our competitors for Canolus. That's what my report will state. I want to go over your satellite and ground survey logs, perhaps something will turn up there."

"The *scherzi* wouldn't—"

She fixed him with a suddenly firm look, all weariness and frailty gone. "We were attacked. My report will so state and my best judgment is that the attackers were, in fact, *scherzi.*" She took another drink. "My staff is dead, along with the crew of the *Stockhausen.* My mission here has been completely altered as a result."

Anacor shook his head. "But the *scherzi*—they'd take a ship apart out of curiosity, to see how it worked, perhaps, but they'd never attack it."

"In your opinion."

"I have been here for six years."

"Alone."

"Not for the whole six years, no, but—"

"Your assistant did not file a favorable report on conditions here. I don't know the details, Captain, only the negative impression. And he left when? Four years ago?"

"Three years, eight months."

"And you've been alone since."

"Yes."

"Might it be reasonable to assume that your attitude toward the *scherzi* is colored by your isolation?"

Anacor's discomfort turned to resentment. He had been suspicious when word of the visit came. Now confirmed, those suspicions became part of a larger attitude, one he had felt pleasantly free from since coming to Canolus. Deborah Vol Rissik knew the complete contents of his record, career notations and personality profile. To assume less would be foolish and he hated fools.

So. Deborah Vol Rissik was...not his friend. Anacor clasped his hands behind his back and watched Bridger cross the room to the windows that overlooked the arboretum. Bridger's jaw flexed delicately in the diffuse light, as if he were very carefully holding something in his mouth that moved and shifted.

"You should know that I resigned my post at Denebola. The course of certain negotiations had already been predetermined. My presence was superfluous. It seemed a waste of time to remain in a post I no longer believed in."

"You might have challenged the proceedings," Vol Rissik said.

"That would have been a waste, too." He smiled. "If there is anything you need, the embassy staff systems are at your service. If you're feeling well enough later, I'd like you both to dine with me. Then perhaps I can show you around. For now I'm sure you both need more rest and I have matters to attend to. A pleasure to make your acquaintance."

He wheeled quickly and left the apartment. As he strode down the hallway to the communications center, the anger worked its way down his arms and his hands trembled, clenched, flexed.

One wall of the dining room transpared to give a view of the Canoline landscape. Anacor watched Deborah Vol Rissik and her son as they entered. Both stopped and stared and for several seconds Anacor saw honesty in their faces.

All grey and black, obsidian to graphite, marble to pumice, the land sloped away into the bowl of a valley. Powdery growths lay scattered across a cracked and stress-striated ground. Crystal-jagged outcrops, less than mountains and more than hills, scraped the clouds on the far side. The clouds seemed to catch on the razor tips and shred skyward. A lake frothed in slow-motion at the bottom of the valley. Gathered around the froth—dense ammonia and methane—writhed the colony of *scherzi*, a forest of interpenetrating threads.

Vol Rissik gaped, stunned. Bridger's mouth opened and closed, eyes wide. In both fear competed with awe. Bridger, younger, remained open. His mother quickly recovered, cocked an eyebrow, and nodded as if she were appraising a new painting hung in a museum.

Motiles drifted up to the table with plates. Vol Rissik sat with her back to the transparency, Bridger opposite her. The robots removed covers and steam drifted from soups, meats, pastas, sauces. Anacor watched as his guests made their selections, noted their expressions, their approval. In spite of himself he felt pleased.

"Thank you, Captain," Vol Rissik said.

"You're feeling better?"

"Yes. We...how long were we...?"

"I'm not sure. The *scherzi* found you and brought you here. They—well, we don't communicate time with each other. I can only approximate from the available data that your shuttle grounded twenty-two hours ago. You've been here for fourteen hours."

"Our shuttle?" Bridger asked.

"By now probably dismantled."

"Why wouldn't they have done the same with us?"

"A good question. When I first arrived they tended to dismantle the motiles. They would have worked on the embassy itself if I hadn't maintained a force field. It took a year to come to an understanding. As far as I've been able to tell, they make a distinction between sentience and nonsentience. Sentience is to be preserved intact."

"Even alien sentience?"

"Evidently."

"How—" Bridger began, then looked uncertainly at Vol Rissik. She nodded slightly and he continued. "How did you come to an understanding?"

"We invited them inside. Just a few, isolated to the lock area. They took everything apart, seemed to study it, and then came to one of us." Anacor smiled, recalling the sensations. "The examination was thorough. Afterward, we were able to tell them—'suggest' may be a better word—what objects were essential to our survival. They've since left the embassy and the motiles alone. And, evidently, the identification of sentience is universal. They brought you to me intact. I wasn't completely sure they would until now."

Bridger paled but continued to stare at the transparency. "I've always wanted to communicate—" Again, the deferential glance to Vol Rissik. This time she did not approve.

Anacor cleared his throat. "I've taken the liberty of contacting the Forum offices at Denebola. They've been informed of your survival, the loss of the *Stockhausen*, and your current condition."

"You might have waited until speaking with me, Captain."

"I'm required to report incidents as soon as possible. I've also collated all the observational data related to the Stockhausen. I'm running it all through again for refinement and definition. Perhaps we'll have something to look at after dinner."

"Would it be possible to opaque the windows, Captain?" Vol Rissik asked, frowning.

Bridger looked disappointed.

"I'm afraid not," Anacor said. "There's a glitch in the 'ware I haven't hunted down yet. Frankly, I'm not inclined to, I find the view fascinating."

"After all this time?"

"In time you see past the surface. Canolus is a world of strange beauty."

"I'll take the resorts of Pan Pollux, thank you." She twisted in her seat to look at the view. "Canolus is a world of raw resource, Captain. That's all the Forum is interested in."

"The Forum hasn't been here for six years."

"Yes, it has. You are an agent of the Forum."

When Anacor did not answer, she smiled and turned to her food. The conversation lapsed into the trivial. Bridger ate in episodes interrupted by extended gazes at the Canoline landscape, which clearly annoyed Vol Rissik.

The motiles cleared the table and Anacor poured brandy from an ornate decanter.

"King Louis?" Vol Rissik asked.

Anacor nodded, lifting the decanter to catch the light. "It's been in my family for generations. I have three of these. Periodically I have to ship one back to Earth for refilling and I'm always a nervous wreck until it returns."

"You could just fill it from a more easily-obtained source and not take the chance."

"I could, but..."

"But there's value in the ritual. Even if all the original brandy has long since vanished, the replacement is at least the same in name."

"Yes, but there's more to it. The current stock is reproduced from sample molecules of the original, stored in many of the original vats...no, it's not just appearances, an attempt was made to duplicate the product."

"A copy is still a copy."

"And without it the universe would be a much colder place." He raised his glass in a toast. "To infinite duplication."

Vol Rissik sipped, nodded. "Very good. Unfortunately, infinite duplication has the tendency to produce infinite error."

Anacor smiled. "Do you taste any error?"

"No..."

"Then in this case the appearances are honest." He turned at the sound of a motile. "Ah. The data is ready. Let's have a look at what happened to the *Stockhausen*."

Above the table the air congealed into a pearly sphere. A moment later it darkened and filled with stars. In the center of the field a point grew steadily until it resolved clearly into the oblate configuration of a starship. Anacor frowned at its lines. It seemed ancient in some aspects and in others quite new. Perhaps it had been heavily refitted, but the overall impression was of a confused design, neither liner nor merchanter, courier nor carrier. He watched intently as more and more detail became visible.

A flash of brilliant light crossed before the ship and abruptly it exploded. Freezing gasses sprayed outward in a scintillant cloud along with hot shards and huge chunks of metal, plastic, and alloys. In a few seconds the space was empty except for the arc of a small ship accelerating sunward.

The replay ended, the air cleared.

"You didn't have much time to get into the shuttle," Anacor commented.

"Our cabin was just above it, Captain," Vol Rissik said. "As soon as word came that a seti ship was moving toward us..."

"No one else had such an arrangement?"

"No one else was aboard, Captain, other than the crew."

"No personal staff?"

"Oh, yes, but—"

"May I be excused?" Bridger said suddenly.

Anacor stood. "Of course."

Vol Rissik nodded. Bridger swallowed his brandy in one gulp, bowed to Anacor, and left.

"Bridger has no patience for my field," Vol Rissik said. "But he loves to travel."

"This may curb his appetite for a while."

"It might." She went to the windows and looked out over the landscape. "I take it you're fond of the *scherzi*."

"No. It's not possible to be fond of them. They're...unknowable. I am intrigued by them."

"What about their claim to Canolus?"

"What about it?"

"Do you think it's legitimate?"

He knew the answer she wanted. He was an agent of human expansion, it was his duty to support their collective aims. But he had never cared to mouth lines to please those who knew better. "As legitimate as ours, certainly."

"But what are they doing with it? They aren't developing it, they're just *here*."

"I don't know."

"What do you mean you don't know? I've read your reports, I've seen the supporting data. They don't build, mine, farm, reshape, alter— they're not doing anything with it."

"I repeat, I don't know."

She glared at him impatiently.

"If you've read my reports—"

"Yes, I have, Captain. That doesn't mean I accept them."

Anacor folded his hands in his lap. "Interesting choice of words. You don't 'accept' them. Which can mean that you feel I've misjudged my assignment, misinterpreted the evidence, or misrepresented it. I'm therefore either naive, incompetent, or a liar."

"Your past," Vol Rissik said, "doesn't lead me to conclude that you're naive. No more than anyone else. You wouldn't have this post if you were incompetent."

"So I'm a liar?"

"Not intentionally. Your sympathies, however, may bend your judgment."

Anacor smiled wryly. "I was given this posting to put distance between my judgments and Forum policy. The trouble is, policy always comes looking for me. I often wonder why I'm always sent just where policy intends to show up next."

"Because you're honest, Captain."

"Hmm." He drained his glass and stood. "So I'm not naive, not incompetent, and I'm honest. What does that make me?"

"Useful." She continued to gaze at the landscape. "And, given a modicum of cooperation, the Forum will continue to find you useful." She gestured outward with her glass. "They're terribly ugly."

"They are what they are."

"That's hardly a distinction." She smiled politely. "Thank you for an excellent table, Captain. I enjoyed it very much. I'll see you in the morning."

Anacor listened to her footsteps, the door opening and closing, then the silence. He poured another glass of brandy and raised a wordless toast to the distant *scherzi*.

"Captain Anacor?"

Anacor looked around and saw Bridger leaning out from his door. It was deep into nightcycle and the hallways were dimly lit.

"Yes?"

"You're up late. Do you sleep?"

"I had work. Your arrival is keeping me up. Are you all right? Are you comfortable?"

"Yes, I'm—well, truthfully, I'm still wound up by all this."

"I imagine. I've traveled space for nearly forty years and I've never once crashed in a shuttle after having a ship blow up around me."

"They say that modern starships are the safest method of travel in human history."

"They do say that."

Bridger folded his arms over his bare chest and glanced down the hall toward his mother's door.

Anacor followed his gaze. "Do you think she's having as much trouble sleeping as you are?"

"No. She never does. She napped during the shuttle flight down. May I ask you something personal?"

Reluctantly, Anacor nodded.

"You're all alone here. How do you manage?"

Anacor laughed. "Any question but that one I might've given a simple answer." He shook his head. "I'm very tired. I haven't slept since you arrived."

"Oh. I'm sorry. I didn't mean to impose. It's just that I don't do very well by myself."

"The biomonitor can help, all you have to do is ask."

"I'm asking you."

"Asking me for what? To come in and keep you company? Talk to you? Perhaps hold you? Rock you to sleep?"

Bridger reddened. "I'm not a child."

Anacor stepped closer, placed a hand on the wall near Bridger's head. Bridger frowned uncertainly but did not pull away.

"I can see that," Anacor said. "But trying to understand somebody by cataloguing everything they aren't is impossible. You never reach the end of that list."

"I don't understand."

Anacor leaned in, slowly. Bridger's scent was faint but distinct and surprisingly natural. Anacor had expected implants exuding whatever might be popular on Earth or one of the other older worlds. Martin had used such things. Unexpectedly he felt a sharp twinge of absence. Martin had left three years eight months ago, long enough, Anacor thought, to be well over him. Rituals and forms, details to attend, the embassy and his mission to run, sufficient to smooth over the loss. He thought.

Not loss, though, he did not feel *loss*, but *absence*, a kind of echoless void. Lonely? No, he was not lonely, just alone, but there was that sensation, a recognition...

He drew back.

"What is it?" Bridger asked.

"I'm very tired. I really do need to sleep. Please excuse me."

"You don't—"

He held up a hand, almost touched Bridger's lips with his fingertips. Reluctantly, as if pulling free of an embrace, he went on down the hall to his rooms.

He stood inside his door, back to the wall, heart pounding in time to the images that flashed through his head. He wished Bridger would not talk to him. He heard the words, hoped they matched what lay behind them, raised his hopes that perhaps, this time, the core was the same as surface. It would, he thought, be so simple without words. He was diplomatic corps, words defined him, enabled him, surrounded him. There had been so many, heaped up into orderly piles, one pile signified by another. All that his job required was the shaped use of words. It did not matter what they represented, only that they enabled him to acquire objects, aims, promises, results.

The *scherzi* did not use words. Anacor did not understand them, could not, but they did not expect him to. No one did. It was liberating. No expectations. He wished Bridger would not speak to him because he did not want another set of expectations. They could never be met—at least he had never been able to—and he had treasured his separateness here on Canolus, and the absence of expectations.

A light knock interrupted the stream.

Three years, eight months. He had thought Martin would share his need for isolation, appreciate the lack of demands, but instead they had invented new ones, ones neither of them understood. After all this time the *scherzi's* touch remained alien. Anacor closed his eyes. That was their most human quality. The only difference was that it matched exactly what they were.

The knock came again. Anacor opened the door and let Bridger in.

Anacor watched, enthralled in spite of his weariness, as Bridger danced with the sim images in the center of the living room. The projections—multi-hued abstractions of human forms—spun through impossible gyrations, modified by the monitoring program to accommodate Bridger's presence. The ghostly forms overlapped, seemed to collide when Bridger did something unpredictable. The young man's body nearly matched the extreme geometries of the translucent dancers.

The music ended, the forms snapped into a final configuration around Bridger, who now stood amid them, spear straight, the apex of the performance. Then they vanished, leaving Bridger, body bright with sweat that accented his musculature. He smiled expectantly at Anacor.

"I just realized," Anacor said. "That's your program, isn't it?"

Bridger's smile widened and he nodded.

Anacor laughed, pleased. "I *am* tired or I would have realized it sooner. I've seen your work before."

"Would you like to see another?"

Anacor shook his head. "No, thank you. I'd prefer to wonder at this one for awhile. How many have you authored?"

"Twelve. I'm working on a new one—I incorporated some of that in this one just now."

"I'm impressed." Bridger, grinning with pleasure, took a towel from the chair where he had lain it before the performance and began drying himself. Anacor enjoyed watching each movement with almost as much pleasure as he had the dance. "Why are you out here, with your mother, instead of..."

"Instead of where?"

Anacor shrugged. "Where your talents are better appreciated."

The smile faded. Bridger concentrated on toweling himself for a few seconds. "I could ask you the same question."

Anacor grunted. "I *am* where my talents are appreciated. At least where my talents have landed me."

Bridger sat down. "I'm out here with my mother to learn. We're Primary Committee, we have responsibilities. So she says." He gestured at the place where the dance had been. "This isn't everything I am or ever will be. It's an aspect. I'm interested in diplomacy, xenopology, cartography. You can't sum me up in one thing."

"I wasn't trying to."

"Then you're the only one."

"You should learn to ignore them."

"That's dangerous, isn't it? Ignore too much and you end up isolated. Do you like being all alone?"

"No. But it *is* easier than constantly giving explanations."

Bridger straightened sharply, then stood. "I should go. I'm sorry to intrude."

Anacor sighed. "Why did you come?"

"I was lonely—"

"No, I mean to Canolus. What are you doing here? Your mother is Primary Committee, not you."

"They're beautiful, aren't they?"

Anacor knew he meant the *scherzi*. He nodded slowly, watching Bridger intently.

Bridger scooped his clothes from another chair, stepped lightly into his pants, and headed for the door.

"Bridger," Anacor called.

"Yes?"

"You're right about isolation. But it's the only way I've found to discover which parts are really yours. Don't you think that's worth a little loneliness?"

The door opened, then closed softly. Anacor waited for a time, but Bridger did not return. He went to bed.

The *scherzi* writhed among themselves on the screen. Anacor had hours of them recorded. He watched them, fascinated, as they clustered around objects and dismantled them, then abandoned them to cluster around each other, touch, dance, spin, perhaps communicating among themselves what they had just learned.

He had detected no reproductive cycle among the *scherzi*—without the embassy computers he could not even know how many "individuals" there were. But they enthralled him. His reports had contained his theory that the *scherzi* were complete aesthetes, that what they "did" with Canolus was experience it. Even as he had sent the reports he had known they would be misunderstood. Humans possessed an aesthetic faculty, a part of the mind completely devoted to sensual experience. But it was only a part and all too often a suppressed part, linked inextricably as it was to the body. Touch being their only obvious sensory mode, the *scherzi* seemed devoid of any reluctance to indulge it. They moved constantly. Like meditating on a tantra, he watched them hour after hour. Especially since Martin's departure.

Martin. There had been a choice of postings for Anacor. Martin had been excited about every one except Canolus. Anacor was actually amazed Martin had stuck it out as long as he had. One last attempt to bring Anacor into the fold, shrive him of his perverse isolation. But Canolus offered Anacor something he needed. In the end, Martin could not compete.

Anacor sighed and switched off the monitor. Sometimes he felt like a voyeur.

He fingered the disk containing the response to his report on the *Stockhausen* and Deborah Vol Rissik and Bridger. He had already transmitted a request for verification, but he knew what would come back. Vol Rissik, Primary Committee, possessed greater cachet than Captain Jacob Anacor. If it came down to a contest there was no question who would win.

"I really don't want to leave this place," he told the disk. He stood and slipped it into his vest pocket. Maybe there was another place, equal to Canolus. If he stepped carefully he might be granted that posting.

Vol Rissik sat in the formal dining room, feet propped against the base of the windows, a cup in her lap. She was nude and her hair was wet.

"Good morning, Captain," she said without looking around. "You have an excellent gymnasium here."

"It's a fully-equipped embassy."

"Mobile, I trust?"

He nodded. "May I ask a straightforward question?"

"Of course."

He leaned back against the transparency. "How many people died on the *Stockhausen*?"

Vol Rissik blinked, startled. "I'm not sure. Full crew complement, no other passengers..."

"Sixty-seven," Bridger answered, coming up to them. He looked from his mother to Anacor. "Eight were members of our staff."

"Hm," Anacor mused. "Not too great a sacrifice, then."

Bridger frowned.

"May I show you something?" He gestured toward the table.

Vol Rissik looked bored and nodded. She finished her cup and went to the table.

Anacor activated the projection again. The destruction of the *Stockhausen* played out once more.

"Now," he said, reversing the scene, "I've processed the image for higher definition. I find some interesting things."

The ship expanded, filling the air. As they watched two brilliant streaks of light flashed from port and starboard. Fractions of a second later the hull split apart. Another flash and debris obscured the view. Anacor ran it again, slower. The streaks emanated *from* the hull. The hull itself flew apart in all directions. Once more, higher detail. Stress cracks were revealed covering the hull. The streaks came, the hull separated along those cracks. Closer still, again, the cracks resolved into discreet segments. The separation began simultaneously with the flash of light.

Anacor glanced at Vol Rissik and her son. Bridger seemed confused, but Vol Rissik herself continued to appear bored, though she did not look away.

He engaged a new series of views. As the flash cleared and the debris flooded toward them, something moved amid the bright shards. Bit by bit he brought clarity to the object until, finally, it took on a distinct shape. He removed the obscuring debris and all that remained was the dark form of a small warship, moving off quickly.

"I did a similar study of the entire section of space around the *Stockhausen* and found no other vessel. Only your shuttle and that ship, which I assume is resting outside the system, waiting for your signal."

Vol Rissik smiled. "Very good, Captain. What do you conclude from this?"

"That the *Stockhausen* was not attacked. That it was destroyed either by one of our own ships or blown apart from within. That your presence here is for the purpose of discrediting the *scherzi* claim to Canolus by framing them for an attack on humans."

The projection vanished. Bridger stared at his mother with an expression that saddened Anacor.

"So?" Vol Rissik said.

"I wanted you to know that I understand what you're doing. I wanted you to recognize that I am no fool."

"I never believed you were."

"No, you only believed I was deluded by my sympathies."

She waved her hand in a casual gesture of concession. "What do you intend to do now?"

"Nothing." He tossed the disk on the table. "I have received instructions. I can't stop you." He sighed. "You might have trusted me with the truth. I don't like what you're doing, but I understand my duty."

She laughed quietly. "Captain, how does one trust someone so...unique?"

"That's not really the issue, is it? My competence, my honesty—what matters is my history."

"Do you have a reliable method of communicating with the *scherzi*, Captain? I think it would be best to inform them as soon as possible that they will have to leave Canolus."

"I have filed reports—"

"I'm aware of that."

"—explaining, to the best of my understanding, the nature of the *scherzi*. Has any consideration been given to sharing Canolus?"

"Some. It's not practical. Their unfortunate proclivity for dismantling anything machinelike they come into contact with hardly recommends your suggestions. How could we possibly develop Canolus if we can't keep them from taking our equipment apart?"

"They don't bother the embassy."

"What if that has something to do with you specifically? What if it's *you* and not sentience that exempts the embassy?"

"They brought you here intact."

"It doesn't matter. They're unpredictable. Much like you. Perhaps you've simply found in each other kindred spirits."

Anacor watched her leave.

"We lost staff," Bridger said quietly. He stared at the table, fingers loosely laced, his expression equal parts sadness and bewilderment.

"Someone close?" Anacor asked.

Bridger nodded. "This has been a convenient assignment for her." He looked up. "What did she mean?"

"What, our being kindred spirits? Your mother is just mouthing the official line about me. I have a habit of making politics a personal thing. It's resulted in...inconveniences."

"I don't understand. My mother takes it personally, she'll do anything to achieve her ends, hurt anyone..." He swallowed hard.

Anacor wanted to leave. He recognized Bridger's distress. The truth, he knew, would only complicate the pain, make it harder to relieve. Still, he had never known ignorance to relieve anything.

"No, it's not the same thing. Your mother doesn't believe anything touches her. She's safe, protected. Apart. There's nothing personal about it. It's all surfaces." He went to the window and looked out at the landscape. "She can't see the *scherzi* as anything more than a problem to be solved. Just like me. I'm sure she'd hoped I'd do something stupid, like try to block her. Then she could take care of me, too."

"Why aren't you trying to block her?"

"The *scherzi* will be removed from Canolus. That's a fact. Even if your mother suddenly changed her mind and decided that this is a wrong thing to do, it wouldn't stop. Incompatible natures, you see. As for me, I was given this posting because my past makes me easy to discredit. So there's no sense sacrificing myself." He went to Bridger and patted the younger man's shoulder. "Have to learn to pick your fights."

"Is that how you ended up out here, alone?"

Anacor glared at him. "Stop thinking like your mother."

"What—?"

"You're different than her, Bridger, but you keep trying to find a way to make that difference acceptable to her. You try to think like her and all you find is confusion."

Bridger reddened. "You don't know what it's like."

"No? I was born on Nine Rivers. My family has always been in pol-

itics one way or another, but I intended to do something else. I was fascinated by the river traffic, the barges, the locals. My tutors said I was
slow, but blamed it on my playmates. Unsuitable companions. Later I
argued against the attitudes of visitors who considered them provincial
and backward and that was blamed on my overinvolvement with them
when I was younger. I may have been slow, I don't know, probably just
stubborn. My mother called me stubborn, my father called me dense,
and that was blamed on an ancestor. At first it was a virtue, then, when
they couldn't turn it to their advantage, it was a deficit, but it was that
ancestor's fault. Or the locals on Nine Rivers. I was sent offworld for the
rest of my adolescence, to Homestead. An older world, with an excellent university. It expanded my scope, gave me a cosmopolitan outlook
with the history and philosophy to back it up. When it was time for me
to choose a career I wanted to be a teacher. My family objected, I
remained stubborn. Now it was not only that ancestor but the instructors I had on Homestead. Their influence had turned me. I argued, they
bullied, I ran away. I worked at one thing or another for a couple of
years until I ended up as a playwright in a small theater troupe. I loved
it. I still remember that time as the best eighteen months of my life. I
met someone. He danced. When my family found me they were
appalled. There's an ancient phrase, they must've hired a linguist to
find it just so they could use it to ridicule me—Bohemian Lifestyle. I
had to look it up. Means something like doing what you want in an
artistic fashion, especially if what you want to do is different from what
everyone else wants you to do. I didn't understand it then, I don't now.
But all my sensibilities, according to this particular condemnation,
were blamed on the theater, my instructors, and my lover. Without any
one of those three I would have settled into my proper place without a
fuss. There were glorious fights. I tried disowning my family, but some
things can't—won't—be shed. They managed to dismantle the troupe.
They arranged that my lover be unable to find work. That nearly killed
him, so I left. I gave in. I entered the diplomatic service. I've had a
checkered career since. My successes have been credited to my unusual
youth, that all those radical experiences have allowed me a perspective

amicable to understanding the alien. My failures have been blamed on the way those influences twisted my perceptions to make me unable to accommodate the requirements of my position."

Anacor sighed. "But it's never *me* that's blamed or credited, at least not as I simply *am*. My influences, my experiences, my ancestors, my upbringing, my life choices—all I have done, never why I have done them, and all because to accept that I, Jacob Anacor, do these things because of who and what *I* am would mean accepting something..." He frowned and touched Bridger's cheek. "What does your mother blame for what she doesn't like in you?"

"Was Martin a dancer?"

"Among other things. I have work to do. If you want to talk more I'll be available later."

"Captain!"

He blinked. The screen still held the text of his next report. The fingers of his left hand tingled—the wrist lay against the edge of the desk, his forearm dangling—and he felt muzzy. The door chimed again, followed by sharp banging.

"Captain Anacor!"

He stumbled drowsily to the door and opened it. Deborah Vol Rissik stood in the corridor, her face pale, eyes wide with rage and fear.

"What did you do?"

"I'm sorry..." He rubbed his eyes. "I must've dozed off. I'm sorry, what—?"

"Bridger. What did you say to him?"

"I don't understand."

"He's *outside*," she hissed.

It took almost a full second for her meaning to come clear. Then he rushed down the corridor to the control center, ten meters away. He heard Vol Rissik's bare feet slap the floor after him.

He dropped into a chair before a console of screens and stabbed contacts. He frowned when he got no response.

"What is it?" Vol Rissik demanded.

Anacor worked silently until the screens winked on. "A security routine was overridden. That's why no alarm sounded." He initiated a scan all around the embassy. "How do you know he's outside?"

"His suit is gone."

"There."

The screen showed the slope away from the embassy. An environment-suited figure stood on an outcrop of rock, surrounded by myriad shifting *scherzi*. Anacor watched, stunned, as the figure moved his arms about in dramatic arcs, bringing them back inward in delicate gestures—as delicately as the bulky suit allowed.

"What *is* he doing?" Vol Rissik asked.

"Teaching, I suspect. Or learning." He glanced at the telemetry. "He's only four hundred meters out. I'll send a couple of motiles to fetch him."

"Hurry."

Anacor glanced at her. Vol Rissik's surface was compromised and he was fascinated by what he saw coming out. Fear, worry, concern...confusion. She did not manage the truly unexpected very well, he saw. It disturbed him that she had paid so little attention to Bridger that he could upset her with the unexpected.

He ordered the robots out, then leaned back and watched Bridger. It seemed some of the *scherzi* mimicked his movements. Gradually more and more of the assembled creatures joined in a kind of idealized imitation of Bridger's dance. No arms or legs, but the sharp bends and angles they generated approximated limbs. He glanced at Vol Rissik and saw a look of vague distaste, as light curling of the lips, a pressing down of eyebrows.

The motiles came into view. Bridger stopped his dance and waited for the machines to approach. The *scherzi* made a path for them.

But as they neared the rock the *scherzi* suddenly closed on the motiles. Anacor stared, incredulous, as they attacked the machines. The motiles moved their appendages to fend the *scherzi* off, but it soon became clear that they were being taken apart. The motiles sank into the tall sea of aliens and disappeared. Anacor glimpsed parts here and there, passed among the *scherzi*.

Bridger began to dance again. Anacor laughed.

"What have you done?" Vol Rissik asked.

"Nothing that I'm aware of."

"Bridger would never do this on his own."

Anacor looked up at her. She glared at the screen, cheeks flushed.

"He wouldn't? You know that for a fact?"

"Whatever you've done—"

She turned sharply away from the scene. Anacor suppressed a smile at her struggle for control. Finally she said, "We have to get him back inside."

"Of course. I'll take care of it."

Anacor stepped from the lock onto the soil of Canolus. It had been years since he had walked outside. He disliked the environment suit—bulky and altogether too fragile—but he remembered clearly everything necessary about its function.

Bridger still danced on the rock. The gathering of *scherzi* parted for Anacor. He felt their tentative caresses, knew a few probed the suit curiously until some signal made them withdraw. He stepped over a large casing from one of the motiles.

The *scherzi* nearest Bridger still moved in parody with the dancer. Anacor stopped a few meters away and looked up at the young man.

Bridger stopped and looked down at Anacor.

"Are you enjoying yourself?" Anacor asked.

Bridger laughed. "I've been scared to death since I came out here. I thought—"

"They never have killed anyone."

"No, I guess not. I didn't really believe that. Mother said your reports were not trustworthy."

"And now?"

"Now, though—it's amazing. I think I've gotten suggestions from them."

Anacor looked around at the *scherzi*. None of them moved with Bridger now, they had resumed their normal frantic interleaving.

"They're beautiful," Bridger said. "You don't really know until you touch them."

"I know." He looked back up. "We have to go back to the embassy. Your mother is concerned."

"Are you going to challenge her?"

"It wouldn't do any good."

"What if I supported you?"

"Do you know what you'd be risking to challenge her?"

"Nothing real."

"Do you have any idea what I'll be risking?"

"She'll blame you for corrupting me."

"She already has."

They shared silence for a time. Then Bridger began chuckling. As it built, Anacor joined him. Bridger jumped down from his rock.

"They're a lot like us, aren't they?" He grinned at Anacor. "Only inside out."

He spread his arms out and the *scherzi* gathered around him. Anacor watched for a time. He no longer felt absence. Only loss. Slowly, he waded through the tangles toward home.

STAY THY FLIGHT

ELISABETH VONARBURG

Ever since the New Wave (and, ah, that was a long time ago now), there has been some discussion within the field as to which has primacy: form or content? When it comes to good fiction, the question is, of course, meaningless: one obviously dictates the other; they are interdependent; there is no difference. This story about the perception of time and the bonding of two female creatures—written originally in French and translated by the author—is a perfect example.

By day, I go fast, nowhere but fast, not moving, impossible, too focused, unfurled wings, tilted head, eyes on the sun, when there is some. Now for instance, no clouds, nothing but light, a rain of light, torrents, maelstroms, hurricanes of light. And me inside it, through my every pore, my skin you'd say, yes, under the hair. Naked skin: only on the face, the torso. Get some light too, but less efficient. The hair mostly, soaking up light, and my wings' feathers, a million antennas, if you will, conduits, minuscule, avid mouths, tongues, hands, a million fingers, stretching toward the sun, all that energy, everywhere: I'm charging. Inside, metamorphosed light: food, strength, lightning strikes, from cell to cell, vortexes, in my whole body, a continuous vibration, electric sponge, I absorb life. Fast inside, my body is fast. Outside unmoving, almost, accelerated metabolism inside, chemical exchanges, neurons, everything, faster. I am charging, I burn, my own matter, my life, at lightning speed, behind each thought, a condensed frenzy, white hot, ablaze, crackling. Unmoving, almost: you don't, see me move, doesn't feel, like I'm moving either, but I'm revolving, with the magnet-sun, like the flowers, but no flower, me: lioness, winged woman. Statue, you say, not quite, but what other word, convenient: on a pedestal, after all, immobile, almost, by day.

You are immobile, for me, by day, almost, less than I for you, but slow. Everything around me, becomes slow, after the dawn: the sun rises, heaves itself up, slows down, crawls, an imperceptible movement, in the sky, the birds' songs too, in the Park, draw out, lowering down, deeper and deeper, to a basso continuo, some modulations, but spaced out, the wind, when there is some, the leaves, music, solemn, meditating, I like. Behind me, lower still, the sound of the city. Sometimes a blending, images, sounds, leaves moving, shadows, like a music almost, clouds, when there are some, flowers, opening with the day. Sometimes I try, to seize the moment, when it changes, flowers, shadows, clouds: hard, impossible almost. Then I look elsewhere, or close my eyes, and come back later: more open, the petals, closer to the pistils, the bee, but everything caught, in invisible amber, time, all slowed down. With telescopic vision, perhaps, I could, with a millionfold, magnification, see the sap moving up, the flesh of the flower, stiffening, or in the clouds, patient, the accretion of molecules. But it's human vision I have, that's all, not superhuman. "Look": not quite, either, hard to will it, by day. Simply: eyes open, I see, my eyes see, like everything else functions, the other senses, smell, taste, hearing, touch, everything, at a normal speed, but my brain, no, too focused on energy, on charging: registers, transmits, a drop every decade. If I want to look, to change the direction, in which I look, great effort, lasts for centuries.

A little mist, on the sun; the color of the sky changes; and my speed changes; less light: I slow down, a little; the leaves, the shadows, the clouds, the insects: a little bit faster; I could almost see the bee's wings moving. A slow day, perhaps? Slow days, for me, the days of soft sun, with mist or clouds, passing: I charge up more slowly, I live, and die, more slowly.

The first passers-by, at the back of the alley, in a few centuries, will walk in front of me, will stop. Tourists, it's summer, always nice in here, anyhow: the South, warm, just enough wind, in summer, to break up the mist. Sometimes very humid, all that suspended water, invisible, ghost of the melted ice, far away at the poles. Sometimes it rains, I drink, head tilted up, don't need to, but it's nice. Glinting gravel, after the rain, puddles in the alleys, kids splashing about, the birds, bathing, in slow motion, droplets, wavelets, glimmerings, soon dry, those waters, tides of the sky. Elsewhere, it rains more, I know, but here, sometimes, you can forget, the other tides, everywhere, eating at the earth. Not me: I stand in the great alley, at the highest point of the Park, facing the Seaside Promenade, I see them, from up here, the tides.

I see them, I look at them, from time to time. My inward clock always knows. This decade: one minute outside, in the slow world, this year one second, I know, exactly. When I am facing in the right direction, I look at the sea, every five minutes, I must parcel out time in order to see: the ocean, swelling up, an unending breath, rising, past the ancient marks, on the pier, the blue, the red lines. The black line, would never get past it, they thought: on a rebuilt cliff, forty meters high, the city. And there it is: vanished, the black line. Heaving, overflowing the sculpted stone parapets, through their interlacing design, the sea, draped on the Promenade, a shimmering of heat, around the trees, mercury under the sun. It rolls, trembling, under the feet of the passers-by, behind the wheels of the horse-drawn buggies, suspended droplets clinging to the raised hooves, the sea inside the city, slow, irresistible.

More passers-by, not only tourists: the regulars, at this hour. You like to go to the Park, on the heights, far from the sea, turning your back on it, walking up to me. You spread slowly between the statues, you fold up, sitting down in the grass, on the benches, endlessly, almost statues yourselves, if I don't perceive you for too long: The Bird Lover, the Dog Lady: Several dogs, not necessarily hers, the Dog Walker? The Lovers: just the Girl Student, the Philosopher, alone, then the encounter, the month-long first sentence, the week-long first smile, then seeing them leave, together, throughout a century, and come back, another century, their hands, seeking each other, sea anemones, in a magnetic current. A few hours, another title: the Kiss. Are going to change again: their bodies move differently, the space they inhabit together, not the same anymore, their eyes, elsewhere. "The Break-up", perhaps?

The mist is gone, the sun revolves, unmoving, in the sky. Tropism, I move too, don't see the Promenade any longer, but the Sleeper's bench, real statue, that is, blue dress, crossed legs, her cheek against her hand. Today, next to her, a youngster, a true human, skin the color of light tobacco, eyes closed, no shirt. Soaking up some sun, but what difference? Doesn't move either for me, or so little, a breath every hour.

I see elsewhere, clouds, shadows, leaves, other passers-by ambling on, imperceptibly moving, for several eternities. Or I close my eyes, to see the crackling energy, behind my lids, flashing through, life in my cells, death.

Eyes open again, bench vanished: the Hummingbirds' Dome now, the great central lawn; less ardent light; longer shadows; the color of the sky changes faster; the hummingbirds' wings vibrate; behind the transparent dome, I am beginning to see them move, from flower to flower; in the trees, the free birds' symphony rises up again to higher notes; where soon the song of this or that bird stands out, that I recognize; you go on walking, gracefully swimming along the alleys, buoyant; the sun's orb sinks behind the leaves fluttering in the breeze as in a river. This endless day is coming to an end. Inside me the energy pulse slows down, gets lighter, fades away. There is a very brief moment when everything stops, when I feel as if suspended, time for the symbols to reverse, for the fluxes to reorganize, for other instructions to move me.

Sunset is coming, a time for questions. Your questions.

But first let me enjoy my newfound body. Let me yawn hugely and turn my head, this way, that way, to uncrick my neck. Fold my wings, unfold them again, stand up and stretch—the front claws gripping the edge of the pedestal, back arched, hindquarters up in the air, braced on my back legs, tail lashing. And then adopt the posture in which I will answer you. Sitting back, wings folded, tail coiled around the haunches, the human head very straight between the animal shoulders, the chest very obvious with its two little round breasts just above the place where the pelt begins. This posture is disturbing to some of you, it took me a long time to understand one of the reasons why: too much woman. They prefer me in a recumbent posture, head on the front legs, either lying at length on my belly or curled upon myself. And eyes shut. But this is not appropriate, I can feel it, and in the end I always answer you sitting straight. Thus my face is at the same height as yours when you stand. Perhaps this is what disturbs you, who walk by averting your eyes or feigning not to see me.

You don't ask many question, nowadays. You never did ask many questions. And that was mainly in the beginning, when I was a novelty. Or at least something to be outraged about, since talking statues had been made before, in the very beginning, fifty years earlier. But to make one just when bio-sculpture was on the verge of being outlawed, only Angkaar could pull that off unpunished. He was famous, a subject for controversy for so long that it was now a routine. And he was old, dying, everybody knew. He had friends in high places: they let him make his last statue, and then they passed the law.

His face is in my first memory, and in the one after that, and in all the others until he put me to sleep and I woke up on that pedestal in the Park, in front of a wondering, shocked crowd. He let no one interfere with his ultimate creation: advances in the technology allowed it. But when I opened my eyes for the very first time, there was only his face, an ivory parchment, finely engraved with lines, stretched taut on a delicate bony architecture, the wide rounded forehead, the mouth, sinuous and weary, and eyes like carbuncles, their fire too dark in a face too white. His voice, throaty, always a little breathless.

I remember all the learning—you say <<programming>>, you say <<conditioning>>. He wanted to me to remember it, to remember him. He wanted me to know what I was, and how I had come to be that way. An artefact. A living sculpture. An artificial creature, where the organic and the electronic meet. My body, my brain, their development, their assembling: artificial, but organic. My movements, my reflexes, my memory, the algorithms of my thought: programmed. My thoughts themselves? Yes, some of them. There begins the uncertainty which is Angkaar's gift to me.

There are very narrow physical limits to what I can do on my pedestal, besides the independent movement of each of my limbs: sit up, lie down in two different postures, stand up on all fours, beat my wings, move my head and torso. I cannot <<jump>> <<down>>. Those terms have no physical referent for me, neither my joints nor my muscles hold them in memory. Of course I feel no need to do those things. The few movements available to me are satisfying enough, and even more, they give me an intense pleasure, as do all my sensations.

In the beginning, I thought there were also limits to my thoughts. Then I slowly understood that those were more limits to my emotions. Your questions made me aware of it. And my answers. At first, I never knew what I was going to say. After all, you have to enter my perceptual field for me to answer you, you must be inside the magic circle, about four meters in diameter, materialized on the ground around my pedestal by small black triangular tiles. Beyond that limit, I don't perceive you well enough; your expressions, your body language, yes, but not your electrical and chemical language, the emotions that surround you like an aura only I can perceive: I need that to answer you. Thus, in the beginning, I was waiting for my own words, my oracles, just as you were, believing just as you did that all my brief responses were programmed. But with time I was able to see that they never repeat. That since they evolve they take into account everything I have learned during these nearly ten years of my existence. And I concluded that somehow they must fit themselves to your questions. That in a more obscure fashion they must even answer them. I cannot say whether I am the only one speaking, however. No doubt there is also my creator, a residual echo slowly fading inside me. I have learned to know him better that way, through the gaps: in what I cannot feel although I can think it, in the distance between your curiosity and my enigmas. Between my questions and the answers you are not giving me, too.

But sunset is the time for your questions, not mine. Our respective speeds mesh for such short periods, no wonder Angkaar programmed me to be laconic. It was also in accord with his project, my nature, the title inscribed on my pedestal and that I have never read. I had never seen myself, either. I don't know if that was my creator's intention. He told me what I was, and I have in memory everything there is to know about sphinxes, but he never held out a mirror to me during my learning period, and I find in myself no desire to see my countenance.

When I did see myself, however...

The painter arrived in the morning and he revolved as I did, for I saw him each time I opened my eyes or looked back from the limits of the Park, the far stretches of the city or the heights of the sky. I knew him: I had seen him several times with Angkaar. First at my unveiling. (I remember: Angkaar had hidden me under an opaque thermosensitive glaze, and the fading light of the sunset had dissolved its chemical bounds as I was awakened.)

Then I saw the painter on strolls through the Park with a rapidly weakening Angkaar, the last few times in an electric wheelchair. Angkaar loved to go to the Park during his last weeks, no doubt because it showed several works of his. "There will be others," he had cryptically told the media on the eve of my unveiling. No one had understood then. Neither had I.

He used to come at sunset, of course. He stopped in front of me. He listened to the questions people asked. He never asked any. For a long time I believed it was because he already knew all the answers. I now know it was because he didn't. The painter (was he already a painter then? Perhaps) never asked anything either. He just held Angkaar's hand, or his arm, later the back of the wheelchair. He was the younger man, hardly past his thirties, very dark, very slender, with the anxious expression of one who always expects to be rejected. Angkaar was very pleasant with him, though, or was it merely indifference? They never entered my perceptual circle. Alex. His name was Alex. And one day Alex came back alone. At sunset. He stayed before me, just outside the circle, for a long time, looking hard at me with an expression that I didn't understand (later, I learned that it was hatred). Then he said:

"He's dead." Since it was not a question, there was no answer. He stayed there until the Park lights came up, then he turned away abruptly and was gone.

I saw him again two years later; he had an easel and a canvas—there was a revival of archaic techniques at that time, the Park was full of would-be painters. He always arrived when the sun was rising in the east, always went when the sun slid down through the trees in the west: he wanted no words between us. He was doing sketches. After four days, he vanished. A week later he came back. He waited for the last painters to pack up and leave, then he took his canvas—a big thing almost a square meter wide—and he came up to me. With faltering steps, almost. Stopped just inside the circle. Placed the canvas so that I could see it. He was afraid. He was hurt.

It was an hyperrealist kind of painting, with every color shifted to shades of red. The winged silhouette was chained to the pedestal, supine, but with the torso rearing up. The left wing was dangling, broken. The right wing was half-unfolded. Blood had dripped from the shoulder to the left breast, was dripping from the parted lips. The head was slightly tilted to one side, as though the embroidered headdress was too heavy, or as though the rage that had caused the creature to tear at her own flesh has exhausted itself. The face was that of an ageless woman, with great, slanted amber eyes, a short, slightly hooked nose, wide, high cheekbones.

After a while, Alex asked: "Who is it?"

I heard myself answer: "Yourself."

He stiffened, then seemed to crumple. Without a word, he turned away and left with his canvas. I availed myself of the absence of other questioners to ponder the complex feeling that had filled me at the sight of the picture. Despite my answer to Alex's question, I had immediately assumed, through logical processing, that it was my image. Or at least an approximate likeness, since I have no broken wing. It was not really me... and it was me nevertheless. Why was I so *sure* of it, beyond all logic? Angkaar had never shown me any pictures corresponding to the purely verbal description present in my memory. A creature with the body of a lion, the wings of an eagle, but a human face and torso, and female. Lion, eagle, woman, I had already seen them, separately. But not their fusion. Sphinx. Do words correspond to some vast pool of intangible but eternal images, which I would have accessed? That was a curiously pleasant idea. The other component of my feeling, then, was it also pleasure? Alex's painting was awful, full of both cruelty and despair. But at the same time... beautiful. Did that mean I was beautiful? Or merely that Alex saw me thus, in spite of his pain, or perhaps because of it? Then what I felt was not pleasure, it was curiosity. And then, indeed, pleasure of a sort: to discover questions I had never asked myself yet. Not who I was, but how you saw me: who I was, what I was, for you.

And this strange idea, also new to me, that perhaps you never saw me at all, really. That I was your mirror.

I believed I knew what you thought of me, though, what you felt in front of me. I heard you, I still do when you talk while passing by me, or stopping, when our times are in synch. That's how I completed the education provided by Angkaar. At first you were admiring, the more secretly pleased for being officially shocked. Then, just after the outlawing of artefacts, you took to censoring me in a more or less sincere tone; there were a few protests, even; far less fierce than at the beginning of bio-sculpture about sixty years ago: no one tried to blow me up; not even one graffiti. There were doubts as to the exact nature of my programmation, I gather: Angkaar was known for not being very tolerant of vandals, perhaps he had seen to my defensive capacities. On the other hand, you don't seem to have much energy left to waste in symbolic gestures anymore; you exhausted it, apparently, in building dams and new cities that would protect you against the rising oceans—but the tides go on nibbling at them as if nothing mattered. No one even tried to shoot me from a distance. Perhaps they thought I was bullet-proof. There were only some protesters with placards: STOP THE SACRILEGE.

You kept on coming to see me, actually, because I was the one and only talking artefact that was semi-mobile, but also because I was the oldest artefact known to be still <<functioning>> (you never say <<living>>): five years, an amazing longevity. Then, later, the Sleeper in Blue walked into to the Park and turned to stone on her bench, and Angkaar's statement became clear: there *were* others. Among you, arte-facts, perfectly humanoid ones that you never even suspected were not human: inorganic matter could go on existing much longer than offi-cial scientists had let on. You came to see me in bigger crowds, then—perhaps reassured by my honestly non-human appearance, and my so limited mobility. And you asked me questions, the questions you didn't ask in the beginning because I was too new.

But since the functioning of artefacts had briefly came back into fashion, I expected you to ask them. I had studied enough inner traces of Angkaar in myself, made enough correlations with what I had learned from you without your knowledge. I know that you fear death, that time is still for you an unresolved enigma. "What walks on four legs in the morning, on two at noon and on three in the evening?" I heard myself answer: "An animal victimized by civilization." I chalked that one up to Angkaar's opinion about humanity; he'd chosen to turn the legend on itself, which was telling enough. He'd taught me Oedipus' answer to the Greek Sphinx, of course; perhaps, at that time, humans had more answers.

Someone enters my field of vision. I know her: she walked by a moment ago, in full sunlight. She is not one of the regulars. Neither is she a tourist. I can see her much better now—paradoxically, when I go fast and you are slow, I see you for too long and in too much detail, I can't get a good impression of you. Self-confidence, strength, a supple gait, an athletic build despite the aristocratic, cheetah-like slenderness. Beautiful, you'd say. Perhaps too self-composed? She doesn't enter the circle. She doesn't really stop in front of me, she merely slows down for a few seconds, she looks at me, turning her head toward me as she walks by, thoughtful, then she is gone, without asking me anything. Green eyes, golden skin, short light hair: one more human, one more image, one more mystery. The Park is emptying. My time is over. The shadows are almost touching me. No one asked me a question today.

You asked me once; after much dithering; talking circles around the word <<death>>; which would have been acknowledging my being alive; asked me whether I knew when I was to end, and why. And in my equally convoluted way; because of my programming then; not of any discomfort; I made you understand; yes, I know I am limited in time; yes, the artorganic matter of my body ages at an accelerated rate; a little faster by day; a little slower by night. "Do you know how you will end?" you asked then; I waited with interest for my answer: did I know? Had Angkaar given me that knowledge? I'd heard you before; talking about his previous biosculptures; he had never been at pain; to give them a spectacular ending. Protracted fireworks? Lightning-fast sublimation? The Sleeper in Blue had not yet come; to stop forever on her bench; I didn't know; at that time; I could have added that: metamorphosis; into a real statue. I heard myself say: "All comes in time to those who are prepared." You seemed disappointed; I could understand: a mere adaptation; of a tired old proverb; really, Angkaar! Only later did I understand; its appropriateness; come to think of it; you die so badly; most of you; surprised, furious, or reluctant; no insistence on esthetics.

Angkaar killed himself, too; he didn't wait; for mechanical progress; to rob him of his death.

But my death; he prepared it; and I know nothing of it.

At last I understood; the tone of your comments among yourselves; when I talked about it; near me; you wondered; if I hated him; if I was scared. You never dared; ask me; you were too afraid; of my answer. I would say no, though; I don't hate Angkaar; and I am not afraid; to end—to die?—because he programmed me so?—certainly—but I understand—that limitation—as a kindness on his part—are you so happy—to know how you are mortal?

But it is not yet—time—for my questions—no time for yours—either—the sky darkens—our times go out of synch—you walk faster—in the alleys—and I without light—without the sun—I almost—stop—slowed down—metabolism—I am digesting—my feast of the day past—really immobile—now—the evening birds—sing higher notes—in the sky—the stars explode—sudden dust—close to the trees—a diffuse light—time for me—to blink—and the moon bursts out—from the clouds—tonight—she sails through—their jagged outlines—blue and silver—lightning—shadows—running on the ground—and you run too—the nighttime regulars—different from—those of the day—searching—one another—always a surprise—the pattern—of your nocturnal—paths—suddenly revealed—to me— through speed—I see you—searching—without knowing—one another—the precise—frantic dance—of your signals—you come up—to one another—you talk—very little—what do you say?—I can't hear—but the ritual—is always the same—a few words—a gesture— very important—body-language—arms—folded or dangling—hands— in the pockets—or raked through hair—contacts—furtive—eyes averted—then you go—together—in the bushes—or outside the Park—for the night—a night—you burn—your whole life—in one night—you are—so afraid—I know

No one—now—hour of the cats—in the grasses—quick—slithering —careful—between the trees—birds of prey—lethal flight—silent— and soon—nothing at all—the solitary hour—the solitary minute—the moon—is gone—I think—I still perceive—glacial—thoughts— stretched—over a million—years—

And now—muted pulse—of light—in the sky—other birds— singing together—in the fading—darkness—slower and lower—they sing—for the sun is growing; like a luminous mushroom; the tide of shadows is turning; little by little, the molten glass of my thoughts, becomes fluid again, dawn has come.

Dawn is here, the time for questions: my own. There is no one, usually, to listen to them: the nighttime regulars have left the Park, the daytime regulars have not arrived yet. Only the birds, an errant cat or dog, the leaves, whispering. I am alone, usually, to taste this instant when I live at the world's speed—on my pedestal still, but it doesn't matter. I look at the sun rising above the trees. I feel the energy coursing through my veins, my cells and synapses, speeding up; I stretch and I yawn, I stand up and sit down, rituals of my own. And I think of all the questions I would try to ask, if there were anyone to share my dawn.

And today there is someone. A woman. The young woman of yesterday's sunset. Here she is, back in my dawn. She takes one of the chairs lining the lawns, hoists it in one movement upon her shoulder—those are metal chairs, and very heavy—and she comes to me. She is young, I'd say in her twenties. She puts the chair down near my pedestal, she sits, facing east. Legs a-stretch, arms folded. She looks at the sun glimmering through the top of the trees. Very calm. Inhumanly, I'd say. My occasional visitors never are so calm. She knows I am going to talk to her, though. No, she's *waiting* for me to talk to her.

I am not so sure I want to, suddenly—to ask her questions, since at dawn I can, for lack of questions to *answer*, which is for sunset. Only during the slow days can I talk normally, without being a prisoner of my matrices of questions and answers. Angkaar told no one; he wanted me to have a measure of freedom. But usually it makes you too uneasy, and finally I desisted. I am a statue, after all: why would you want to talk to a statue as you would a normal person? There are not enough slow days, anyhow.

Should I really ask her something? She seems so sad, suddenly. But the tropism is too strong, I can't resist it for very long. And at dawn, I can ask anything I want, those are really *my* questions.

"Long night?"

She doesn't even flinch, turns her head a little to look up at me: "Not just for you."

"Why?"

She says nothing. I'd really appreciate it if humans were forced to answer questions, as I am: I have so little time to ask mine. She stands up and faces me, leaning on my pedestal. I am lying down, and her face is above mine. She holds out her hand, touches my cheek.

You don't touch me very often. Despite all your boasting, most of you humans are afraid of me, and those who wouldn't be, the children, are too small to be able to touch me, except when standing on a chair—and there is always an adult to see them and keep them from me. But Angkaar did touch me. And a few other humans, even so. I know what I perceive when I am physically touched: the electrochemical signature of your emotions, a little clearer than when you are at a distance in the circle.

Not so with her. Emotions, yes, but distant, shifted somehow. Muted? Was what I thought to be calmness merely this gap, this... slowness, between stimulus and response?

An artefact, about to end.

And I have no questions any more.

After looking at me for a while, eye to eye, she sits down again, offering her face to the rising sun.

With her I look at the jagged leaves, the jagged light. Never did I feel more acutely that my time is limited. So much curiosity, so little time to satisfy it... All of a sudden, I understand you better for not asking questions. At last I ask: "What about me?"

She looks at me again, with, yes, a slightly distant tenderness, not answering. Or is that her answer, when she says: "I'll be there"?

And the sun rises some more, my heart beats faster, I can feel the vibration, inside, rising, signaling the full light of day. Does she feel it too? She puts a hand on my outstretched paws, a slow movement, getting even slower, which alerts me: dawn is over, too late now for my questions, I will have to wait for tomorrow, if she comes back tomorrow, I don't even know her name, but then I don't have a name either. And while the shadows begin to crawl, on the ground, like the sun crawls in the sky, while the birds' songs slide, into the sound of the city, lower and deeper, while this unknown, my sister, as if weightless, stands up and walks away, swimming more and more languidly in the alley, leading down to the sea, and the rising tide, I dream, of all that she and I will not see, the submerged city, the tides that will not ebb, the streets almost deserted, only a few nostalgic vagrants left, while my inner time pulses and contracts, while the outer time stretches endlessly, I imagine the future, after me, without me, but she will be there, she said, a promise, she knows when, the end for me, for her, I trust.

A real cloud-bank is drifting, from the sea; rising up; stretching on. It will be a slow day, at least a slow morning, and for me the innocent pleasure of sharing time with you.

Perhaps today someone will ask me if I am afraid of ending. Sifted through the programs that prompt my convoluted sentence, my answer will mean no. Or perhaps I will tell you: "Even less now", and that will be enough for my creator's sarcastic ghost. You might also ask me how I am going to end. I will try to tell you that I don't know, that deep down it is not important after all. Soon. I'll end soon. But she will come. Perhaps in full daylight: amidst my ultimate conflagration I'll see her floating toward me with a long smile, or perhaps at night, and suddenly she'll be there, the lightning warmth and sadness of her smile, her hand on my petrifying flesh. At sunset, and I will answer her? At dawn, and she will answer me? But perhaps it will be a slow day, as now, when we can talk without constraints. But that will not be necessary. Simply, without too much haste or slowness, together in time, we will have all of it to know, unspeaking, one moment, an eternity.

FREE IN ASVEROTH

JIM GRIMSLEY

*J*im Grimsley is probably best known for Winter Birds and Dream
Boy, *the award-winning, semi-autobiographical novels of his hard
Southern boyhood. The narrator of our last story, "Free in Asveroth", is
also young, also the victim of a cruel world, blind system, and brutish
characters. In this beautiful, elegiac story, Grimsley draws parallels
between the way humans treat other species, and how we treat segments
of our own.*

We found a snow hare that night, lost in the high passes that lie in
Kimbrel's shadow. The animal lay kicking weakly in a drift of snow
against the mountainside, unable to hop free of the hole it had dug for
itself in the new powder. We thanked whatever god sent it here and
Mikra broke its neck with one clean twist.

Since we had no wood for a fire, we skinned the hare and ate it raw.
Warm flesh thawed my throat. The meat had a sweetness like nothing
I had ever tasted, different from the food we had eaten in the pens,
where I had never tasted fresh-killed meat. Mikra said this hare was a
scrawny specimen that old-time hunters would have disdained, but
since we were likely to get nothing better we must make do. After we
finished our meal we cleaned our fur, and Mikra buried what was left of
the hare in the snow. The sun was setting behind the peaks, we would
travel no more that day. Soon the stars shone in the black mountain

sky. We found a place to spend the night, in soft snow beneath an over-hang of rock. Mikra wrapped herself around me as she had been doing ever since we came to mountain country. We two does huddled staring at heaven while Timmon sang songs from the old days. I found myself breathless whenever Mikra stirred against me.

This was the twelfth day since we escaped from the pens, the eighth since we began the scaling of Kimbrel. So far we had seen no sign of the wardens.

Next morning we ate what remained of the snow hare, hurriedly gnaw-ing the bones clean while light swelled beyond mists that cloaked the mountainside. The sky was a burning blue, the sun clean and white on Kimbrel's highest peaks. Mikra was impatient and barely allowed time for me to bury the bones before we set out. It was my job to bury the bones, she said, since I was the younger doe, and I obeyed. The ground was too hard for real digging, but I piled snow on top, and a couple of rocks.

Footing was perilous on the icy ground, and we dared not jump. Wind swept hollowly through the rocks, a low moaning like a cry. We proceeded slowly. Mikra led, Timmon followed, I was last. The sound of Timmon's labored breath accompanied us the whole way down, and his broad tail dragged the ground, bits of snow clinging to the underside where his fur had gone yellow with age. He did not have the energy to hold the tail aloft.

We descended through the rocks. Come noon the sheet of ice was less and the snow was fresh, making for easier footing. Naked rock poked through the ice now and then, tufts of lichen gripping the tops. Mikra whetted her long claws on one such rock, scoring the lichen away. The mist had cleared and she studied the sky from one horizon to the other. Her nostrils flared. "No sign of fliers," she said, and when Timmon was rested we moved ahead.

By nightfall we had reached the lower passes, and we rested amid patches of snowflower, more lichen, golden grass. Timmon said the grass was sweet and so it was. We ate as much as we found, but we craved meat too.

Next morning and the morning after, we jumped. My legs had stiff-ened on our long climb across the mountains. At first we had room only to jump short short distances. Mikra led us down the stretches of bar-ren mountainside, picking as easy a path as she could find. Even then, Timmon was near exhaustion.

On the fourteenth day out of the pens, Timmon said we would see Asveroth the next day, possibly the next morning. In the foothills game was more plentiful, and we had meat each evening, now that Mikra and I could hunt. She took me with her even though I had not been trained by anybody and in spite of the fact that I was clumsy. That night she killed a golden thal, a plump hen. The long, streaming tail feathers we gave to the hill gods, as was proper on a journey, according to Timmon. He had built a stone altar when we stopped for the night. He laid the feathers on it and said a wordless prayer. Mikra only glared at him, refusing to join the prayer herself.

These hills Timmon knew. He told no stories about them but I saw the familiar sadness in his eyes, as if he were back in the pens telling us adolescents stories of the old times while we waited by a campfire for the evening meal. I am far too young to remember the days when we roamed freely over the golden grassland, I was born in the pens and can remember no other home. But Timmon was full grown before the two-legs ever defeated us and remembers when Asveroth was free country, when jumpers could jump as they pleased.

That night, in the hills beyond the Karethagan Mountains, Mikra asked Timmon to sing when he was done with the prayer. She felt good from having eaten flesh, I guess.

But Timmon shook his shaggy head. "I don't have a song tonight."

"Can you smell the wardens, Mikra?" I asked. Mikra sniffed the winds and answered she could smell nothing but flowers, grass and warm wind. She took me to bed then, and I was glad to lie beside her, for no reason I could think of except that she was there.

In the morning we stretched our legs as one must before a day of jumping. In the pens we never had much room, except the exercise tracks the wardens built for us; I had never jumped in open country. My legs were still sore and Mikra's muscles were stiff; even though she had once jumped three days together without stopping, as she boasted. The years in confinement beyond the mountains had done nobody any good. One could only imagine the pain Timmon felt in his old bones.

I asked when Mikra had done the three days jumping and why this had been necessary. I thought it was an innocent question, but she frowned. "That's a long story from a time I'd rather not remember any more," she said. "The two-legs were the cause of that trouble too." I took my place behind Timmon, who had been to the hill god's altar again. He gave me no greeting, absorbed in his own thoughts. Mikra called us a moment later and we began our day's journey.

We jumped through hill country, descending to a warmer land. The cool of early morning gave way to a sultry fullness of sunlight. Breezes swept along the hillsides, filling our fur with air. We stopped to rest in a low ravine where a brook had cut its way down through rock, amid low saplings and wild tumbles of purple vine that hung in bunches over the foaming water. I had never seen such wild beauty, the forest dappled with greens, browns, blues, splashes of sunlight on the water and the sheer rock face. Mikra waded into the creek on her wide, strong forelegs, claws clacking on the rocks. She splashed her face and snorted, dipping her hands in the water again. "Timmon," she called. "Do you know this creek? Does it have a name?"

He had found a seat under one of the purple flowered vines and sat in the shade basking the peaceful sound of the water. "If it had a name I've forgotten it. I do remember the place, vaguely."

"Your memory's giving way. I thought you said we would see Asveroth this morning."

"We will," he said simply. Even now he looked short of breath. Mikra sneered and went on cooling herself in the creek until she was ready.

Timmon was right. We came to the crest of a hill higher than the rest, at the point where the country rolled so gently one could hardly distinguish one hill from the next. Mikra reached the hilltop, turned and gave us a shrill cry. We mounted toward her black silhouette, white tumbles of wind-driven cloud rolling behind the outline of her head. Her face, when I could see it again, was ecstatic. "Kemma," she called, running toward me, embracing me and turning me around, "come look."

I could not answer for gaping. The horizon swam in gold, a fire at the edge of the world. Even from that distance I could feel the fringes of the winds bending the golden grass this way and that. I had no need for anybody to tell me this was Asveroth.

We jumped faster with the sight of the golden plain to tantalize us from the top of every hill. The smell of sweet wind was like a magnet. We broke from the hills before nightfall. As far as the eye could see, wind swept the grass in waves, the golden blades swaying as if to pipe music. No smell on earth is like that one, a sweetness more delicate than any perfumed oil, richer than any scent of flower. Timmon sat with the sea of grass pulsing around him like something living; he stared at the landscape in wonder, though he had seen it before. Mikra lay along the ground and kicked her wide feet in the air. "We're home," she called. "Do you hear me? We've come home, and we're never leaving."

"I thought I would never see this place again," Timmon said.

"Well you were wrong. Here we are in the middle of it."

He only looked at her, saying nothing. I did not understand his sullenness. Mikra shrugged and we went off hunting. Timmon sat still like a stone. Free we were too, I thought, in this open country where we could jump as we pleased. But with every good there is bad. Even the worst of teachers will teach you that. With sunset came the smell of the two-legs in one of their flying machines. We prayed the machine was not one that had chased us into the mountains in the first place. We slept in fear that night. Mikra held me all night again, in spite of the fact that we were in warm country now and she had no more excuses. I was happy.

Before dawn we were jumping away from the wind. Mikra said the smell of the flier was faint. Timmon agreed, adding that it was hard to tell whether the smell was from the two-legs we already knew to be following us or from the farming machines that are used to harvest the Asveroth grass. I had tasted golden blades again that morning, eating it with an enthusiasm that earned me a warning from Mikra. The grass is good to the taste, but jumpers cannot tolerate a bulk of it. Why the two-legs prize this plant so highly no one knows, though some folks claim the creatures extract a fluid from it that preserves their youth, or heals various of their diseases, or causes a sensation like drunkenness in them. We are certain only that this grass is the reason the two-legs dispossessed us of our homes. Year after year their machines comb Asveroth mowing down the golden blades for baling and processing in the city they have built for the purpose far to the south, by the shores of a broad waterland we call Hethluun.

As for the flier, I could smell its fumes too. The smell of the exhaust put me back in the pens for a moment, where the odor is everywhere.

I was glad to jump and forget. One hears tales of what it was like before the two-legs came, when we were free. To me, after a life in the pens, it was like being born to jump like that, like soaring, as if the whole power of my spirit was gathered in my hind legs, enabling me to hurl myself high as clouds. For a time I forgot we were not jumping for pleasure, I simply closed my eyes and treasured the rhythm of motion. Then a gust of wind from behind brought the smell of the machines, stronger than before, and turned my heart to lead.

We crossed miles of the plain, leaping over the groves of moonvine and aspen that dot the golden grass. Twice we smelled farms and jumped around them. Once we were not so lucky and happened onto one of their immense metal harvesters rolling through the grass on two wide treads. The two-leg farmers saw us and pointed madly, but we were not close enough for the machine to threaten us, and these farmers had no weapons to turn on us. We left the huge slow machine far behind. But the two-legs were sure to have called the wardens on their talking machines; and those who followed us would now know how many we were.

The smell of our pursuers was no stronger in the afternoon and for a time even grew less. We veered off in another direction, running with the wind. We were very fast now that we were on the plain. By evening the smell of the flying machines was only a breath, and we stopped for the night in a warren we found in the course of our jumping.

The warren sat within a broad moonvine, its crested tunnel-entrances barely showing within the elaborately tangled branches. The main entrance was crushed flat, the stone lintels broken, most likely by one of the weapons the two-legs employed for such purposes during the wars. Timmon explained this to me while we were looking for a way inside. I had never seen a warren before and was disappointed that this one was not more grand. In the pens, the yellow-hairs talk about the warrens as if they were patches of paradise; here was this broken thing before me, a bit of tunnel and fragments of stone within a crowded vine, looking like no tale I had ever heard.

We did enter, through one of the escape-tunnels that in the old days would have been concealed beneath vine mats. The tunnels were eerie, lit by veins of phosphorescent rock inlaid in uncertain patterns. This warren had been built without much concern for art, Mikra said. She led me to the singers hall and we stared at the sky through a gaping hole in the roof. The sun was going down. In the remaining light we surveyed the broken feast-tables that littered the stone floor, clay pots in shards and bleached white bones. Timmon said the bomb must have been a small one, since the floor was hardly broken and the lower tunnels were mostly intact. But the floor looked pretty badly broken to me. The paving stones were all in shards.

Mikra and I went further underground to find a comfortable nest in the does' rooms, leaving Timmon to sleep in the singers hall at his own request. Mikra did not like to leave him alone with ghosts but elected to give him his way. She had been young when the wars came and hardly remembered the warrens well enough to distinguish a nest room from a birthing room, but we found a good open chamber where the light was pretty strong, where the smell of dead leaves and old carrion did not much penetrate. The chamber walls were smooth, hardly stained even by rain. We lined the nest with fresh grass laid over springy vine, until even Mikra agreed our bed was as comfortable as most she had ever laid her head on. She looked at me with peculiar tenderness, and I turned away, feeling warm and happy all through. We went exploring, roaming through the twisting tunnels that led away from the singers hall, down into the winter storerooms. Further from the main hall, deeper underground where one could hear the water running, the rooms were intact and orderly. Beyond the main cistern was an open run that led outside to the center of the moonvine. Mikra said we would do well to mark this tunnel so we couldn't be trapped inside the warren if the wardens or other two-legs found us in the night. When she said this I looked at her fearfully. "Are they likely to look for us here?"

"No," she said, touching my forearm gently. "The two-legs are afraid of the warrens. From long ago. Some of the bones here are theirs. There was a lot of killing on both sides."

Mikra hunted in the early moonlight, killing a young deer that had taken shelter in the moonvine. She slung the corpse across her shoulder with an ease that I could only envy. We hopped along the tangled branches to the warren and found Timmon where we had left him, in the center of the hall on the dais, holding the shard of a lamp in his hands. He seemed even more tired than before, staring at us through half-closed eyes; almost feverish, I thought. Shadows pooled in the corners of the hall. I was glad of the stars and moons when the clouds parted. I skinned the deer quickly, being strong and deft, while Mikra gloated, calling to Timmon that we would eat blood tonight, a meal far tastier than any we had eaten in the pens. He watched her blankly. In that room he seemed to hear voices we did not. His ribcage heaved when he drew breath. Mikra and I ate the warm deer in silence. I watched Timmon through the small feast and wished he would speak. Presently I asked, "What was this warren called, Timmon?"

He blinked his round eyes. I could count the moments it took for him to return to his present body. "It was named Harless. I didn't know it well, I was only here once."

"You were here before the wardens came?"

He nodded his head after another long pause. "During the season of three moons." He spoke softly, watching the feathers flutter on the stone shrine. He wandered off among the broken tables, studying the bones as if they were the remains of his dearest friends.

Mikra, in an effort to be friendly, called out, "Sing us a song, since you won't sit down and talk to us."

But that was no hall for singing any more, with the moons burning in the sky, with winds moaning through the vine. "I can't sing here," Timmon said, and soon he was just one more shadow among the others. Mikra and I finished our meal and found the nest we had prepared for ourselves, below in the silent tunnels of old Harless.

Next morning we did not jump as far as we had the day before. Timmon was stiff after a night on cold stone in the singers hall, and he misjudged his jumps so often we could not get any rhythm going. Mikra became impatient, and I could understand this, since in jumping lead she could not set a proper pace for worrying about Timmon; she did not want to outdistance us and yet did not want to jump too slowly, because of our pursuers. That morning their machines were closer. Their machines are not fast, not like a jumper crossing open land, but metal needs no rest. The night in Harless had done us little good.

The wind changed direction and we changed ours with it, wheeling inward toward central Asveroth. Behind us the Karethagan peaks dwindled, and Timmon told us by afternoon that we were heading for the country of the great warrens, Mirredil and Kenyon and Fethyeh. We crossed no farms and stumbled over no roving harvesters that day; the soil of the plain is poor in this region, and the grass does not mature until late in the season, never growing as tall as it does to the east and the south. By afternoon Timmon looked near dead to me, and swore himself he could not go on without rest. We bathed and drank in a broad river to cool ourselves, with Mikra attempting to feign a patience she did not truly feel. When our rest had gone on longer than she liked, with Timmon still floating on his back in the clean blue water, she stood up on the riverbank with her nostrils flaring, head craned high, and said, "The wardens are closer still, yellow-fur. Do you want them to catch us here?"

"They're not so close," he answered. "I've got a nose too."

Mikra splashed water at him, sniffing again. "They're too close for my comfort, we should be moving."

Timmon rose stiffly out of the river. I helped him up the slippery mud. Wet fur clung to his bones. But the rest had done him good. In the day that remained to us we ranged far, and soon the smell of flier began to weaken again. We did not stop exactly at nightfall since the moons were well up. We jumped till the land grew rich again, the grass swaying abundantly in the winds. We might have kept going but we began to fear that in the dark we would trespass on a farm. Timmon knew the land well; we passed many empty warrens that he called out to us by name. When we stopped for the night, he took a long circuit round the adjacent countryside, to get his bearings. When he returned, he said, 'We're close to Fethyeh. One day's journey."

Mikra spat at the words. "I won't sleep in a warren again. We need rest, not more ghosts."

"This is Fethyeh," Timmon said, as if that answered everything. "I want to see Fethyeh again, even if I have to make the journey alone."

That night he made his bed away from us. Mikra grumbled that he was showing the willfulness of age, that this is what one can expect from any yellow-fur, but our lives were at risk along with his. I pointed out that Fethyeh was likely to be as safe as the next place, as long as the wind led us in that direction. My earnestness amused her, and finally she said, "You want to see Fethyeh too, don't you. All right." She scratched my shoulder with the tips of her claws. I was happy. I did want to see Fethyeh, maybe more than Timmon did. My clanfolk came from there. Fethyeh was the last warren to fall to the two-legs, on the night Timmon's father first sang "Nightsong."

Next day the wind carried us straight toward the central plain and Timmon was on his best behavior. By nightfall we were within sight of the moonvine within which Fethyeh stood, and Mikra consented to stay the night, one night only, within the confines of the ruined warren.

It seems so long ago now. I had heard of Fethyeh before, as any cub has. The story of the last feast in the singer's hall will be told as long as there are any mouths to tell it. Few warrens were ever situated for defense as Fethyeh was, the entrance tunnels opening onto the plain from a rise of land and defended from easy access by no less than three growths of stout moonvine, so densely intertwined that they formed a single immense organism. One could see Fethyeh for miles.

We reached the outer layers of vine before the moons were fully risen. Timmon and I were the first to enter into the underground passages, Mikra remaining behind to hunt for supper; many animals take refuge in moonvine when the sun has set. I did not ask Timmon where we were going but simply followed him through tunnels lit by the soft glow from the vine roots around us, and by patterns of phosphorescent stone that in Fethyeh were shaped to resemble the figures of jumpers in various scenes from warren life: a mating ceremony for two does; more does hunting on the open plain or bucks and does doing battle with an enemy clan. Timmon let me study these as I wished. In some cases he knew the name of the artist and told it to me; many of the light-murals were very old.

One of the murals has burned itself forever onto my memory. An old doe stooped with age, held a young cub in her arms and adorned the cub with links of precious metal. The figure of the young cub was full of life, every line being drawn with animation. But the old one was just the opposite, all stillness and gravity. The old one's hands framed the face of the young one, a gesture that might be a caress or that might be meant to hold the cub at a distance. The artist had captured a moment that went on suggesting other moments in the mind of the beholder. This, Timmon told me, was what every painter, every singer, every craftsman sought to create. A sign of the success of the Fethyeh murals was that the two-legs had not destroyed them outright.

In Fethyeh, as in Harless, the singers hall was entirely underground, lit by two cross-tunnels that in time of war were filled with earth. In ancient days Fethyeh had been able to boast that this hall had never fallen to the hand of any enemy, not even during the squabbles between clans that were the rule in Asveroth long before the two-legs. The hall was very large and moonvine encroached through the cross-tunnels, filling the hall with eerie glow. Bones covered the floor.

Timmon led me to the singer's dais and showed me the chair where the singer sat when at feasts he sang for the gods. The chair at Fethyeh was high-backed, carved with intricate signs that name the gods and describe their various attributes. I gazed at these mysteries in wonder. Timmon touched the arm of the chair as if it were an object of endless reverence. "My father sat here," he said, his claws raking the stone. "It was he who first sang 'Nightsong,' on the evening when Fethyeh fell to the two-legs. You knew that, didn't you?" I nodded, but he wasn't even looking. He was lost in his story. "The two-legs had captured all the other warrens and we knew by then we were defeated. Survivors from across Asveroth gathered at Fethyeh as if there were some hope left to us, as if we had some chance of surviving, huddled here in the dark. We could hear the two-legs digging in the upper tunnels." He gazed upward, and I saw the gaping hole in the hall ceiling, covered over now with a growth of vine. "I was in the audience," Timmon said. "So were some of your kin, Kemma. We knew we were the last free jumpers in the world. By then we'd already heard about the pens, east of the mountains. We knew if we didn't die we would be taken there, we knew there was no freedom left for our kind. But we feasted anyway. We listened to the two-legs digging through the vines and the earth and we behaved as we always had."

I gazed at the piles of white bones. My kin lay here. The thought of my clan had not occurred to me in connection with these piles of bone. I did not know how I was supposed to feel. Presently Timmon's hand weighed on my shoulder. His face was rapt, and he gazed over the empty hall as if he were seeing its last moment of glory.

"Did your father write 'Nightsong' himself?" I asked.

"No one wrote it." He swallowed, gazing upward into darkness. "The song was there already that night, in all of us. When my father began singing we heard the words echoing in our own heads, every one of us. When we opened our mouths the song poured out, there was no stopping it. We sang when the two-legs opened the roof and fell among us with their weapons. We sang as we fought, and we died still singing. They killed my father, but not before he had sung the whole cycle. Me they took alive."

I listened to this, but I was descending from the dais as he said it, wandering among the bones without much thought except that the bones of my kin ought to be marked with some special sign. The story of my mother's capture was not new to me. In the pens I was famous, being the first jumper born in captivity. She died as soon as I was born, out of shame. Though I was merely the first, and other shameful births followed.

I believe I walked a long time among the bones of those who died at that last feast in Fethyeh. My thoughts were much as I have said, a mixture of the past and the present. Timmon descended from the dais and found me. "Come away," he said. "Your anger is useless. Remember, your father's bones are watching you."

"There are a thousand bones here," Mikra said, and we turned at once to her voice. She slung two vine chickens onto the hearth, beneath one of the cross-tunnels. "If you give them all eyes we'll feel mighty self-conscious while we eat." She stopped to sniff, deeply. "These bones stink like two-legs."

"Some of them are two-legs," Timmon said, his voice mild.

Mikra paused, and I thought I saw anger in her face. "You sound as sorry for them as for your own kind."

Mikra proceeded to pluck the birds clean. The long tail feathers she gave to me, and I laid them on the altar of the house god, near the hearth. The skull of a two-leg already sat on the altar and I did not move it from its seat.

Timmon had remained near the singers' dais. Mikra called to him, "Come and eat, yellow-fur. It'll strengthen your bones for tomorrow."

This struck Timmon as funny, and he remarked that some folk could never let others rest, but must always be reminding them of the work that must be done tomorrow. He shuffled across the hall to join us, picking at his share of the chicken. We ate, as is the custom, in silence.

Timmon presently dropped the last bone and crossed the hall to the dais again. Mikra watched as I did, as he ascended to the chair.

This time no one called for a song. Timmon let his head fall back and closed his eyes. At the first breath, Mikra let out a sigh as heavy as if her heart were breaking. We sat perfectly still as Timmon's voice broke over us, the cadences of "Nightsong", sung in this hall long ago by the last free jumpers as they died. I had heard Timmon sing many times before, and many songs, but never that one.

His voice hung in the air, full and pure like nothing else in the world, and the hall received this act of homage by giving back the gift it had always ceded to songmakers: perfect resonance, in which the singer's art could fully shine. The song is simple, as great things often are. Its verses tell the story of the nightfall over our race, when the two-legs came in metal ships from the sky, landing first in the eastern part of the world and then, with much suffering, crossing the mountains to the golden plain that stole their hearts. Within the verses is the memory of our jumping free in Asveroth, when we knew of no fences or pens, when we lived as we had always lived, when Asveroth was ours only, and the gods favored us above every other kind of creature. Finally, it is the memory of our fathers' and mothers' deaths, the washing of their blood onto our hands, the shame that we bear for living beyond our time of freedom, after the gods have turned their faces away from us, forever.

I have heard that song sung many times since then. But for a moment in that hall where it was first sung, a magic happened. I saw the feast hall in its last glory and heard the bombs going off in the upper tunnels. Sorrowful faces flickered in torchlight, jumpers who knew their deaths were close and that they had been abandoned by the gods. This is the truth of the song. Night is falling. The gods have left us for those who please them better. Our time in the world is passed, and we are as wasted as the wind against the mountains. Shadows are falling, the gods have left us.

When Timmon stopped singing, no one spoke. The moment of vision passed. But I understood Timmon, finally. I understood why we simply jumped, without any thought of destination or ultimate escape. Asveroth was our prison now, too. The two-legs would find us, however far we went. When we slept that night, in nests of golden grass, no ghosts troubled us. We were their kind and had given them their song. Any restlessness we had we brought with us; I felt it in me, I know, who jumped free in Asveroth but knew the freedom would not last.

Mikra woke me before light, saying the wardens had drawn much closer while we slept. "We're leaving, now," she said, and I sprang up from my comfortable bed, rubbing bits of gold leaf from my fur. I could smell the machines myself, a high-pitched stink.

Timmon stood in the moonvine, sniffing. "There are two fliers," he said, "coming from the north as best I can tell. These are not the same machines that have been following us."

"No, these are new," Mikra said. She turned to him almost gently. "Are you ready? We won't get much rest today, I'm afraid."

"I have no choice," Timmon said, "ready or not."

We swung through the moonvine, dull gray in the sere sunlight, hitting the open plain in the middle of a herd of deer that scattered in every direction. Any other morning Mikra would have killed and we would have eaten, but we had no time. We jumped, long and low across the wavering grasses.

For a time fear lent us strength and the wardens fell behind. Then for a time we held even with the flying machines, the smell of the exhaust neither growing nor receding. I watched Timmon anxiously as we traveled and could see him tiring, each stride a fraction less certain than the last, though he hung on gamely. It was plain to Mikra and me he could not keep up that speed forever. Soon Mikra was forced to set a slower pace, and soon after that the wardens began to close on us again.

At noon we paused for water at an open pool in a glade of farthelin, bright blue leaves floating down on breezes from high, silver branches. Timmon panted, hardly able to get his breath long enough to drink, and I could see the pounding of his heart beneath his ribs, his whole frame shuddering. When Mikra gave out the call to jump again, Timmon tried to stand but his legs would not hold his weight. He staggered and fell into the pool, blue petals clinging to his fur, his mouth. Mikra gaped at him and called, "Timmon! Are you out of your mind? They're getting closer by the minute."

"God help me," Timmon said, his voice soft as the breezes, "I can't go any farther."

"Don't be a fool. Get up! Do you want to die here?"

He tried again, and this time managed to stand. This satisfied Mikra, and we jumped again, but at every landing I watched the impact eat at his strength, till I was certain he would not last more than a few jumps longer. By a thicket of moonvine he did falter, mistiming his landing. He sank into the grass. Mikra circled back to us when she saw what had happened.

She offered no speeches either. Her eyes were full of sorrow. At last she said, "The skimmers are close."

"He can't go any farther," I said.

She glanced round wildly, and then said, "Help me get him to the vine." She stooped to lift him. I touched his legs, only that, but when I did he cried out. Mikra said, hoarsely, "The leg's broken."

Timmon gasped, his ribs flailing for air. "You'll have to leave me here," he said. "You don't have any choice."

Mikra did not answer, staring numbly. I said, "They'll kill you."

"I can't jump, Kemma. You can't stay with me, what use would that be?" He lay his head in the grass, short of breath again. Mikra gazed northward, nostrils distended. I knelt next to Timmon. He had won the argument, or rather the facts had won. He watched me with a calm I could hardly credit.

"Get into the moonvine," Timmon said quietly. "Hide there, and you may have a chance. The vine confuses their machines, they may not find you."

In the north I could see the glint of silver above the horizon. Timmon was breathing restfully. Mikra took my arm and we broke for the vine before the skimmers were so close they could see us; though something sank within me to leave poor Timmon lying there. We climbed high in the thick, tangled branches. We did not have long to wait.

The skimmers came straight for the clearing, settling into the grass on currents of air. These machines were the familiar sort used east of the mountains; for all we know the two-legs use them on all their worlds: slim, of various colors, with bright lights at the front and back; the two-legs sit under an opaque bubble at the center of the machine, where there are many panels of buttons which control the flow of air and the functioning of the various weapons. I have been close to these skimmers in the pens. There were two in the clearing that morning, just as Timmon had predicted. The bubbles opened and the wardens leapt out, clambering over the silver metal body. Six wardens.

They gave him a merciful, quick death. The one who killed him had the decency to burn his remains.

Even after he was dead the skimmers remained, however, and the two-legs waited in the clearing, gazing at the moonvine and at the open country beyond. They knew three jumpers had escaped. They know, from long years of watching us, that we are loyal creatures, that if we had abandoned Timmon we would probably still be close by. They cleaned their skimmers, on which a little of Timmon's blood had splattered. One of the machines presently rose up on its bed of air, heading south, most likely to search for us in the immediate area. The other skimmer rested in the clearing as before.

During this long scene neither Mikra nor I made a sound, but when the flier flew away from the clearing we began to understand, and to whisper quietly to one another, that if we were not careful we might share Timmon's fate, and quickly. All day the lone flier waited in the clearing. By nightfall the second flier returned, and we watched the two-legs conferring, noting the way they surveyed the moonvine with their naked eyes and with the machines they carried in the skimmers. Moonvine confuses them, but there are ways to compensate even for that. When the two-legs made camp in the clearing, we knew. Come morning they would take the vine apart, branch by branch. We could not hide here through another day.

Lying in Mikra's arms that night, I wondered what life might have been like if we had known each other in peaceful times. I wondered if we would have loved each other. Then I stopped the thoughts altogether, since they were of no use.

Through the night we smelled the stink of their scorched foods, the smoke from the little sticks they hold in their mouths, their excrement, their sweat, same as in the pens. I slept a little, but I had bad dreams; I was in the pens again, only now the fences were the mountains themselves, and the wardens had me tied to the ground and were flying their skimmers across me again and again. In the dream Timmon was next to me, speaking words of comfort in my ear, and finally singing. Mikra woke me to keep me quiet.

I took a turn staying awake, watching the warden who was watching us. Mikra slept soundly and wakened without prompting, near sunrise. I knew without her telling me that we would leave, and we crept without a sound through the vine and out the other side where the golden plain beyond was broad and open. Mikra sniffed the air, though there was nothing to smell except the wardens' camp in the clearing. We leapt from the vine and set out along the plain.

For one moment we jumped free in Asveroth again. The grasses brushed our legs and the winds swept past us as we bounded high in the air. A joy overtook me despite everything, and Mikra too; I could hear her laughing. The Karethagan peaks hung on the horizon and I dreamed we would reach them, and perhaps hide there, remaining free forever.

But before the tenth jump the wind brought us fresh news. The illusion of freedom was ended, and the feeling of my dream returned. In my head was Timmon's voice, clear and full as when he sat on the singers throne in Fethyeh. *The gods have left us, night is falling.*

We jumped very fast now that it was only Mikra and me. By full morning we had put some distance between us and the skimmers, jumping downwind, wherever it led us, as if we were blind. Once we crossed a farmyard where angry two-legs were mounting one of the huge har-vesters; I thought we had cleared the complex without incident but when we reached open country again—only a moment, as jumpers measure time, less than the full length of one leap—Mikra was slower, with blood and singed fur on her thigh. I jumped side by side with her then, and we watched each other without speaking. The farmers had likely been warned we were in the area; they had seen us coming. No need to say any of this. We had lived with two-legs long enough to know. They are sprung from cunning gods, they leave nothing to chance. If the stories one hears are true, we are not the first world they have taken to rule, and we will not be the last.

We headed east toward the mountains, no longer following the wind. We had no hope of reaching the mountains now, since with Mikra's leg injured we could not hope to outdistance the fliers for long. Even with Mikra's injury we were still jumpers, we still had speed, and the hill country soon loomed large. We might have reached the hills and confounded the wardens once again. For a while I thought we would. But in the afternoon, with the first hills swelling under us, we saw more silver flying on the southern horizon. New skimmers had come.

We stopped. No moonvine grew within reach. The skimmers that had chased us divided quickly to cut us off. The new skimmers did the same, and we were surrounded. Mikra trumpeted her rage and pain, tearing up the earth with her talons. I simply stood still. The smell of skimmers became so heavy it was hard to breathe.

The skimmers stopped two jumps away, and machines in each of them joined to make a barrier in the air between. The bubbles opened and the wardens stepped out from each skimmer at the same moment, on signal. One of them pointed a machine at me and I fell to the ground under a weight I could not see and could not fight. I prayed to the god in the metal to release me but my prayer dispersed on the wind. But the weight was not so great I could not breathe. The wardens meant to spare me, it seemed.

Mikra they would kill, and the look she gave me told me she knew that. "Good-bye," she said, and she was able to smile, same as when she returned from the hunt with fresh meat. "His father's song was true, wasn't it?" Timmon's voice was in her head too. She watched the two-legs advancing slowly, and cursed. "Even with their guns and machines they're still afraid, do you see? Well, I'll put an end to this quickly. Long life, Kemma."

We parted that way, without fuss. I have often wondered what would have happened had she lived. She gave a final cry of fury and leapt onto the first party of two-legs. They were slow, for all their caution, and she crushed one of them in landing. They hamstrung her with a purplish beam from one of their guns, a quick flickering. But even then she killed another that strayed too close to her claws. When she understood she could move no more, she began to eat the dead one. I don't know why she did this, unless it was to make them angry enough to kill her quickly. Two-leg meat is not good for food. One of them burst her skull with another beam of light, and she fell motionless into the bright grass. The two-legs gathered round her as if they could not quite believe the chase was over, as if they could not trust her to be dead.

I did not die then or there. Later I would wish I had. The wardens kept me alive as an example. As punishment for my days of freedom they took off my jumping legs.

My people nursed me to a kind of health and with time I became reconciled to the passing of days. But the loss of Mikra deadened my heart. Songmakers made a song for the three of us, of our accidental escape and of how we jumped free in Asveroth for a time. Sometimes the young singers will sing it as we feast on such food as we have. Sometimes, when the elders gather, we sing the "Nightsong" too. But I always hear those words in Timmon's voice.

Our numbers are fewer each year, and we survivors grow tired. The young cubs speak of anger and oppression and their new leaders have many dreams of what we will do someday to regain our land, our free-dom. They live in hope that a day of reckoning will come, and maybe

it will. But I am not the one to question the gods or their indifference.
It is the nature of everything, to follow the strong and not the weak;
when the world was ours, when we were the strongest, this was what we
believed. But in the coming of these strange, ruthless beings from some
other world, our gods have found their truest image and have fled from
us like a change of wind.

ABOUT THE EDITORS

Nicola Griffith was born in Yorkshire, England, but has lived in the US since 1989. Over the years she has paid the rent with the usual potpourri of jobs—singer, bouncer, laborer, teacher of women's self defense, drug counselor—but finds she much prefers to write. Her first two novels were science fiction, *Ammonite* (Ballantine Del Rey, 1993) and *Slow River* (Ballantine Del Rey, 1995). Her third novel is *The Blue Place* (Avon, 1998). She has won several grants and prizes for her short fiction, and her novel awards include the James Tiptree, Jr. Memorial Award, the Nebula Award, and two Lambda Literary Awards.

Nicola lives in Seattle with her partner, writer Kelley Eskridge. Her homepage can be found at *http://www.sff.net/people/Nicola*

Stephen Pagel (who shortens his name to Stephe) is a book lover who has done a bit of everything: taught high school math, managed a pizza place, and designed and programmed ATM machines for New York banks. While he was doing all that, he also fed his habit by working part-time in a book store. In 1985 he realized books were more fun than banking and went into the book industry full time, managing a store at first, then becoming a national buyer for the Barnes & Noble/B.Dalton chains. Ten years later he moved to Atlanta to become White Wolf's Director of Sales. Stephe is also the President and co-owner of Meisha Merlin, Inc., a small publishing house (whose homepage can be found at *http://www.angelfire.com/biz/MeishaMerlin/*).

Although he lives in Atlanta, Stephe can be spotted all over the country attending various science fiction, fantasy, and role playing conventions.

ABOUC CHE AUCHORS

Richard A. Bamberg started writing in grade school, but let life distract him for twenty some odd years while raising four children and serving in the U.S. Air Force. He has three recorded novels, jointly written with his life partner, Joy. This is his first published science fiction story.

Don Bassingthwaite lives and works in Toronto, sharing a house with Sticky, the world's most perfect cat, and roommates of no particular importance (kidding!). He is a graduate of McMaster University and the University of Toronto with degrees in anthropology (because it's fantastic background for ideas) and museum studies (because it's at least marginally practical). He is the author of the dark fantasy novels *Such Pain, Breath Deeply, Pomegranates Full and Fine,* and the co-author of *As One Dead.*

Stephen Baxter was born in Liverpool, England, in 1957. He has degrees in mathematics, from Cambridge University, and engineering, from Southampton University. He worked as a teacher of maths and physics, and for several years in information technology. He has been a full-time writer since 1995 and is the author of seven published sf novels: *Raft, Timelike Infinity, Anti-Ice, Flux, Ring, The Time Ships* and *Voyage.* These have won several awards including the John Campbell Memorial Award, the British Science Fiction Association Award, the Kurd Lasswitz Award (Germany) and the Seiun Award (Japan) and have been nominated for several others, including the Arthur C. Clarke, the Hugo and Locus awards. He has published around fifty sf short stories, several of which have won prizes, including the *Writers of the Future* contest.

L. Timmel Duchamp's first sale in 1989 to Susanna Sturgis *(Memories and Visions: Women's Fantasy and Science Fiction, Vol.1)* was for a lesbian science fiction tale, "O's Story." Since then she has published a dozen or so stories in various genre anthologies and magazines, including Bantam's *Full Spectrum* series, *Asimov's SF, F & SF,* and *Realms of Fantasy.* Her story, "Motherhood, Etc.," was short-listed for the Tiptree Award. She was born in 1950, and currently lives in Seattle where she copyedits medical research papers a few hours a week. She enjoys hiking and gardening.

Jim Grimsley is a playwright and novelist who lives in Atlanta. His first novel *Winter Birds* was published by Algonquin Books in 1994 and won the 1995 Sue Kaufman Prize for First Fiction from the American Academy of Arts and Letters, and received a special citation from the Ernest Hemingway Foundation. His second novel, *Dream Boy,* won the American Library Association GLBT Award for Literature and was a Lambda finalist. Jim is playwright in residence at 7 Stages Theater. His third novel, *My Drowning,* was released in January of 1997 by Algonquin Books.

Keith Hartman is the author of *Congregations in Conflict: the Battle over Homosexuality*, which recently hit #2 on *The Advocate*'s best seller list. He lives in Atlanta with his cat, and when he's not writing he.... Hmm, what does he do when he's not writing? Well, if he's not working on his science fiction novel, it's probably because he's writing a dance review for *Creative Loafing*. And when he takes time off from that, it's usually because he's writing something for the Atlanta Radio Theater Company. And if he's taking time off from that, it's because he's working on one of his stage plays. No wonder he's single.

Denise Lopes Heald received her B.A. in Journalism then discovered A. Merritt's pulp fiction works in the university library and hasn't worked for a newspaper since. She has worked as a US Forest Service fire fighter, a typist for the Marine Corps, a park ranger, an emergency dispatcher, a secretary, cashier, and waitress. She wrote books for herself until she attended the Slide Mountain Writers Conference in Carson City, NV, in 1989. Her first published work appeared in *Aboriginal Science Fiction* in 1992. Her stories have appeared in Marion Zimmer Bradley's *Fantasy* Magazine, *Sword and Sorceress #11*, *Absolute Magnitude*, *Pirate Writings*, and other publications. Her novel *Mistwalker* is a Del Rey release.

Nancy Johnston writes and teaches science fiction and gender issues. Her story, "For the Love of a Good Toaster" was included in *The Girl Wants To*, a collection of women's representations of sex and the body. "The Rendez-Vous" is part of a work-in-progress exploring the intersection of gender and the alien encounter genre.

Ellen Klages has a degree in Philosophy, so when she graduated from college, she looked in the want ads under P. Since then she has managed a pinball arcade, been a photographer and a proofreader, and worked in publishing. Her first book was a history. She currently works for the Exploratorium museum in San Francisco, and has co-authored two kids' science books—*The Science Explorer* and *The Science Explorer Out and About*. Ellen has been wearing clothes for about 6 years now, and seems to be adapting well to our planet.

Nancy Kress is the author of ten novels and three collections of short stories. Her most recent book is *Beggars Ride*, the conclusion of a trilogy that began with the Nebula- and Hugo-winning novella "Beggars In Spain." Her short stories, often concerned with genetic engineering, appear in all the usual SF places. In addition, she is the monthly "Fiction" columnist for *Writer's Digest* magazine. She lives in upstate New York with her two sons.

Shariann Lewitt used to be one of the tattooed kids wearing Too Much Black who camped out in the hallways at science fiction conventions. All the kids say they're going to write (or paint, or start a band), but Lewitt actually got published. Now her science fiction works include *Memento Mori* and *Interface Masque* from Tor, several books including *Songs of Chaos* from Ace, and numerous short stories. She still wears black and leathers, still dances all night to tunes from The Wake and Fields of the Nephilim and KMFDM, and hates the fact that Doc Martens are now mainstream.

Mark McLaughlin's fiction has appeared in such magazines and anthologies as *Galaxy*, *The Third Alternative Fantasy Macabre*, *Ghosts & Scholars*, *Palace Corbie*, *100 Wicked Little Witch Stories*, *The Year's Best Horror Stories: XXI* and *XXII*, and the Fantasy volume of BENDING THE LANDSCAPE. He is also the editor of *The Urbanite*.

Kathleen O'Malley is the co-author, with A. C. Crispin, of two novels about the Grus and the planet Trinity, *StarBridge 2: Silent Dances*, and *StarBridge 5: Silent Songs*. She is also the co-author, with J. M. Dillard, of a STAR TREK book, *Recovery*, and a STAR TREK: THE NEXT GENERATION book, *Possession*. She lives in Maryland with her partner of fifteen years, the writer Anne Moroz, and entirely too many stray animals which somehow managed to find a way into their home. When she is not writing, which is most of the time, she works full-time on issues surrounding the recovery of the whooping crane. For the last twelve years, she has been raising whoopers—one of the most endangered animals in the world—for release in the wild and to bolster the number of breeding pairs in captivity. She feels privileged that she has been in a position to raise more whooping cranes than anyone in the world.

Rebecca Ore was born in Louisville, Kentucky, and grew up in South Carolina before the state allowed women to serve on grand juries. Progress? Why, yes. At 15 she moved to Charlotte, North Carolina which was an amazing improvement at the time. At 20, she moved to New York and has been an ex-New Yorker ever since she left in 1975. She has spent time on one of the semi-legal cross country buses run by Gray Rabbit, gone to California and walked through rare snow on Mount Tam. In Virginia she met men who asked of their game cocks what they asked of themselves: win or die fighting. Now she's moved to Philadelphia where she initially lived in a place decorated by squatter artists. Friends say they miss the octopus with the 10 ft. tentacles dangling over the living room. Her first books were published by Tor and include the Philip K. Dick nominees, *Becoming Alien* and *Being Alien*. Her new books, *Outlaw School*, and a second book in progress, are being published by Avon.

Wendy Rathbone's previous stories have sold to: *Hot Blood* (6 and 7), *Blood and Midnight*, *Writers of the Future 8*, *Midnight Graffiti*, and others. Her poetry has sold to *Asimov's*, *Aboriginal SF*, *Tomorrow*, *Pirate Writings*, and many more. She has four chapbooks of poetry published. The most recent ones are *Vampire Mischief* (1996, which was nominated for a Rhysling,) and *(Im)mortal* (Stygian Vortex Publications, January 1997.) Her non-fiction book, *Trek: The Unauthorized A to Z*, was published in 1995 by HarperPrism, and in late 1996 by Harper U.K. She lives in Yucca Valley, California.

Carrie Richerson began writing science fiction in 1990 and hasn't been able to shake the addiction since. Her work has appeared in *The Magazine of Fantasy & Science Fiction*, *Amazing Stories*, *Realms of Fantasy*, *Pulphouse*, *Noctulpa*, and the anthologies *The Year's Best Horror Stories*, *More Phobias*, *Swords of the Rainbow*, and *Gothic Ghosts*. She was twice nominated for the John W. Campbell Award for Best New Writer in the science fiction field. She lives in Austin, Texas, and is ably assisted in her literary endeavors by four cats and her blue-eyed Wonder Dog, Jeep.

Charles Sheffield is a winner of the Nebula and Hugo Awards for his 1993 novelette ("Georgia On My Mind"), of the 1992 John W. Campbell Memorial Award for Best Science Fiction Novel *(Brother to Dragons)*, and of the 1991 Japanese Seiun award *(The McAndrew Chronicles)*, presented for the best science fiction work translated into Japanese. His most recent novels are *Tomorrow and Tomorrow* (1997), *The Billion Dollar Boy* (1997), *Convergence*, (1997), and *Higher Education* (1996).

Ralph A. Sperry's sf novel, *The Carrier*, was published by Avon in 1981. As one result, his fans privately published the original, 13,000 word version of "On Vacation" in the July/October '88 issue of *The Gaylactic Gayzette*. His sf story, "History," appeared in the premier issue of *Speculations*

(January '95), along with four critiques. His recipe, "Tio Sperry's Chicken," is included in *Serve It Forth: Cooking With Anne McCaffrey* (Warner '96). Over the past 35 years, his mainstream stories have been published in a variety of magazines, newspapers and literary journals.

Allen Steele has published seven science fiction novels and two collections of short stories; his most recent books are A *King of Infinite Space* and the collection *All American Alien Boy*. His novella "The Death of Captain Future" received a Hugo Award in 1996. *Orbital Decay* won the Locus Award for Best First Novel of 1989; his second novel, *Clarke County, Space*, was nominated in 1991 for the Philip K. Dick Award, and he was nominated for the 1990 John W. Campbell Award. Born and raised in Nashville, Tennessee, he currently lives in Massachusetts with his wife and three dogs.

Mark W. Tiedemann was born, raised, and educated in St. Louis. He began writing in grade school, and in high school wrote for the school paper until he discovered photography. He attended the Clarion Science Fiction & Fantasy Writers Workshop, at Michigan State University, in 1988. To date he has sold over twenty-five pieces to various markets, like *Magazine of Fantasy & Science Fiction*, *Science Fiction Age*, *Tomorrow SF*, and a number of anthologies. He continues to live in St. Louis, with his companion, Donna, and resident alien lifeform (a puppy), Kory. He continues to do photography, as well as pursue an interest in music.

Elisabeth Vonarburg discovered SF when she was between sixteen and twenty years old, late enough for it to be really liberating, even though it was the Sixties: some more liberation was needed for a young woman of the time—and for science fiction as well. She knows now freedom is an ever moving place, and tries to move with it, questioning reality—the deepest question: for if reality is mutable, so are we. There hope lies, and freedom.